EVERYTHING GIRL

Emily Mayer

Emily Mayer

For my Mom and Dad who always told me I could. And for Ryan who made me believe it. I love you.

1.

I sipped my second cup of coffee at my desk, dividing my attention between a newspaper article that was supposed to run in the *Tribune* next week and my boss, Ben, who was in the middle of a very heated argument. I watched as Ben resumed pacing, making sure he wasn't facing my desk, before my gaze drifted back to the article. My eyes landed on a picture of Ben leaving a hotel with Mrs. Slater, the wife of a city commissioner. At three p.m. On a Tuesday. I cringed at the next picture of the two locked in an embrace that was nowhere near close to professional. Leaning forward, I tried to locate Ben's hands in the second picture. It was like a skeevy *Where's Waldo?*

"Evelyn, my office!"

"Shit," I hissed. Ben's voice had startled me, causing me to jump and sending hot coffee onto my hand. I shook off the scalding hot liquid before grabbing my tablet with my non-coffee-burnt hand, then made my way into Ben's office.

He sat behind his desk with his back to me, staring out the large windows that overlooked downtown Chicago.

"Ben, what's going on?" I asked tentatively, sliding into a chair.

He swiveled around, let loose a sigh, and scrubbed both hands down his face.

"You've seen the new article the *Tribune* is running next week?"

The original article was supposed to be part of their *40 Under 40* series, in which they featured forty of Chicago's most influential citizens under the age of forty. Unfortunately, a photographer from the *Tribune* had spotted Ben with the commissioner's wife and the story had changed direction.

"I did. It's... not great." I offered, unhelpfully.

"Yeah, well the board agrees with you." He sighed. "They want me gone before the article is released."

I sat up straight in my chair. "Gone? What does that mean, exactly?"

"They want me to lay low until this whole thing blows over. They're worried about what this 'scandal' will do to our stock prices." His voice held a note of defeat I didn't like. This was the same man who had negotiated multi-million-dollar contracts without breaking a sweat. He had been described as cunning and ruthless, both in his professional and personal life. Ben practically grew up following his uncle around the boardroom. I doubted anyone knew this company as well as him.

"So what are you going to do?" I asked, watching as he picked up a pen to twirl between his fingers.

"I'm going to lay low—for now." He sighed, eyes focused on the pen. "It's important that the board of directors and our shareholders don't lose confidence in me."

"How are you planning to 'lay low'?" I asked.

"I'm going to Montana," Ben responded, finally dropping the pen back to his desk and looking at me.

"I'm sorry—did you say Montana?" I wasn't quite sure I heard him correctly. "Did you mean London?"

"No, I said Montana," he confirmed, one of his eyebrows winging up.

"Montana," I repeated. "The state?"

"Yes, Evelyn. The state of Montana. You know, the place where I spent my childhood. Where Pinehaven Ranch has been located for the past hundred years." He spoke slowly, like I was a very small child who didn't fully understand English yet.

I did, in fact,I know that Ben's family owned a ranch in Montana, courtesy of the article. The Danver family had started out as small-time ranchers way back in the mid 1800s. By the time Robert Danver took over the ranch in the early 1900s, he was inheriting one of the largest working ranches in the western United States. He also had the good luck of finding an oil field on their ever-expanding property. While the oil well hadn't been enough to give them oil-money status, Robert thought it would be wise to invest his money in something other than cattle. He'd traveled to Chicago to meet with a finance guy at Sterling & Sterling and happened to meet Laura Sterling, the daughter of the owner. The two married less than a month later and the Danver-Sterling dynasty was created.

"Wow, Montana. That's..." I cleared my throat, trying to come up with the right adjective. "A big state."

He shrugged. "I'm overdue for a visit anyway."

"Okay, and how long are you planning on visiting?" I asked, glad I'd grabbed my tablet.

"A month?" His statement came out sounding like a question. "And I'd like you to come with me. I have no intention of stepping down from Sterling despite whatever bullshit the Tribune is peddling, so your legal background might be helpful if anything comes up while I'm there. Think of it as a working vacation."

I fought the urge to point out that the story wasn't exactly bullshit but the concept of a working vacation was. "You want me to go to Montana for a month?"

"Don't say I never take you anywhere nice." Ben said, a trace of his normal confidence resurfacing. "Pinehaven is still a working ranch. We're in the process of acquiring a piece of land adjacent to the current property. Then there's federal contracts for grazing on federally-owned land that need to be reviewed, contracts with beef wholesalers—and I'll make it more than worth your while."

My mind reeled. This man knew my weaknesses. Contracts and money. Not that I was greedy—I would be perfectly happy as long as I could pay my law school loans and afford a latte every day.

I pulled out my phone to scroll through my calendar. It was wide open. Wide, wide open. Much like I pictured Montana.

"I guess I could make that work," I said unconvincingly. "But wouldn't you rather hide in Paris? Or on a warm island with a beach?"

"I'm not hiding. I'm laying low," Ben grumbled. "I'll give you until the end of the day to make a decision. And I'll need you to rearrange my schedule for the next month regardless of what you decide."

I made my way back to my desk, making a list of things I would need to get done before the end of the day. My email icon dinged and when I saw my name in the subject line of the newest email, I opened it right away. It was from Ben to HR and the board. He was informing them of his travel plans and requesting appropriate compensation for his executive assistant, who would ideally be making the trip with him. My eyes widened almost comically when I saw the amount he was approving for my time.

An executive assistant wasn't my dream job. In fact, if you had told me a year ago that I would soon be an executive assistant, I would have said you were crazy. I wasn't a total snob—there was absolutely nothing wrong with being an executive assistant. They were some of the hardest working people here. But I had meticulously planned my career trajectory the minute I received my acceptance letter to law school. In truth, I had been planning for my career practically from childhood. While my sisters wanted to play house, I wanted to play work, so I was often cast as the reluctant husband in exchange for my sisters' participation as my employees.

Everything had gone perfectly according to my plans. At least for a while. I'd landed a coveted internship my first year of school, made law review my second year and graduated at the top of my class. When I was chosen from a pool of highly-qualified candidates for an associate position in Sterling & Sterling's legal department, I felt unstoppable. All my carefully made plans were finally coming to fruition. Even the long hours in a tiny cubicle devoid of anything that would inspire happiness didn't faze me. I faced it all with a sense of contentment, knowing it was just the next step in my plan. Another box to be checked.

It took a year of missed birthdays, holidays, and weddings spent tucked away in my cubicle for me to realize I absolutely hated the life I had so carefully planned. The realization left me feeling totally adrift. I had no contingency plan. I was a planner by nature. I made lists, I planned, I organized. Nothing made me happier than checking items off lists. Planning made me feel like the world could be neatly organized, like everything had its place and was manageable. I had been so completely focused on this one goal that I hadn't even considered the possibility that I might need a backup plan. Planners did not fail! And this felt like the ultimate failure.

When the opportunity to become an executive assistant to the CEO came my way, I shoved aside my pride and plans, and took the position. It hadn't been a bad year either. I was making more than I did as a new attorney—which was incredibly depressing—and Ben was a really good boss. I actually got to see my family, and sunshine. I had even added a couple of stamps to my passport. As I looked at the number in that email one more time, just to make sure it was real, I accepted the fact that I was about to add a trip to Montana to my list of new experiences.

2.

I spent most of the morning and early afternoon frantically trying to rearrange Ben's schedule and making to-do lists. I also felt compelled to search for Pinehaven Ranch on the internet, just to reassure myself it had indoor plumbing. My knowledge of working ranches was limited to the reruns of *Bonanza* that my grandpa liked to nap to in the afternoons.

It wasn't until almost three in the afternoon that I finally felt like I had made enough headway to break for lunch. I peered into the refrigerator, digging for yesterday's lunch-meeting leftovers, which I had shoved somewhere toward the back. Somehow I never managed to actually eat any lunch at lunch meetings. They should have been called anti-lunch meetings, or "see how long you can sit in a group with very serious professionals before your stomach makes loud noises that resemble whales mating" meetings.

Finally I spotted the carton of chicken fried rice with my name on it. "Aha!"

"Evelyn!" An excited voice I recognized as belonging to my friend Anna had me abandoning my search for the yogurt I remembered stashing in the fridge at some point.

I straightened, smiling, to see two of my friends from the office standing in the kitchen's entryway. Anna and Hilari were executive assistants to two of the vice presidents who worked on the same floor. The two women had taken me under their wing when it had become obvious that I had absolutely no idea what I was doing as an assistant. Seven years of school and I was suddenly totally useless. The experience had been humbling, to say the least.

I was as grateful for their friendship as I was for their help.

We often worked the same long hours, and sometimes went out for dinner or drinks after we left the office. Anna and Hilari were also my go-to for all the office gossip. Nothing escaped them. I had yet to discover their sources.

"Is it true you're going to Montana with Ben?" Hilari asked, sitting down at the small table closest to the window. See what I mean?

"It's true. I had no idea Ben grew up in Montana until I read that stupid article. I mean I knew the Danver family started out in ranching, but I don't think I realized Ben was raised on the ranch. It's almost impossible to imagine Ben growing up on a ranch, isn't it?" I asked, taking an empty seat at the table.

"Impossible," Anna agreed. "But more importantly, you're going to get to meet his brother!"

"Why do you sound so excited about that?" I asked, shoveling a large forkful of fried rice into my mouth.

"Seriously, Evelyn? Where have you been? Please tell me you're joking," Hilari exclaimed, her large blue eyes widening with astonishment.

I only shrugged. To be completely honest, I was much more interested in the fried rice than in hearing about Ben's brother. I shoveled another large bite into my mouth, knowing they didn't need my encouragement to continue.

"Well, you know Ben *has* a brother, right?" Hilari asked. I nodded my head yes. I was, in fact, vaguely aware that Ben had a brother.

"And about his days on the circuit?" Hilari prompted.

"Circuit?" I questioned around a mouthful of rice. The only circuits I was familiar with were court circuits, and judging by the context clues, that was not what we were talking about here. Nobody gets excited about court circuits.

"Do you know anything about Ben's family? Anything at all? I don't know how you missed this. I love you, Evelyn, and I can't believe I'm actually saying this, but you need to pull your head out of the books a little more." Hilari said, rolling her eyes dramatically.

"She missed the last time Jack was here, Hil!" Anna turned to me and continued. "We didn't know anything about him either until he came into the office, which he almost never does. Anyway, Jack—that's his brother's name—was huge on the rodeo circuit five or so years ago. He won everything. He was really amazing. And ridiculously hot. Naturally, he was a real ladies' man, so it wasn't super surprising when he got engaged to Leigh Decker. They looked perfect together. Supposedly he was going to retire after the national championships but he got injured really badly during his ride. He was tossed off the bull and trampled. It was so awful I couldn't even watch the video. I don't know how he survived, really," Anna said. Hilari was nodding in agreement.

"Okay," I said, waving Anna on with my fork, "is that it? Hot cowboy with a supermodel fiancée who gets injured?"

"What, is that not enough for you?" Anna threw her hands up, frustrated by my lack of enthusiasm.

"Then, at some point during his recovery," Hilari said, "model fiancée breaks off the engagement. Jack kind of turns into a real manwhore. He was spotted with a different girl basically every week, and then he just disappeared." She gave a dramatic poof of her hands.

"Disappeared? What does that even mean?" I asked skeptically. "Is he missing? I think Ben would have at least mentioned having a missing brother."

"No, he isn't missing," Anna huffed, "he just totally disappeared from the spotlight. Every once in a while a tabloid will run a sighting of him somewhere or try to pair him up with a woman, but it's always at a ranch function. His fiancée probably destroyed him."

"He's at the ranch all the time then?" I asked.

"Well, yeah, he runs the ranch now. He never went back to riding in rodeos after his accident," Anna said.

"Great. Stuck in the middle of nowhere with two disgruntled Danvers. This just keeps getting better and better," I said, dropping my head into my hand with a sigh.

"You're thinking about this all wrong! You're going to be stuck in the middle of nowhere with one of the most gorgeous men I have ever seen. How is that a bad thing? I mean, what are the odds that Montana is swarming with attractive women?" Hilari said.

"Oh sure, I'll show up and he'll suddenly realize that he had it all wrong with the leggy, beautiful blondes—short brunettes are actually his type," I responded.

"Variety is the spice of life," Anna pointed out optimistically.

They spent the rest of lunch trying to convince me that the prospect of spending any amount of time on a ranch with an unhappy Ben and his reclusive, possibly also unhappy, brother was much more exciting than it sounded.

3.

By the time I made it back to my tiny apartment, I had to stumble through the dark to find the light switch. Fall had officially found Chicago, and the sun was setting earlier and earlier. Fall was my absolute favorite season, since Christmas didn't technically count as a season, but I did start to miss the sunshine. It felt like I left for work in the dark and came back home in the dark.

I slumped down on the couch and kicked off my shoes. Closing my eyes in relief, I nestled deeper into the cushions. The bedroom was less than ten feet away, but it seemed like an impossible task to drag myself the extra few steps when the couch was so comfortable and so *right here*.

A series of loud buzzes woke me and I reflexively swung my arm out, expecting to find my phone in its usual spot on my nightstand. When my hand found the television remote, I groaned, remembering I was on the couch and my phone was still in my bag by the door. I groggily made my way to my bag and dug around for the offending phone. I smiled when I saw the messages were all from my sisters.

My sister Corinne had messaged, *Celeste was exhausted from her play date at the pool. She passed out at 7! Date in 30?*

Yes! See you ladies in 30, Elise had responded.

I smiled as I typed my response. *I'm in too!*

The three of us seized every opportunity to video chat with each other. After Corinne had Celeste, it had become increasingly difficult to find time to talk face to face. Celeste was three and a half and a handful, but my sister loved every single crazy moment. It had always been Corinne's dream to have a family—she had mothered Elise and me pretty much since birth. Corinne had started dating a surgeon when he was still in medical school. They had dated for years before Corinne learned he had been having an affair with another surgeon for most of their relationship. She had been completely devastated, and Elise and I had felt totally helpless watching Corinne piece her life back together after the breakup. She was the oldest of the Mercer girls and we were used to her telling us what to do, not the other way around.

After the nasty breakup, Corinne had announced she would never date another doctor, because they were all womanizing narcissists. So when she announced that she was dating a pediatrician and she really liked him, we had all been shocked. If I'm being honest, I'd been a little surprised when Corinne first introduced Ted. On the surface, Ted seemed to be the exact opposite of Corinne in every way. His dark features stood in stark contrast to Corinne's honey blond hair and pale blue eyes. Ted wore horn-rimmed glasses and a bow tie most days, while Corinne always looked like she'd just stepped off a runway. She turned heads even now, at six months pregnant with a toddler in tow.

It didn't take long for the family to understand why she had fallen for him. He was kind and laughed easily. He took Corinne's boisterous personality in stride, and it was apparent that he absolutely adored her. When Celeste was born, Ted became the picture of a doting father.

I pulled my laptop out from my bag and sat it on the coffee table. I went to the kitchen and poured myself a glass of wine before settling back on the couch. Grabbing my laptop, I decided to do a little research before my sisters called.

I typed in the name *Jack Danver* but the search results didn't yield anything promising. Chewing on my lower lip, I refined my search, typing in *Jack Danver bull riding*. Article after article appeared in the results this time.

"Jackpot."

I clicked on the first article that appeared. I saw a picture of Jack waving to an excited crowd in the middle of what looked like a dirt-covered arena. He was dressed in what I imagined was standard cowboy attire: cowboy hat, chambray shirt, and black chaps covering a pair of blue jeans. He was quite possibly the most attractive man I had ever seen. 'Attractive' didn't really even do him justice. He was posing with one hand on his hat, the hat hiding his eyes in shadow, with a slight grin that suggested he knew just how good-looking he was. I thought he looked like every cowboy fantasy ever, all rolled into one man.

Maybe it was the wine and sleep deprivation but I found myself wondering what it would be like to be the girl he was searching the crowd for as he waved in that picture. What If he was so isolated on that ranch that he actually thought I was hilarious and sexy, not slightly awkward and shaped like a lumpy potato?

I forced myself to stop daydreaming and continued my super-healthy internet stalking. I scrolled through the search results until I found an article about Jack and Leigh. It was from a tabloid magazine, speculating on the cause of his broken engagement.

"For the second time in less than two weeks, Leigh Decker appeared at an event without her fiancé and without her engagement ring," I read aloud. I scanned the rest of the article. A picture zoomed in on her left hand, obviously missing a ring. Further down, the article had a shot of the formerly happy couple. I felt a strange stab of jealousy. Leigh was the kind of beautiful that was almost hard to believe existed in the real world. She looked like she belonged on the red carpet, even in the outfit she was wearing as she walked down the street on a shopping trip with friends. Her long, platinum blond hair was perfectly styled in loose curls, and she was wearing stiletto boots that made her already long, lean legs look like skyscrapers. She wore a stylish crop-top sweater that would have made me look like I'd accidentally purchased something from the children's section. There was nothing about her effortlessly glamorous look that I could have pulled off, even on my best day.

"I couldn't look like that unless... I had another body," I said, taking a drink of wine. And then a second drink for good measure because honestly, those legs. It was like I could actually feel the wine drowning my short-lived hope of capturing Jack's attention.

By the time I had paged through several other articles with pictures of Jack, my fantasy relationship was good and dead but my libido was very much alive. I was so focused on my internet stalking that I almost threw the laptop when the chat icon started ringing loudly.

"Get it together, Evelyn," I chastised myself before hitting the accept button.

I waved at the camera as Elise's smiling face appeared on my screen.

"Evie! Why are you so red? Did you just get back from a run?" Elise leaned closer to her screen to get a better look.

"What? No. I'm not red, and you know I don't run. It's probably just the wine," I said, raising my glass for Elise to see. There was no way I was going to admit my flush was due to ogling hot pictures of a cowboy I didn't know on the internet.

"Oh, wine! Good idea. I'll be right back!" Elise said, heading off camera. Elise was only nineteen months older than me, making her the middle sister, but she was the tallest of us three girls. Her height had earned her a volleyball scholarship, and was always a point of jealousy with me and Corinne, who had barely managed to sneak past five feet. Elise had honey-colored hair a few shades darker than Corinne's, and it was currently dyed a light lavender, making her bright blue eyes look almost violet. She could have easily been an actress taking Hollywood by storm. Tall and athletic, Elise was all effortless beauty. Her laid-back personality sometimes gave people the impression that she was the stereotypical dumb blonde, but Elise was the farthest thing possible from an airhead. She was a registered dietician, and counseled patients at a weight loss clinic run by a health insurance company.

A request from Corinne to join our video chat appeared on my screen. Her smiling but tired-looking face appeared next to Elise's.

"Hi ladies! It's so good to see your faces, your adult faces!" Corinne exclaimed, waving.

"Let me say hi to my nephew," I demanded.

"Your nephew is being a real pain. Feel free to ask him to ease up on the heartburn. Oh! and tell me what my feet look like. I miss them," Corinne said, angling her camera toward her round belly.

"Hey baby boy, your aunties can't wait to meet you," I said, kissing the screen.

"We love you already, but cut your mama some slack, kid," Elise added. Corinne swung the camera back up to her face.

"I spent all day listening to a bunch of toddlers. I need to hear about someone else's life right now. Are you both drinking wine? You are so mean," Corinne pouted.

Elise proceeded to tell us about her newest client at the clinic, who was significantly overweight and a difficult but hilarious case. He refused to follow the program she designed for him despite his increasing difficulty getting around, because he was the other half of a bluegrass duo called Fat and Sassy. Fans would be so disappointed if Fat Bill was skinny. Elise had spent the better part of an hour trying to convince Bill he would still be very sassy and talented even if he lost weight.

"What's new with you, Evie?" Corinne asked when Elise finished her story.

"I have to go to Pine Hollow, Montana, with Ben," I said with an exaggerated pout.

"Montana? What's in Montana?" Corinne asked.

"Ben's family has a ranch there. The *Tribune* article that was supposed to be about Sterling & Sterling and its young, ambitious CEO didn't actually turn out to be about the company and its young, ambitious CEO."

"Uh-oh," Elise said.

"Yeah, a photographer captured pictures of Ben leaving a hotel with the wife of a city commissioner. It's basically a tabloid piece disguised as serious journalism," I explained.

"Not to be mean here, but Ben doesn't exactly have a great track record with women. This is definitely not the first time he's caused headlines for sticking his dick where he shouldn't have. And there was the whole issue with the executive assistant before you—he's had a long line of assistants who were a little *too* personal. He isn't exactly an innocent victim here," Corinne pointed out.

"I know he doesn't make the best decisions when it comes to women. I don't think he has much of a defense in that department at all. But the story was supposed to be about a young CEO successfully running an international corporation, and it turned into a tabloid story. Ben might be a womanizer, but he's a brilliant businessman. One look at the annual earnings report is enough to prove how good he is at running the company," I said, feeling a little defensive of Ben. He was a great boss and made me feel valued.

"Okay, but what does any of this have to do with his family's ranch in Montana?" Elise interjected.

"The author of the article sent an advance copy to Ben and the board of directors as a courtesy before the article appears in the paper. They weren't happy. I'm not sure exactly what they said, but there was a lot of yelling. I think this is Ben's version of laying low until the whole thing blows over," I said.

"But why Montana? I mean, the man has his own jet! He could pretty much go anywhere in the world to lay low, like a beach or Europe. Montana seems... drastic," Corinne said.

"Drastic and awful," Elise agreed.

"His mom and younger brother still live there—it's been in their family forever. Maybe he wants to be near his family for support? He helps run the business part of the ranch too. I absolutely cannot picture Ben being on a ranch, let alone growing up on one. I keep imagining him riding a horse in one of his Armani suits."

"At least it sounds like you won't be alone in the middle of nowhere," Corinne said, trying to sound reassuring.

"I suppose. His brother Jack was a rodeo champion. He was pretty famous until he had an accident. He was even engaged to a model. Leigh Decker," I said.

"Leigh Decker—the supermodel, Leigh Decker? She was on the cover of *Sports Illustrated* last year. Wait, what? Is his last name Danver too? I'm looking him up right now," Elise said as she began typing. "Oh my gosh, Corinne, seriously, you need to see this guy! He is *gorgeous*. I'm about to start panting."

"I'm looking at him right now! Is he even real? He looks like he should be on the cover of a romance novel. A very, very good romance novel," Corinne said.

"He is really good-looking, isn't he? Ugh," I groaned, lowering my head to rest on my arms.

"Why are you making it sound like that's a bad thing, Evelyn? This trip is starting to look a whole lot better. You're going to be stuck on a ranch in the middle of nowhere with a real-life cowboy who looks like a freaking naughty dream come true. How is that a bad thing?" Elise asked.

"Do you know what I would give to be stranded in the middle of nowhere with him right now? Do you know what I would *do* to him if I was? So much, Evie, *so* much," Corinne added.

"Honestly, what do you think is going to happen? I'm very clearly not his type. You saw the pictures of his fiancée and his rebound ladies—not to mention all the women who were pretty obviously his rodeo groupies. Did either of you see a single picture of him where he isn't with at least one gorgeous woman? I doubt he'd notice me if I was the only woman in all of Montana."

"You're going to be in his house, so I'm pretty sure he's at least going to notice you, Evie," Corinne pointed out. "And according to Google, the proper term is *buckle bunnies*."

"And you might *be* the only woman in Montana, so there is that. I mean what is Montana's population size, anyway, twenty people and some buffalo? I'm kidding! Geez!" Elise said, laughing at my disgruntled look. "I think there are actually buffalo, though..."

"Okay, I will admit that I very briefly imagined a Jack-Evelyn situation, but I need to be realistic. There's no sense getting my hopes up about something that is never going to happen. He isn't going to be interested in the chubby brunette who works for his brother," I replied, unable to keep the annoyance out of my voice.

"Why do you always do that? You make it sound like you're the Hunchback of Notre Dame and you're not! You're beautiful, Evelyn. I don't know why you're the only one who can't see it," Corinne scolded. Elise was nodding her head in agreement.

I didn't want to talk about my lack of confidence about my appearance, so I attempted to steer the conversation to the obvious flaw in my sisters' plan.

"It doesn't matter. What would happen if he did—against all odds—find me attractive? I'd move to Montana and live on a ranch? He doesn't seem like the type to move to Chicago, even for the deep-dish pizza. It would never work," I said.

"Jesus, Evelyn, you haven't even met him and you're already planning your breakup! You can't plan an entire relationship with anyone, let alone someone you don't even know yet," Elise said.

"Furthermore, who said you have to date him? It is possible to have fun with someone without being seriously involved with them, you know. Live a little for a change. And he looks like someone who knows how to have a lot of fun. A roll in the hay, if you will." Corinne wiggled her eyebrows suggestively.

"First, I am legitimately worried for Ted's safety with your hormones right now, Corinne. Second, you both know I'm not good at the whole casual, relaxed thing. I don't know how to be casual. The whole idea of spending who knows how long trapped on that ranch is starting to make me want to quit. I'm dreading this trip even more now," I said.

They spent the remainder of the video date trying to convince me that I needed to relax. I couldn't help but feel like I'd had the exact same conversation with Anna and Hilari earlier. But despite the nearly identical pep talks, I still found myself lying awake late into the night worrying—and, if I was being honest, fantasizing about what Jack looked like in those chaps.

4.

Morning came way too soon. I'd spent most of the night going over what I needed to pack and everything I'd need to get done before Ben picked me up. I didn't think I'd slept more than a few hours. Sitting up, I felt a dull ache in my left temple, and I groaned. A migraine was the last thing I needed this morning. I grabbed two aspirin before starting a pot of coffee, even though I knew I'd spend the entire flight trying to remember if I had turned off the coffee pot before leaving my apartment.

My first task was to finish packing. Being someone who excelled at planning and making lists meant I was a terrible packer. I tended to pack for every possible contingency or scenario that could arise on any given trip, which often required multiple suitcases crammed with clothing. You never know when there might be a blizzard on the beach! It didn't help that, according to my research, the weather was all over the place in Montana during September. My inability to pack light was a problem when we flew on commercial airlines, but luckily, we were taking the corporate jet for this trip so overpacking wouldn't be an issue.

Three suitcases later, I finally felt like I was prepared for whatever Montana might throw my way. I moved on to making sure most of my appliances were turned off and the perishables were all thrown away. Ben called me as I was on my way back from taking out the garbage to let me know they would be there in ten minutes.

"Do you have a lot of luggage? Rodney packed for twelve people so we don't have a lot of room left in the trunk."

"How do you define a lot? More or less than three suitcases?" I responded, fumbling with my keys.

"I don't understand what you two packed for. You realize there are stores in Montana, right?" I could almost hear him rubbing his forehead with his free hand.

"Actually, I wasn't sure there would be stores in Montana, thank you very much," I quipped.

"Just be ready in ten minutes."

It took almost the entire ten minutes for me to lug my suitcases down the stairs of my old brownstone. I loved the historic feel of the building, but sometimes I wished they had updated it to include an elevator. This was definitely one of those times. The car pulled up and Ben hopped out, smiling. It looked like the stress of yesterday had already been forgotten.

"You better hope there isn't a lot of traffic this morning or it's going to be a long car ride with all that luggage on our laps," he said, grabbing two of my suitcases.

"I can't help it. You know I like to be prepared," I said, dragging the last bag toward the back of the car while trying to take gulps of coffee from my traveling mug.

"What are you preparing for? Armageddon?" he mumbled with his head in the trunk.

It took a few minutes, but Ben was able to cram all the luggage into the vehicle. Even more miraculously, the trunk closed—after he gave it two solid slams.

Once inside the car, Ben began making introductions.

"Rodney, this is my executive assistant, Evelyn Mercer. She'll be helping out as needed during the trip. She's smart enough to do both our jobs and probably do them better, so don't hesitate to use her as a resource. Evelyn, this is Rodney Ashcroft."

Rodney extended his hand to me and almost crushed my fingers in a handshake that would have made the Hulk grimace.

"Pleasure to meet you, Evelyn. I was just telling Ben how valuable a good assistant is. My girl just left me after ten years and I'm practically helpless without her."

I gagged inwardly at "my girl," but I smiled outwardly and allowed the two to slip back into the conversation my arrival had interrupted. Rodney was a junior partner at Porter, Crane & Wright, one of the largest mergers and acquisition firms in Chicago. Sterling & Sterling used them for all our acquisitions that were too big to be handled in-house. When Ben had mentioned he would be joining us on this trip, I had briefly considered resigning effective immediately.

Rodney was notoriously smarmy. He wore a wedding ring, but never missed a chance to corner female employees to introduce himself and "offer his assistance."

Obviously, Rodney had forgotten that we'd met several times before when I was working in the legal department. He had managed to corner me shortly before I took the job with Ben. I had been poring over a contract looking for mistakes, and was startled when he leaned over me to see what I was working on. He'd said he liked to introduce himself to all the newer associates, because he recognized how valuable all the players were to the success of the team. I had to concentrate to keep myself from visibly cringing and leaning away from him. It wasn't uncommon for the girls from multiple departments to exchange horror stories over lunch after one of his visits. Rumor had it that his wife was equally transparent in her extramarital activities—two gross peas in a sleazy pod.

Rodney and Ben continued their conversation for the duration of the trip to the airport, and I was grateful for the chance to rest my eyes. The dull ache in my left temple was still trying to work its way up to a migraine. I was dreading the thought of a long flight with a migraine *and* Rodney, who was the human equivalent of a migraine.

Much to my dismay, once on the plane, Rodney chose the seat directly across from mine and immediately tried to lure me into a conversation. Even the pre-flight speech one of the two flight attendants who would be assisting with our flight was in the process of giving didn't deter him.

"So Evelyn, Ben tells me you're also an attorney. Quite the

career change—going from attorney to executive assistant, I mean."

"It was. I think I made the right decision though," I responded, purposely trying to keep my answers simple enough not to warrant a follow-up question.

"Got tired of spending all your time in the basement with us bottom-feeders, huh?" Rodney said with a chuckle.

I knew that, in reality, Rodney had a large office with windows facing the Chicago River and a view of Millennium Park.

"My new office is a little bit nicer than my cubicle in the basement." I managed to force a smile.

While one flight attendant instructed us where the emergency life vests were located, the other appeare with coffee, saving me from having to continue the conversation with Rodney. I sipped my coffee and tried to close my eyes the rest of the fight, only joining in the conversation when I had to.

"You seem deep in thought, Evelyn. Care to share?" Rodney asked, leaning forward in his seat to address me as the pilot finished his reminder to buckle our seat belts as we prepared for our descent.

"Just trying to remember whether I turned off the coffee pot," I responded, hoping I sounded friendly and not nervous. I was not a good flier. Planes just seemed liked airborne coffins that could drop out of the sky in a fiery inferno of death at any minute. Smaller planes were even worse. To be fair, I'm not sure a corporate jet counts as small, but it didn't feel as steady as a commercial airplane.

I peered anxiously out the window, searching for any sign of a runway as the plane began to make its descent. The horizon was filled with trees, and it seemed almost impossible that a runway could be lying somewhere below. Just as I was beginning to really worry, I saw a tiny strip of cement appear in between the trees. I watched as it got closer and closer, growing steadily larger but still not looking wide or long enough to be a runway. I closed my eyes, gripping the armrests, until I felt the familiar jolt of the plane landing safely.

Opening my eyes, I saw that the 'airport' was actually little more than a four-lane road with a few buildings at the far end. Ben unfastened his seatbelt and smiled at us.

"Welcome to Montana," he said, gesturing toward the door like a game show host.

I turned my attention back to the window and watched as two men wearing bright orange vests appeared from one of the buildings and moved toward the plane. Parked at the far end of the runway near the row of buildings was a large black truck with a man leaning casually against the front, watching the scene unfold. I wondered if this was the famous brother I had spent an embarrassing amount of time fantasizing about since my internet stalking last night.

The thud of the staircase hitting the ground jolted me back to the moment, and I realized Ben and Rodney were gathering their things and making their way to the exit. I unbuckled my seatbelt and slipped my jacket on. I focused on climbing out of the plane without tripping. It was harder than I expected – my attention was divided between avoiding Rodney's helping hands and the figure slowly approaching the plane.

Ben walked out to meet the man and wrapped him in a quick embrace. Rodney and I followed behind Ben like ducklings behind a mama duck while the "ground crew" started to unload our luggage. When the two men separated, I took the opportunity to covertly examine the man I assumed was the former rodeo star while he was distracted. My eyes traveled up denim covered thighs that definitely looked like they were capable of holding onto an angry bull for eight seconds, to a button-up chambray shirt stretched across broad shoulders. I swallowed, as my eyes traveled the rest of the distance up to a face that left me feeling slightly dazed. Everything about him seemed to be just a little bit more than Ben somehow. He was just a little taller than Ben, his brown hair a few shades darker, his muscles a little broader everywhere, and he made my heart do something wildly erratic it had absolutely never done for Ben.

"Rodney, this is my brother, Jack. He looks a little rough around the edges, but don't be fooled—the man has a head for business." Ben smiled broadly as the two men shook hands.

I braced myself for one of Rodney's speeches, but it seemed Rodney was also busy sizing up the newcomer to our party, and he responded with a courteous hello. I didn't know the man was even capable of limiting himself to just one word.

"Jack, this is my executive assistant, Evelyn. I decided I couldn't do without her this trip." Putting one hand between my shoulders, Ben propelled me forward.

I took Jack's reluctantly extended hand and shook it firmly, trying to maintain a confident smile. Judging by the scowl on his face, he was not pleased at the news of an unexpected guest, but I was determined not to let my nervousness show.

"It's nice to meet you, Jack," I said, trying to keep my voice steady and resisting the urge to break eye contact. His brown eyes were warm despite his obvious displeasure. Somewhere in my mind the roughness of his hand registered—which seemed like a strange thing to notice, all things considered.

He responded with a curt nod and dropped my hand like it was diseased. Ben directed us toward the truck where our pile of luggage was stacked and waiting to be loaded. I listened as Ben and Jack made small talk about the ranch and the flight here, with the occasional interjection from Rodney.

Jack made quick work of folding back the bed cover and began loading our luggage into the truck while Rodney and Ben hopped into the cab, deep in conversation about the procurement clauses they had been discussing on the flight. In an attempt to earn myself some type of goodwill, I reached for one of my suitcases and tried to swing it over the side of the truck into the bed. But my swing came up short, and the large bag came tumbling over the edge toward me. I lunged, trying to simultaneously shield myself from the wayward bag and catch it before it hit the ground. I heard myself grunt as I fumbled, trying to control the avalanche of bag tumbling toward me. *What did I even pack that was this heavy?*

"Evelyn, get in the truck before you kill yourself. Let Jack get the bags," Ben called from the passenger-side window.

"It's fine," I half-mumbled, half-yelled, "they just always put these handles in such awkward spots. No one's arms work like this." I swung the bag with more force this time, successfully clearing the side of the truck. Avoiding everyone's eyes, I slid into the cab.

So much for goodwill, I thought.

Rodney seemed to have found his voice and was busy describing his last wilderness adventure—where he had managed to land a "real nice twelve-point buck;" mounted the antlers in his office, even—to his captive audience. Literally, we were captive, or at least I felt captive, since hopping out of the truck to watch Jack load luggage didn't seem like much of an alternative. I rolled my eyes, facing the window, and thought of plausible scenarios in which Rodney actually killed a large deer. I knew the most believable explanation was that he'd hit the poor creature with his Jaguar on the way home from a steak dinner.

Jack joined us just in time to catch the end of Rodney's story and even he looked a little skeptical. He made a non-committal noise that was mostly drowned out as the truck's engine roared to life.

"Rodney, the hunting out here is unbelievable—right, Jack? We get all kinds of sportsmen during the various seasons. In fact, we used to host some of the parties. Jack can take you out if you're interested. I don't have the patience or I would offer," Ben hastened to explain, shrugging his shoulders at the obviously irritated looks coming from his brother.

"Yeah, that would be great. I bet you have a lot of big game out here. Better than deer. Do you ever get any wolves?" Rodney asked.

I glared at him, not even trying to hide my disgust. As far as I was concerned, wolves were the dogs of the forest, and I loved dogs. Jack peered at him through the rearview mirror; I thought I saw his lip curl a little before he answered.

"No, we don't get a lot of wolves. People around here let them be unless they give us trouble. You're looking at a lot of elk and moose. Someone gets a bear on occasion," Jack responded evenly.

"Now a bear would be something. We don't get many in Illinois, huh?" Rodney said, slapping the back of Ben's seat, totally oblivious to the shift in mood.

I was grateful to be excluded from this particular conversation, and used the opportunity to give the rapidly changing scenery outside the window my full attention. I could tell we were gaining elevation. There would be sudden breaks in the tree cover where rocky patches peeked through, seeming to slope down into smaller patches of green. Everything seemed to be bigger. *This is why they call it big sky country*. I saw the reflection of my smile in the window.

"Hey, Evelyn are you still with us?" Ben asked from the front seat. "You're awfully quiet back there."

"Just taking in the view," I answered, smiling at him. "What type of trees are those—the bigger ones that look like... like they have a Christmas tree on top of them?"

"Lodgepole pine," Jack responded, not even bothering to glance my way.

"Oh." I was startled by his response, even though I should have known he would be one of two people in the truck likely to answer. "I don't think I know that one."

Of course you don't. I chastised myself for sounding like an idiot. *You wouldn't have asked if you had known.* Why, why, why could I not just answer like a normal human being? I looked back out the window, hoping no one would see the slight reddening of my cheeks. The trees were so tall I had to crane my neck with my face pressed very close to the glass to see their tops. Some of the pines seemed to have a golden hue that reminded me of marigolds, and the green and brown landscape was punctuated with bright purple. One of my hands came to rest on the edge of the window. Montana might not turn out

Emily Mayer

to be the total wasteland I had been imagining, but I was still convinced being stuck with two disgruntled Danvers and Rodney was going to be torture.

5.

My gaze remained fixed on the landscape for the rest of the ride. I was in awe of all the vibrant colors. I had thought of Montana as being all tall grass and flat land. This was an entirely new part of the country to me, and I couldn't help smile at the discovery.

When it appeared, as if out of nowhere, the house looked like it had always been a part of the landscape. The front of the house rose to a point, like an A-frame, and appeared to be one big window made to overlook the mountains. The rest of the house stretched outwards from both sides of the large window and was composed of a combination of wood and stone siding. A large porch on one side of the house was lined with rockers and dotted with window boxes filled with bright flowers. It looked like a home you would see on the front of a magazine.

I noticed several barns and fenced-in areas just behind the house, which I assumed were for animals. Closer to the house was what appeared to be a large garden and a chicken coop. There was not one single part of the sprawling ranch that I didn't immediately love. It felt strangely like coming home.

The truck's driver, however, didn't seem to share my enthusiasm. In fact, I didn't think he had cracked even the tiniest smile since greeting his brother back at the airport.

As the truck approached the house, the front door swung wide open and a woman walked onto the porch and waved. A large dog was right on her heels, managing to sneak out of the door just before it closed. The dog raced to the end of the porch and began to howl. The woman swatted good-naturedly at the dog in what I guessed was an attempt to stop the howl-

Emily Mayer

ing. I smiled at the scene.

When the truck came to a stop, both the woman and the dog came bounding toward it. When Ben stepped out, the woman immediately wrapped him up in a hug. The hound dog was enthusiastically jumping and drooling on Jack, who was trying to remind him he had only been gone for a couple of hours. I circled around the back of the truck to stand beside Rodney, because standing next to Rodney actually seemed like a more appealing option than being alone on the other side with Jack.

"I'm so glad you're here, Ben! Break your mother's heart, staying away so long," she said, pulling back to smile up at him.

"I know, I know. I should have come home sooner," Ben responded affectionately, pulling her into another hug and kissing the top of her head.

"I'm sure you remember our attorney, Rodney," Ben said, extending his arm in Rodney's direction.

She took Rodney's hand and smiled warmly. "Of course. It's good to see you again, Rodney." I thought I heard a hint of forced friendliness in her voice.

"Thanks for having me. You have a beautiful home," Rodney responded enthusiastically, shaking her hand.

"And who do we have here?" she asked, turning her gaze toward me. Normally, I would have been uncomfortable with the attention shifting to me, but everything about the woman exuded warmth. Her short brown hair had hints of grey just peeking through in some places, and she had those tiny wrinkles at the corners of her eyes that only come from smiling often. She was a lot shorter than either of her children, but she had the same rich brown eyes.

"Mom, this is Evelyn, my new assistant. She's great, you'll love her. Sorry to surprise you with an extra guest, but I didn't think I would ever talk her into coming." Ben winked at me like this was some joke we shared.

"Well, surprise or not, we're glad to have you here, Evelyn,"

32

she said, her warm smile never faltering.

I took her hand, easily returning her smile. "It's nice to meet you, Mrs. Danver. Ben didn't actually tell me I had the option of not coming. I'm sorry if I'm an unexpected guest."

"Oh, no need to apologize! We have plenty of rooms and I love having guests. But please—call me Mary. You're going to be here for a while and 'Mrs. Danver' will get tiresome for everyone," she responded graciously.

A brown blur rounded the truck enthusiastically greeting Ben before smashing its nose into my leg, almost knocking me to the ground. I reached for the side of the truck to steady myself and looked down to see the dog from the porch peering up at me, his tail wagging furiously behind him. I couldn't help laughing as I dropped to my knees to greet the adorable little guy. I was met with enthusiastic kisses and head butts.

"Hello, you handsome boy. You are just the sweetest thing, aren't you? Yes you are. I just love you already," I said, scratching his ears and underneath his chin.

"I think the feeling is mutual," Ben laughed. "Hank Williams, give the poor girl a break!"

"I don't mind. His name is Hank Williams? Like the 'I'm So Lonesome I Could Cry' Hank Williams?"

"The howling and big ears reminded Jack of Hank Williams. Their granddad was a big Hank Williams fan—the musician, not the dog," Mary explained.

I stood, only to have Hank Williams lay down across the top of my feet, making it impossible for me to take a step. I shrugged my shoulders in response to the laughter the dog's theatrics elicited.

"Well, I hope you like that dog more than I do, because I think you have a new boyfriend," Ben said, still chuckling.

"What can I say? It was love at first sight for us both," I said, stooping down to give his belly some pets.

"Why don't we head inside? I'm sure you'll all want to get settled before dinner. Don't worry about the bags. Jack can have some of the guys take them to your rooms. Jack, put

Evelyn in the lilac room. I think she might like her own bath-room," Mary said, turning toward the house.

"Up, Hank Williams," Jack ordered.

Hank popped up and trotted behind Jack toward the barn, releasing my feet. The inside of the house had the same warm, beautiful design as the outside. The entryway had a nook for coats and boots, and it was currently occupied by several hats and two dusty coats. Beyond the entry, a large staircase wound up to the second floor where part of the hallway was visible, lined with framed pictures. Just to the right of the staircase a large stone chimney climbed the wall of a cozy living room. Everywhere I looked, warm woods lined the floors, walls, or bookcases. It had a Joanna Gaines feel to it that I loved.

"I'm sure you can show Rodney and Evelyn to their rooms while I finish dinner," Mary instructed Ben.

"I think I remember where everything is," Ben responded playfully, earning him a smile and small laugh from his mother, who very obviously adored her oldest son.

"Actually Mrs... Mary, would you mind if I followed you to the kitchen? I forgot my water on the plane," I asked.

"Of course! The kitchen is this way—you're always welcome to help yourself, Evelyn," Mary replied, motioning for me to follow her down the hallway just to the left of the stairs.

I noticed a large office on the right, whose large windows overlooked the barns and fenced-in areas. It was the perfect place for the office. I hoped it would be where we would be working during our stay.

"You really do have a beautiful home," I said, echoing Rodney's earlier sentiments but without the extra helping of creepy.

"Thank you. It was truly a labor of love! My husband was a big dreamer, and I'd like to think I kept him grounded. When he got the idea to move to the ranch fulltime, I absolutely refused to go along with him unless he convinced me this wasn't just a passing fancy. So, he built me a house. Nothing says permanent like a house."

"I would say this house is a pretty compelling argument. And I can see where Ben got his negotiation skills."

Mary laughed as we entered the kitchen. In contrast to the dark earth tones the rest of the house was decorated with, the kitchen was a bright yellow with white cabinets that made the entire room seem open and inviting. I suspected a great deal of time was spent in this room, gathered around the breakfast bar lined with stools or the large farm-style table just beyond the cooking area.

"The glasses are over here," Mary said, opening the cabinet to retrieve a glass. "Again, you're welcome to help yourself to anything you find in here. Goodness knows all the boys do."

"Thank you," I said, gratefully taking the glass from Mary. I hadn't realized how thirsty I was until we walked into the house.

"I hope you don't mind that I had Jack put your things in a separate room. You're welcome to stay in Ben's room. I just thought it might be nice to have your own space too," Mary said nonchalantly.

"We don't… I mean, we've never… umm… I mean… I just work for him. I don't even know why he hired me. I called him an idiot to his face. I mean, I didn't know it was his face but still," I stammered, surprised at the implication that Mary thought I was sleeping with her son. I was a nervous rambler. The more nervous I got, the more I rambled.

Mary raised her eyebrows in surprise.

"You called him an idiot?"

"Yes. Of course, I didn't know Ben was Ben. He had just gotten rid of his last assistant the day before, and was sitting at her desk rifling through some papers. I just assumed he must be Ben's assistant. I had never been up to the executive floor; I pretty much had no idea what happened outside of the legal department, which is like a cave. My horrible boss had me run some documents up to Ben for him to review and sign, because I went through three years of law school to track down signatures. I found a couple of pretty obvious mistakes on the elevator ride up and I pointed them out to him when I handed the documents over. I told him his boss probably would have missed them, because he must be an even bigger idiot than my boss if he actually let her run the merger and acquisitions department. "

Mary was listening intently, her grin widening as I rambled on.

"And how did you end up going from the legal department to his assistant?" Mary prodded when I didn't continue.

"The next day I got a message telling me to go to Ben's office immediately. I was pretty sure his assistant had told him I'd called him an idiot, and I was going to be fired as soon as I stepped off the elevator." My hands started sweating just remembering that elevator ride. "I had finally saved up enough money to quit at the end of the month, but quitting and being fired are two totally different things. As you can probably imagine, I almost died when I saw Ben sitting at his actual desk. For no reason I can possibly think of, he offered me the job as his executive assistant. "

"You didn't mind going from an attorney to an assistant?" It was the obvious question.

"I told him no at first, because it did seem like a huge step back career-wise. Law school wasn't easy or cheap. He offered me a pretty big raise but I still said no. He told me to think about it and give him my final answer on Tuesday, because he had to leave for London on Wednesday and his assistant usually traveled with him. I'd never been to London, so I said yes. I absolutely hated my job anyway, so I chose London." I shrugged.

Later I had learned the real reason Ben had been so desperate to hire me. He'd had what could only be described as a very unprofessional relationship with his last assistant, which did not end well. The company had paid her a large settlement to avoid her leaking the relationship to the press, and the board finally put their collective foot down. They gave Ben two weeks to find a new assistant they approved of, or they would find an acceptable replacement for him. I was the perfect solution. I was smart and career-focused, as evidenced by my tenure in the legal department. Most importantly, I looked nothing like any of his previous assistants. The board readily approved of Ben's new hire.

Despite his track record, Ben was a great boss. He never yelled or insulted me like my previous boss had. He always asked my opinion. I felt more valued in my new role than I ever had as an attorney, and I'd learned a lot about how the company operated in the months I had been working with him. It wasn't the job I had imagined for myself, and I had no idea where it fit into my long-term plan, but I was happy for the moment.

Jack walked through the door, pausing when he saw we were in the middle of a conversation.

"Am I interrupting?" he asked, looking slightly nervous and a lot like he wanted to bolt.

"Not at all. Actually, if Evelyn is all set, why don't you show her where her room is so she can get settled in before dinner," Mary said.

"No, no, that's not necessary. I'm sure I can find my own way," I said, walking toward the door for emphasis.

"Don't be silly. Jack doesn't mind, do you, Jack?" Mary asked.

"Nope, it's no problem," Jack replied, looking very much like it was a problem.

I once again tried not to look as nervous as I felt at the prospect of being alone with Jack. I waited for him to take the lead and followed behind him silently. I reminded myself that there was no way he could dislike me on sight. He had probably just been confused when Ben introduced me. He was used to Ben's assistants looking more like women he would date.

The framed pictures I'd noticed earlier caught my eye as we walked down the hallway, and I slowed to take a better look at them. They were all photographs, some of them in black and white and so old they were worn yellow.

"Are these all family pictures?" I asked without thinking, curiosity winning out over my nerves.

"Most of them are," Jack responded. He moved behind me to look at the picture that had caught my attention. "Those are our great-great grandparents, Louisa and Theodore Sterling. I think that was taken in Boston."

"Louisa and Theodore started the company, right?" I asked.

"You did your homework," Jack said, walking down the hallway away from me.

I scampered after him, trying to keep up, and we walked the rest of the way down the hall in silence. I was grateful Mary had insisted on having Jack show me the way to my room. The house was bigger than it looked, and we passed several doors down a winding hallway before we stopped.

"Here you go, this is your room," Jack said, opening the door for me and standing aside.

"Thank you," I said, trying to avoid eye contact as I crept past him into the room.

"If you need anything, just let someone know. Ben's room is down the hall to the right. Third door after the corner," he said casually.

I felt a flare of unexpected anger and snapped, "Great, I'd hate to get lost."

I had no trouble meeting his eyes to glare at him as I slammed the door. *Why does everyone just assume I'm sleeping with Ben?* But some small part of me acknowledged that what bothered me most was that Jack thought I was sleeping with his brother. I didn't really care to think about what that meant. I was completely willing to just chalk it up to lack of sleep and a long plane ride.

6.

Pulling myself out of my thoughts, I looked around the room. The walls were painted a soft lilac which was beautifully set off by the white crown molding. A distressed-wood dresser and matching nightstand gave the room an almost rustic quality. The walls were decorated with pressed flowers that had been placed in distressed white wood frames, complementing the molding. A large four-poster bed sat in the middle of the wall, across from picture windows that overlooked a large field leading up to the mountains looming in the distance. It was obvious that every detail of the room had been lovingly planned. I couldn't wait to crawl into the large bed, which had been decorated with lots of plush pillows that seemed to be calling out to me.

I pulled my phone out of my bag to let my family know I had arrived.

I sent the first message to my mom, knowing she would be checking her phone waiting to hear I had landed safely.

Me: *Landed safe and sound. Montana is BIG. Love you.*

Scrolling down the message list, I found the well-used group message my sisters and I talked on throughout the day.

Me: *Made it to Montana. The house is beautiful! And big.*

Almost immediately, I heard the familiar ding notifying me that I had a message.

Elise: *Evie, I love you but no one cares about the house! Did you see his brother?*

Corinne: *Please tell me he's even hotter in real life than he is in pictures, Evie! I need to live through you right now.*

I smiled reading my sisters' responses. Technology made living away from each other seem almost bearable. I'd spent the first half of my life wishing I was an only child, and the second half wishing I lived closer to my sisters. Life was weird like that.

Me: *He's fine. We didn't really talk much.*

I purposely avoided the details I knew my sisters were actually curious about. A little part of me wanted to avoid having to tell my sisters that Jack had pretty much ignored me the entire ride—when he wasn't acting like I was carrying the plague. Another part of me wasn't ready to admit that Jack was probably the hottest human being I had ever seen. He needed to carry a warning label: *DO NOT look directly at heat source, may cause eye damage.*

Elise: *Fine is not an answer! Unless you mean fineeeee.*

Corinne: *I really don't care whether he's a great conversationalist, Evie. I spent all morning watching cartoons with Celeste, and I haven't seen my lady parts in months. MONTHS! Give me something to work with over here!*

Me: *Sorry, I have to change for dinner. I don't have time for a lengthy description of his hotness right now. Wine date later? Tomorrow night maybe?* I responded, hoping to keep them at bay a little longer.

Corinne: *Fine. But don't think this means you're getting out of this!*

I tossed my phone onto the bed and turned my attention to the suitcase laying by the dresser. Living out of a suitcase was never something I could tolerate for more than a few days. It always made me feel unorganized and unsettled. I surveyed the luggage, chewing on my lower lip while trying to assess how much I could unpack before dinner. I made a quick to do list and got started.

7.

The sunlight I had been inching farther and farther across the bed to avoid had finally reached my face. I groaned, admitting defeat. One more roll and I would be on the floor. Aware that it hadn't been the best idea to indulge in a second glass of wine last night in an effort to survive dinner, I tentatively opened my right eye to assess how badly my migraines would punish me for that decision.

Dinner had been a complex balancing act of trying to engage Mary in conversation while also avoiding eye contact with Jack and dodging Rodney's quick hands, which always seemed to find a way to rest on an arm or shoulder.

At one point, I thought I caught Jack watching as Rodney's hand traveled from my shoulder to my back while he was regaling the room with a much-exaggerated retelling of a contract negotiation he had just completed. Involuntarily, I glanced up and met his eye, instantly triggering a blush. I'd felt it starting at my chest and slowly creeping to my cheeks, and I winced now, remembering how quickly I had averted my eyes. Had he attributed the blush and awkwardness to the accidental eye contact or Rodney's freely roaming hands? Neither possibility was particularly appealing, but I doubted he would assume I'd had too much wine after just one glass.

When I had slowly opened my right eye without the familiar shooting pain immediately appearing, I cautiously opened my left eye and sat up. There was just the familiar dull ache that promised to be a migraine later if I didn't pay attention to it. Swinging my feet over the side of the bed, I opened the nightstand drawer where I had stashed some of my medicine in case I needed it in the middle of the night. I always made sure I kept a few pills on my nightstand when I was traveling; it wouldn't be wise to stumble around a dark and unfamiliar room trying to find my medicine.

So much of who I was had been shaped by my migraines. My need to carefully plan every aspect of my life stemmed from always having to be prepared for the possibility that a migraine would ruin my plans and then I'd have to scramble to compensate for the lost time. The knowledge that pain was always lurking just below the surface had made me a little more cautious, a little more anxious, than most people. I'd never been as carefree as Elise, who never had the need to follow a plan and whose spontaneity often inspired a combination of horror and envy in me. Even Corinne seemed to have the ability to roll with all those bumps in the road that instilled almost crippling fear in my overly anxious heart.

Despite it all, I had never allowed my migraines to hold me back. In a very significant way, they had made me tough and determined, too. Whenever a migraine forced me to throw in the towel during a study session in law school, I would be in the library the next day before the sun came up, making up for the time I'd lost in the dark with an icepack pressed to my forehead. I worked extra long when my head felt fine, so as not to fall too far behind the next time a migraine sent me to bed for countless hours. I had been careful to surround myself with friends who didn't disappear after a few canceled plans, and people who weren't put off by my need for quiet nights in with friends instead of noisy, crowded bars.

A loud grunt from the other side of the bed made me smile as I gulped down the two aspirins. A loud pawing and whining had startled me after I'd crawled, exhausted, into bed last night. Hank Williams had been eagerly waiting outside my bedroom door to be admitted, and jumped right into bed with me when I opened the door. At first I had protested the intrusion, but it quickly became apparent that he was not going to leave the bed without the use of force. The dog was like my own personal heater and didn't seem to mind if I stuck my cold feet underneath him.

"I know, Hank. I'm not happy about getting up either. At least you wake up looking handsome," I said, scratching my bedmate behind the ears. Hank lifted a paw to cover his face and gave a whimper of protest.

"You're a real drama queen," I said, getting out of bed and heading to the bathroom. I needed a quick shower to clear my head and wake me up before I faced my first day on the ranch. Right now, having my own bathroom attached to the room seemed like a pretty good tradeoff for not having a balcony. I was fully aware that my "quick" showers usually turned into standing under the hot water until I almost fell asleep. It was one of the few habits my former roommates had found cause to complain about.

After standing in the warm water long enough for all the stress of the previous day's travel to be burned off, my skin and my muscles had turned to pudding, making me want to crawl back into bed instead of getting dressed to face the day. I surveyed the clothes I had hurriedly unpacked last night. I had no idea what to expect from today since Ben hadn't exactly given me an itinerary for this last-minute trip. I'd be lying if I said I wasn't thinking about seeing Jack again when I finally settled on a pair of dark, slim-fitting jeans and a soft pink tunic sweater that I knew complemented my dark hair and pale skin. I pulled my hair to the side and secured it into a thick braid that hung over my left shoulder. I decided to go for a casual look with my make-up, and stuck with eyeliner and mascara. Then I pulled on the soft leather ankle boots Elise had sent me last Christmas and headed downstairs.

Following the smell of coffee, I managed to find my way to the kitchen—and immediately came to a halt at the sight of the five men scattered around the room, eating and talking loudly. No one had seen me enter the kitchen, so I seriously considered sneaking out again before anyone could spot me. But the need for coffee quickly overpowered my desire to not be trapped in a room with five strange men. Well, four strange men and Ben, whom I recognized sitting at the breakfast bar talking to an older man dressed in jeans and a chambray shirt.

I crept along the counter toward the coffee pot, trying not to draw attention to myself. I was not great with strangers to begin with, and without at least one cup of coffee in my system I was totally hopeless. Not to mention that even in my uncaffeinated state, I recognized Jack sitting at the large farm table. Next to him were two very attractive guys who would have made me tongue-tied and awkward even fully caffeinated on my very best day.

"Well, Evelyn, nice of you to finally join us," I heard Ben say.

Busted. I turned slowly to see Ben smiling at me over his coffee mug. The group of men had stopped their conversation to watch me. My slow, slow brain was crying for coffee, and scrambling and failing to come up with words. I was vaguely aware of making some sort of grunting noise that I was pretty sure I would have been horrified by if my brain wasn't totally frazzled.

"Coffee."

Coffee? Good one, Evelyn.

Staying committed to totally ignoring Ben's previous comment, I managed to pull a more coherent string of words together. "Where do you keep your coffee mugs?" I asked, keeping my eyes focused on Ben.

"If you're the last one up by an hour and there aren't any more mugs hanging on the rack," Ben said, motioning to two rows of empty hooks hanging on the wall next to where the coffee pot was stationed on the counter, "there are more in that cabinet." He pointed to a cabinet just over my left shoulder.

"Ha ha," I deadpanned, opening the cabinet and reaching for a mug. I filled the mug to the brim and lifted it to my mouth, inhaling the slightly bitter aroma as I silently gave thanks to the coffee gods.

"There's cream in the fridge and the sugar is on the shelf

there," said the older man who had been talking with Ben when I came in.

"Thanks, but I'm not big on cream or sugar," I said, giving him a genuine smile. I took another small sip, eyeing the man over the rim of my cup. His skin was tanned and worn, with lots of lines that suggested he laughed and smiled often. His blond hair was streaked with grey and his blue eyes seemed to twinkle, confirming my suspicion that he was not unused to laughing. In his chambray shirt and well-fitted Levis, the man was a total silver fox. It did not escape my notice that I was sipping my cup of coffee in a room filled with ridiculously attractive men, who were all watching me.

If Hilari and Anna could see me now... I chuckled to myself, taking another long sip.

"Well, and here I thought you'd be one of those city girls Ben is always running around with, asking for non-fat grass-fed milk and fake sugar. If you tell me you don't like kale, we're keeping you," he said with a good-natured smile.

"No worries there, Sam," Ben said, giving me a mischievous grin that I knew was a big part of the reason he was currently in so much trouble. "I'm pretty sure Evelyn's never even tried kale."

"Hey! I've tried kale before, thank you very much. You made me try that kale-apple-mango smoothie thing," I said defensively.

Ben threw his head back and laughed. "How could I forget? You gagged and spit it back into *my* cup."

"I almost died!" I exclaimed, shuddering at the memory.

I heard chuckles from the table, and was reminded of the other three men in the room. Ben turned toward the man he called Sam.

"Evelyn, this is Sam, the foreman of the ranch. He's the only one who knows this place better than Jack."

"Pleased to meet you, Evelyn," Sam said, dipping his chin slightly in my direction.

I returned his smile easily and followed Ben's hand as he

motioned toward the table.

"You remember Jack," Ben said. Jack was looking at me, a slight scowl marring his handsome features. Either he was not a morning person, which I could absolutely respect, or he was still not happy I was here. We stared at each other briefly, and a weird silence lingered after Ben's introduction. Finally I couldn't take it any longer.

"Of course," I said, attempting a smile in his direction. It only seemed to make his scowl deepen. *Well, okay then.* Wanting to end the entire interaction—or lack thereof—I immediately darted my gaze to the very handsome man sitting next to him on the bench.

He looked to be about the same age as Ben, and bore a strong resemblance to Sam with his sandy blond hair and blue eyes. He was dressed in a worn pair of jeans and a white t-shirt that hugged every muscle—and there were a lot of muscles. I seriously questioned what was in this state's drinking water and if it could be bottled, because Jesus, I was fighting the urge to pinch my arm to make sure I was in fact awake and not dreaming.

"This is Cole, Sam's son. He has a spread about twenty miles or so south of here but shares grazing pastures with us. Cole and Jack also work the breeding program together," Ben said, turning my thoughts to the words *breeding program* for reasons that would have made Corinne proud.

"Hey, Evelyn. It's nice to meet you. I promise not everyone here has manners like a grizzly," Cole said, charm oozing from his smile. I noticed him flinch slightly and caught the movement of Jack's leg under the table.

"Hi." I heard my voice come out, part whisper and part sigh. I felt myself blushing. Clearing my throat, I tried for a sturdier voice. "It's nice to meet you too, Cole." *Much better.* I sounded like an adult and not a teenager at a One Direction concert.

I followed Ben's gaze as it traveled to the last diner in the room.

"And this is Gabe, head trainer, occasional cowboy."

Gabe was by the far the largest of the group gathered in the kitchen. His dark hair made his almost silver eyes pop out of his tanned face. With his sharp, chiseled cheekbones and a nose that had clearly been broken a few times, he would never be described as handsome, like Ben or Cole. Or Jack. But one corner of his mouth pulled up slightly, revealing a dimple, and it changed everything about his hard features. My heart stopped for a second, then started beating frantically against my ribs like I had just finished running a marathon. Not that I had *ever* run a marathon, but that was how I imagined it would feel. He was completely devastating. I could almost feel my hormones rapid-firing as I stared at him, desperately clutching my mug. That was all I could seem to do—just stare, and maybe drool a little.

Hank Williams came lumbering around the corner, nose pressed to the ground. I tore my eyes away from Gabe and greeted my little four-legged savior. Mary turned the corner a minute later, carrying a small basket wrapped in white cloth.

"Ladies gave me a lot of eggs this morning. They must know how much you all eat," she said, smoothing down a wayward piece of hair with her free hand. Mary smiled at me as she set the basket on the counter.

"Good morning, Evelyn. Please tell me one of these boys offered to feed you some breakfast," she asked, slowly eyeing each of the men in the room. They all looked down at their plates, suddenly interested in their breakfasts again. Mary made a disapproving noise in her throat, one of those noises only a mother can make.

I thrust the coffee mug in her direction, still a little dazed from that dimple.

"Oh, it's fine. I'm not really much of a breakfast eater. More of a coffee person."

I heard Ben snicker around a mouthful of toast. I glanced in his direction with an expression that I hoped conveyed how much I wanted to strangle him.

"Not much of a breakfast person, huh? Because I've defin-itely seen you take down an entire stack of pancakes, more than a couple times."

"First of all, thank you for mentioning how many carbs I can eat in one setting. Girls love that, for future reference. Sec-ond, it was dinner. Everyone likes reverse dinners."

I heard a masculine chuckle but was too self-conscious to figure out its owner. Instead, I took another sip of coffee and peered out the large window, suddenly aware that I was the center of attention again.

"Well, I certainly can't have a guest go without breakfast, so how about I whip you up some pancakes to go with that coffee? You haven't had pancakes until they've been made with fresh eggs and cream," Mary said, opening cabinets and pulling out a pan and mixing bowl.

"Oh no, you don't have to go to all that extra trouble for me. Really. Coffee is fine," I said as Mary moved past me to open the fridge and pull out various ingredients.

"It's no trouble at all!" She breezed past me again with her arms full, and began scooping and pouring.

"At least let me help you," I offered, watching her pour a generous amount of cream into the bowl.

"Thank you for offering, but I'll have these ready for you in no time." She gave me a reassuring smile.

I watched Mary whisk the ingredients together and pour the thick batter onto the sizzling pan. Conversation hummed all around me mixing with the sizzling sound of the pancakes. Just as Mary was reaching for the spatula, Rodney wandered into the kitchen. I felt my mouth drop open as I took in his appearance. Rodney was dressed like he had just stepped out of a John Wayne movie. A red button-up shirt was tucked into a pair of tight jeans that looked like they had been painted on to his body. A thick tan belt with a large, shiny buckle matched his gaudy cowboy boots, which I was confident had never seen a cow or a horse or dirt. Completing the entire look was a wide-brimmed cowboy hat. He kind of reminded me of

Woody from *Toy Story*, if Woody wasn't allowed within five hundred feet of children or a school.

Rodney clapped his hands together, smiling enthusiastically at everyone in the kitchen.

"Oh good! I didn't miss breakfast while I was getting changed. A man's gotta eat before a big ride, am I right?"

I heard the sound of throats being cleared and coughs clearly attempting to mask laughter. Before I could close my mouth and fix my face, Rodney noticed me leaning against the counter. His smile turned into the slightly lecherous grin that always gave me chills—the bad kind.

"Hey, Evelyn. You look extra pretty this morning. I think this country air is already doing you good. Then again, anything would be better than that stuffy pantsuit you were wearing yesterday."

I had to fight to keep my face from showing my annoyance. Thankfully, I didn't have to try to open my mouth to answer without barfing, because Rodney, good old Rodney, never needed another person to participate in a conversation.

"I hope you're joining us on our ride this morning. It would be nice to have a lady break up all this testosterone."

I could feel myself epically losing the battle not to roll my eyes, but I was way past the point of caring. All my energy was needed to keep my hands firmly planted around the mug and not wrapped around Rodney's neck. As if sensing my control was fading fast, Mary came to my rescue with a plate of pancakes that looked like fluffy heaven.

"Rodney, can I make you some pancakes? Or would you prefer eggs?"

While Rodney rambled on about the importance of protein in the morning, I surveyed the room and weighed my seating options. One hand holding a surprisingly heavy plate of pancakes and one hand holding my mug, I forced myself to start moving toward the breakfast bar where Sam had taken a stool to eat, figuring the third stool was the least intimidating option.

"Oh honey, I put the syrup and silverware on the table for you," Mary called, halting my progress.

I turned to see that Mary had indeed set a spot for me at the table while I had been distracted by Rodney's ensemble. I silently cursed him for being so obnoxious. My eyes locked on the fork laying on the table in the open spot next to Jack, and I felt like I was in the cafeteria on the first day of high school. I took my spot and reached for the syrup, never lifting my eyes to the other occupants of the table. I could have reached across the table and kissed Cole when he chuckled quietly.

"That is some outfit. I'm going to enjoy watching him try to mount a horse in those pants."

Gabe graced us with one of his devastating smiles, and I had to actively remind myself to chew. I did not want to choke on my pancakes. With my luck, Rodney would be the one to give me the Heimlich—and if I was lucky, he would wait to cop a feel until *after* I was breathing again.

"I bet he got that entire outfit from a costume store," Gabe added.

The theories flowed around me but I stayed silent, focusing on taking small bites of pancake instead of shoveling them into my mouth like I wanted. Mary was absolutely correct. These were the best pancakes I had ever eaten. I almost moaned when I took the first bite. But I was self-conscious about eating at a table with these men I didn't know, who were all easily the most handsome men I had ever laid eyes on. From the corner of my eye, I watched Jack's arm moving: picking up his cup to take a drink, lifting the fork to take another bite. Always returning his arm so close to mine.

I was so absorbed in watching Jack's arm and trying to take small bites that I didn't notice Rodney sit down on the bench next to me until I felt his hand land on the strip of skin my braid had left exposed on my neck. He squeezed it lightly which made me jerk reflexively to the left, hitting Jack in the arm I had just been fixated on. Jack jerked to *his* left, completing the chain reaction of horror. Still leaning away from me like I was infected with a contagious disease, Jack shot me a questioning look. I could feel his eyes take in my scrunched shoulders and then the unwelcome hand on my neck. Without saying a word, he straightened and quietly moved down the bench. I had no idea whether he was moving to get away from me or to give me an escape route, but I slid into the opening he left, effectively dislodging the hand on my neck.

"So, you never did answer my question, Evelyn. Are you going on the ride with the menfolk this morning?"

"Uh, no," I said, shooting Rodney some serious side-eye. "I'm sure Ben has lots of work to get through this morning, with the unexpected trip and everything."

"No work this morning. Get settled in and explore the ranch," Ben said from somewhere behind me.

I snapped my head around to glare at Ben, then widened my eyes and twitched my head toward Rodney. I hoped he got the message that under no circumstances did I want to spend an entire afternoon with the Wyatt Earp wannabe. Ben just gave me his most charming smile, like he didn't realize I was trying to avoid going along.

I was going to murder him. Slowly. This poor man obviously underestimated the skill set required to survive growing up in a house with two older sisters.

"I really should at least answer some emails. I haven't had the chance to reply to Katrina Kent's invitation to the Arts Gala, and I know how much you're looking forward to going with her this year. I would just hate for her to think you weren't interested and find another date. You know, I should probably send her some flowers too. Roses, I think," I said, in an overly innocent voice.

Ben had taken Katrina to dinner over a year ago, and ever since then she'd been operating under the assumption that Ben was going to propose at any minute. There had never even been a second date, but that hadn't stopped her from leaving at least four voicemails a week and dropping by the office once or twice a month. I ran more interference than an offensive lineman.

I couldn't stop the smile of satisfaction that took over my face when Ben choked on his toast. He needed to cough several times before he could answer.

"I thought you already declined that invitation."

"Did I?" I said, shrugging, false sweetness oozing from my voice.

"You did, because you know that woman is completely insane. And she laughs like a hyena."

"Katrina Kent? A little crazy might be worth it since she got all those enhancements." Rodney held two cupped hands up to his chest, presumably referencing Katrina's very large, very fake breasts.

I shot a look Rodney's way. Taking small bites was getting easier; this conversation was making me lose my appetite.

"Not worth it. She sent me one of those pictures that predicts what your future children would like—after our first, and only, date."

Sam whistled, shaking his head, as the men around the table laughed.

"Oh! Do you still have the picture?" Mary asked, turning away from the sink to face Ben with a hopeful expression. "Don't look at me like that, Benjamin. At the rate you two are going, that picture will be the closest I come to getting a grandchild." She waved the spatula accusingly at her children.

I couldn't help but laugh at the outraged expression on Ben's face.

"Okay, back to the original point of this conversation. Evelyn, you don't have to come with us on the ride this morning."

At the word "us," I spun my entire body around to face Ben, my back brushing lightly against Jack's arm.

"*Us*? As in you're going to ride a horse?"

"Yes, Evelyn, I'm going to ride a horse," Ben said, his voice laced with annoyance at my obvious disbelief.

"Do... you know *how* to ride a horse?" I asked, still having a hard time picturing Ben getting on a horse on purpose. In my defense, I knew how much he spent on his suits and his dry cleaning, and I'd forced to wait on him to finish getting ready more than once.

"Stop looking at me like that. Why is it so hard for you to believe I can ride a horse? I did spend a lot of time here growing up. What do you think I did all those summers?"

"Do you want an honest answer?" I responded, raising one eyebrow slightly.

"You know I can fire you, right?"

"One man's loss is another man's gain," Rodney chimed in, aiming that signature creepy grin my way.

I shot him a look that hopefully conveyed my thoughts on that comment. My side-eye game was strong this morning.

"Actually, if you don't need me, I was thinking about going for a walk. I saw a lot of what looked like really pretty trails on the way here that I'd love to explore a little," I said with genuine enthusiasm.

"Oh, honey, I don't know about you going out alone. This isn't like one of your parks in the city," Mary said, turning from the sink to give me a concerned look.

"I wasn't planning on doing any serious hiking, don't worry. Just take in some of the scenery. I thought maybe I could take Hank Williams with me? He seems like good company for a walk."

At the sound of his name and the word *walk*, Hank lifted his head and gave an enthusiastic wag of his tail, then plopped back down to resume his nap.

"Well," I said, drawing out the word. "He'll definitely make sure I don't wander too far. I don't know what his official job is around here, though, so I don't want to steal him away if someone needs him for something."

Mary and Sam chuckled. "Hank Williams is a professional napper. If he isn't following Jack around, he's hunkered down in a sunny spot," Sam responded, bending down to give Hank an affectionate scratch behind the ears as if to say *no hard feelings*.

Emily Mayer

I rose from where I sat, sandwiched between Jack and Rodney on the bench at the table, and brought my half-empty plate to join Mary. Taking a spot beside her at the sink, I reached for a towel and started to dry the dishes despite her protests about me being a guest. It seemed like the least I could do after those life-altering pancakes.

"It's okay if I take him then?"

"I'm sure Jack can part with him this morning. He can show you where his leash and harness are kept," Mary said, handing me a dripping frying pan.

8.

We worked in silence for a few more minutes, Mary washing dishes and silently passing me each one while the men in the room carried on multiple conversations around us. I silently marveled at the number of dishes it took to cook for all these people, and felt sorry for the poor chickens. *They must need to lay an insane amount of eggs to keep them all fed. Not that I know how much effort it takes to lay eggs. I don't actually know much about chickens at all. I think I remember reading somewhere that chickens don't lay eggs. Maybe it's hens?*

When the stack of dishes waiting to be washed no longer resembled one of the mountains just outside the window, Mary drew me out of my silent chicken debate by removing the dish towel from my hands.

"Thank you for your help, Evelyn. I can take it from here. I think the boys are about ready to start their ride, so why don't you have Jack show you where Hank's stuff is?"

At hearing his name, Jack turned toward us and gave his mom a look that effectively communicated how thrilled he was by that idea. I could barely contain my eyeroll. My eyes were getting a lot of exercise this morning. He looked like he was being asked to go with me on the walk, not show me where a leash was kept. *Unreal.*

He grabbed the same faded red baseball hat from a rack by the door, and mumbled something that could have been "Come on" as he walked toward the hall. I wasn't sure if the mumbled command was directed at me or the dog, but Hank Williams didn't look like he was going to be moving any time soon so I quickly abandoned my spot at the sink and once again started to follow Jack.

Taking big strides to catch up with this man, who was not slowing down to wait for me, I met him at a bench positioned just inside the front door. He crouched down and pulled out one of the baskets tucked into a cubby underneath, and removed a leash attached to a harness. He stood, handing me Hank's gear.

"Try to keep him on the leash. He's pretty good about coming when called but if he gets his nose on something, he can be pretty stubborn, and he's been known to wander off following a trail. Otherwise, he shouldn't give you too much trouble."

"I think I can handle that," I said, returning his scowl with a smile, hoping it would ease the tension a little.

Everything about this man made me feel unsettled and awkward. He was so ridiculously handsome, and I suspected he would probably be totally impossible to look at if he smiled. But that was clearly never going to be a problem at this rate. It was bad enough that a mere mortal like myself had to share the same space as this man, this man who had dated models, but he looked at me like I was the worst thing that had ever happened to him. I honestly did not know how to respond to that kind of instant dislike.

Jack glanced down, taking in my boot-clad feet before returning his gaze to my face.

"Are you wearing those boots?"

"Oh, umm, yes. These are the only boots I own. Besides snow boots. I own a couple pairs of snow boots, but there's no snow and these are pretty warm so." I silently pleaded with myself to stop talking.

"Those don't look like good boots to hike in," he responded evenly, apparently unfazed by my monologue about boots. I glanced down to take in the boots he was glaring at as if they had personally offended him.

"I wasn't planning on doing any actual hiking. The trail that passes right by the far barn—the biggest one," I said, to clarify "—it looks pretty easy and like it might have some nice views for pictures. And like I told your mom, I'm not planning on going very far. I just really don't want..."

I stopped myself mid-sentence before I admitted that I really did not want to go on a ride or any activity that included Rodney. Jack stood quietly watching me for a moment, waiting for me to finish my thought. When it became clear I wasn't going to continue speaking, he moved one hand to adjust his hat. It seemed reflexive, as if it was something he did often without even thinking about it.

"Just stay on the trail, yeah? And bring some water with you just in case."

I nodded my head in agreement, and he sighed as if it physically pained him to remain in my presence even a minute longer than absolutely necessary.

"Do you have any questions about anything?" He gestured toward the leash that hung limply at my side.

And then. *And then.* In a moment that would probably haunt me for the rest of my life, I asked the question that was tumbling around inside my head, the one from moments earlier in the kitchen.

"Do chickens lay eggs? I mean, obviously I know where eggs come from, even though we don't have a lot of chickens in the city." I laughed uncomfortably before I plowed on, fully committed now. "Although, I read somewhere that urban farming is getting really popular now since people are all of a sudden so concerned about where their food comes from. Plus, you know, organic is like an entire movement now. And chickens are the obvious choice. I mean for urban farming. Because they don't require a lot of space, and people living in cities don't really have big backyards, or any backyards at all. So anyway, I know roosters are boys and nature's alarm clock"— I gave an awkward chuckle—"but is a hen different than a chicken?"

His eyes widened briefly, as if trying to fully absorb all the crazy I had just hurled his way without warning. Then he blinked slowly—once, twice, a third time. Every blink sent a fresh wave of shame crashing over me.

"A hen is a female chicken."

The blush that had started as soon as the word *chicken* left my mouth was now covering my entire face. My cheeks were flaming. I could feel the heat radiating from them.

"Great! Well, enjoy your ride!" I practically shouted, then turned and walked away with my head bent in shame before either of us could say another word.

Mercifully, the kitchen was empty, so I was left to wrangle Hank into his harness alone while my skin tone slowly faded from bright red to its usual shade of pale. I was extra grateful for the lack of people in the kitchen when it became painfully obvious Hank was not going to get up while I struggled to put the harness on his sleeping body. At least one of my embarrassing scenes wouldn't have an audience. Men of all kinds of species were actively conspiring against me this morning.

A few minutes—and lots of pleading, complete with a bacon bribe—later, Hank and I set off on our walk. The late morning air was crisp and the wide sky didn't seem to contain a single cloud. Mornings like this really didn't exist in the city. It was so quiet as Hank and I walked past the barn that I could hear the nicker of the horses as we passed. Then the trail opened into a wide field. Hank walked a zigzag path, nose pressed to the ground, occasionally pausing to sniff the air. I pulled my phone out of my pocket and stopped to take some pictures of the ranch.

We wandered down the trail that way, Hank stopping now and then to sniff the air and me stopping to take pictures, until the field narrowed into a forest. I looked around at the dense underbrush contrasting with the tall trees that seemed to stretch into the sky. Flowers managed to poke through the foliage and fallen leaves creating bursts of color among the shades of green and brown. I could hear water somewhere in the distance, getting louder as we made our way through the little patch of forest. At one point, the trees grew so dense that they seemed to block out the sun and everything was cast into shadow. Hank plodded along, nose working a path back and forth in front of him, seemingly unconcerned with the changing scenery.

A few feet later, the trees opened into another wide field, revealing a river that apparently cut through the forest somewhere. It was so pretty that it almost didn't seem real. I dragged Hank off the path toward the river, pausing to take more pictures. Near the riverbank I found a large rock that looked like the perfect place to take a break. Jack was correct when he said my boots weren't made for hiking. My toes were starting to feel pinched and I was sure blisters had started to form on all ten toes. Settling onto the rock with Hank stretched out beside me, I slipped off my boots and socks, wiggling my toes in front of me. With my poor toes freed, I lay back on the rock next to Hank and felt the sunshine wrapping me up in its warmth. Closing my eyes, I could hear the sounds of the river combining with Hank's soft snores next to me.

I'd always thought I was more of a city girl. But this—*this* felt like someplace I could get used to seeing every day. My love of the city was mostly based on what I thought would be best for my career, I supposed; it probably didn't have much to do with any real love for living in a city. I liked the convenience of public transportation, and it was nice to be able to disappear in the hustle every once in a while. I didn't hate the abundance of coffee shops everywhere, either. But most importantly, cities were where all the biggest law firms were located, so the city was where I'd thought I needed to be. Now that law firms didn't matter anymore, living in the city was just what I was used to doing. It was also the last piece of my stupid plan, which I was clinging to while I tried to navigate life without a plan. The city felt safe. Anything else seemed like I was admitting total defeat.

This place was so beautiful and so different from anything

I had seen—it wasn't difficult to imagine why Ben's great-grandparents had fallen in love with it. I'd been here less than a day and already *I* was a little in love with it. Since learning about Jack's existence, I had wondered why he would have chosen to work the ranch instead of working at the company. Chicago seemed like a much better place for a young, single guy to live. But now it wasn't so difficult to understand Jack's choice.

Jack himself, however, was not as easy to understand.

My mind wandered back to all our encounters, trying to come up with a rational explanation for his behavior. Aside from the chicken rant and body-slamming him when Rodney's hand had landed on my neck at breakfast, I couldn't think of anything I had said or done that could have caused him to dislike me so much. Could Ben have said something about me? Honestly, I doubted it. I thought of myself as the vanilla pudding of human beings. No one had a super strong opinion one way or the other about vanilla pudding. Maybe he assumed I was just another idiot girl sleeping with his brother to advance a personal agenda?

I sighed, mulling over the possibilities in my mind, unable to decide on either a reason for his dislike or any solid plan for changing his opinion. It was going to be a long trip if I couldn't come up with a way to make him think I was less awful—or make myself stop caring about what he thought.

The air near the river was already noticeably cooler, and when a cloud crept across the sun, it left me shivering. I opened my eyes, realizing I must have dozed off for a little, and rolled my head over to find myself nose to snout with Hank Williams.

"Ready to head back?" I asked, sliding off the rock and waiting for him to slowly lumber down after me.

We walked back the way we came, me stopping to take pictures when something caught my eye now that the sun's disappearance behind the clouds seemed to have changed the landscape so much, and Hank stopping to paw or sniff at certain spots.

As we got closer to the ranch, I noticed a single horse in a fenced-in enclosure, away from all the other barns. I hadn't seen it when I'd started my hike. The fenced-in area only had a small lean-to shelter and two pails hanging off the fenceposts. Even from a distance, I could tell this horse was in bad shape. His ribs were clearly visible, and it looked like patches of his coat were missing. I didn't know why I felt like I needed to get a closer look, but I steered us toward the little paddock anyway.

I sucked in a sharp breath when I got close enough to take a good look at the poor creature. Not only were his ribs showing, but it looked like someone had beaten him and left the wounds to become infected. One of the pails was filled with food that looked largely untouched, and the other pail was filled with water. His ears were pinned all the way back, and he seemed to be eyeing me with suspicion.

"What happened to you?"

"He's a sorry sight, all right." I let out a little yelp of surprise. I had been so focused on the neglected horse that I hadn't heard Gabe approaching. He was casually leaning against the fence, watching me watch the horse.

I nodded in agreement. "Who did that to him? Did... did Jack do this?" I asked, keeping my eyes on Gabe's face as if I'd somehow be able to tell if he lied to me.

He reared back like I had slapped him, surprise lacing his voice.

"*Jack?* No. We don't use whips on horses. Jack doesn't even keep them around. He rescued the horse from a farm two counties over. Believe it or not, that's a racehorse. Pretty good one, too."

"I don't understand. If he was a good racehorse, how did he end up here?"

"Some ass—er, jerk thought he could beat him back into

shape after an injury. It didn't work, and they couldn't use him as a stud so they just left him in a field to rot. Jack bought King-pin—that's his name—and brought him here just before you all came in."

The disbelief I was feeling must have been written clearly on my face.

"Jack rescues horses. Tries to rehabilitate and rehome them if he can. Most people around here know that, so they'll call Jack if they see someone mistreating a horse. It's pretty rare, but it does happen."

"He doesn't look like he's doing much better. Why is he out here all alone? Shouldn't you call a vet?"

Gabe let out a low whistle, shaking his head from side to side. He turned to face me fully, a grin unleashing those dimples that should be registered as a national treasure.

"You don't think too highly of Jack, huh? He's a grumpy, pain in the as—butt, I'll give you that, but he knows horses. King here just about took our heads off trying to load and unload him in the trailer. He might not look like much, but he put up a heck of a fight. Won't let anyone near him. Jack made him a special feed blend to help him put on weight, but King's not eating much either."

I looked back at the poor horse who looked so pathetic standing in the field alone, and my heart felt heavy in my chest. Ignoring his comment about Jack, I wondered out loud, "What will happen to him if he doesn't let anyone help?" My voice was almost a whisper, weighed down under the sadness of it all.

"Don't worry, darling. If anyone can help King, it's Jack. Never seen anyone better with horses. He comes out here every day to talk to him. Jack tries to earn their trust. Most of these horses are pretty short on that—can't say I blame them —but it's easier to work with horses if they trust you. Horses are pretty good judges of character."

We stood side by side, leaning on the fence and watching King for a moment. Then Gabe nudged me with his shoulder.

"You hungry? I'm starving. Let's head back to the house and see what Mary's got going. Hey, if we're lucky, we can catch the rest of Rodney's story from the ride today. I bet he fought at least one mountain lion."

I couldn't stop the laugh; it started so deep it felt like it was almost from my toes.

"I'm betting he really did get that outfit from a costume store. It takes a brave man to wear jeans that tight," Gabe continued, shaking his head slowly, dimples still in full force.

"I like the outfit!" Gabe's eyebrows leapt up his forehead at my response. "I do. In all that denim and those boots, I can hear him coming." I shuddered involuntarily.

Gabe laughed, eyeing me sideways. "His hands do seem to have a problem with wandering."

"Don't I know it! Sometimes I swear he has an extra pair hidden somewhere. I can't keep up."

"Guess I should be thankful I'm not his type."

"Oh, give it a couple of days. I could totally see him developing a mad man-crush on a real-life cowboy."

It was Gabe's turn to shudder. "I say we agree to throw Jack under the bus if that day ever comes," he said as he held the door open for me.

"Done," I agreed, stepping into the kitchen. I was very aware of the wall of muscle that was his chest as I passed.

"And I said to Sam, if you gave me a rope, I'd show those cows..." Rodney's voice carried from the table where he was, in fact, telling everyone tales from his ride this afternoon.

Gabe and I snickered like two kids sharing an inside joke. Mary shot us a questioning look.

"Where did you two come from? Gabe, hat," Mary said, gesturing toward Gabe's head.

"Yes ma'am." He took off his hat and hung it by the door. I couldn't decide if I liked him better with the hat on or off. If I had a sly bone in my body, I would have snuck a picture to send the girls to get their input on this very important issue. "Found Evelyn and Hank out by Kingpin's paddock; thought I'd bring her in for lunch."

Mary's face morphed into a sad expression.

"Poor boy. I hope Gabe told you not to go near him. He's all skin and bones but he can still do a lot of damage if you don't know what you're doing."

"He did. Well, he told me Kingpin wouldn't let anyone near him, and the part about almost taking their heads off getting here. The stay-away part I sort of figured out on my own."

Sam's deep laugh drew my gaze toward the table. I couldn't help but notice that Jack was watching our exchange with his usual scowl. I also couldn't help but notice that it looked like he had just gotten out of the shower. His hair was damp and he wore a button-down plaid shirt that was rolled up to his elbow, revealing strong forearms. Not fancy, just clean. I could swear I still saw the path where his fingers had combed through his hair.

"Take a seat, you two, lunch is about ready," Mary said, drawing my focus away from the disconcerting man with perfect forearms sitting at the table.

9.

Later that night, I found the study empty, so I decided to settle in with my laptop to answer a few emails. Somehow, I had managed to snag a seat in between Mary and Ben for dinner, avoiding having to sit beside Jack or within hands'-reach of Rodney. Jack had completely ignored my presence for the entire meal, except the occasional glare or handing me the rolls when I asked for them. I got a head-nod and a frown for a reply when I thanked him.

I took out my phone to send my sisters some of the pictures I had taken on my hike. Elise responded almost immediately.

Elise: *Gorgeous! I would rather have seen a picture of the hot brother though.*

Me: *What do you want from me? I'm not stealthy at all and I don't think I can just ask him to pose for pictures to send to my nosey sisters.*

Elise: *Uh yeah, whatever gets it done. Take one for the team Evie! I have to go. Date number two with Joe tonight.*

Me: *Joe? I thought you weren't into him after your date last week?*

Elise: *I don't know. First dates are always hard. Maybe I was too quick to judge.*

Me: *I want full details later! Have fun and don't do anything I wouldn't do!*

Elise: *I wouldn't be going on a date then ;o) xoxo*

I rolled my eyes at Elise's comment. I dated, but school and then work had made it hard to date seriously. No one wanted to start a relationship with someone who was so busy with work they'd only see each other once a week. Being career-oriented was a totally acceptable choice, I told myself as I started working through emails using my usual sorting system, separating them by importance and order to be answered. My phone's buzzing startled me out of my email sorting. It was a video chat invitation from Corinne. I switched the call to my laptop and a tiny little face way too close to the camera greeted me.

"Hi Celeste!" I said to her adorable little chin. I heard my sister's voice in the background.

"Here, sweetie, let's back up a little so your auntie can see us. There we go," she said as their entire faces came into view. "Hey, Auntie Evie, we loved your pictures. Didn't we, baby girl?"

Celeste shook her head enthusiastically.

"Yes, sooo pwetty Aunt Evie!"

"We thought we'd say goodnight to you, right, Celeste? Do you want to tell your auntie what we did today?"

Celeste started jumping up and down, waving her little arms around like a maniac.

"Yes! Yes! We went to the zoo! And we saw lots of amnals and daddy let me have two drinks of his soda."

"So fun! What was your favorite animal?" I asked.

She responded almost immediately. "The manadees!"

"Manatees are very cute," I agreed. Ted sat down next to Corinne and bent down to wave into the camera.

"Hey, Evie. Great pictures. Looks like you're enjoying Montana more than you thought you would. What are you ladies talking about?"

"Manadees! They are my favorite," Celeste told her dad.

"Oh yeah? We like the manatees now. What happened to the elephants? I thought they were your favorite," Ted asked the little girl, who was now busy pulling a shirt onto a teddy bear.

"They were, but I like manadees now because they are like Mommy."

"They're like Mommy?" I asked, genuinely confused by the

comparison.

"Uh huh. They have big middles and are soooo slow."

I heard a strangled noise followed by a low chuckle and then an "*oomph.*"

"Mommy! No hitting! Say sorry to Daddy."

I was biting my lip so hard to keep from laughing that I thought I might draw blood, but I couldn't keep the tears from leaking out of the corners of my eyes or my shoulders from shaking.

"Mommy's hand just slipped. Right into Daddy's stomach."

I heard a distinctly masculine chuckle come from the doorway. My eyes snapped up to see Jack leaning against the door, his body just inside the room. His smile widened as my eyes found his, and my smile faltered. I forgot about the family on the screen halfway across the country as this man stood watching me. Not scowling. Not pretending like I didn't exist in his space.

Corinne's voice broke the spell his smile had cast over the room. "Anyway, we better say goodnight to Auntie Evie. Night, Evie, we love you!" Corinne said, blowing me a kiss. Celeste leaned into the camera to kiss it like she always did when we said goodbye.

"Night-night, Aunt Evie, love you." Her sweet little voice brought back the smile that had dimmed when I'd seen Jack in the doorway.

"Night-night, baby girl, sweet dreams! I love you the most!" We ended our conversations the same way every time we talked. The first time I had forgotten to add *the most* to the end, Celeste had asked, "you love me the most, right?" My heart had almost exploded. Ever since, I made sure to add *the most.* It was pretty much the truth. I really did love her the most. I'd figure out how to handle the addition of a baby brother, since I'd love that kid like a crazy person too.

Corinne leaned forward as she scooted to the end of the couch to stand.

"And for the record, I totally agree with Elise. Those pictures were great, but I'd much rather see a picture—"

"OKAY BYE CRAZY LOVE YOU TOO!" I shouted loudly over her, snapping the laptop lid shut before Jack could hear her say his name.

I looked from the desk toward the door where Jack had been standing. He stepped fully into the room, uncrossing his arms to slide his hands into his pockets. My gaze lingered on his jean-clad thighs maybe just a few seconds too long. We stared at each other for one heartbeat, then two. His chin dipped down before he said in that deep, almost raspy voice, "I didn't mean to eavesdrop."

I could have sworn his cheeks turned just the tiniest bit pink. I did my best to smile at him warmly, hoping this might be a turning point.

"It's fine. I didn't mean to be in here for so long. I got carried away checking emails and then my sister called."

"Was that your niece?"

"Yeah. She's three and totally brutal. My sister, Corinne, is super pregnant." I felt like I should defend her after the manatee comment.

The sound of his warm chuckle rumbled through me. I really, really liked that sound. So much so that I would probably spend too much time later on, thinking of ways to make it happen again. After I was done fantasizing about the sound. Obviously.

An awkward silence settled over the room. I scrambled to come up with something to say, though I was terrified of breaking this temporary truce. There was also a very real possibility that I would word-vomit again and we could both relive the horror of the urban farming verbal onslaught. So many great options. I looked down at my hands, which were busy taking out their anxiety on the hem of my sweater. Nervously clearing my throat, I prepared to make small talk.

"I was just going to update some paperwork, but it's nothing that needs to get done right now." I breathed out a small sigh of relief that Jack had spoken up first. "I can come back later."

"No, no, I was finished working. Let me just grab my stuff and I'll get out of your way." I was already busy scooping up notebooks, pens, and highlighters into my arms, and balancing everything precariously on top of my laptop. I stood and moved toward the door, cautiously skirting around Jack without making eye contact, as if he were a wild animal I didn't want to upset. I held my laptop pressed close to my chest, like it could shield me from one of his fierce scowls, which I had become all too familiar with over the past two days.

He just stood silently watching me make my exit. No longer smiling, but not scowling—just watching with a neutral expression on his face. I smiled hesitantly.

"Okay, well, umm… have a good night then," I fired off, turning so quickly to flee that I caught my shoulder on the edge of the door frame. Groaning inwardly, I shuffled quickly to the side to avoid a second run-in before hustling out the door and down the hall, conscious of the throb in my shoulder.

I made my way back to my bedroom, carefully avoiding the voices drifting through the house. The run-in with Jack was enough for tonight. I did not want to get cornered by Rodney. I had done an excellent job of avoiding him today, and that was a winning streak I didn't want to break.

Safely back in my room, I quickly changed into my pajamas and snuggled under the covers with my Kindle. Reading was a love I had rediscovered after my career plan went down in flames. I'd pretty much stopped reading for fun during law school. After the massive amount of reading I had to do for school and internships, the last thing I wanted to do was read more. I'd kept a running list of books I wanted to read after I graduated, but the list had remained untouched until I'd started working for Ben. I was making up for lost time now, though. I was crossing at least a book a week off my list. My Kindle had become an accessory I never left home without, safely tucked into purses and totes and suitcases. The list had also been responsible for several burned dinners, one flaming pancake, and a casserole that sat in an oven I forgot to turn on for two hours. Honestly, the line between hobby and addiction was getting pretty thin these days.

A few pages in, I heard a series of small thuds at my door. I put my book down just as another series of thuds was followed by a sad, sad whimper. Hopping out of bed, I padded over to the door and opened it just wide enough to let my four-legged visitor in.

"Hi, Hank Williams." I gave him a good scratch behind the ears. "Are we going to make this a regular thing?"

Hank ambled over to the bed, leaping up and settling into the warm spot I had just left.

"You know there are rules about this kind of thing, right? I think it's three dates before you sleep with a guy now. I don't know. It's been a while since I dated, but I'm pretty sure you're at least supposed to buy me dinner first. And you're definitely supposed to ask what side of the bed I want if there's going to be a sleepover."

I slid in next to the already sleeping dog, reaching over his body to retrieve my Kindle. Snuggled up next to Hank—who had stretched out even more and begun to snore—I didn't make it more than a few pages before my eyelids got heavy and I caught myself reading the same words over and over again. Giving up the fight, I sat my book down and snuggled closer to Hank.

I would be lying if I said one of the last thoughts that drifted across my tired brain before I fell asleep wasn't the sound of that warm chuckle that seemed so at odds with the man who owned it.

10.

The next few days fell into an easy routine. I spent most of each day working on a new proposal with Ben or answering emails, and spent the rest exploring—usually with Hank Williams in tow.

There was a flood of email to respond to after the article about Ben was published, and I got pretty creative with ways to say 'thanks but no thanks' to the various requests. I did my best to hide the worst ones from Ben after I overheard a heated conversation between him and Mary about the article. Mary was not happy to read about all the scandals Ben was somehow connected to, but she also seemed really concerned about his feelings. Ben also hinted that he had "caught shit" from some of the guys on the ranch about the article.

While I spent a lot of energy avoiding Rodney, I had gotten to know Cole, Gabe, and Sam better. I learned that Cole's mother had died when he was little. Cole was quieter and less of an outrageous charmer than Gabe. He reminded me of the workhorses I saw on the ranch, steady and reliable, and it drew me toward him. He was married to his high school sweetheart and had a two-year-old daughter who was basically the sun in his sky.

Cole's father Sam had never remarried after his wife's death. Sam had worked on the ranch most of his life, and Mary had been like a mother to Cole. He was a treasure trove of embarrassing stories about Ben, which I exploited as much as possible, like any good employee would.

Gabe was definitely the character of the group. I was beginning to think he purposely went out of his way to make me blush—which honestly was not that difficult. After almost a full week here, I still couldn't handle myself when he brought out both his dimples. He had also become an ally in helping me avoid Rodney and his grabby hands. One night at dinner, he had inserted himself into the tiny space between Rodney and me, shooting me a wink that made my stomach flip a little. He even readily agreed to pose for a picture to send the girls, as long as I gave him complete "artistic control" and read him the responses. I had to hand him my phone to read the text messages, because there was no way I could read them out loud and ever look him in the eye again. Yeah, the girls were not disappointed.

Even Jack and I had managed to find a comfortable routine where we both tried our best to avoid being in each other's presence, though he shot an impressive array of glares and scowls in my direction when we accidentally found ourselves occupying the same space. That night in the study when we'd shared a smile had apparently changed nothing. By the next morning, Jack was back to being irritated by my existence. And it really was *me*. I saw him laughing with the guys, giving Mary a quick kiss on the head before heading out in the morning, forcing a smile through one of Rodney's stories. I watched him patiently work on training a new horse, smiling and patting him affectionately. It was only me who seemed to bring out his grump. Sure, he wasn't necessarily Mr. Personality in general, but he didn't treat anyone *else* like they were a human rash.

I tried not to let it bother me too much. Some people were just never going to like you, no matter what. I could still be pleasant while hoping he stepped in horse poop. I was an adult.

The desire to avoid another awkward breakfast had me grabbing a muffin to go with my cup of coffee and heading out the door before anyone found me. The sun was just coming up and once again I was in awe of how pretty it was here. It was the kind of peaceful that settled deep in your bones. I ate my muffin sitting on one of the rockers, just taking it all in. After finishing the homemade muffin—which put all other muffins to shame—I headed out to the paddock where King was still being kept. From what Gabe had said, Jack wasn't having any luck getting King to eat much, or getting near enough to examine the horse's sores. I tried to stop by at least once a day to say hi to King.

I didn't know a lot about horses. I'd spent a couple of summers at riding camp as a kid, but I figured that probably made me the least qualified person in all of Montana. But for whatever reason, I felt like King should know there were nice people here. People who thought he mattered. All living things needed that, right?

So I told King about Chicago, about deep-dish pizza, and about the book I was reading. I even told him that Jack might be a grumpy jerk, but he was really trying to help him. I counted it as progress in our relationship that King had stopped pawing the ground whenever I leaned up against the fence to have our talks, and that he didn't pin his ears back as soon as I started talking anymore. He was either starting to like me, or was giving up hope that I would ever leave him alone. Either way, it was progress, and beggars can't be choosers!

"Good morning, King," I called softly to the horse. I leaned up against the fence facing him, coffee mug cradled in my hands. "They just don't make mornings like this in Chicago. I could get used to waking up to Montana mornings. I mean, I might need to get an espresso machine because I miss my lattes, but I could really get used to this place. What do you think, King? Could you get used to this place?"

King watched me warily, ears alert.

"I really think you should give it a shot."

We eyed each other cautiously for a minute, and then King took a tentative step in my direction. I gasped. King startled at the sound, pausing momentarily, but then took another small step toward me. This was the first time King had responded to me with anything other than a snort or pawing at the ground. He came a few steps closer before stopping. My heart was beating wildly in my chest as we stood there looking at each other.

Don't mess this up, Evelyn. Oh God, can I look him in the eye? I don't think you're supposed to look dogs in the eye. A horse is pretty much a big dog, right? All those Planet Earth *shows I watched and I retained nothing!*

My thoughts were racing as fast as my heart. I took a few deep breaths, trying to mentally get my shit together before I scared us both. Slow as a snail, I moved one foot forward in the dirt, the other foot following. *Slow. Slow. Slow*, I chanted in my head as I crept down the length of the fence in King's direction.

"I'm going to be honest with you, King. I don't know anything about horses," I said in a quiet, soothing tone I usually reserved for babies. "But I'm trying really, really hard not to mess this up, because I feel like we just took a really big step in our relationship. This is like getting a drawer in the bathroom or taking someone home to meet your mom."

Inching forward as I tried to gauge King's reaction, I kept my voice steady despite the frantic pounding of my heart. This little bit of trust felt important—like the most important thing in the world. A few more steps in his direction and we would be so close. Close enough that if I leaned over the fence, I could touch him.

King had different ideas though. My last steps sent him retreating back to the far corner. I sighed, disappointment replacing the excitement I had felt earlier. I leaned against the fence, giving King a sad smile.

"It's okay, big guy. I think we made some serious progress here this morning. Rome wasn't built in a day, and I promise

I'll be back tomorrow. I know you would miss our little chats even if you aren't ready to admit it yet."

I sipped on the coffee that had been forgotten when King took that first step forward. When Gabe told me that Jack wasn't making any progress with King the other night, I didn't ask him what exactly counted as progress. Gabe had said King was still barely eating, and he hadn't been able to look at his sores yet. I had a feeling that I was having better luck with King, which obviously confirmed that horses were excellent judges of character.

Sure, I knew nothing about horses besides the basics and what little I remembered about those summer camps from over a decade ago, but I really felt like I could help King. Helping him felt like something I had to do. I couldn't explain it. I just felt this overwhelming need to see him healthy and happy. But since I knew next to nothing about horses, I also realized I was going to need help. And help meant Jack. Getting Jack to agree to let me help King was going to be climbing-Mount-Everest hard. I was going to need a really convincing argument to get him to agree to the idea rapidly forming in my head.

"You're a lawyer, Evelyn!" I said out loud. "Or were a lawyer. No, technically you still have a license to practice law so that makes you a lawyer. This is not a big deal. You just have to convince the grouchiest man on earth, who also happens to hate your guts, to let you help him out. Easy peasy."

Liar, liar, pants on fire. I needed a plan and a backup plan, and backup plan for my backup plan. But planning was what I did best!

11.

Coffee finished and plans made, I headed back to the house with way more energy than was normal for a human being this early. I swung open the kitchen door a little too hard, sending it crashing into the wall.

"Oh, hi, sorry," I said on an exhale. Mary, knife in hand mid-chop, was staring at me with a startled expression on her face. "Have you seen Jack?"

Mary blinked at me a few times before clearing her throat.

"Uh, I think he's out in one of the barns. He wanted to get an early start riding along the fences today. Are you okay, sweetie? You look a little flushed and you missed breakfast. Ben thought you might have a migraine."

"No, no, I'm fine. I grabbed a muffin," I answered, already turning back toward the open door. I needed to keep moving before my nerves caught up with me. The longer it took to find Jack, the more likely it was I would talk myself out of pitching my idea to him. "Thanks, Mary. Bye, have a good morning!"

Almost jogging, I stuck my head in the first barn, looking for any sign of the man I usually worked so hard to avoid. Looking around, I didn't see any sign of him. I stepped into the barn and called out.

"Hello? Jack?"

Only the sounds of horses enjoying their breakfast answered me. I turned to head out when I heard a noise coming from the far end of the stables. I made my way toward the tack room, giving myself a pep talk along the way. With equal parts dread and eagerness, I stepped into the surprisingly large room. The white walls were decorated with saddle blankets, bridles, and other things I didn't have names for, and lined on all sides by saddles. The room smelled like leather and horse. It was a strangely delicious and soothing combination. I inhaled deeply, letting the smell calm me.

Standing by one of the far walls was Jack, his hands full of rope. Too busy to acknowledge me, apparently. I stepped a little farther into the room, reaching out my hand to run my fingers along the smooth leather of saddle after saddle as I went.

"Good morning, Jack," I greeted him, as if I hadn't noticed he was ignoring me.

"Evelyn."

He didn't bother turning to face me, just tossed out my name as he hung one bridle up and moved another out of the way. I briefly wondered if he had a favorite one, and if he was searching for it, before I plowed ahead.

"I was wondering if I could ask you about something. I had an idea and I thought maybe I could run it by you."

Did this stubborn, unreasonable man answer me? Did he so much as turn around to acknowledge that I was speaking? No, he did not. He just continued moving things around like it was the most important job in the history of jobs.

Well, if he thought ignoring me was going to somehow deter me, he was wrong. I did not grow up with the queen of the silent treatment for nothing. Elise could go days pretending someone didn't exist. *Sorry, cowboy, this is not my first rodeo.*

"I was hoping you would let me help you with King."

Jack's arm stilled mid-reach. *Excellent; that got his attention.* He turned to face me, face completely neutral, giving nothing away. He just watched me. Not curious, not angry, not even surprised. The man might have missed his true calling. If the whole ranching thing didn't work out for him, I'm sure the CIA would take him in a heartbeat. Interrogating people would be a breeze for this guy. I mean, my hands were starting to sweat at an alarming rate and I was just asking a simple question.

"See, I have this theory King would do better with a woman. Specifically, me and—"

"No," he said, turning around to continue with whatever it was he'd been doing before I interrupted him, a clear dismissal of both the idea and me.

But I wasn't going to let him off the hook that easily. "Why not?"

He sighed the sigh parents give children when they ask for the fiftieth time if they can have a cookie, then turned around to face me. He took off his hat and ran a hand through his hair in an obvious sign of frustration. My ovaries sighed a little at the sight of his messed-up hair, because I was female and breathing. My eyes traveled from his hair back to those brown eyes.

"Why not?" I repeated with more force, straightening my spine.

"Because you don't know anything about horses. You'd either be in the way or end up getting hurt. I don't have time to babysit some city girl who wants to play cowgirl for a week. That's why."

I felt my jaw drop as he finished hurling the words at me. I was stunned. Stunned and angry—so angry. How dare this man, who had made absolutely no effort whatsoever to get to know me, make so many assumptions? Shoving all my anger way, way down for later—and there *would* be a later—I reminded myself this was about King.

"I know a little about horses; at least enough to not get hurt. And I do not need a babysitter." I emphasized the *not*. "I understand—"

"I said no, Evelyn. Forget it."

Cutting me off for the second time, Jack turned and walked through the door at the opposite end of the room, which I assumed led to, most importantly, wherever I was not.

"That went well," I said to the saddles and bridles.

I hadn't imagined a scenario where Jack was super enthusiastic about the idea, but I hadn't thought he would be a total ass either. Was I going to let it go just because Jack the jackass said no? Nope. Was I concerned that I was resorting to calling him childish nicknames in my head? Also no. Was I going to lie awake tonight reliving the horror of this conversation and plotting revenge? Probably. I was a girl with a backup plan, though, and right now I needed to find my backup plans before Jack huffed and puffed and blew my little dream house down.

Heading out of the barn, I spotted my backup plans loading tools and coiled wire into the bed of a large red pickup truck. Gabe and Cole were too busy chatting to notice me approaching them.

"Hi, guys," I said cheerily, like someone who had not just been thoroughly insulted and then completely dismissed.

Cole swung a large seven-gallon cooler into the truck bed like it weighed less than a feather. I could have watched those two work all day. *Focus.* I needed to focus on the task at hand.

"Hey, Evelyn, what's up?" Cole stopped to wipe his arm across his forehead.

"Well, I actually had a favor to ask you and Gabe. It's nothing major."

Gabe stopped what he was doing to come stand next to Cole. In a tight grey Henley, the man was a walking dream.

"A favor, huh?" Gabe quirked an eyebrow, throwing a little grin my way. I was slowly getting used to the effects of those devastating grins and was no longer rendered completely stupid every time he shot one my way.

"Yep. I was hoping you guys could teach me about horses and..." I said, drawing out the word a little. "Teach me how to ride a horse. Re-teach really. I've ridden lots of horses. So many horses. It's just like riding a bike. Right?"

Both men looked at me like I had just asked them if they'd seen Bigfoot running around the field this morning. Why was it so hard for all the men on this ranch to believe I wanted to learn to ride a horse? It wasn't like I'd walked around in designer jeans and stilettos all week.

"You want to learn to ride?" Cole repeated back to me slowly.

I nodded my head enthusiastically.

"Yes, I definitely want to learn to ride. Or re-learn, really."

"Where exactly in Chicago have you been riding all these horses?" Gabe chimed in.

"I rode horses at summer camp... when I was in middle school..." I looked at the bed of the truck, purposely avoiding eye contact with either of them.

Silence stretched on for what felt like hours instead of a few seconds.

"Not that I think it's a terrible idea, but why the sudden interest in riding?" Cole asked—a totally reasonable question. I appreciated that these two weren't immediately shutting me down.

"It's *not* sudden, not really. I just haven't gotten a chance to ride that didn't involve Rodney offering to go along and give me a leg up." I shuddered involuntarily, remembering the offer from just yesterday that had made me want to gag. Both men seemed to remember the conversation and cringed.

"Fair enough," Cole said.

"I bet Jack can—" Gabe began, but I cut him off.

"No need to bring Jack into this. He's so busy doing stuff around here and being all grumpy and making assumptions."

For the second time in our brief conversation, they looked at me like I had completely lost my mind. I sighed, pushing the toe of my boot around in the dirt.

"I already asked Jack and he said no. A very solid no."

"Jack said he wouldn't teach you? That doesn't sound like him. He might be a moody fuc—guy, but I can't see him refusing to teach you to ride," Gabe said.

One day I was going to put Gabe out of his very polite misery and tell him that I knew all the bad words, and even used them. Frequently. Especially in my head whenever Jack was around.

"I have to agree with Gabe here, Evelyn. Jack's stubborn but not unreasonable. I can't see him telling anyone they couldn't learn to ride."

I fought against the urge to roll my eyes. Jack was the most unreasonable human being I had ever encountered. He had acted like I'd asked him to help me build a nuclear bomb to drop on a herd of puppies, not let me help him with King.

"Listen, just hear me out before you say no, okay? I may have actually phrased it as asking if I could help Jack with King. And he said he does not have time to, I quote, 'babysit some city girl who wants to play cowgirl for a week.'" Their eyes widened in surprise. I was honest enough with myself to admit I was more than a little satisfied by their reaction.

"But I really think I can help King. I heard Jack telling Sam that he wasn't making any progress with him the other night, and I have a theory about it. I've been going to King's paddock every day to talk to him. Today, he walked over toward me. He got so close I could almost reach out and touch him. So I thought that maybe King would respond better to a woman. Which when you think about it, totally makes sense. He was mistreated by a bunch of men, so of course he's going to have a hard time trusting a man. And Gabe, you said building trust was important."

I took a deep breath and let it out slowly, fully aware I had just given them an earful. Cole eyed me warily, but not like I was an idiot—which I took as a good sign.

"And you told all of that to Jack?" he asked.

"No. I made it to the *help with King* part before he said no and walked off."

Gabe was looking at me with an expression I couldn't quite place. Something told me I should be nervous, that his expression meant trouble.

"So, let me see if I have this right. You asked Jack to let you help him with King. He said no and now you want us to help you learn to ride so you can prove to Jack that you don't need a babysitter. That sound about right?"

"Yep, that sounds about right. But less devious than you're making it sound. Remember, it's for King, the poor, sad horse who needs a friend."

Cole chuckled, and Gabe kept giving me that look that I couldn't quite place. I threw in the last weapon in my arsenal.

"I know teaching me to ride would mean extra work for you guys, so I was thinking I could help you out with stuff around here. If you wanted," I added.

Gabe gave me one last look like he was making up his mind about something and then turned to Cole.

"Evelyn, can you give us a minute?"

"Sure, yeah, of course."

I moved around to the front of the truck, just far enough away that I couldn't hear them but still close enough to watch them discuss whatever it was Gabe wanted to say. He was talking animatedly, using his hands, that easy grin still in place.

Something he said must have been pretty unexpected, because Cole's head snapped back in surprise, then his hand came up to rub those lightly whiskered cheeks thoughtfully. Gabe kept talking, undeterred by Cole's reaction.

I was starting to get nervous—or maybe *concerned* would be a better word. How did giving me riding lessons require this much discussion? Sure, Jack had said no to my plans to help King, but he hadn't said anything about me riding a horse. It was only a small technicality that teaching me to ride was intended to convince Jack to change his mind. It wasn't like I was asking them to sneak me into King's paddock when no one was looking.

A smile started at one corner of Cole's mouth before stretching out wide, and he started shaking his head slowly. I knew I should be concerned. Every reasonable fiber of my being told me that interaction spelled trouble. But I wanted this badly—so badly I was willing to ignore all those reasonable voices. I wanted this more than I had wanted anything in a long time. Well, anything not food-related. So, I tuned out all those voices echoing around in my head saying this was no good and watched as the two men seemed to come to some sort of agreement and made their way back to me. Both wore broad smiles that did not seem to match the situation.

"We'd love to help you. Cole and I will teach you to ride, and you can help us out a little around here. Might be good for you to learn a little bit about ranching. You know, so nobody has to babysit you while you're here."

Gabe's voice was teasing and he smiled at me good-naturedly. I knew he was just parroting the words Jack had used on me earlier. It didn't matter. No amount of teasing could dampen my enthusiasm. I was bouncing on the balls of my feet, barely able to contain my glee.

Clapping my hands together, I half-yelled, half-sang my thoughts. "Thank you, thank you! I promise you won't regret this!"

Cole gave me a look that could only be described as a mixture of skepticism and hopefulness. I chose to ignore all their weird looks, shoving them down somewhere below Jack's earlier angry words to be examined later. Right now, I was just going to bask in my victory.

"We're going with Jack to see what parts of the fence need replaced before winter, but while we're gone, you can muck out the stalls. Figure that'd be a pretty easy job to get you started. I'll show you where the equipment is and find you a pair of gloves that aren't too big."

Cole motioned for me to follow him into the barn.

"Yes! I can muck stalls, no problem," I responded, following close on his heels while trying to remember if I knew what mucking stalls meant. I thought it meant cleaning the stalls out, but I wouldn't bet money on it.

Following Cole toward the tack room—the scene of my verbal assault earlier—he stopped in front of a wheelbarrow and tools that looked like the ones I used to use helping my dad in the yard growing up. *Okay, nothing crazy, I can do this. I know what a rake is, and a shovel's a shovel.* Cole dug around on a shelf that was just high enough to hide the contents from my eyes until he found what he was looking for.

Thrusting a pair of thick blue gloves in my direction, he instructed, "Put those on for fit. I think they're the smallest pair we have around here. Might need to make a trip to town soon if you're serious about this plan," he added, glancing down at my sneakers. I was wearing a pair of grey and pink Nikes that he was eyeballing like they were a pair of heels. Nikes were perfectly respectful shoes for doing things. They were doing-things shoes! I shrugged, pulling on the gloves. I held my hands out in front of me and wiggled my fingers in front him.

"They're a little big but I think they'll work fine." I moved my hands around dramatically to reinforce my words.

"Looks good. Everything you need should be here. If you run into a problem, just ask anyone around. It's usually easiest starting at the far end and working your way back but you can do it however you want. Most of the stalls should be empty. Skip the ones that aren't; don't be a hero. You don't have any-thing to prove to Gabe and me, got it?"

"Yes, absolutely. No problem."

"All right then. Do you have any questions before we head out?"

"Well... just one. What exactly does mucking out a stall mean?"

12.

After a very patient demonstration—so much more patient than I deserved—I was left alone with a wheelbarrow,
some tools I wasn't convinced I knew how to use, and a mostly
empty barn. Moving to the first stall, the one Cole had suggested, I stepped into the empty space, which smelled like
things that couldn't be found in Chicago.

"Okay, you can do this. Just like raking leaves with Dad.
Only smellier."

I looked down at my new, clean Nikes and said 'so long.'
I didn't think there was going to be a future for us after this
was all over. I started raking out the old stuff, trying not
to cringe every time I stepped in something that squished. I
made pretty quick work of raking the contents into a pile and
then shoveling them into the wheelbarrow waiting outside.
Grabbing the handles, I lifted up to move to the next stall. Not
realizing there was a difference steering an empty wheelbarrow and one filled with something, I took quick steps forward
sending the wheelbarrow lurching suddenly to the left.

"No no no no no!" I jerked it to the right trying to keep the
stupid thing upright, but I jerked too hard and the movement
sent the wheelbarrow crashing to the ground, spilling everything I had just shoveled into it.

I whimpered, looking at the mess, and gave myself until
the count of ten to get over it. Letting out a huff of breath to
blow away the hair that was already spilling out of my ponytail, I grabbed the shovel and got back to work.

Seven stalls later, I felt every single muscle in my arms

—muscles I hadn't even known I had. I looked at the row of stalls I had left and sighed loudly. It seemed to go on forever. I couldn't even remember seeing that many horses on this ranch. I actually felt tears starting to build up in my eyes, and I whimpered again.

My arms felt so heavy and my legs were starting to feel like I had done four million squats. The rake felt like it was made of bricks. For a brief second, I regretted turning down Hilari and Anna's invitations to go to their spinning class. Every single week. I'd tried hot yoga with them once and almost died. I thought yoga was supposed to be relaxing, but I'd felt like an unhappy pretzel in an oven.

Hank Williams, who had been napping on a pile of hay in the corner most of the time, lifted his head just long enough to let out a little howl of his own.

"I know, Hank, I know." I drew out the last word.

Drawing on the one and only thing I had going for me, I called up the words Jack had hurled my way earlier and let my stubbornness take over. Moving stall to stall, I tried to ignore the muscles that cried out every time I bent or shoveled or lifted or breathed. I focused on Jack calling me a city girl who needed a babysitter, and King, who needed a friend. I was running on rage fumes when I heard Mary calling my name from somewhere in the barn.

"I'm here," I called, popping my head out of the stall I was in. I had finished and was wheeling my way out of the stall by the time she found her way to the far end of the barn.

"Goodness, Evelyn, look at you! You missed lunch and Sam said he hadn't seen you all day. What on earth are you doing?"

Mary's eyes roamed over me, taking in my dirty, disheveled appearance, her eyes moving from my shoes to the hay I could feel sticking out of the sad remnants of my ponytail. I could also feel something that I hoped was dirt smeared on my forehead from where I had pushed my hair out of my face earlier.

My stomach rumbled loudly, right on cue. I never missed meals. I was usually planning lunch before I finished breakfast. Missing meals almost always led to a migraine, and I just genuinely liked to eat. I had the physique to prove it. I must not have been able to feel the hunger over all the throbbing in my limbs.

"Umm... mucking stalls?" I shrugged and then immediately winced when my shoulders protested loudly at the movement.

"I see that. Why are you mucking stalls?"

I panicked a little, debating how to answer what should have been an easy question. No part of me wanted to explain to Mary that her youngest son was quite possibly the biggest ass in Montana and had given me an epic verbal beatdown for asking a simple question. But I also didn't want to lie to this woman, who had been nothing but kind to me since I had arrived. I decided to go with a version of the truth that I hoped wouldn't make anyone look bad, even if I really wanted to make it known that Jack was the bad guy in this scenario. I knew it. My muscles knew it. Cole and Gabe knew it. That would have to be good enough.

"I asked Cole and Gabe if they would give me riding lessons. I thought I could help out around here as a thank-you. You know, since I'm making extra work for them. But it turns out I'm basically useless so..."

I gestured toward the wheelbarrow, without actually moving most of my arm.

"Ben and Gabe are making you do chores for riding lessons?" Mary's eyebrows jumped up her forehead.

"No! I asked them to let me help out. I like being helpful and they were nice enough to agree to teach me. Like I said, I offered. Besides, I should know how to take care of a horse too, right? I mean, that *is* part of riding."

I hoped I sounded more enthusiastic and persuasive than I felt. Mary looked at me silently for a few seconds before making up her mind. I would have been so shitty in the courtroom.

"Well, it's very thoughtful of you to want to help out, but if you're going to be doing work around here, you can't go around skipping meals. Why don't you take a little break and come to the kitchen with me? I can whip you something up. It looks like you could use a nice cool drink, too. How long have you been out here?"

"Oh, um, I don't know, what time is it?" I realized I hadn't stopped once to check the time.

"Just about three thirty."

"A long time." I tried to laugh casually, but even I could hear what a sad sound had come out of my mouth. "I think I'll just keep working. I'm almost done anyway. Might as well just keep going. I brought plenty of water, so I'm staying hydrated."

Honestly, I was afraid if I stopped moving long enough to sit at the table and eat, I might not be able to get back up. It was safer to just keep moving. Mary made a disapproving noise in her throat.

"Okay, but I'm bringing you a sandwich. You won't be much help to anyone if you pass out. I don't want to hear any arguments, either."

"Thank you, Mary, a sandwich would be great." I smiled genuinely. She wasn't going to get any argument out of me if she wanted to make me a sandwich. I wouldn't say no if she offered to feed me the sandwich, either, at this point.

True to her word, Mary returned with a chicken salad sandwich on bread I was pretty sure was not store-bought. I devoured it, savoring every single bite. It was the best sandwich I had ever eaten, and I had eaten many, many sandwiches in my twenty-seven years.

Mary left with an empty plate and the promise that I wouldn't miss dinner. Hank Williams, who had perked up as soon as the sandwich appeared, followed Mary back to the house. His loyalty stopped at food. I could respect that.

13.

I finished the last couple of stalls, each one taking longer than the one before it, and dragged myself to the house. I paused to take off my shoes just outside the door, where I had seen boots lined up in messy rows before. My slow procession stopped when I reached the bottom of the staircase. I peered up. It seemed a lot longer than I remembered. I whimpered for what felt like the hundredth time today.

The staircase I had so admired the first time I saw it now seemed like an insurmountable obstacle. I took one step and then another, slowly making my way up while reminding my aching legs that there was a warm shower waiting for them at the top.

Ben chose that moment to casually walk down the stairs like it was nothing. His steps slowed as he got closer, taking in my appearance.

"What the hell happened to you?"

"Your brother's an ass, that's what happened," I fired back, not stopping my ascent. 'Keep moving' was my official mantra today.

"Jack?" His voice thick with disbelief. Why everyone had such a hard time believing that Jack could be an ass was beyond me. I grunted.

"Forget it. It's fine. I just want to take a shower. If I'm not at dinner, I'm dead and it was nice knowing you. You were a great boss."

Ben's loud laugh echoed through the empty space.

"I'd offer to help, but I'm pretty sure that would count as sexual harassment and I'm supposed to be keeping a low profile."

"Ha ha," I deadpanned. "You are so funny. Don't forget, I control your calendar. I can make your life miserable."

Ben laughed again, holding up his hands in surrender.

"You got me. See you at dinner. I promise to send a rescue party if you're a no-show."

I gave a wave and powered on. I wasted no time undressing once I closed my bedroom door behind me. In a move that went against everything in my nature, I left my clothes wherever they fell as I crossed the short distance to the bathroom. I wasn't big on baths, but if I'd had more time, I would have loved to sink into a tub of hot water with a glass of wine and a couple of ibuprofens. Instead, I settled for two ibuprofens with water and turned the nozzle for the shower to just shy of scalding and waited for the water to warm up.

Stepping into the hot spray, I groaned so loudly I would have been embarrassed if anyone had been around to hear me. I stood motionless, letting the heat of the water work its way into my skin, and deeper, into all those newly-discovered muscles I'd made frenemies with today. I stood there until my arms felt up to the task of washing my hair and then the rest of me. I stayed under the water until my limbs felt like jelly and my eyes were heavy.

It took so much strength to pull myself out of the shower, but I had promised Mary I wouldn't skip dinner. Pulling on my favorite pair of worn jeans and an old college sweatshirt, I piled my hair on top of my head and applied just the smallest amount of makeup, in the hopes it would make me look less tired than I felt.

I traveled down the hall and then down the stairs slowly, the effects of the shower and the ibuprofen fading the more

I moved. I vaguely remembered someone telling me moving was the best thing for sore muscles. I decided that person had probably never had a sore muscle in their entire life. I could hear the buzz of conversation as I got closer to the kitchen. Sam, Ben, Gabe, and Jack were already seated around the table, each with a beer in hand. I saw Rodney's lower half sticking out of the refrigerator, and it sounded like he was still attempting to dominate the conversation despite his head being buried inside it.

Smiling my way, Gabe scooted over and patted the spot next to him. I returned his smile and made my way over, then eyeballed the bench that stood between me and sitting. I heard Gabe chuckle. Gingerly, I lifted one leg up and carefully swung it over the bench, fighting to keep the misery from showing on my face. My hand had other ideas, though, and moved to Gabe's shoulder totally of its own volition. Any other time, I would have taken a moment to appreciate the muscular shoulder my hand was gripping. Then again, any other time I wouldn't have touched that shoulder without an invitation. The second leg followed the path of the first one, and I lowered myself to the bench like someone four times my age.

Gabe looked at me, that easy grin still in place, and winked. I was too tired to handle that dimple. It was going to fry the little bit of my brain that was still working.

"The barn looked real good, Evie. How you feeling?"

"Evie, huh? And like I got beat up by a shovel and its wheelbarrow partner in crime." I returned his grin with a tired one of my own. Gabe chuckled, shooting me a two-dimpled smile, and nudged me gently with his shoulder.

"I heard one of your girls call you that. I like it. You want me to grab you a beer? I think you earned one today."

"A beer would be great, thank you."

Mary announced that dinner was ready and the table began to clear. I decided to stay seated. It wasn't like I was going to beat anyone to the front of the line. At this point, I was considering just drinking my dinner. Beer had a lot of calories. Nutrition was overrated, anyway.

Gabe returned to the table balancing two plates and a beer. I'm sure the smile I gave him when he set the second plate and beer in front of me was ridiculous.

"Don't look at me like that. I just didn't want to have to watch you try to stand up," Gabe said, taking a large bite of potatoes.

"Have I told you today that you are my absolute favorite cowboy?" I asked him, reaching for the cold beer and taking a long drink. I was a little in love with this man right now.

"Uh-huh," Gabe mumbled around his food. "I'll remember that."

I ate quietly, struggling to keep my eyes open and to keep up with all the conversations happening around me. Sam and Jack were discussing the various states of disrepair the fences were in, Gabe and Ben were talking about some sports team, and Rodney was telling Mary about a shop he found in town. I learned that Ben had taken Rodney into town to run some errands earlier. From what I heard around the table, Jack wasn't aware that I had been the one to clean out the barn—which meant he didn't know about the deal I'd made earlier with Gabe and Cole.

"Evelyn."

The sound of my name drew me out of my thoughts.

"Sorry, what was that?" I looked up and saw everyone's eyes on me. I felt a blush start to spread across my chest and up my cheeks.

"I was saying how much you must be looking forward to having another woman around here at dinner. Mary said

Cole's wife was coming up tomorrow. Nice break for you from all this testosterone, huh?" Rodney laughed at his own joke. I wasn't sure he realized that his comment might have been slightly offensive to the other woman in the room, who at this point should have been nominated for sainthood. Raising two boys must have given her a high tolerance for stupidity.

"It's been a real struggle," I confirmed, my sarcasm obvious to everyone but him.

I already knew Cole's wife and daughter ate dinner up here regularly. Margot had stayed home with their daughter, Letty, this week, because Letty was fighting a cold and being a "little nightmare." Cole's words, not mine.

If anyone else had made the comment, I would have admitted that I was really looking forward to meeting Margot. I already decided she had to be amazing to have snagged Cole. There was no way I was going to tell Rodney any of this, though, and risk accidentally starting a conversation with him.

"There's a band playing at Rowdy's tonight, little bar in town. I think we're all going to grab a drink and listen, if you want to come with us. Break up that testosterone?" Gabe leaned in to whisper.

"Do I want to go to a bar where there is dancing with Rodney? Nope. No thank you. I kind of just want to go to sleep, honestly. Thanks for the offer, though."

"Can't say I blame you. But we both know you'd be using all your dances on me."

He was absolutely right, although I suspected I would be fighting off every other female in the bar.

"You think so, huh? And we both know you would just be holding me up at this point. There wouldn't be any dancing happening."

"I'd take my chances. Do you think you can handle a riding

lesson tomorrow morning?" One of Gabe's eyebrows slid up that handsome forehead as he asked the question, making it sound more like a challenge.

"Yep! I'll be fine." I couldn't help giving a little squeal. "I'm so excited!"

Gabe barked out at a laugh, obviously caught off-guard by the level of my enthusiasm.

"Okay, city girl. Take it easy." My smile turned to a scowl at the use of that nickname. "You think you can make it to the barn by six?"

"Let's stick with Evie, cowboy, and six is fine. I'll be there!" But six was pretty early, so I followed up with an important question. "What's your policy on drinking coffee while riding, though? Asking for a friend."

"You and your coffee." Gabe shook his head. "Sorry, no drinking and riding."

I may have mumbled something about it being more un-safe for me to operate a horse while uncaffeinated, earning an-other laugh from Gabe.

"You ready, Romeo, or did you change your mind about going?" Jack's abrupt question made my head snap in his dir-ection, and this time I didn't manage to hide the grimace the sudden movement caused.

"Worried about the competition, old man?" Gabe fired back easily, clearly unfazed by what I was pretty sure was an insult.

"Nah, just thought I'd give you a chance to bow out grace-fully," Jack teased back, a small grin appearing.

I wasn't sure what this back-and-forth was actually about, but I was fairly confident that it involved women—confident enough to roll my eyes in their general direction. Men are boys forever. Ben felt the need to prove that point.

"Hey now, I think you both forgot I was in town. God knows the poor women at Rowdy's need a break from your faces."

Gross, gross, gross. And that was my cue to jump into this idiot-fest.

"You keep your hands to yourself. You are officially out of the running for whatever contest this is," I said, pointing to Ben and wagging my finger. Turning to Gabe, I said, "Make sure he doesn't do anything that's going to require antibiotics later."

The last part earned a strangled laugh from Gabe, and even a chuckle from Ben—who didn't look the least bit embarrassed, despite the fact that his mother was seated at the table.

"Yes ma'am," Gabe obliged.

Gabe's agreement seemed to be a sign that it was time for them to head out. Dishes were dropped into the sink, thank-yous and goodbyes given to Mary, and hats grabbed off the rack by the door. I was promptly told to go to my room and rest by Mary when I tried to help her clean the kitchen. I didn't put up much of a fight—just enough for Midwestern politeness. Hank Williams followed closely behind me as if even he was aware that, once I crawled into bed, I was not getting up again.

Sliding under the cover, I sighed with relief. Everything they said about physical labor was true. I looked longingly at my Kindle but decided I didn't even have the energy to read. I reached to turn the lamp off.

My phone's loud ring stopped me mid-reach. Picking it up off the nightstand, I saw "mom" on the screen. I waged a brief internal battle between the desire to sleep and being a good daughter.

"Hi mom," I greeted her after hitting the answer button. Being a good daughter had won.

"Hi, Evie. I hope I'm not calling too late. I keep getting the time difference messed up." I heard a muffled "Okay, give me a minute," and then, "Your dad says hi and he loves you."

"Tell him I love him too, and I was still up, so no worries."

"You sound tired, sweetie. Did you have a migraine?" Concern edged her question.

"No, I just spent the day mucking out stalls and I'm exhausted. I hadn't realized there were so many horses on this ranch."

"Why were you mucking out stalls, Evelyn?" she half-asked, half-demanded, in the way only mothers can manage.

"It's kind of a long story, actually. " But even I knew how pathetically evasive that response sounded. Mom was not having it.

"Well, then, I guess it's a good thing I'm retired." She waited silently on the other end. I knew there was no way she was going to drop it. She was a master in the art of waiting you out. My mom could wield silence better than a mime.

I couldn't exactly put my finger on why, but telling my mom about King and Jack felt like poking a raw wound. I didn't know why so many emotions were wrapped up in those two. But I took a deep breath, petting Hank Williams for comfort, and told her about King and wanting to help him. Then I told her about Jack and how cold he had been since I got here, and what he had said to me when I asked to help. Finally, I told her about the deal I'd struck with Cole and Gabe and how they had been nothing but nice to me—the opposite of Jack in every way.

"I don't know, Mom. I just feel like I have to help King. I can't really explain it, I guess. It just feels important. Is that crazy? It is right?"

My mom made a thoughtful noise in her throat. Silence stretched across the phone. There were times when I loved how thoughtful my mom always was and there were times when it made me want to scream. This was one of the latter.

"I think it makes perfect sense, actually. You were always trying to bring home hurt or stray animals when you were little, so I can't say I'm all that surprised. Do you remember the time you brought home those rabbits you found in the backyard because you were worried they'd freeze to death?"

"Yes! How could I ever forget those rabbits? And all the babies they had in my closet."

I snickered, remembering the look on Mom's face when she opened my closet door and a whole herd of bunnies came hopping out. How I had managed to keep their existence a secret for so long was one of the greatest unexplained mysteries in Mercer family history. The bunny family was promptly packed up and delivered to a rabbit sanctuary. Yes, there is such a thing as a bunny sanctuary, and yes, it is as adorable as it sounds.

"Do you think my plan will convince Jack, though? I feel like I've thought of everything that could go wrong, but I don't know. It's hard to make a plan to change his mind when I don't even know why he dislikes me so much in the first place. And I really think the reason he doesn't want me to help is because he doesn't like me."

Mom sighed. She was one of those magical creatures: a mother who never seemed to raise her voice. Even with three teenage girls, I could rarely remember my mom yelling, unless it was to be heard over our screaming. However, that didn't mean she never called us out on our nonsense. I could always count on her to tell me I was being stubborn or ridiculous —which always felt slightly harder to hear when it was said quietly. Quiet is always so much more reasonable-sounding than shouting.

After a few more seconds of silence, she said, in that patient voice that was such a large part of the soundtrack of my childhood, "Evie, you can't plan people, sweetie. I know you need everything to fit into a neat little plan, but people don't work like that. I don't know if Jack will feel any differently once you prove you're at least capable of not getting hurt, but I think it's worth trying."

"Ugh. I just wish I knew why he hates me so much. I get along fine with everyone else here—well, except Rodney, but that's because of Rodney. I can't think of anything I could have done or said."

"Some people don't need a good reason to not like someone. I have a feeling you're not the problem, though."

I couldn't contain the yawn that snuck out.

"Get some sleep, Evie. Let me know how your lesson goes tomorrow. I love you."

"I love you too. I'll try to send some more pictures tomorrow."

14.

I didn't remember my head hitting the pillow after hanging up with my mom, so when the alarm on my phone sounded, I startled awake, knocking it from the nightstand. I tumbled out of bed after it, frantically trying to hit the snooze button. It wasn't until I silenced the alarm that my body seemed to catch up with me. I curled up on the floor and moaned.

"Everything hurts," I whined to Hank Williams, who had moved to hang his head over the edge of the bed. "Be a good dog and bring me some pants. Please."

A rooster started crowing and I rolled onto my back, trying to stretch my limbs. I was literally up before the roosters. I lifted my tired body off the floor, ignoring the loud protests from my muscles, and made my way into the bathroom. I washed my face and braided my hair without even bothering to look in the mirror. There were at least three hours left before I started caring about my appearance. Gabe would just have to deal.

Moving as fast as my body would allow, I pulled on a pair of jeans and the same crewneck sweater I had worn to dinner. Then I crept out of my room, leaving the door cracked slightly for whenever Hank Williams decided to get up. He might be the only living creature who hated mornings more than I did. I tiptoed down the hall and down the stairs, making my way into the kitchen. My first stop was the coffee pot. I noticed a note lying on top of it.

Evelyn,

There's quiche in the fridge for you to heat up before your lesson. The coffee pot is ready to go, just hit brew. Good luck!

Mary

Tears started welling up in my eyes, blurring my vision. I blinked hard, clearing my throat and sniffling. I was not emotionally prepared to handle that much kindness so early. I ate the reheated quiche and chugged the hot coffee as fast as I could without burning my mouth, then headed out looking for my teacher.

I found him saddling a large horse, who eyed me suspiciously as I walked toward them.

"Good morning, Gabe." I said, offering my hand for the horse to smell. Whiskers tickled my hand and I laughed. The horse let out a huff of breath before turning away to eye the hay in the corner.

"Hey, Evie, you ready for your first lesson?" His voice was still rough from sleep, and I noticed he hadn't bothered to shave this morning. It must have been a late night, and that made me like Gabe even more for showing up early to give me a lesson when I was sure he would have loved the extra sleep. My hormones also appreciated the lack of shaving, but for completely different reasons.

Gabe unhooked the lead lines from the wall and started leading the horse from the barn. I fell into step next to him.

"I'm ready, but some of my muscles are not as excited about it. You look a little rough yourself."

Gabe laughed, coming to a stop in front of a ring. He unlatched the gate and led the horse through it. I followed him in, stopping to lock the gate behind me.

"This nice old lady is Photo. She's taught a lot of kids around here to ride, because she's such a patient woman. Isn't that right, sweetheart?" Gabe stroked her nose affectionately, and I swear she swooned a little. No species was immune to those dimples. *I feel ya, girl.* "Do you remember if you rode English or Western at summer camp?"

"English, but I have ridden with a Western saddle before." I left out the part about it being on a guided beach walk in Mexico. *Details.*

"Well, look at you. Do you want me to give you a leg up, or do you think can you mount by yourself?"

"Nope, I remember how to mount a horse." *Lie.*

I told my muscles to quit their whining and placed my right foot into the stirrup. I heard Gabe make a noise that sounded like a confused cough, and I shot a glance in his direction. His lips were pressed tightly together and he was clearly trying to keep from laughing.

"What?" I asked him, my foot still in the stirrup.

"You planning on riding poor Photo backward?'

I looked at my foot and then up at the saddle.

"You passed the first test! Nice job. You're going to be a great teacher." I slid my foot out of the stirrup and placed my hands on my hips. I needed a minute to regroup from that one.

"Uh-huh. Glad I'm up to your standards." Gabe played along.

Placing my left foot in the stirrup this time, I reached up to grab the horn and came up short.

"Ooomph."

I added a little extra hop and managed to get my hand around the horn on my second try. *Okay, all right, not so bad.* I tried to pull myself up while simultaneously trying to swing my other leg over Photo. My right leg made it to the hump on the back of the saddle, coming to an abrupt stop. Gravity chose that minute to bring me down—literally. I felt myself slowly sliding down, down, down.

Emily Mayer

"Umm... okay... ahh... oof... er, just..." More incoherent sounds tumbled out of my mouth. "Shit... nooo..."

My sore muscles were no match for gravity. I slid until I was a sad, awkward tangle of legs on horse dangling inches from the ground. I said a silent prayer that the ground would open and swallow me up before my butt hit it, or that Gabe would disappear into thin air. Both went unanswered, and I hit the ground in a heap of limbs and shame.

"Listen, you can never tell anyone about this, okay? Promise me, Gabe," I begged, looking up at him from my spot on the ground. I could hear him fighting to contain his laughter. Chest heaving and eyes squeezed tight, he was trying to pull himself together—and failing miserably.

"I think we both know I'll never promise you that. It's probably going to be the first thing I tell Cole when I see him."

"You're such a girl." I rolled my eyes at him from my spot on the ground.

"I don't think anyone's ever called me that before. I gotta hand it to you, Evie. I've never seen anyone mount a horse quite like that. Is that what they're teaching kids at riding camps?"

He walked toward me and extended his hand. I reached out, accepting it gratefully.

"Shut it. You won't tell anyone, will you, girl?"

Photo turned to look at me, giving a little sound that I took as a 'no, we ladies have to stick together.' *Right on, sister solider.* I attempted to brush the dirt off my jeans, eyeing the saddle.

"You know what, I've decided to let you help me mount after all."

"Oh, you're gonna *let* me help, huh?" Gabe snickered again. If nothing else, he was getting some serious entertainment out of this whole thing. "How nice of you!"

"That's just the kind of person I am." I shrugged, barely managing to keep a straight face.

"All right, enough talking, get into position and let's get on with this," he said, moving behind me. Glancing over my shoulder at him, I wiggled my eyebrows suggestively. Well, as suggestively as I was capable of.

"I bet you say that to all the girls. Such a charmer!"

Gabe was momentarily stunned, mouth gaping and eyes wide, before he threw his head back and let out a laugh from deep in his stomach. He shook his head slowly, taking me in.

"Jesus, Evelyn, I didn't know you had it in you."

I didn't either. And I definitely didn't think the Evelyn from a week ago would have been able to say that. Never in my life had I been this comfortable with a man who looked like Gabe. Usually I was all shy eye contact and awkward silence around men who looked like they should be in a magazine —and those were best-case scenarios. Something about Gabe made it easier. Or maybe it was just being out here, so out of my element? It felt strange and freeing. I liked it.

"Seriously, leg up." I snickered, but Gabe cut me off with, "Don't even say it."

This time, with Gabe's help, I managed to gracelessly but successfully mount poor Photo. Making a mental note to sneak her an apple when this was over, I reached forward to rub her neck and thank her for being patient.

After handing me the reins and adjusting the stirrups, Gabe gave me a crash course in riding. I gave Photo a little nudge and we were off. She set off at a slow, steady walk and I began to relax a little. Gabe gave me instructions to sit up and keep my heels down.

"Looking good, Evie," I heard Cole shout from somewhere

behind me. Turning my body carefully, I spotted him leaning against the fence on the far end of the enclosure next to Gabe.

I waved, a large smile in place, equally pleased by the praise and the nickname. Just as we turned the corner to head back in their direction, I heard the sound of gravel crunching under tires. Jack's black truck was making its way up the winding drive that led to the house. I watched the truck's progress as it made its way to the end of the drive. The driver's door opened and Jack's long legs exited, followed by the rest of the surly man—who just so happened to be dressed in the same clothes he'd left in last night. *Interesting.*

I heard Gabe shout something at him, but I was too far away to make out the words. Cole had turned to face Jack and was shaking his head. Jack shot something back at the men without even turning in their direction on his way into the house.

Unreal. What. A. Pig. He might not have time to babysit me, but apparently he had plenty of time to have a one-night stand with whatever poor creature had been lured in by that face and the way he looked in those jeans. I'm sure he had his shirt sleeves rolled up to show off those forearms, too. She never stood a chance! Also the temperature must have shot up twenty degrees because my cheeks suddenly felt flushed. *Must be the altitude up here...*

This is why your parents tell you not to judge a book by its cover, I thought. How could someone so, so attractive on the outside be so awful on the inside? It really didn't seem fair. I guessed it was just the universe's way of balancing the scale. I was sure the rest of his gender appreciated his abrasive, surly personality. Jack would have made for some stiff competition otherwise.

Once I was close to the two men—who were gossiping like middle schoolers—I asked Photo to stop the way Gabe had demonstrated. I thought about attempting to dismount without help, but an image of myself dangling off Photo again was all it took to shoot down that idea.

"Hey, hello! Who's in charge of this lesson?" I called out. Cole unlocked the gate and stepped into the enclosure, closing it behind him before heading in my direction.

"How's it going?" He stroked Photo's nose.

"Good, I think. I should probably head in, though. Ben wants to go over some proposals before a conference call later this morning." I left out the part about my legs begging me to get down. Loudly.

"Okay, hop on down."

"Hop on down? How?" I eyed the distance between me and the ground.

His right hand covered mine, guiding it to the horn.

"Hold on to the reins and horn the whole time, that's the most important thing to remember. Just take your right foot out of the stirrup and swing it over Photo. Kick your left foot out before you hit the ground. That's all there is to it."

I looked down at Cole doubtfully. He made it sound so easy. My hands started to sweat a little. I did *not* want a repeat of my earlier performance, and my butt didn't want to make contact with the ground from this height.

"You're overthinking this, Evie. I'll be right behind you. I won't let you fall, okay?"

Taking a deep breath, I dismounted, landing on the ground feet first.

"I did it!" I yelled, doing a little happy dance. I might have been a little too excited about dismounting without making a scene, but a win was a win. "Even the Russian judges would have given that dismount at least a nine."

"I told you it'd be fine. So, how'd it feel to be back in the saddle?" Cole asked, taking the reins from me.

"It felt great! Well, my legs don't feel great, but I forgot how much I liked riding."

Cole smiled, handing me the reins he had slipped over Photo's head.

"We might just turn you into a cowgirl yet. Lead Photo back and I'll show you how to get her tack off and brush her."

"Sounds good."

We walked together for a few seconds before he added, "So I hear the mounting style they teach in summer camps is a little backward..."

15.

I made my way back to the house once Photo was settled in her stall munching on an apple. I needed to take a shower since I assumed Ben would not love the idea of spending all day stuck in a room with me covered in dirt and smelling like horse. Every step sent pain shooting through the muscles in my legs.

Freshly showered, I pulled on a pair of cropped leggings and a light pink tunic sweater. I decided to add a scarf and take the time to apply a little makeup. It still felt weird to "go to work" in leggings, so I told myself a scarf and makeup made the whole thing less casual. With my wet hair piled on top of my head, I grabbed my laptop and work bag before heading out the door.

My first stop was the kitchen, because the coffee I'd chugged earlier had worn off. The nice thing about ranch life was that there always seemed to be coffee left in the pot. The house was so quiet as I walked toward the office that the sound of boots and the closing of a door seemed to echo through the hall. Just a few feet ahead of me, Jack was stepping out of the bathroom, turning to head in my direction. I stopped walking and considered creeping back to the kitchen to avoid him when I realized he hadn't noticed me yet. But I hesitated too long. His steps halted as soon as his eyes landed on me, and my traitorous heart skidded.

I figured I had two options. I could smile and pretend like I hadn't spent too many hours over the past couple of days dreaming about kicking him in the shins—or I could let loose the petty girl I usually managed to keep in check, and ignore him like he wasn't even worth acknowledging. I settled on a compromise between the two, like the adult I pretended to be, and forced myself to start putting one foot in front of the other, clutching my laptop tightly to my chest like it could deflect whatever words he hurled at me. I gave him a smile that even I knew looked forced as I moved past him, pressing myself as close to the wall as I could to avoid his wide shoulders. He didn't return my smile; he just stood watching me pass by and making me regret not letting that petty girl win.

He made an exasperated noise that sounded like he had let all the air in his lungs out at once. I didn't even bother stopping to look back. I was not a glutton for punishment.

"Evelyn."

My heart stopped at the sound of my name called out—so softly, so differently than that same voice had used it yesterday—but my feet ignored my heart and kept moving me forward. I clutched my laptop a little tighter to my chest, blaming the caffeine for whatever it was my heart kept doing. I didn't loosen my grip until I was safely inside the office.

Ben looked up from his laptop's screen, concern etched on his face as he took in my appearance.

"Are you okay?"

Why couldn't Jack be as nice as his brother? It made no sense that such a jerk could come from such a nice, thoughtful mom who had produced a similarly nice human being, even if he was kind of a man-whore.

"I'm fine! Just need more coffee." I forced my shoulders to relax and plastered a smile on my face.

"Yeah, I heard your lesson got off to a rough start. Thought I might need to bring in a cushion for you to sit on."

I mentally took back everything I'd thought about him being such a nice guy.

"Unreal! Does everyone know about this? Who told you?"

I slumped into the chair across from him, setting my work bag on the floor.

"Welcome to small-town life. Everyone knows everything ten minutes after it happens. I'm thinking about putting the pictures in the e-newsletter—"

"THERE ARE *PICTURES*?" My shrieked question interrupted him mid-thought. I was going to kill Gabe. Kill. Him.

"Jesus, I didn't know the human voice could get that high. Relax. There are no pictures."

I directed the most withering glare I was capable of at him before turning to my laptop.

The morning passed quickly, turning into afternoon with only a grumble from my stomach reminding me about the time. Rodney took a break from bothering whomever he had undoubtedly been bothering to go over some of the proposed contracts that Ben and I had discussed on an endless conference call. Even I had to begrudgingly admit that Rodney was incredibly good at his job, which made the fact that he was a total creep extra unfortunate—a point he drove home when I stood to stretch my cramping muscles. My irritation was only slightly dampened when I saw he had brought lunch for us.

"You know, I think there are definitely some advantages to the whole office-casual attire idea. I can't say I thought it was a good idea before, but I'm going to have to seriously consider instituting casual Fridays when I get back." He made a show of ogling my backside as I stretched, making me drop back into my chair as fast as my brain could process his words.

Ben, who had been eyeing us like a science experiment gone wrong all afternoon, narrowed his eyes, looking from me to Rodney.

"Well, I'm going to clean up for dinner since we have guests joining us tonight." Rodney stood, squeezing my shoulder.

Ben watched Rodney leave and then turned to me, waiting a minute before clearing his throat and rubbing the back of his neck. It might have been my imagination, but he seemed to be having a hard time looking me in the eyes.

"Listen, Evelyn," he started. I was pretty sure he was now blushing. "I know I can be pretty oblivious at the office—maybe just in general—but you know you can always talk to me about anything that might be bothering you."

What the hell? He looked like a parent about to give their kid the sex talk. Was he waiting for me to respond?

"Uh, thank you. I appreciate that, so umm... thank you?" The last part sounded more like a question than a statement.

Ben let out a huff of breath, more pink creeping up his neck into his cheeks. "Here's the thing. Everyone knows Rodney is a total sleazeball and that he can be a little handsy. I guess I've just gotten immune to it. I don't know. Maybe I don't notice it as much as I should, or assumed you would say something? This is new territory for me." He paused to run his hands through his hair. "Jack said Rodney had to be making you uncomfortable, that he was basically harassing you non-stop, and that I needed to say something to Rodney or he would. So I'll talk to Rodney if he's making you uncomfortable at all."

What the... what? Jack was worried I was uncomfortable? My brain was struggling to absorb all the information Ben had just unloaded on me. The same man who regularly made me feel uncomfortable—worse than uncomfortable—was worried I was being manhandled. It was much more likely that Jack was just uncomfortable watching Rodney paw at me. There was no way he was concerned about my well-being. Was there?

"Evelyn? Are you still with me?" Ben's voice startled me out of my thoughts.

"Oh yeah—sorry. I definitely wouldn't say I'm comfortable

around him, but he hasn't really crossed any lines." I shrugged. Realizing I was probably minimizing the situation to end this conversation, I added, "It might be a good idea to remind him about how damaging a sexual harassment lawsuit could be for him personally, though, and probably how sexual harassment is defined. I think all the women in his life would appreciate that."

"Yes. I can absolutely do that." He paused like he was debating something with himself. "I need to have a serious talk about personal boundaries with him. I don't think I could live with myself if I didn't and he was out there terrorizing you or the rest of our female employees. But, if he crosses a line or you've just had enough, tell me. I would never fire you for telling me something like that—you know that, right?"

"Of course I do! I promise I would have said something to you if I was upset." The same voice that had chastised me for minimizing the situation also questioned whether that was a true statement.

"Well, I know I need a drink. Let's call it a day. You want a beer before dinner? I think Margot and Letty should be here soon."

Ben stood and walked toward the door, waiting for me to follow.

"I'll just pack all this up and meet you in the kitchen. I hate leaving a mess." I scrunched my nose, looking around at the papers scattered about the desk.

Ben laughed. "Of course." He rolled his eyes, shaking his head slowly. "I'll have a beer waiting for you when you're done being your neurotic self."

"There is nothing crazy about wanting to be organized!" I yelled at his retreating back.

"Whatever you say, Evelyn, whatever you say."

I organized the papers scattered around the desk and

placed them in stacks or folders. After packing up my laptop and notebooks, I made a quick stop in my room to drop off my stuff before heading toward the kitchen.

The sounds of male laughter echoed through the hallway and I smiled at the now-familiar sounds. All the guys were seated around the table, talking with beers in hand. Mary was in her usual spot in front of the stove.

"Mom, what do you need help with? You've been in front of that stove all afternoon," Ben asked from his spot.

"I appreciate the offer, Benjamin, but I like my food edible." Her comment earned a round of laughter from the men gathered at the table.

"I'm not a very good cook," I said, moving away from the entrance to make my appearance known. "But I can set the table and chop things. I also stir. Mostly things I microwaved, but I'm pretty sure that still counts."

"Hello, Evelyn—I didn't see you come in. How are you feeling?"

I moved to stand next to her at the stove, leaning my hip against the counter. "Good! My muscles may never forgive me, but they're starting to feel less angry. It could be all the ibuprofen talking, though."

She smiled sympathetically, turning away from the pan she was frying chicken in to look me over.

"I thought you were hobbling a little bit when you came in. Why don't you just sit down and relax?"

"No, really, I don't mind standing. I've been sitting all day, and it feels really good to stretch a little. I'm sure there's something I could help you with."

I prayed she wouldn't ask me to help with the cooking. Saying I wasn't a very good cook was an understatement. I had burnt a pancake beyond recognition. Literally. I sent the picture of the smoking disc to my sisters, and they couldn't tell it was supposed to be a pancake. I thought the spatula melted to it would have been a dead giveaway.

My mom had insisted all of us learn to cook, growing up. It was my least favorite life lesson. Both my sisters were great cooks; Corinne was beyond amazing in the kitchen. I was a total disaster—so bad that my dad confessed he was eating before he came home the nights it was my turn to make dinner. The sad part was, I was more upset that he wasn't bringing me any of the food he was sneaking than I was about the fact that he thought my cooking was so bad.

"You can set the table if you wouldn't mind. Everything's already out." Mary pointed to the stack of dishes on the counter with her tongs.

"I can do that," I replied, picking up the stack of plates and heading toward the table.

I immediately realized my mistake. Setting the table would mean placing a plate in front of the people already sitting there. As in, Rodney and Jack. Those were two close encounters I could do without.

My feet started to drag, prolonging the inevitable. I decided to just rip the Band-Aid off and get the worst over with first. I stepped next to Rodney, making sure to stand just out of his reach. Reaching forward with the plate in my hand, I tried to set the plate in front of him while angling my body away from him at the same time. The plate fell to the table with a clatter.

"Sorry about that; it slipped right out of my hand," I lied.

Trying to dodge Rodney's hand, which had started to travel in my direction as soon as the plate hit the table, I moved quicker than my sore muscles could handle, sending my hip crashing into a corner of the table. I winced. A warm pressure settled over the spot on my hip that had just been rudely introduced to the table. Strong fingertips rubbed a slow circle over the sore spot. I could feel the heat of his hand through my clothes. Turning my head just slightly, I set the plate down—much more gently this time—in front of Jack, fully aware my cheeks were a shade of red that could lead Santa's sleigh through a snowstorm. Jack moved his eyes from the hip he was still holding to meet mine. I gave him an unsteady smile.

"Thanks," I mumbled before moving quickly to my right, forcing his hand to release my hip. I set the next plate in front of Sam, nodding when he thanked me, careful to avoid looking at Jack. I could feel his eyes still on me.

The front door crashed open, almost making me drop the rest of the pile. Tiny footsteps were followed by an excited squeal.

"Uncle Jack!"

A little girl with a stuffed unicorn clutched under one arm ran as fast as her legs could carry her toward Jack. He had turned his body completely away from the table and bent with outstretched arms ready to catch the girl hurtling his way. Scooping her up, he smiled the warmest smile I had ever seen. The kind of smile that crinkles the corner of your eyes. A smile I had not thought this man was even capable of making.

"How's my best girl? Are you feeling better?" said this strange new version of the man I knew as he kissed the top of her strawberry-blond, pigtailed head.

"Mmmhmm." She nodded her head and held up the unicorn to Jack, who bent down and kissed its horned head like it was the most natural thing in the world. Like he had done it a hundred times before.

And I just stood there watching this interaction, plates in hand, confusion radiating off me. I felt like I had entered into some sort of alternate universe instead of the kitchen minutes earlier. Who was this person who had done nothing but scowl or snap at me unnecessarily? Why was I suddenly so jealous of a stuffed unicorn? Jack-without-a-scowl did something to my insides I was not prepared for—not prepared for at all.

"Am I going to get a plate or am I eating dinner off the table?" Gabe asked me.

I tore my eyes away from the pair to shoot Gabe some side-eye. The look he gave me made me seriously concerned that he knew exactly what was going on inside my head.

I was saved when a woman walked through the door carrying a covered tray and asked, "Letty, did you take your shoes off before running through Grandma Mary's kitchen?"

Letty looked up at Jack and then down at her shoe-covered feet. Gabe spun quickly to his right and slid both shoes off her feet, winking conspiratorially at Letty. The smile she gave him could only be described as adoring. Even little girls were not immune to the man.

"Yes." Letty drew out the word, continuing to gaze at Gabe.

The woman I assumed was Margot gave Letty a skeptical look. She moved to give Mary a hug, smiling at Cole as he walked through the door. "Your daughter is a liar."

"No!" Letty's word dissolved into giggles as Jack stood, scooping her up into a little ball. He handed her to Cole and pulled Margot into a hug.

"Hey, Go."

He kissed the top of her head affectionately. I moved like a robot, dropping plates into spots while my eyes stayed glued to what was happening across the kitchen. Margot returned the hug like this was a regular thing, like someone who had not been on the receiving end of scowls and biting remarks. *What the hell?* It couldn't be any clearer. Jack just didn't like me. Not other people. Not women in general. Not city people. *Me.*

"Hey, yourself. I missed your ugly mug this week," Margot said, returning his hug easily. "Ben, it's so good to see you! I'm sorry we couldn't make it up here sooner."

This was Ben's cue to get up and exchange hugs. Letty peered at him shyly from her dad's arms as Ben tried to convince her that she really did remember her favorite uncle. Was there any woman who could blame me for swooning over this scene? I was having a hard time accepting this was real life. And not panting.

I finished setting the table, trying to avoid being remembered for as long as possible. I was never great at big crowds or being the odd one out. My quietness worked against me, and on more than one occasion I'd been accused of coming off as cold or unfriendly. Networking was my worst nightmare. I tried to remind myself that I knew everyone in the room; I would even consider Gabe and Cole friends. I spent an obscene amount of time with Ben on a regular basis, and Mary and Sam were probably two of the nicest humans on Earth. This was fine. Everything was fine.

"Margot, this is a business associate from Chicago, Rodney." Rodney moved to shake Margot's hand at the introduction, and Cole suddenly appeared at his wife's side, wrapping a protective arm around her waist. Ben introduced Letty, who buried her head in her dad's neck. Girl was a good judge of character already. I braced myself, knowing what came next.

"And this..." Ben said, motioning me forward. I moved to stand next to him, reminding myself to try to look friendly. "...is my executive assistant, Evelyn. She basically runs the show at this point."

Rodney felt the need to emphasize this by placing his hand on my back and announcing, "We're all glad Ben found Evelyn."

Catching me off-guard, Margot pulled me into a hug. "I'm so glad I finally get to meet you!"

As soon as she released me, before I could even answer, Jack took my elbow and moved me to stand next to him. He was giving Rodney a look that was alarmingly similar to the scowls I had been the recipient of so many times. I must have looked as startled as I felt, because Margot felt the need to apologize.

"Sorry, I'm a hugger!"

Panic was starting to take root in the pit of my stomach. I didn't want to seem unfriendly—I already liked Margot. My confusion had nothing to do with her hug.

"I don't mind. I come from a big family of huggers, so I'm totally used to hugs." I gave her a genuine smile, feeling re-assured by her open, warm expression. "It's really nice to meet you, too."

"All right, everyone, dinner's ready. I made your favorite, Letty-Lou," Mary announced. Letty hopped out of Cole's arms and reached for Mary's hand.

It took me almost a full minute to realize I was the only one not making my way towards the table. New Jack had left me a little stunned and a whole lot of confused.

16.

Dinner was loud and filled with laughter. It was so much like family dinners from when I was growing up that I was more than a little overwhelmed by nostalgia. I had managed to snag a seat next to Margot and Letty, who spent all of dinner telling me about Sparkle, her unicorn, and chatting about all the things two-almost-three-year-olds find interesting. Margot managed to sneak in a few questions about Chicago or how I was liking Montana so far. Every once in a while, I would feel eyes on me and look up to find Jack watching me, that neutral expression firmly in place. I would look away quickly, feeling my neck heat, and return my attention to Letty.

After dinner, the boys moved to the porch with fresh drinks, talking all things ranch. Letty trailed behind them while Margot and I helped Mary clean up from dinner. The conversation between us was easy and comfortable. When the last dish was dried and put away, Margot turned to me and asked if I wanted to take a walk with her. We wandered past the boys, who were making their way toward one of the barns, Letty holding Ben's hand. Margot followed my eyes.

"So, you and Ben... you're really not sleeping together?" She slapped her hands over her mouth, her eyes going wide. "I am so sorry! I don't know what's gotten into me. I blame being pregnant. These hormones are already making me crazy."

I laughed, waving my hands in the universal sign for *it's fine.*

"Don't worry about it! No, we're not sleeping together, and we never have. But I have eyes that work just fine."

"I know, right? I never thought I'd be such a sucker for seeing men with kids, but ever since we had Letty, it's ridiculous. It's pretty much how we got baby number two." Margot glanced back toward the group, sighing. "Ben is really good-looking, isn't he? I didn't really believe you all weren't sleeping together."

"Those good looks are what get him into so much trouble." I shrugged. "I was basically approved as a hire by the board of directors because they didn't think Ben would sleep with me. Kind of a blow to my self-esteem, but it paid really well and there was lots of traveling so I got over it. We just never had that kind of connection. I mean, he's a really great guy, if he isn't sleeping with you, but—I don't know, he feels more like my older brother. I know that sounds so weird, since he is my boss and all, but it's true."

"I think you might be the first woman on earth able to resist one of the Danver brothers' charm. I never thought I'd see the day."

"You seemed to manage it okay," I pointed out.

Margot smiled, placing a hand on the small bump that was just starting to peek through. She was one of those people who just seemed to shine a natural light wherever they went. Her blue eyes sparkled with warmth, luring you in, making you feel instantly at ease.

"Have you seen my husband? I might be biased but I think he holds his own against those Danvers."

"Can I... um... agree with you? I don't know what the rules are about that, but I think it would be pretty obvious I was lying if I didn't agree, right?"

"Girl, yes! And when that man puts on his cowboy hat..." Margot's voice trailed off, a wistful look on her face.

"You get baby number one?" I finished for her. She laughed, nodding her head. "I used to think there was nothing better than a guy in a well-tailored suit, but this place is making me question that. I mean, there's gotta be something in the water here. They could open the ranch to tours and it would be overrun with women as soon as word spread. I'm not even kidding."

Margot reached over and squeezed my arm.

"I'm so glad you're not awful! I thought you were going to be like all the other women Ben has dragged out here—like talking to a stick with hair. I was so excited to meet you after Cole told me about you. You're just as great as he said you are."

My cheeks warmed at her compliment. It was probably more than a little pathetic how pleased I was to hear that Cole had told Margot I was great. But it is what it is, and I was so happy that I couldn't contain the smile that spread across my face.

"Thanks. I was pretty excited to meet you too. Most of the guys here have been really great, but it's nice to have someone to talk to about how good they look in those jeans. I don't think Ben would really appreciate that conversation. And it would be weird to thank Mary for her gene pool."

"'Most of the guys'? You said 'most of the guys' have been really great."

I wished I could take back that word. Why couldn't I just have said 'the guys'? Margot clearly thought Jack was great. He called her Go! They obviously had a good thing going, and no one liked to hear someone talk badly about their friend. I sighed, considering my next words more carefully.

"It's nothing. I don't know why I said it. Jack just doesn't like me very much. It's fine. I mean, not everyone is going to like me."

"Jack? What makes you think he doesn't like you?"

I groaned inwardly. I looked down at my feet, then out over the gorgeous field that ended in mountains. I looked everywhere but at the person walking next to me, whom I really didn't want to hate me. She must have sensed I was hesitating, because she squeezed my arm lightly and gave me a reassuring smile.

"Hey, it's fine. It's not like I don't know Jack can be an ass. I love him, I do. But I've been around for a while. I had front-row seats to the broken engagement and the mess that followed it."

Those few words of reassurance were all I needed to open the floodgates.

"He just doesn't like me. He's always scowling at me and going out of his way to avoid me. I thought I was just being overly sensitive at first. It wouldn't be the first time I got my feelings hurt over something stupid I imagined. But I asked him if he would let me help him with King, because I really want to help and Jack said he wasn't making any progress. He literally said he didn't have time to babysit some city girl who felt like playing cowgirl for a couple weeks." I shrugged. "I just can't think of anything I could have done or said to make him dislike me so much."

We had stopped moving and I'd been watching the expressions wash across Margot's face. She seemed genuinely surprised by the time I had finished speaking. It seemed to take her a second to process what I'd said, because she was staring at me like I had just grown another head.

"That's terrible! I can't believe he said that. I mean, I really cannot believe it. I've never heard him be mean just to be mean. Yes, he was absolutely miserable to be around after Leigh, but he wasn't mean. He wasn't a prince to the women he slept with after, but he seemed pretty honest with them about expectations—not that that makes it okay. Wait! Did you—I mean did you and Jack…"

"*What?* No!" I practically shrieked. "No, absolutely not. He can't even stand to be in the same room with me for more than five seconds. I swear he looks at me like I make him want to barf most of the time."

"Okay, sorry, I had to ask. I saw the way he moved you away from Rodney before dinner, the way he grabbed your elbow. I thought maybe there was something there. I mean, I wouldn't blame you if you had. Jack is—well, you've seen him."

"Yeah, I don't know what that was about. I'm surprised he didn't go wash his hands right away."

I was fully aware that I sounded like a child, but I wasn't about to take it back. Jack wasn't the only one who got to act like a child. Not that I wanted to be lumped into that particular group with him.

"I'll say something to him. You shouldn't have to deal with his attitude."

"No!" I grabbed her arm, feeling slightly frantic. "Please don't say anything to him. It's not like I live here. We barely see each other. It's fine, really. I know I'm not super outgoing, but I'm not a total troll either. It's his problem."

"And his loss! You're great. I don't know what his problem is. Are you sure you don't want me to say something? I hate that he's being mean to you. This place isn't exactly overflowing with women my age, so I can't have him chasing you away! See, it's totally selfish."

"I'm sure, thank you. Rodney has basically made me a ninja, so I'm super good at avoiding people. Plus, Jack told Ben that if Ben didn't tell Rodney to leave me alone, he'd say something himself. So he must not totally hate me."

Margot _hmm_ed, looking at me with a thoughtful expression on her face.

"Well, that's interesting." Her thoughtful expression turned into a smile that said she knew something I didn't, but before I could ask what was interesting, she turned back toward the house. "We should get back before Letty finds a pile of dirt to bathe in."

We walked back to the house, mostly quiet. I had to fight the urge to ask Margot about what Jack had been like before the accident. If he had changed much since then. What kind of person he was when he didn't dislike you on sight. I had almost convinced myself I didn't really care about those answers by the time we made it back to the house, but much later, lying next to a snoring Hank Williams, I admitted I was a liar.

17.

The next couple of days seemed to fly by. I worked with Ben for however long I was needed, then helped Cole or Gabe around the ranch. We would cram a riding lesson in whenever there was time, and I started to get more confident on Photo. I checked in with King a couple of times a day, telling him about my lessons and how I was making new friends with all the muscles in my arms and legs. He took more and more steps in my direction with each visit. Margot and Letty joined us every evening, and I loved spending time with both of them. Pine-haven was really growing on me.

Even Jack and I managed to find a comfortable routine. He was no longer acting like I kicked his dog all the time, so I worked extra hard to try to avoid him. It made perfect sense in my head. I was seriously concerned Margot had said something to him, even though she promised me she hadn't. I was getting good at avoiding him—I had it down to a science, sneaking past open doors and pivoting to head in the opposite direction whenever I saw him or heard his voice.

It was a gorgeous afternoon and the air was crisp. Mid-September had brought cooler weather with it. I had practiced cantering today, and the speed had made the wind feel extra cold against my skin. My face still felt a little frozen as I finished putting Photo's gear away.

"I can't tell if you're getting heavier or my arms are getting sorer," I grunted, trying to lift the saddle up onto its spot on the rack.

"I don't think the saddle is getting any heavier."

A deep voice that did not belong to the saddle answered. I spun around, arms still stretched over my head trying to keep the precariously balanced saddle from falling down, to see the person I had been avoiding leaning against the door frame. The saddle chose this moment to decide that no, it would not go quietly. It came tumbling back down, landing awkwardly between my shoulder and neck.

"Ow, okay, just…" I tried to push the saddle off me and back up to the rack, failing pretty spectacularly. I blew the loose strands of hair off my face and turned back to Jack. "Did you need something? I'm almost done here so I'll be out of your way in a second."

The stupid saddle lurched forward on my shoulder, and a hiss escaped my lips as it settled onto that ultra-sore part just below my neck. Jack moved forward quickly, stepping directly into my space. He lifted the saddle easily off me and onto its spot as if it weighed less than nothing. I was trapped between the wall and his chest. His flannel shirt stretched across broad shoulders as he reached up. It looked cozy.

Despite my best efforts at resisting his closeness, I inhaled the smell of him—horse and leather and something distinctly Jack. It was a pretty heady combination, one I couldn't even pretend to hate, which made me dislike him even more. How dare this man smell so good? So good he made my body work against my brain. It was rude. He probably did it on purpose, like a Venus flytrap wrapped in flannel that was annoyingly snug.

Good, Evelyn, I thought to myself. *Cling to your anger. Anger is the right feeling here. Always the right feeling with Jack.* I peered up at him and away from his gloriously muscled chest. He looked down at me as he lowered his arms, a grin pulling his mouth to one side.

"Are you okay?" he asked, not stepping out of my space.

"What?"

This close I could see that his brown eyes had flecks of gold in them. His square jaw was covered in stubble that was just a shade lighter than his rich brown hair. He must not have shaved today. I noticed he had a small scar just above his lip.

"A saddle just landed on you."

Shit. I felt embarrassment stain my cheeks. I pulled my eyes away from his and looked down at my dirty shoes. Maybe I could act like a normal human being if I wasn't looking into those brown eyes that turned my brain to mush.

"Oh yeah, sure. Happens all the time."

I cringed. So much for acting like a normal person.

"I noticed," that deep voice said, so close I could almost feel it.

"It's... wait, what?"

I felt his gaze on the top of my head. I moved my eyes from my shoes to his chin. His chin seemed safe. It was a good strong chin. God, why did I keep finding things I liked about his face? I should be focusing on how much I did not like his behavior, like any sane person would be doing. Like I had no trouble doing with Rodney, but my mind kept reminding me of all the ways he was nothing like Rodney. And my heart—I had no idea what it was trying to do.

"Things seem to have a habit of falling on you. Suitcases, saddles..."

"Did... did you just make a joke?" I lifted my eyes to meet his, not missing the unmistakable warmth that seemed to pervade his features.

"I did. You didn't laugh, though, so not my finest work."

I only managed a weak, "Oh." I didn't know what to say. I felt so nervous my hands were starting to get damp, while at the same time a weird warmth was spreading from my stomach to my limbs. Everything about this man threw me off balance, whether he was being grumpy or nice. I was never on solid footing.

The silence stretched between us for several beats before Jack let out what sounded like a frustrated breath.

"I saw you out there on Photo today. You looked good. Gabe said you're a quick learner."

I met his eyes, trying to judge the sincerity behind his words.

"Thank you. I forgot how much I liked riding."

It felt like I was tiptoeing on ice with him. I wasn't sure if the ice was solid or it would break, sending me plunging into frigid waters again.

"Yeah, not too many horses in Chicago." His eyes moved away from mine, making their way to my shoes. "Those aren't great for riding. You need to get some boots. Some real boots, not those things you had on earlier."

I threw my hands up in the air.

"What is *with* you all and these shoes? Nikes are athletic shoes—you know, for sporting stuff. Horseback riding is a sporting thing, so they're perfectly acceptable."

"Sporting stuff, huh? I don't think it works like that, but nice try. Listen, I have to run to town tomorrow; you should come with me. We can stop and get you some boots that would be better for riding."

I stood, mouth slightly agape, trying to process his words. There was a pretty large part of me that was convinced the saddle had fallen on my head and knocked me out. Obviously, I had a head injury.

"I'm sorry, what?"

Jack's mouth moved from a grin to a full smile, obliterating whatever ability I had to form coherent thoughts.

"You should go with me into town tomorrow. Get some boots." His boot-clad foot moved to nudge my Nikes lightly. "If you're not working."

My frazzled brain could only process single words as it frantically tried to understand the sudden change in the man standing a little too close for two people who weren't even friends.

"Boots? Like cowboy boots?"

Jack chuckled, that warm deep noise that rumbled through my entire being. God, that was a noise I could get used to hearing. And then that elusive smile widened as if he knew exactly what kind of effect his laugh was having on me.

"Yeah, I think you earned a pair of cowboy boots."

I felt conflicted, staring up at this man who might be offering me an olive branch in the form of footwear. I remembered all the scowls and the words he had so carelessly tossed my way, but I also remembered the way he was with everyone else. The way he joked with Gabe and Cole, or the ease with which he showered Margot and Letty with affection. How could I not want to experience a little of that side of Jack? It didn't mean I had to forgive him, but I could give him a chance to earn my forgiveness.

"Okay, sure. If Ben doesn't need me to work and you're sure you don't mind, that would be great, actually."

"I wouldn't have asked if I minded."

He sounded so sure, looking at me with those warm brown eyes, that it was almost hard for me to remember how much he *would* have minded not too long ago. All of a sudden, I couldn't seem to stop looking at the very same man I had been trying to avoid. And then his hand was moving toward my face, tentatively, like I might bite. I felt his fingertips gently brush against my forehead before disappearing into the hair just above it. I leaned into him just a little and fought the urge to close my eyes and lean into his open palm completely. Just as quickly, his hand was retreating back to his side, a piece of hay pinched between his fingers. I tried to swallow against my dry throat. It was like my whole body forgot how to work properly at the brief contact.

Hank Williams chose that moment to walk into the tack room and headbutt my leg for some attention, blessedly breaking the tension. I breathed a sigh of relief, bending down to greet the little intruder.

"Hey, Hank Williams, what have you been up to?"

Jack cleared his throat before stooping down to give Hank a quick scratch behind the ears.

"I better get back. I'll see you later."

I looked up from Hank, giving Jack a weak smile. I watched him walk through the door, taking the time to admire the back of him, before I pulled Hank into a hug.

"What just happened, Hank? This is a dream, right?"

Hank began to enthusiastically lick the side of my face, managing to slobber in my ear. I laughed. It was a loud, un-controlled noise that bordered dangerously on the hysterical. I pulled my phone out of my pocket and scrolled to the group chat with my sisters. I needed help translating whatever it was that had just happened.

Me: *I need an emergency meeting or something. This is not a drill! I repeat, this is not a drill!*

My phone was beeping in my hand before I even made it out of the barn.

Elise: *What's happening? Did you tear your pants again? I swear to God, Evie, if this is another coffee emergency…*

Me: *Excuse me, tearing your pants in half while bending down to pick up a pen at work is absolutely an emergency. And I ran out of coffee on a holiday! Everything was closed, Elise. I could have died!*

Elise: *Sometimes I think you missed your true calling, Miss Dramatics. Can you wait 20 minutes? I have one more call to finish.*

Corinne: *Yes, 20 minutes! Celeste will be taking her nap, God willing.*

Me: *20 minutes is perfect. See you both then!*

I tucked my phone back into my pocket and hurried to the house. I managed to take a shower in record time. Settling back against the pillows, I set my laptop on the bed and waited for my sisters to call. A few minutes later I was looking at their faces and feeling a ridiculous sense of relief. The afternoon had been such an emotional rollercoaster that I was seriously in danger of crying.

"Okay, Evie, spill it. What's going on and why do you look like you're about to cry?" Corinne said, her voice like balm to my frayed nerves.

"I just really miss you ladies. It's really good to see your faces." I swiped under my eyes, catching the few tears that had managed to escape.

"Evie, what's wrong? Do I need to fly out to Montana and kick someone's ass? Because I will," Elise said.

Corinne nodded, adding, "I'll fly out there and give you a hug. I'm too short to kick anyone's ass, and also I think that's frowned upon when pregnant. Very Jerry Springer."

I laughed, sniffling a little, and feeling so unbelievably grateful that these two amazing humans were my sisters. All those years of fighting over anything and everything had slowly turned into the best friendship anyone could ask for. It made me regret even more all the moments of their lives I had missed trying to make all those stupid, stupid plans come true.

"I don't know what happened. Jack was nice to me. I mean really nice. He found me in the tack room and offered to take me with him into town tomorrow so I could get boots. And then he got a piece of hay out of my hair."

Silence followed. Elise held up her hand.

"Wait a minute. All this"—she waved her hand up and down in front of the screen—"is because Jack wants to take you to get boots? And he got hay out of your hair?"

"Help me out here, Evie. I feel like we're missing something," Corinne added, frowning a little.

"It's just, well—you remember how I told you he doesn't seem to like me at all? Like how he's always trying to avoid me or scowling, but how he's so sweet to Margot and Letty?"

I waited for both to nod before continuing.

"It's like all of that changed overnight. I don't know. It feels weird. *I* feel weird. I don't know what to think."

"Okay, let's start at the beginning. What happened today, in detail? The last thing I remember hearing about Jack is that he called you a cowgirl wannabe that he didn't feel like babysitting or something, and then how weird it was to see him being all sweet to Letty and Margot. Is that right, or did I leave something out?" Corinne prompted, using her concerned mom voice. Normally I wanted to strangle her when she used her mom voice on me, but right now it seemed fair.

"No, that's everything. Actually, no—a couple days ago, Ben asked me if Rodney was making me feel uncomfortable—"

"Uh, hell yeah he is! It's about time Ben said something," Elise interrupted.

"It was probably one of the most uncomfortable conversations I've ever endured, second only to mom's 'sex is not a recreational activity' talk." My shudder was echoed by shudders from both sisters. "Anyway, he apologized and said he would say something to Rodney. Then he admitted Jack had told him to say something to him or *he* would, because he thought Rod-

Emily Mayer

ney was manhandling me."

"Whoa, I didn't see that one coming," Elise said.

Corinne nodded her head in agreement, adding, "That is pretty unexpected."

"I know! And it felt like he hasn't been trying so hard to avoid me. So, obviously, I've been working extra hard to avoid him. I was putting Photo's saddle back in the tack room when he came in and helped me. Then, like we were just two friends who do friend things all the time, he said I should go with him tomorrow so I could get a pair of cowboy boots. Just like that. And he made a joke! A freaking joke! Who does that?"

"He's clearly a monster," Corinne deadpanned.

"Don't joke with her, Corinne; she's obviously a woman on the edge."

"Thank you, Elise. Like I was saying, after he told a joke, he said I was really coming along in my lessons, or that I was a quick learner or something like that. He was standing really, really close and my brain stopped working. It was definitely a compliment though. I mean, I was speechless. I just looked at him. And he has these really pretty, warm eyes. They just kind of suck you in and you can't think at all. At all!"

I sucked in a deep breath. I couldn't stop the words that were spewing out of my mouth like a tidal wave.

"Then he just reached up like this"—I demonstrated the way his hand had grazed my forehead before it reached the piece of hay in my hair—"and pulled a piece of hay out of my hair."

"Uh-huh," Elise said, looking a little dazed. "What exactly is the problem? Because it sounds to me like Jack is actually trying to be a nice human being, which is a good thing."

"What's the *problem*?" I huffed. "I liked it! That's the problem! I should have kicked him in the shin and said 'Thanks but

134

no thanks, you scowly asshat.' I need to go back in time and slap some sense into myself, obviously."

"Okay, time travel is clearly not an option here, so—and don't get mad at me for asking, but—Evie, have you considered the possibility that you might like Jack a little?" Corinne suggested.

"*No!*" I shouted. Lowering my voice back to a normal level, remembering that I was in a house full of people, I continued, "How could you say that? It's totally ridiculous."

"Umm, have you seen him? Because I could forgive a whole lot of bad behavior for someone who looked like Jack in a pair of jeans," Elise said.

"Yes, I'm sure! He's been nothing but rude to me. I mean I might like to look at him but that's where it ends. Give me a little credit here. I do have some self-respect."

Elise rolled her eyes. "Maybe he realized he was being a jerk and decided to get his shit together?"

"I don't think so. It doesn't make sense. Why would he all of a sudden decide he was going to be nice? That doesn't happen. People don't just wake up and say 'Today is the day I stop being mean.' I think this might be a trap." I tapped my chin, trying to think of Jack's ultimate goal. Maybe he was going to frame me for stealing the boots and have me arrested? I also considered that I might be watching too much *Dateline*.

"I'm sorry, did you just say you think this is a trap?" Corinne said, disbelief lacing her voice.

"Yes," I nodded. "A trap makes the most sense."

"Yeah, because that's not crazy talk," Elise responded.

"Evie, I know you. You do not do well with change at all. You like to put everything into these neat, tidy little boxes and then you freak out when life refuses to stay organized. That is clearly what is happening here," Corinne said.

"What are you talking about? That makes no sense," I fired back. I could admit that I preferred organization and plans, but my need for planning had nothing to do with the Jack situation.

"You can't fit Jack into any of your usual boxes and it's freaking you out. He's surly and kind of mean, but you like him. It's throwing you off your game," Corinne said matter-of-factly.

"I absolutely do not! Stop saying that! It's annoying and not helpful."

"Let me ask you this then," Elise said. "What did you say? Did you say yes to his invitation?"

"Of course I said yes! It would have been rude to say no, and I really do need boots and..."

"And?" Corinne and Elise asked, almost in unison.

"And I don't know. I'm an idiot. Montana is making me stupid. There's too much fresh air and I haven't had a latte in over a week. My brain is rotting. I have brain rot." I dropped my head into my hands and groaned.

"Sure, they're always warning about the dangers of fresh air," Elise responded. I was starting to wonder why I'd thought it would be a good idea to ask these two for advice. "Listen, Evie, I think you should go with Jack tomorrow and get a pair of boots. Try to have a good time and stop overthinking everything."

"I agree with Elise. I do not think this is a trap, and I highly doubt he is planning to dump your body on some backwoods road. Who knows why he decided to start behaving like a decent human being? Stop trying to figure it out and just enjoy the change."

"Now, more importantly, what are you going to wear? Let's move this to your closet," Elise ordered.

After I had shown them almost everything I'd packed and they decided on an outfit, I let Hank into my room and climbed into bed. I tried to read my book, hoping it would quiet all the thoughts tumbling through my mind. But it just made me even more frustrated when I had to read and re-read the same pages over and over again. I finally gave up the book and snuggled under the covers, tucking my cold feet under Hank Williams, who gave a small grunt of protest. I spent the rest of the night tossing and turning, coming up with all the possible ways tomorrow could go wrong. And it *would* go wrong. I was sure of it.

18.

The next morning, I dragged myself out of bed, then into the shower and into the outfit my sisters had picked out. I left my thick, wavy hair down in all its untamed glory and debated putting on more than my usual bare minimum of makeup before deciding against it. I didn't want to give Jack the impression I'd put any extra effort into my appearance. Even if I technically had.

Hank Williams and I made our way downstairs and toward the kitchen, both of us dragging our feet. Mary greeted me with her usual smile and a cup of coffee.

"Good morning, Evelyn, Hank Williams."

Ben sauntered into the kitchen, looking like he was not going to spend all day working.

"Hey, Evelyn. Morning, Mom. Are those omelets? I'm going to have to get a personal trainer when I get back to Chicago."

Ben pulled his mom into a side hug with one arm and patted his still very flat, toned stomach with his free hand.

"You're going to have to add personal training sessions to my benefits package, since this is technically a work trip and it's not humanly possible to resist your mom's homecooked meals."

"You do know we have a gym in the building that's free for all employees, right?" Ben asked, taking a large bite of hash browns right from the serving plate.

"I've heard rumors of such a place, yes." I nodded my head.

"Never cared to confirm those rumors, huh?"

"Nope. That's not true, actually—I did go the day they were giving out free donuts to anyone who signed up for a group class. Anyway, what's the plan for today? Did you need me for anything? I thought you might want me to look over those contracts one more time before sending them out."

I was also willing to organize his sock drawer, organize all the files on his laptop, or move rocks around the yard. Anything that meant I had a good, reasonable excuse not to go with Jack into town.

"I thought you were going to town with Jack today?" Mary asked, taking a seat at the breakfast bar next to Ben.

"Oh yeah, I was planning on it. Just wanted to make sure Ben didn't need me to get anything done before we left," I lied, shoveling a forkful of omelet into my mouth while trying to smile convincingly at the same time.

"You're going to get a kick out of this town, Evelyn. It looks like it should be the movie set for a small-town-America movie. It's no Chicago, but it is the definition of small-town charm," Ben said.

"I'm really looking forward to it." The lies were just rolling off my tongue this morning. I briefly glanced down to confirm there was no smoke coming out of my jeans. Nope. Good to go.

"I think Jack just wanted to get a few things done around here this morning, then he'll be ready to go. I told him to take you to Joan's for lunch and not to rush through his errands like usual. I'm sure you'll want to look around a little. Ben's right—it's no Chicago, but there are plenty of cute little stores to explore," Mary added, in what I was sure was an honest attempt to be helpful.

"Oh no, I wouldn't want to be any trouble. If Jack has things he needs to do back here, I don't want to slow him down too much," I stammered.

"Nonsense. He wouldn't have asked you to come along if

he didn't want you there, and you both have to eat," Mary said with an air of finality.

We finished the rest of our breakfast largely in silence, Ben checking emails on his phone and answering the occasional question from Mary. I could barely finish the delicious hash browns, which was insane because I never let a good potato go to waste. My nerves about the trip to town were starting to make me increasingly nauseated. I just wish I knew what version of Jack would show up today. Or what to do with the friendly version of Jack. Friendly Jack actually made me more nervous than the surly version.

I helped Mary and Ben clean up after breakfast, then moved to one of the rocking chairs to finish a second cup of coffee. The surprisingly comfortable chairs overlooking the ranch and beyond had become one of my favorite places to enjoy the morning. I loved the sounds of the ranch, the animals all busy with their own morning routines, and the scenery was gorgeous. I would love to see this place in the winter. I wondered if Mary decorated the house for Christmas and how amazing it would be to sit around the large fireplace in the living room. A part of me was strangely disappointed at the thought of never seeing Christmas here, of never seeing this place again.

The sound of male voices drew my gaze to the large barn. Jack, Gabe, and Cole exited and made their way to a truck with a large horse trailer hitched to it. Gabe and Cole got into the truck, leaving Jack to watch them pull away. I watched him as he walked toward the house, his steps relaxed and confident. The old red baseball hat covered his brown hair, leaving the ends sticking out. A dirty, long-sleeved top stretched over those broad shoulders and chest, looking like it was made especially for him. I could almost feel the minute those brown, sometimes almost gold, eyes found me on the porch. A few more steps brought him to where I sat.

"Morning," his voice still sounded rough from sleep. "You still coming with me today?"

I nodded my head, tilting it back to look up at that handsome face, and tried to order my scattered words before speaking.

"I am. If it's okay."

"It's okay." He reached up to take off his hat and run his hand through his hair, completely unaware of the effect it had on me. "Let me just get cleaned up and we can head out."

"Sure. Sounds good."

I spent the next twenty or so minutes giving myself another pep talk. I told myself to get my shit together—and I meant it this time. Being a weirdo was not going to help at all. I even managed to smile at Jack as he walked through the door, wearing a clean grey Henley and pair of jeans that made my stomach do a little dance. He returned my smile, pulling on a shearling-lined coat.

"Ready?" I noticed he hadn't bothered to shave the light stubble lining his strong jaw—and I also noticed that I liked it.

"Yep," I said, standing and reaching for my bag.

"You planning on staying the night in town?" He was looking at my bag with an eyebrow raised. I made an outraged noise, clutching my favorite Kate Spade tote to my side.

"This is a reasonable bag for a day trip!" I said, turning to follow him off the porch. "I like to be prepared for things."

He stopped at the passenger's side of the truck and opened the door for me. I mentally congratulated myself for managing to conceal my surprise. I tried to climb into the truck gracefully. Jack closed the door behind me, then moved around the truck to the driver's side.

"Trucks are not made for short people," I said, watching him slide easily into the driver's seat. He laughed, glancing over at me.

"Letty uses a step stool. I can grab hers if—"

"Do not finish that sentence, Jack Danver," I warned him. He laughed again. I was quickly getting addicted to that noise. God, I hoped there was a twelve-step program available for this sort of thing.

I studied his profile as the truck drove off the ranch and onto the road. He glanced over at me and gave me a quizzical look before directing his eyes back to the road.

"What? Do I have something on my face?" He brought one hand up to rub over his whiskered jaw.

Answering truthfully, that I just liked looking at him, seemed like a pretty terrible idea, so I reached up to touch my head.

"You have a different hat on."

"Is that bad? Do you not like this hat?" He adjusted the hat in question, moving the brim from side to side. "It's a good hat."

"It is a good hat. I just didn't think you owned another one."

A slow smile spread across his mouth, making me smile in return.

"I own more than one hat. The red one is for working, is all. It's good and broken in the way I like it."

An easy silence—one I could never have imagined possible just a day ago—settled over the car, and I watched the scenery roll past my window. Jack turned the radio to a station playing country music. A few songs later, he broke the silence with a question.

"So Miss Prepared, what's in the bag?"

Turning from the window, I picked my bag up off the floor

of the truck and began rifling through the contents.

"Umm, let's see... I have granola bars in case I start getting hungry and we aren't close to someplace to eat." I pulled out the two bars then dropped them back into the bag. "I usually get a migraine if I skip meals, so I try to carry an emergency snack. I have mittens for if the temperature drops; September can be weird like that. My hands are always cold. I have extra socks to try boots on with... umm, my Kindle... things like that."

When I looked up from my bag, Jack was shaking his head back and forth slowly, eyes still facing the road.

"How heavy is that bag? Why do you have a Kindle in there?"

"It's not heavy!" *Another lie.* "I always pack my Kindle. I like to read."

"You like to read," Jack stated. It wasn't a question, just a statement.

"Yes, a lot. I didn't get to read a ton during law school, or after, when I worked in the legal department at Sterling. I missed it. I kept this list of books I wanted to read the whole time, and now I'm making up for lost time, I guess." My cheeks pinked at the amount of unsolicited information I had just provided. Jack just looked at me like he was taking it all in. I thought he was going to let it pass without comment when he moved his eyes back to the road.

"What do you like to read?" he asked.

"Anything. Fiction, nonfiction—but I like fiction the best for sure." I faced out the window, needing a break from his probing gaze.

"You're full of surprises, Evelyn from Chicago."

19.

The rest of the ride was spent mostly in silence, the only noise in the cab coming from the radio. It wasn't awkward, though. Every few minutes, one of us would think of a question to ask. I would ask about something I saw out the window or something about the town; he would ask something small about my life. Nothing deep, nothing groundbreaking.

I finally saw a roof peeking up above the bend in the road just ahead and I instantly straightened in my seat, looking forward to seeing the town. I sucked in a sharp breath when we reached the top of the hill and I could see almost the entire town spread out in front of me. Pine Hollow really was as charming as Ben had said it was, like something out of a movie. The buildings were almost all brick or had siding painted a soft pastel color, or some combination of the two. Trees and potted plants decorated the sidewalks and windows, adding even more color. Benches were spread along the sidewalks, under trees and just outside store doors. The streets all seemed to lead to a large, green space that looked like it was used as a community park. A gorgeous white gazebo stood in the center.

And then I saw it.

"Is that... is that a horse tied up outside that building?" My wide eyes turned to find Jack grinning at me. I noticed that my hand had moved to grasp his forearm at some point. A little stunned, I tried to slowly move my hand back to my lap without it seeming awkward.

"Yeah, most county residents use cars but you get the occasional horse parked somewhere." Jack steered the truck confidently down the streets toward a large white-washed building.

"Is this place even real?" I shook my head, still trying to take in everything. "If you tell me there's a little bakery that serves lattes, this might be my new favorite place."

Jack chuckled, putting the truck into park.

"Well, it's your lucky day. Pine Hollow has its very own latte-serving bakery." He opened his door and slid out of the truck easily, all his motions so confident.

I swung my door open and exited the truck much less gracefully. I scrambled into the store behind him, calling out, "Do not joke with me about lattes, Jack!"

I caught up to him, taking quick, quick strides to match his longer legs. He looked down at me and smiled.

"I've seen how you are about your morning coffee. I think I like living enough not to joke with you about caffeine."

"Good," I said, turning away from him to look around the store. It looked like a pet store combined with maybe a hardware store. Almost nothing looked familiar. "So, what is this place?"

I felt a gentle pressure on my hip lightly steer me into a hard body. My startled gaze jerked from the hand on my hip, still gently tugging, to the man attached to it, and then to the pole directly in my path.

"There's a pole," Jack said, dropping his hand away from my now lonely hip. "It's a supply store. I have an order of feed I need to pick up, but you can find just about anything you'd need for the ranch here."

"Oh. So sort of like a Home Depot for ranchers? I try to avoid Home Depots."

"Oh yeah?"

"Yeah, I'm pretty sure it's my least favorite place on earth. Well, to be fair, any home improvement store. We spent hours and hours there with my dad growing up. One time, I got... you know what, never mind."

I could feel Jack's eyes on me. Shame heated my cheeks. Why couldn't I just stop talking?

"You got what?"

I waved my hand around in front of me. "Don't worry about it."

"You can't leave me hanging like that, Evelyn." My name on his lips was like my own personal variety of kryptonite.

I groaned. I couldn't believe I was actually going to tell him this story.

"I got one of those lugnut things stuck on my finger once. We were pretending to have a wedding." I shot Jack a sidelong glance when he snickered. "We had been there for hours!"

"Who was the groom?"

"Ugh. I was the groom. I was always the groom. It's the plight of the youngest sister."

Jack's lips were pressed together so tightly that the skin around them was lined with white. He swiped a hand across his mouth like he was trying to physically wipe the smile off his mouth.

"What happened?" he managed to squeak out.

"My dad had to find someone to cut it off my finger," I mumbled, keeping my eyes on the shelves to my left.

I didn't think my face could possibly get any more red. I was so embarrassed that I was starting to sweat a little. Jack's eyes were once again squeezed shut, and his chest was visibly vibrating with suppressed laughter. Thankfully, just then we reached the counter in the very back of the store, which was apparently our destination. Jack only gave me one last look before he turned to the man standing behind it, and I could have sworn there were unshed tears in his eyes.

"Hey Jack, you here for the feed order?" the man behind the counter asked, leaning forward to shake Jack's hand.

"Yeah, I need to pick up a wire twister too." Jack returned the man's handshake.

"Sure thing." He searched through a haphazard looking stack of files until he found what he was looking for, then pulled out a sheet of paper and passed it to Jack. "Look that over and make sure it's right. I'll have the guys get your order ready to load if it looks good."

Jack looked over the piece of paper. "Looks good," he said, and handed it back to the man, who was now watching me with an openly curious expression.

"Since this oaf has no manners, I'll have to introduce myself. Bill Hayes." Bill leaned across the counter, hand extended in my direction, wearing a large smile. I slipped my hand into his and gave it a friendly shake.

"Evelyn Mercer. It's nice to meet you, Mr. Hayes."

"Likewise, and please call me Bill. Are you staying out at Pinehaven?"

"Yes, I came with Ben. I mean I work for him. I'm his executive assistant at Sterling."

"Ahhh," Bill said, like something I'd said made sense to him.

"All right, you've met. I'm going to pull the truck around back and load up. Take it easy, Bill." Jack turned and started walking back the way we had come.

I waved at Bill, walking backward after Jack.

"It was nice to meet you, Bill."

"Nice to meet you, Evelyn. Hope to see you around."

I turned and scampered after Jack. It was starting to feel like I was always chasing after him. I didn't care for it. Not that he didn't have a very nice back. I slowed my steps in silent protest, mostly because I wasn't sure we were at the 'launching a formal complaint' level of friendship yet. He would either have to wait for me to get to the truck or he could drive off without me, which I was betting was not an actual possibility.

Jack was waiting for me at the truck, reclining against the hood like waiting for me was something he regularly did. I looked down at his boot-covered feet.

"I can't seem to keep up with you." My gaze traveled up those long, toned legs to meet his eyes. I wondered if he realized my words held more than one meaning.

He stood and graced me with one of those smiles that were becoming less and less rare.

"Sorry, I'll try to slow down. I guess I'm not used to someone—" His sentence came to an abrupt stop and he glanced away before returning his eyes to mine.

"Someone what?" I prompted, half-terrified of what he was going to say but not able to let it drop.

"Someone with such... with much... shorter legs. "

Supermodels. He was used to supermodels. One in particular, who—according to my recent internet stalking binge, because I really was a glutton for punishment—was releasing a country album next month. Fun stuff.

"Hey! Are you calling me short? I'll have you know I'm five-four."

His eyebrow quirked up skeptically.

"Ish. That's a perfectly respectable height, thank you very much." I moved to the passenger side and opened the door. "These trucks are just unreasonably high."

Jack nodded his head, clearly feigning seriousness.

"Totally unreasonable." He shut the door for me, adding, "I'll try to remind myself to take Letty steps."

The slamming of the door did not drown out my outraged gasp. I waited until Jack was seated next to me before shooting him my best angry glare.

"Did you just insinuate that I'm the same height as Letty? You just said I'm the same height as a child!"

Jack shot me a sly grin that made my stomach flutter in ways I was not at all happy with, and did not match the outrage I was supposed to be feeling.

"Nah, you've got at least another year before you catch up with her."

I swatted him on the shoulder playfully. I was slightly offended, but the offended part of me was losing to the part that loved the teasing version of Jack the most.

"You're just lucky I really want those boots."

Jack steered the truck to the back of the building and backed it up to a platform where bags were stacked on a forklift. Men were moving all around the warehouse. The back of the building seemed to be so much busier than the store in front.

"I'll get these bags loaded, and then we'll go after your boots."

I slid out of the truck after him and made my way to the raised platform behind it. I took a moment to appreciate the sight of Jack bending to pick up bags and loading them into the truck bed. All those muscles stretching and straining. There was no way anyone with a pulse could resist sneaking a peek. I glanced from side to side, fully expecting to see a crowd of females gathering to watch. *Huh; just me.* I stepped up onto the platform and moved to the pile of bags. I bent to pick up one of them, trying to decide the best way to lift it since it was basically half my size.

"What are you doing?" I stood up to see Jack watching me, hands on his hips, head tilted slightly.

"Helping you load the truck." I pointed from the pile of bags to the truck as if he needed a demonstration to accompany my words.

Jack took his hat off to run one hand through his hair before settling the hat back on his ruffled hair.

"I appreciate that thought, but these bags are actually really heavy. Someone will be over to help me load in a minute."

"I *am* someone, and I pretty much have a ton of new muscles just waiting to be used today. So this is no problem."

I resumed my position, reminding myself to lift with the knees, not the back. I didn't really know what that phrase meant exactly, but I remember my dad reminding me to 'lift from the knees' when we were moving the furniture into my apartment. I managed to lift one corner of the bag just slightly before dropping it back on the pile. I cleared my throat.

"I just lost my grip. My hands are cold so..." I blew into my hands and then rubbed them together furiously, putting on what I hoped was a convincing performance. I took a deep breath and tried to lift the nine-hundred-pound bag again, painfully aware that Jack was watching me. What was in this food? Was the special ingredient lead?

I groaned inwardly and lifted with all the strength my puny muscles possessed, but the bag barely budged. My head sank forward in defeat. I saw two distinctly male hands land on the opposite side of the bag I was still gripping.

"We lift on three?"

Bless this man. He was clearly wrestling to contain a shit-eating grin but made no mention of my pathetic attempt to be helpful. I nodded my agreement, and we lifted the bag, lopsidedly, into the truck bed on three. The universe must have decided I'd had enough embarrassment for one hour, because two guys magically appeared to help load the truck before I had to admit defeat.

"Okay, well, it looks like you've got this handled so I'll just wait in the truck," I said, stepping off the platform. I heard Jack's low chuckle at my back as I opened the door and hoisted myself into the truck to wait.

20.

It took no time for the three to finish loading everything, including a wire twister that took an extra ten minutes and three conversations to locate. Jack was very particular about wire twisters. Whatever those were.

"Are you ready to get your first pair of cowboy boots?" Jack took his eyes off the road to shoot me a questioning look.

"Yes! Very ready. I normally hate shoe shopping, but I'm really excited about these boots. Is there like a super-secret handshake I get to learn now? Oh! Or an initiation ceremony?"

I had decided by this time that there was no point in trying to hide all my crazy. It was clearly too late.

"Are you joining a cult or getting a pair of boots?" Jack asked, eyes on the road, smile on his face.

"I don't know, you tell me." I raised my eyebrows conspiratorially, not even trying to hide my goofy grin.

Jack shot me an appraising look, a serious expression crossing his face.

"You have to be able to lasso a steer with one hand behind your back before we teach you the handshake."

"Noooo," I cried dramatically. "I knew it. I'll never get to learn the handshake."

Jack threw back his head and laughed, a deep smooth sound that I immediately catalogued as my new favorite sound. He pulled up in front of a store and put the truck in park.

"All right, let's do this."

I watched him exit the truck, appreciating the view of his backside, before hopping out and following him into the store. The first thing I noticed was the overwhelming smell of leather. The second thing I noticed was an entire wall of boots in every color and size. The wall of boots faced an entire wall of hats. This was no Neiman Marcus.

Jack came to stand next to me as I peered up at the wall of boots.

"Whoa." I tore my eyes away from the wall and faced him. "That is a lot of boots."

"Yeah, people are pretty serious about their boots around here."

"I'm feeling a little overwhelmed. I don't think I did enough research."

"It's not—wait, did you just say you did research?" Jack turned to face me. My cheeks heated a little under the scrutiny.

"Uh, yes. I don't know anything about all this, so I thought I should be prepared."

"Uh-huh. So you did some research?"

I nodded. "Yeah. You know, best brand for comfort and durability, fit. Stuff like that."

"I honestly don't know what to do with all that. Where does your research say to start?" Jack glanced at the wall and then back to me.

I looked up, up, up the wall of boots. Craning my neck, I shrugged.

"My research may not have prepared me for the Great Wall of Cowboy Boots. I definitely think I should defer to the expert here."

Jack was still looking at me with that one handsome eyebrow raised.

"Am I the expert?"

I nudged him with my shoulder and pointed down at his feet, which were currently sporting a pair of boots.

"Yep, you're the expert here. I can help with snow boots, but that's where my expertise ends. Chicago winters are brutal."

"These are not cowboy boots, you know that, right?"

I looked at the tan boots. A boot worn by a cowboy was a cowboy boot as far as I was concerned. God, even Jack's feet were attractive, all covered in boots that looked like they had actually been worn to work and not to walk down a city street. There really was something to the whole working-man fantasy.

I voiced my thoughts out loud. "To-may-to, to-mah-to. You're a cowboy and those are boots."

"Okay, that's not actually how that works, but let's just move on. I think the women's section is over here. I'm really not an expert at shoe shopping. Maybe we should have brought Margot with us."

I followed him to the part of the wall that had colorful boots with intricate patterns worked into the leather. Some of the leather had been dyed shades of pink and purple, clearly marking this as the women's section. Unless there was a segment of male ranchers who liked pastel-colored boots—who was I to judge?

Jack picked up a pair of pink boots and held one out for me to see. "These are pink."

I nodded my head and plastered a serious expression on my face. "Very good, that *is* pink. You know your colors."

"I meant you might like them. Don't women usually like

pink things?"

I rolled my eyes and took the boots from him, placing them back on the shelf.

"Not this woman."

I walked down the row, past boot after boot, Jack trailing patiently behind me until I found the one. A pair of tan boots that looked like they had ivy growing up the side caught my attention. I picked up one of the boots and turned toward Jack.

"What about this?"

I handed him the boot and watched as he turned it over, moving it from hand to hand.

"It's a good boot. Do you want to try it on?"

"Yes! I love it."

"Let's take them to the counter and get your size, unless"—he flipped the boot over, looking at the sole—"you're a size six."

I barked out a laugh, shaking my head. "Yeah, no. Nothing on me is a size six."

My face immediately flooded with heat as my brain caught up with my mouth. Why was there never a hole opening to swallow you up when you needed it? I looked at Jack, who was holding the boot and watching me with a thoughtful expression on his face. I briefly considered the possibility that he was trying to guess my pants size, since I had ruled out the size of pants worn by all his girlfriends. I wondered if that was one of his criteria for a girlfriend: *Size 0-6 only need apply*.

Jack's steady, smooth voice drew me out of my thoughts. "Let's take these to the counter, see if they have them in your size."

I followed him to the counter where he asked a teenage girl, who made googly eyes at him the whole time, if they had the boots in a size seven. Poor kid. I could totally relate to the struggle of remaining sane when staring into those brown eyes.

Seated on a chair with a pair of size seven boots in hand, I dug through my bag to find my extra pair of socks. Jack's hand fell on my arm. I stopped my search to look at him seated in the chair next to me.

"What are you looking for?"

"My trial socks," I said, holding up the pair of extra socks. "For trying on shoes. I don't like to wear dirty socks in case I don't end up getting the shoes. The next person doesn't have to worry about my dirty socks being in their shoes."

Jack scrubbed a hand over his face. I could hear his palm travel roughly across the whiskers growing on his jaw. The sound made my mouth water a little. I swallowed. I might ask the counter girl if she wanted to start a support group with me.

"Evelyn, I never know what to do with you."

I gave him a weird smile and proceeded to switch socks, trying not to think about what Jack meant and whether 'not knowing what to do with me' was a good thing or a bad thing. I slipped my right foot into the boot and stuck it out in front of me.

"I think it fits." I put the left boot on and stood, rocking back and forth on my heels. "What do you think?"

"They look good on you. Do they feel okay?"

I took a few steps away from him and then turned to walk back the way I came.

"They feel good. I think these are my boots."

"You're sure? They don't crowd your toes or anything? You don't want to try any other pairs on first?"

"Nope, I'm sure. These are it." I pulled my phone out of my

bag and snapped a picture of my feet. I went to slip my phone back into its spot when I had an idea. I backed up until the wall of boots was directly behind me, and motioned for Jack to come stand beside me.

"Jack, we need a picture," I said, looking up at him. He sighed dramatically and gave me a look that said my request was actually physically painful to him. I smiled right back, a cheesy, over-the-top smile.

"You want to take a selfie? I can't believe I'm even considering this. Fine, but only because this is your first pair of boots."

He moved to stand next to me, and then, to my complete surprise, Jack wound his arm around my waist and tucked me into his side. I was monetarily stunned, standing stiff like a mannequin. Turning my head to look up at him, I gave him yet another weak smile, aware that my cheeks were turning red at an alarming rate. He just glanced down at me with a 'let's do this' look. I took another second to enjoy being this close to Jack while my brain wasn't working, the heat from his body warming my side.

I stretched my arm out as far as I could, but I only managed to capture our noses and below. I tried to readjust my arms, standing on tiptoe, but still only got our noses on the screen. The chest pressed so close to mine vibrated. I let out a disgruntled huff and turned to the man next to me, who was not even bothering to hide his amusement.

"You're going to have to take this. My T-rex arms aren't going to cut it."

Jack let loose that toe-curling laugh and took the phone from me. He was so close that his laughter stirred those little strands of my hair that never behaved. I was turning to a puddle of goo right next to him, and he had no idea.

"You ready?" Jack asked, face turned toward my phone. I

heard a click before I had a chance to properly pose. I mean, if I was going to be in a picture with a real-life fantasy I was damn well going to make sure I only had one chin. I snapped my head in his direction and shot him a look, nudging him with my shoulder.

"Hey! I wasn't ready. You can't sneak attack me like that." I heard the click again. "Jack! This is serious."

I saw that impossibly perfect smile and was momentarily dazed, staring into it, until I heard the click again. He laughed at my indignant huff.

"Okay! Okay, get yourself ready and tell me when."

I turned toward the camera and smiled. Jack pulled me in a little closer, causing heat to creep back into my cheeks and my smile to grow impossibly wide. Two clicks later, Jack unwound his arm from my waist and handed me back the phone. I felt the absence of his arm like a warm blanket being ripped off. I shivered. What was happening?

We walked the short distance to the counter in silence, and I paid for my boots and shot sympathetic looks at the still-frazzled clerk.

"You ready for some lunch?" Jack asked when we reached his truck.

"Sure. Can we walk though? I'd love to look around a little."

"Everything's pretty much in walking distance, so we can walk if you want. Are you going to be warm enough, though?"

"Yes, I'll be fine, thanks." I dropped my bag in the passenger seat and then joined Jack on the sidewalk. We walked side by side, which was a nice change from me following him. I made the decision to ignore the little voice warning me that this was too good to be true. If this was the only day I got with friendly Jack, I was going to enjoy every second of it.

21.

It turned out that Jack was a pretty great tour guide. He pointed out historic landmarks and places he thought would interest me as we walked. I couldn't decide if I was more fascinated by the sights or by how much Jack was speaking. He didn't even complain when I asked to check out some of the stores we passed along the way. When I saw the sign for Joan's Diner just ahead, I was tempted to ask Jack to keep walking just so I could listen to him talk a little more. The grumbling in my stomach, however, had me following Jack inside the adorable diner, which smelled like a strange, but not unpleasant, combination of grease and ice cream.

Jack led me to a booth and handed me a menu.

"It smells so good in here. What do you recommend?" I said, looking over the menu.

"Joan's is famous for its burgers. Well, famous around here."

I hmmed, pretty much already settled on the grilled cheese sandwich. I almost never passed up a grilled cheese sandwich when it wasn't listed on the kid's menu.

Two glasses of water clinked on the table, and I looked up. A pretty redhead wearing a tight white shirt and an equally tight black skirt was smiling at Jack. A red apron tied loosely around her waist was embroidered with *Joan's*.

"Hey, Jack. We missed you last night," she pouted in a sugary voice that had just the slightest twang to it.

My eyes pivoted from her face to Jack's, trying to catch his reaction.

"How's it going, Shelly?' Jack asked, shooting her a familiar grin that instantly made me not like Shelly at all.

I darted my eyes back to Shelly, since I was apparently just a spectator at this point. I was surprised she'd even brought me a glass of water.

"I'd be a lot better if I didn't have to dance with Sam Evans last night. You know he's all left feet. You really left us girls hanging." She made a little pouty face.

Jack chuckled, clearly more amused by that little display than I was.

"I said I might be there. Shelly, this is Evelyn. Evelyn, this is Shelly. Shelly is Joan's niece."

Shelly turned to look at me, wearing a forced smile. "Well hi, Evelyn, it's nice to meet you."

I didn't actually believe Shelly was happy to meet me at all, but I returned her smile and offered a "Nice to meet you" in reply.

"I don't think I've seen you around here before." Shelly's voiced oozed with fake friendliness. I knew she really wanted to ask who I was to Jack and what I was doing with him.

"I'm here with Ben. I mean I work for him at Sterling. I'm his new executive assistant." I stumbled my way through the explanation in spectacular fashion. I really needed to work on my introduction skills.

"Really?" Shelly said, sounding doubtful and blatantly giving me a once-over. "You're certainly a change. Is Ben going to be joining you?"

Shelly had obviously decided I was no threat to her claim on Jack, whatever that was. A gross feeling settled into my stomach as I watched Shelly turn back to Jack, dismissing me. Was this who Jack had spent the night with? It seemed like they knew each other pretty well, and she was not happy he was here with another woman. I swallowed down the lump forming in my throat—stupid, stupid jealousy I had no right to feel.

"No, it's just us today. Evie needed to get a better pair of boots to wear around the ranch."

God, why did hearing him call me Evie in front of her make my heart flop around inside my chest? My heart had no loyalty. No loyalty at all.

"Around the ranch? Goodness, it sounds like you're settling in to stay a bit."

I shrugged a shoulder casually, not willing to offer any explanation that might ease her worry.

"Cole and Gabe have been giving her riding lessons. She needs something besides tennis shoes," Jack said on my behalf. He shot me a smile that did not go unnoticed.

"I'm surprised one of Ben's girls would be interested in learning to ride. Wonders never cease." Shelly's smile was turning straight *Mean Girls* and I bristled at the accusation lacing her words. Did she not have other tables?

Jack cleared his throat, finally seeming to sense the tension brewing at the table. Shelly and I tore our gazes away from each other and I looked at the man sitting across from me, who I thought looked a little smug.

"We should probably order. I don't want to be unloading the truck in the dark," Jack said, that easy grin sliding across his face.

"Of course. I know how dark it gets out your way." She really couldn't resist getting one last jab in. "Do you want your usual?"

Well, I guess she had one more in her.

"Yep. Thanks, Shelly." Jack handed her his menu.

"And what about you, Evelyn? We don't have those fancy

salads I'm sure you're used to, but I'd be happy to suggest something."

Lord, give me strength.

"Thanks for the offer, but I think I'll go with the grilled cheese," I said, just barely managing to not throw the menu at her.

I watched Shelly saunter off with what I imagined was a little extra sway of her hips. I barely contained my eyeroll.

"Grilled cheese?" Jack's question snapped my attention from Shelly's retreating backside.

"Grilled cheese is my favorite. You almost never find it off the kids' menu so I couldn't pass it up. It's a totally underrated sandwich. I don't think it gets the respect it deserves from the culinary world, you know?"

Jack chuckled, making those brown eyes crinkle at the corner. "Sure, I can respect a good grilled cheese. I guess I just think of it as a sick food."

"A sick food?" I asked.

"Yeah, my mom always used to make it for us with tomato soup when we were sick. It's still my go-to whenever I feel rough."

I smiled at the image of Jack eating tomato soup and grilled cheese.

"I bet your mom makes awesome grilled cheese. Mine was a grilled cheese purist. White bread and a slice of American cheese. It's still the ultimate comfort food."

Quiet settled over the table, and I looked away from Jack and watched the condensation slide down my glass. It was a comfortable silence, but everything felt like too much all of a sudden and I didn't understand any of it. Sitting here talking to Jack like we were friends when I didn't have a clue if he even liked me as a human being suddenly felt stifling. My sisters' words came back to me. I took a deep breath, determined to get out of my own way and just enjoy this moment.

Thankfully, Jack excused himself to use the restroom, giving me a second to regroup. I watched him walk toward the door with the same ease he did everything. When he disappeared around the corner, I reached into my bag to retrieve my cellphone. I smiled, feeling the happiness I always associated with my sisters when I saw I had a bunch of texts from them waiting for me.

Elise: *So... how's it going? Did you find a pair of boots?*

Corinne: *Or did you knock boots ;o)*

Elise: *Hahaha! I see what you did there...*

Corinne: *Did you like that? I'm pretty proud of myself for that one.*

Elise: *You should be. Maybe the quiet is a good sign? It's hard to respond to a text if your hands are busy.*

Corinne: *Yes! Is it too much to hope for pictures? God, I need to have this kid soon. Even I think I'm a total creep.*

Elise: *I think the word you were looking for there was pervert but yes.*

I laughed quietly to myself, reading their messages and debating how to respond. I pulled up the pictures on my phone and scrolled through the ones Jack had taken earlier. I could feel my heart fluttering wildly in my chest as I looked at them. I'd been there when they were taken, but I felt like I was looking at someone else's photos. Jack was smiling that dazzling smile that made me dizzy, and his eyes had a shine that looked a lot like happiness. I was tucked into his side with an equally wide smile that was totally out of sync with how I'd felt when the picture was taken. I didn't look shocked or confused; I looked like it was an everyday occurrence to be standing so close to Jack with his arm wrapped around me.

I took a startled breath when I got to the first couple of pictures he had taken before I was ready. Jack was grinning into the camera and I was smiling up at him. It looked like a couple's picture. We looked like a happy couple taking a picture together. The next few were worse—so much worse. I was laughing up at him with a look that couldn't be mistaken for anything other than adoration, and he was looking down at me with humor etched across every feature of his face. My thumb swept across the screen before I made my decision.

Me: *So this happened...*

I attached the picture of my feet wearing my new boots.

Elise responded almost immediately.

Elise: *Those are gorgeous! Corinne would be proud. You are so legit now!*

Me: *So legit. Also this happened...*

And I attached one of the pictures of Jack and me smiling at the camera.

Elise: *Whaaaaattt?!!*

Me: *And also this...*

I attached one of the shots that could have been a couple's picture posted all over social media to make everyone jealous.

Elise: *HOLY SHIT!*

Corinne: *How did this happen? I feel like I missed something again. Did I miss something? Why does this look like a cheesy couple's picture I would judge on Facebook?*

Me: *I don't know what's going on! I think I just had an out-of-body experience or was possessed. Yep, possessed. I was possessed by the not-awkward-or-shy Evelyn who asks gorgeous men who might actually hate her to take a selfie together. I never take selfies! I hate them! And he took the pictures.*

Elise: *Yeah, unless he's a crazy good actor, I think it's safe to say he does NOT hate you.*

Corinne: *He is gazing at you, Evie. And what a gaze it is. The man is beyond gorgeous.*

Elise: *I honestly might crop you out of those.*

Corinne: *No judgment.*

Me: *I feel like these pictures don't accurately reflect what's happening in real life. Does that make sense?*

Corinne: *Why? Is he still being a grumpy ass?*

Elise: *I would probably still forgive him if he looked at me like that, but I don't understand why you look so happy if he's still being an ass.*

Me: *No, that's the thing! I'm not happy. I mean I was happy, but I was too surprised to feel anything else. Like my brain wasn't even able to process what was happening when he suddenly wrapped his arm around me and started snapping away. He's not being an ass at all, which is just adding to the confusion pile.*

Elise: *I hate to say it, but do you think maybe when your brain stopped overanalyzing every little thing you were able to just let yourself enjoy the moment? Let your real feelings shine through?*

Corinne: *I love you, Evie, but I think Elise may have a point. You do tend to get in your own way.*

"Everything okay?"

My head snapped up from my phone as Jack slid back into the booth, a concerned expression on his face. I slipped my phone into my bag and gave him a reassuring smile.

"Yeah, just catching up with my sisters."

Shelly appeared with our food before Jack could ask a follow-up question. I suspected this might be the only time I would ever be grateful for her presence.

"One heart attack on a plate, or your usual," she said, placing a plate with a huge burger in front of Jack before placing my plate in front of me. "And one grilled cheese. Do you need anything else?"

I shook my head, and Jack offered a 'no.' Shelly promised to be back to check on us, leaving us alone with our food. I picked at a fry, suddenly self-conscious about the amount of carbs piled on my plate.

"You're pretty close to your sisters?"

I watched as Jack took a bite of his cheeseburger. I was momentarily distracted watching his jaw chew and the bob of his throat as he swallowed. This could be a very, very long lunch. I cleared my throat.

"We are really close. Annoyingly close sometimes." I tilted my head to the side, slightly studying his face. "How about you and Ben? I didn't really get the impression you two are very close."

"Why do you say that?" Jack asked, sounding more curious than offended.

I shrugged my shoulders. "I don't know. I never heard him talk about you. And you just seem so... different, I guess?"

"We're actually not that different. We both needed to chase that rush. We just chose different ways to do it."

"Needed? Past tense?" I hoped I wasn't poking a wound that could still be raw, but Jack didn't seem upset by the question.

"Past tense, at least for me. And we both got all that Danvers charm."

I rolled my eyes playfully before adding, "Sure, and all that Danvers humility. So humble."

Jack laughed. "Yeah, I don't think anyone has ever accused either of us of being humble."

There were so many questions I wanted to ask him, but I decided to quit while I was ahead. Finally turning my attention to my food, I took a bite of the greasy, cheesy sandwich that smelled the way I imagined heaven would. I groaned, closing my eyes as the buttery goodness hit my tongue. Cheese, real butter, and carbs are truly the ingredients to happiness. I opened my eyes to find Jack watching me, a muscle twitching in his clenched jaw.

"Are you okay?" I asked.

He gave his head a tight nod. "Fine."

"Okaaay."

I took another bite of my sandwich, the butter melting away whatever carb-related nerves I'd had earlier. I hummed, savoring the flavors. Jack paused with his hamburger halfway to his mouth.

"Are you going to eat that entire sandwich like that?" Jack asked, his voice almost hoarse.

I studied his face, trying to discern the emotion in his voice.

"Like what?"

He let out a low groan in response, before shaking his head and taking a large bite of his burger.

"What? It's so good. Nobody uses real butter anymore, and this is definitely real butter."

"You're killing me, Evelyn. Just eat the sandwich so we can get out of here, please."

22.

We finished the rest of the meal in silence, interrupted only by a very persistent Shelly, who was ridiculously attentive to two people just eating sandwiches. Jack insisted on paying for my meal to celebrate my first pair of boots. As we wandered out of the store, Jack directed our steps toward the promised land—a.k.a. the latte-serving bakery.

"Ugh, I don't know if I have room for dessert. I think that milkshake was a bad idea." I screwed up my face, regretting the sheer amount of food taking up valuable pastry room in my stomach.

"Do you want to skip the latte then?"

"Uh, that's just crazy talk."

"You just said you had no room!" Jack fired back, a laugh softening his accusation.

"There's always room for a warm, caffeinated beverage. It's a scientific fact." I nodded my head for extra emphasis.

"I must have missed that day in biology class," Jack responded, his voice laced with good-natured sarcasm.

I shrugged casually. "Probably. But hey, at least you can say you learned something today." I nudged him with my shoulder, trying to keep a serious expression on my face.

He returned my nudge with one of his own. "Oh, I would say I learned a lot today."

I lost the battle against smiling. We came to a stop in front of a cute blue storefront with a neon pink sign announcing *Sweetheart's Bakery* hanging in the window. My mouth started watering just reading the sign. Jack opened the door, motioning for me to step inside.

I walked past Jack, smiling up at him as I passed, my shoulder accidentally brushing against his chest as I went. I stopped just inside to inhale the familiar smell of espresso and baked goods. God, I missed that smell. If a smell could be a happy place, that combination would be mine.

"Hello!" A blond head popped up from behind the counter. "Oh, hey, Jack!"

"Hey, Tessa." I felt Jack's hand land on the small of my back, gently propelling me forward with him. I almost stumbled over my feet in surprise at the contact. "How's it going?"

Tessa's eyes darted quickly between Jack and me before she responded, "Good—just making a mess back here as usual."

"I can see that. You've got a little flour here," Jack said, pointing to a spot on his cheek at about the same place where a large streak of flour was smeared on Tessa's face.

"Oh great." Her hand shot up to scrub at the spot, and I immediately took note of the two rings on her finger. A sigh of relief escaped against my will. "I was trying a new cupcake recipe this afternoon and things got a little out of hand."

I couldn't help but laugh at the look of frustration that crossed her face.

"Who did you bring with you?" Tessa asked, eyes moving to me while still rubbing at the spot on her cheek.

"Hi, I'm Evelyn." I gave a small wave. "I'm staying at Pinehaven."

"She came from Chicago with Ben, for work," Jack clarified. "She's going through latte withdrawal."

I nodded my head in agreement. "It's true. It's the only thing I really miss about Chicago."

I felt Jack turn his stare toward me.

"I can totally relate! I grew up here, but I went to school in Boston. I got hooked on designer beverages while I was working at a coffee shop there. Pine Hollow was a coffee wasteland before I moved back. I mean, not to brag or anything, but the only place to get a decent cup of coffee before I took over this place was Joan's."

"Then I'm really glad you're here, because I'm desperate for a latte." I know my voice conveyed the amount of excitement I was feeling about how close I was to steamed milk in a cup.

"Do you want anything else? Jack?" Tessa asked.

"I'll have a black coffee to go and a pecan roll."

My head swiveled around in Jack's direction. "A pecan roll? You're getting a pecan roll?"

Jack shot me a questioning look while his hand snaked around to the back pocket of his jeans. He turned his attention to his wallet.

"What? You said you didn't have any room left. I still have plenty of room."

"Ugh, *how*? How do you still have room left? It's so unfair." I reached inside my tote, digging around for my wallet. "Speaking of fair, let me pay for this. You got lunch."

Jack shook his head.

"Nope, we're still celebrating your first pair of cowboy boots."

"But—"

"No buts," Jack interrupted before I could finish. His eyes found mine and whatever fight I had in me died instantly.

"Well, thank you, then."

I tore my eyes away from his to watch Tessa making our drinks behind the counter.

"How long will you be in Pine Hollow, Evelyn?" Tessa asked over the hiss of the steamer.

"Oh, um, I'm not actually sure. Ben had some... work he needed to do at Pinehaven. He wasn't sure how long it would take." I hoped Jack wouldn't judge me for the half-truths that filled my answer.

"I hope you've been able to explore a little. Pine Hollow is small and big at the same time, and it's pretty great. It really grows on you." Tessa snapped lids on two to-go cups and grabbed a pecan roll from display case.

"I've been able to do some exploring, and you're right, it's pretty great out here." I felt Jack's stare land on me again as I reached out to take my cup from Tessa. The warmth of the cup seeping into my hands matched the warmth spreading through me from Jack's stare.

"It's always good to see you, Jack, and Evelyn, it was nice to meet you. Come back next time you need your latte fix," Tessa said, handing Jack his change.

"Thank you! It was nice meeting you, too."

"Good luck with those cupcakes, Tessa," Jack added as we made our way out of my new favorite place in the state of Montana.

We walked in a comfortable silence, both of us momentarily absorbed in our drinks. A cool breeze rustled the trees lining the street, and a shiver worked its way through me.

"Are you cold?" Jack asked, glancing at me over his coffee cup.

"A little." I took a tentative sip from my cup, testing the temperature. "Oh wow, this is really good." The steamed milk warmed me from the inside out.

"It stacks up against the big city coffee shops?" Jack asked.

"Oh, yeah. That Tessa makes a mean latte."

Jack chuckled next to me, sending a wave of warmth through me that rivaled the latte.

"I'm glad you liked it. I know how much you were looking forward to it. I think everyone at home knows how much you were looking forward to it, actually."

"I may have mentioned it once or twice," I acknowledged, taking another sip.

"Just once or twice. Do you want my jacket?"

I briefly considered what it would be like to be wrapped in Jack's jacket, but quickly vetoed the idea. There was a real possibility I would never recover from the experience.

"Thanks, but a warm drink should do the trick." I held up my cup, giving him a grateful smile.

We walked the rest of the way to his truck, largely in silence. The sun darted in and out of clouds during our walk, casting shadows on the sidewalk as we went. Jack opened the door for me when we reached his truck, shutting it behind me after I made the climb into the passenger's side seat.

I looked over at him as he fastened his seatbelt. He was somehow even more handsome in the late afternoon light. Jack returned my gaze for a minute, then turned his attention back to the road.

"What did you think? Of Pine Hollow?" His voice was almost hesitant asking the question.

"I loved it. It really does seem like something straight out of a movie set."

Jack turned to look at me, eyes hard under the brim of his hat. He dipped his head toward his chest seeming to decide on something that he apparently was not sharing with me. Eyes back on the road, he offered one word in reply. "Good."

I spent the next handful of miles wondering if he was ever going to eat the pecan roll resting in the cup holder between us. I imagined in agonizing detail how good it would be with this latte.

"Jack?"

He glanced briefly at me before responding, "Yeah?"

"Are you going to eat the pecan roll, or is it just a prop?"

That hat-covered head whipped back in my direction. He made a noise that was a little bit of a sigh and a little bit of a laugh.

"Is that your way of asking me to share?"

"Yes." I drew out the word, nodding my head.

Jack picked up the bag, dumped out the pastry, and tore it in half. He handed me the bigger half without saying a word.

In that moment, holding the bigger half of a sticky pecan roll, I was finally forced to admit to myself that my heart might seriously be in danger.

23.

The next morning, I woke up with a smile on my face thinking about the ride home with Jack, and the way he slid into the seat next to me at dinner later that evening with a smile just for me. I took a minute to snuggle further into the covers, listening to Hank Williams snore softly somewhere next to me, before getting up.

As soon as my head left the pillow, a bolt of pain shot from behind my eye and down my neck. I winced as a wave of nausea chased the pain. My head dropped back to the pillow as I tried to fight the urge to barf and adjust to the pain. I whimpered, rolling over toward the dresser in search of my phone. The light from the screen sent more bolts of pain through my head. With one eye closed, I sent a short text to Ben.

Me: *Migraine.*

I switched my phone to silent and reached for the medication I had stashed in the nightstand the night I had arrived. I swallowed the medication, fighting back against the nausea, and slowly laid my head down. Hank Williams didn't seem to be in any hurry to get out of bed, so I figured I would deal with letting him out later.

My stomach had other ideas, though. I threw back the covers and raced to the toilet. My knees hit cool tile, and my stomach tried its best to get rid of anything it could. When it finally gave up, I swished my mouth and rinsed my face with cold water.

I dragged myself back to the bed, crawling under the covers. I tucked my legs to my chest and tried to calm down enough to sleep. Instinctively, I reached out to pet Hank Williams, who had squirmed closer to me. I wanted to believe it was out of concern, but it was more likely he had been hit by a blast of cold air when I threw back the covers, and was looking for extra warmth.

A soft knock on my door woke me.

"Evelyn, is it okay if I come in?" Mary's soft voice felt like a kick to the head.

"Yes," I managed to croak.

I heard the door open slowly, and her cautious footsteps approached the bed.

"Oh, sweetheart, you look miserable. Ben said you had a migraine. I just came to check on you. Do you need anything?"

A new head. I didn't bother opening my eyes. I would rather apologize later for being rude than apologize right now for puking on her. I was sure she would agree with my judgment call.

"No thank you," I managed to croak, then I had an idea. "Actually, do you have an ice pack I could borrow?"

"Of course; I'll run it up to you. Is there anything else I can get you?"

"No, just the ice pack." I tried to smile but it felt more like a grimace.

"Okay. I'm going to take Hank Williams with me so he doesn't bother you. Come on, Hank Williams, let's get some breakfast."

Hank perked up at "breakfast," and climbed off the bed, the tapping of his claws on the hardwood echoing through my head. I heard the soft click of the door, then silence. A few minutes later, the door creaked gently and quiet footsteps approached the bed. Mary's hand gently brushed the stray hair off my forehead, a cold pressure replacing her hand as she settled the icepack over my eyes.

"There you go. Are you sure there's nothing else I can bring you?"

"Yep, I just have to try to sleep it off. Thank you." My voice sounded pathetic to my own ears, little more than a whisper.

"Okay. I'll be back to check on you in a bit. Just call if you need anything."

Mary tucked the blankets tighter around me before leaving. I sniffled back tears. I couldn't remember the last time someone had taken care of me when I had a migraine—probably when I was home on break from college. I had forgotten how nice, how comforting it was to have someone take care of you. I breathed out a deep sigh in an effort to keep the sniffle from turning into full-on tears. I missed Hank Williams.

I managed to take more medicine at some point, and Mary continued to check on me as promised. I watched the shadows in the room change from morning to afternoon to evening.

A knock punctuated the quiet, the sound heavier than the light rapping of Mary's fist against the wood door.

"Evelyn?"

Jack's voice was soft and low. My heart banged wildly around in my chest.

"Come in," I said, my voice coming out rough and cracked.

The familiar creak of the door opening had me thrusting my arm under the cover in a moment of panic trying to remember if I had pants on. I felt the edge of my sleep shorts and breathed a sigh of relief. I was pleasantly surprised when I felt only a dull thrum in my head after cracking my eyes open. Adjusting to the darkness, my eyes settled on Jack walking cautiously toward me.

He set something on my nightstand before sitting down on the edge of my bed, so close to me that I caught a whiff of that smell that always seemed to make my heart skip a beat.

"How are you feeling?" he asked in a hushed voice.

I gave him a small smile. "I'm okay."

I cleared my throat, hoping to sound a little less like death, and shoved myself up to rest against the headboard. There would be no coming back from puking on Jack. His eyes dipped briefly to my chest before shooting back up to my face. My face flushed at the realization that I was wearing a thin cotton shirt without a bra. I was suddenly grateful that it was difficult to see in the darkness. I tried to move my arms up to cover my chest without being obvious.

"I brought you some ginger ale. I thought it might feel good on your stomach."

I groaned, hiding my face behind my hands.

"Please tell me you couldn't hear me barfing."

Jack's warm, quiet chuckle washed over me, blanketing me in its warmth. It felt like a tangible thing wrapping itself around me, and I felt it everywhere.

"I didn't hear anything. We had to move the cows this morning so I was long gone before you got acquainted with the toilet."

"Good, that's good." I breathed a sigh of relief. "Ginger ale sounds amazing, actually."

Jack leaned over to retrieve the can and I took the opportunity to shamelessly admire his profile. Even with a migraine, I still knew a good thing when it was right in front of me. He opened the can and handed it to me. Our fingers brushed lightly, making my stomach flutter for a very different reason than it had when I'd woken up this morning.

"Thank you."

"You're welcome."

I took a sip, loving how the cold bubbles felt on my throat. Once I was sure the first sip was going to stay put, I took a big, greedy drink that was dangerously close to a gulp.

His eyes traveled across my face as a heavy silence settled over the room. This poor, broken brain of mine scrambled for something, anything to break the silence. Jack's hand moved off his leg. It reached toward me slowly and tentatively, like I was one of his battered horses whose reaction he couldn't trust. His fingertips brushed just above my eye, catching the loose hair, and sweeping it back behind my ear. He brushed the shell of my ear for the briefest of seconds.

My breath caught in my lungs. There was a real chance my heart was no longer beating. Still, still—everything in the room was still as Jack's eyes moved between mine.

"Okay. I'll let you rest."

"Okay," I echoed. Heart resuming a fractured beat, air flooded my lungs, leaving me a little dizzy.

"Come down later if you feel like it. Mom made you some chicken noodle soup, but I can't promise it'll be there tomorrow. Gabe loves that soup," Jack said, rising from the bed.

"Tell him to stay away from my soup." I tried to force some lightness into my voice.

He smiled down at me. "I'll do my best, but like I said, no promises."

With that, he headed toward the door. He paused, already halfway out the door, and turned back to face me.

"I hope you feel better soon. Everyone missed you today."

He was out the door before I could shake off my surprise and find the words to answer him.

"I missed everyone too," I answered to the door, my words drifting through the quiet.

24.

Somewhere around eleven thirty that night, I finally gave up the struggle for sleep and accepted that I was going to have to do something about the riot coming from my stomach. I honestly wasn't even that tired anymore. One of the many problems of having a knock-you-down migraine all day is that you aren't tired when you should be, and you can't stand the thought of lying in bed for another minute, but you're way too wiped out to do much of anything else. Jack's impromptu visit to my room hadn't done much to help the situation. My mind was a constant whirl of whys and what-ifs.

I slipped on one of the cute sports bras I'd bought the day I convinced myself I was actually going to start taking yoga with Hilari and Anna. They were good for lounging in, with leggings and oversized sweaters, so the bras lasted much longer than my motivation. I pulled on an oversized sweater, remembering how cold the nights could be now. I grabbed the ice pack off the bed and made my way carefully down the dark hallway.

Pausing at the top of the staircase, I listened for any signs of life below. I was still wearing my sleep shorts and didn't feel like running into anyone. When I was confident there was no one lurking downstairs, I crept down toward the chicken noodle soup that I hoped was still waiting for me. A light in the entryway mingled with the dim porch lights to cast a small path down the hallway leading to the kitchen. My movements were still cautious, but I was surprised at how well I already knew the twists and turns in this house after just two weeks.

My hand moved along the wall of the kitchen until I found

the switch, and light filled the room. I paused for a minute to take in the total silence. Weird for the room and weird for me. Silence seemed so unnatural in this room that was always filled with so much noise. The absence of cars driving down the street or doors opening and closing felt foreign too. The city was never quiet, no matter how early or late. A loud growl from my stomach cut through the silence, setting my feet in motion.

"Yes!" I exclaimed in a hushed voice.

The soup was still waiting for me in the fridge. I smiled widely when I saw a note on the lid telling Gabe to leave it for me. Reaching into the cupboard, I pulled out one of the large mugs and heated up the soup. I decided to eat on the porch, grabbing a blanket from the couch before stepping outside.

I passed the chairs and settled onto the porch swing. The night air was crisp and cool enough to make me grateful for the warmth of the blanket as I settled it around me. I ate a spoonful of the soup, savoring the unexpected deliciousness. It was unreal. It definitely did not taste like the canned soup I was used to heating up on the stove. I totally got Gabe's obsession now.

The squeak of the screen door opening startled me, causing a little bit of soup to splash onto my hand. I licked it off, turning toward the sound. Jack was standing on the porch, wearing a pair of loose gym shorts and a grey Grizzlies t-shirt, his eyes trained to the spot where my mouth met my hand. His feet and head were bare, his hair rumpled and a little wild. My heart made an almost painful motion in my chest.

"Jack?"

"Hey, what are you doing out here?" His voice was even deeper than usual.

I lifted my mug for him to see. "I was hungry, so I heated up some soup. It's such a pretty night. I think you can see every single star," I answered, turning away to look toward the sky for my sanity's sake. I heard his hand run over the stubble of his chin, making me shiver involuntarily.

"Be right back," he said as the door shut behind him.

A minute later, he reappeared with a blanket. I kept my eyes on him as he moved to the swing. I thought his movements were a little more stiff than normal, and he definitely winced when he took the spot beside me on the swing. The question I wanted to ask died on my lips when he reached over to settle the blanket around both our shoulders. He lifted the edges of the blanket covering my legs and spread it out to cover his legs, too.

Jack must have felt the question in my eyes because he said, "It's a little cold tonight," as he leaned back, setting the swing in motion.

"Oh," I responded, before giving my head a little shake and finding the question that had died a quick death a few seconds earlier. "What happened?"

"Happened?" He shot a questioning glance at me.

"You were limping a little and I saw your face when you sat down."

I ate another spoonful of soup, giving him space to decide whether he would answer me. He dragged a hand through his hair, tugging lightly at the ends that were long enough to curl just a little.

"I spent a lot of time riding today. Sometimes my hip and leg get a little stiff. I came down to get something for it when I saw the kitchen light on and the door open."

I chewed on my bottom lip, thinking about what I wanted to say next. Something about the dark and the quiet of the night made me feel a little less cautious, a little braver than I knew I would have been in the daylight. Or maybe I was just more tired than I thought, making my brain sluggish.

"From your accident?" My voice came out soft, hesitant.

Jack sighed, never pulling his eyes away from the scenery.

"Yeah, from my accident."

His answer wasn't angry or harsh, just resigned. We both were silent for a minute, the sound of the swing's gentle movement filling the night.

"Jack, can I ask you something?"

He turned to meet my stare and gave me a strained grin. "Did you ever notice that nothing good ever follows that question?"

My eyes bounced between those warm brown eyes that reminded me of whiskey in this light.

"Is that a yes or no?"

"Go ahead, ask away." He stretched his legs out in front of him like he needed to physically brace himself in preparation.

"Do you miss it? The rodeo."

Those big hands—which I knew were rough but could be used so incredibly softly—moved to drag down his face. When his eyes found mine again, there was a tiredness in them I hadn't seen before.

"That's not an easy question, Evie. I miss some things, and other things not at all. I always knew I would be done with it someday, but I hate the way it came to an end. I fucking *hated* physical therapy, and every single thing that came with getting hurt."

"I've never been to a rodeo," I offered before voicing a follow-up question, my courage bolstered by the honesty in his answer. "What do you miss?"

"Somehow it doesn't surprise me that you've never been." He turned away from me again and blew out a quick rush of air. "I miss the adrenaline rush, the sound of the crowd after a great ride. I sure as hell don't miss getting thrown around by an angry bull or sleeping in shitty motels."

"I would be seriously concerned if you missed being thrown to the ground by a very large, very angry bull," I said, trying to lighten the conversation after the heaviness of those confessions.

Jack chuckled, finally giving me back his eyes. "What about you?

"Me?" I questioned.

"Yeah, you. Do you miss being a lawyer?"

I mentally kicked myself for opening the door to this question, but fair was fair. It was my turn to sigh and look away. I took a moment to organize my thoughts.

"No, I don't miss it at all. I miss the idea of it, and if I'm being honest, I miss saying it. Like when people ask, 'So Evelyn, what do you do?' I miss that, I don't know, sense of satisfaction I always got from saying, 'Oh, I'm a lawyer.' God, that sounds so dumb and snotty." I cringed. "But I don't miss actually *being* a lawyer at all."

I took another bite of soup, letting the warm liquid heat all the places that had gone cold when he asked the question. Thinking about the past, about the future, gave me intense feelings of anxiety. Almost verging on panic. I fought the feeling, focusing on the soup and the stillness of the night.

"Is that what you wanted to be, growing up?"

"Yes. No. God, I don't even know anymore," I sighed. "I think that's the worst part. I have no idea why I went to law school. I just had this stupid plan that I had to follow."

"What was the plan?" His stare never left the side of my face. I could almost feel it boring under my skin.

"Get into a top-tier law school, make law review, get an internship, stay at the top ten percent of the class at all times, graduate with a job at a firm with a partnership track available," I recited almost robotically.

"Jesus."

"Yep, Jesus." I nodded my head, turning to look at him.

"It seems like you kind of hit it out of the park, though." Jack gave me a sympathetic smile.

"I did. It was pretty awful, actually. Like 'it makes my stomach hurt just thinking about it' awful." I scrunched up my nose, thinking about that tiny little cubicle and the feeling it had given me every morning when my alarm went off.

"Why did you do it then?"

His expression was all curiosity, no judgment. I exhaled another sad, sad sigh trying to come up with an answer.

"It's kind of hard to explain. I was just so focused on the plan that I didn't think about it. I like plans. A lot. As long as I was sticking to the plan, checking things off the list, I was happy. Or I thought I was, anyway. By the time I figured it out, it was too late."

I gave a slight shrug of my shoulders, trying to play it off like it hadn't, wasn't still, devastating me. Like my whole world didn't feel like it had slid off its axis and was spinning wildly. Jack looked at me like he knew I was lying. I wondered if it was written all over my face or if he just understood what it was like to lose a dream. I turned away, needing a reprieve from that knowing look, and focused my attention on my soup, hoping he was going to let me off the hook.

"So what now? I'm guessing working for Ben isn't the new plan."

Right, then. Guess there would be no letting off the hook.

"Maybe you should think about law school if this whole ranching thing doesn't work out." I gave him a weak smile. My voice was light and teasing, completely at odds with how I felt. "It's the right-now plan. I didn't have a backup plan, so..."

My voice trailed off, and I turned back to look up at the night sky so Jack couldn't see how wet my eyes were suddenly. The panic was welling up in my chest at a rate even faster than the tears. I blinked hard and tried to clear my throat quietly. *Breathe, Evelyn. Breathe.* I repeated the words over and over.

"Lucky for Ben. I don't think his last assistant could spell 'assistant.'"

I let out a strangled noise that could have been the love child of a laugh and a sob. I faced him hoping the darkness would hide the tear that managed to slip out despite the smile forming.

"I'm sure she had an impressive resumé."

Jack laughed, his left hand moving to rub his thigh just above the knee. The movement seemed second nature, almost involuntary. My eyes moved of their own volition to watch his hand. Warmth bloomed in my chest and spread outward. I forced myself to look back at his face.

"Sure, a real impressive... resumé. Now I *know* she couldn't spell that word."

I laughed a much more convincing laugh, smile stretching my cheeks, tears and panic forgotten for the moment.

"Harsh, but probably true. Don't you have to be up early? You should head to bed."

My mouth said the words, but my heart screamed for him to stay here with me in this little blanket cocoon.

"I do. You can put that on the list of things I wouldn't miss about being a rancher," he said, giving me an easy smile.

"You love it, though."

It was a statement, not a question. I knew he loved it the way I knew the sun would come up tomorrow and the day after that.

"I can't think of anything else I would want to be," he said, in a tone that left absolutely no room for doubt.

The look he gave me was the effortlessly confident Jack I knew. This Jack I could totally picture stepping into that rodeo arena—not just because I had searched the internet for him so much—and I could totally understand why he'd always had so many buckle bunnies following him around. Moral of that story: I needed to stay off the internet. This Jack also made me feel uncomfortable in my skin in all kinds of ways. The temperature under the blanket spiked at least ten degrees, and I was choking the life out of the mug of soup.

Jack fought back a yawn, stretching his legs even farther in front of him. His bare leg brushed mine, causing me to swallow a noise that would have sounded suspiciously like a moan if I had allowed it to escape. This was it. This was how I died. Spontaneous combustion caused by a leg brush. What was wrong with me? It was my migraine. My brain wasn't fully recovered yet. Yep, that was definitely it.

"Go to bed," I ordered, silently applauding myself for sounding unaffected.

He got up slowly, favoring his left side a little, and careful to make sure the blanket stayed tucked around me as he stood. Leaning forward so close that I could feel his breath wash over me, he wrapped the blanket that both our shoulders had shared tightly around me. My eyes traveled from where he still held the ends of the blankets in his hands, up toned arms and past broad shoulders, to meet his eyes. We stayed like that, so close our breaths mixed and merged between us, for long seconds, and I was sure he could hear my heart thudding wildly in my chest. Jack released the ends of the blankets abruptly and took a few steps back.

"Goodnight, Evelyn. I hope your migraine is gone tomorrow."

Just like earlier in my bedroom, Jack was through the door

before I could respond, but unlike earlier, I didn't bother with a response. All my thoughts were jumbled somewhere between my chest and my stomach.

I finished my soup and sat swinging on the porch a little bit longer, completely content to watch the stars and listen to all the sounds drifting around the ranch.

When I finally did make my way back to bed, it was with the blanket Jack had tucked around us and the promise that I would ignore the uncomfortable feelings beginning to take root—starting tomorrow.

25.

Thankfully, my migraine was mostly gone when I woke up the next morning. There was only a weird pressure somewhere in the back of my skull and a tightness in my neck. A long, hot shower helped ease the tension in my muscles, and I made my way toward the kitchen, excited to get back to my new routine.

Mary greeted me first, dropping a spatula onto the counter to pull me into a tight hug.

"Good morning, honey. It's good to see you up and about. How are you feeling?"

"Much better, thank you. I think your soup must be magic," I said, returning her hug.

"I'm just glad Gabe left you some. I don't know what it is with that boy and my soup," she said, releasing me and turning her attention back to the eggs.

'That boy' swaggered into the kitchen, gloves clutched in one hand, and pulled me into a side hug.

"I'm all man, not a boy, and your soup is amazing. Glad you're feeling better, Evie. We missed you yesterday." Gabe kissed the top of my head before releasing me and heading to the table.

"Excuse me, 'man,'" Mary said, correcting her previous statement. "How do you two want your eggs?"

"Scrambled, please," I answered, making my way over to the coffee pot.

"I can do scrambled this morning. Evie," Gabe said, dragging out my name, "want to bring me a cup of coffee too?"

I laughed, shaking my head. "Only because you left me some soup, and I know now what a sacrifice that was."

I grabbed two mugs and filled them to the brim. I slid into the spot next to Gabe and placed the steaming mug in front of him.

"Do you think you'll have time for a riding lesson today?" I asked over the brim of my cup.

"Sure, we'll make time, but you know you can take Photo out around the ring whenever you want to practice. You don't need me and Cole to help you get her tack on anymore."

"Really? You think I'm good enough to take her out on my own?" My voice sounded surprised and excited.

"Definitely. Don't try anything crazy and keep it in the ring for now, but you can walk, trot, and canter all you want."

"I am so legit now. I have cowboy boots, and I can operate a horse unsupervised." The smile on my face was so wide it almost hurt my cheeks.

Ben and Cole walked through the door, both wearing jeans that had clearly spent some time around dirt this morning, and wearing matching grim expressions on their faces. Whatever retort Gabe was working on was replaced by a knowing look and shared glances between the three men. My eyes bounced between the three, and then toward Mary to see if she was as confused as I was about the whole look thing going on. She was wearing the same frown as everyone else in the kitchen, so it looked like I was the only one left out.

Mary was the first one to recover. "What kind of eggs do you boys want?" she asked, turning her attention back to the stove. "Is Jack coming in?"

Her voice sounded like she was trying to force it to be casual when every part of her was practically screaming with concern. Her question confirmed my growing hunch that all the shared looks and frowns somehow involved Jack.

"No, he's not coming in for a while," Ben answered trying to force the same casualness into his answer. "I'll ride him out something to eat."

"Okay, good. That's good." Mary nodded her head. "Now, how do you boys want your eggs? I have scrambled going right now."

Cole and Ben came to sit at the table, coffee mugs in hand, and took seats on the opposite side of the table.

"Scrambled is fine with me, Mary, thanks," Cole forced out through a yawn.

"I'll be the difficult one this morning and ask for over-easy," Ben said, rubbing his eyes with the heel of his hands.

"I think it's pretty safe to say you aren't the difficult one this morning," Gabe said, giving the two men across us from a half-hearted grin. They answered with equally half-hearted chuckles and little shakes of their heads.

I had absolutely no idea what was going on. I felt like I'd woken up in a different reality and I had to put all the pieces of the puzzle together to escape back to the real world. The only thing I knew for sure was that Jack was at the center of it all. I sipped my coffee and toyed with the idea of asking what was happening. The Jack from last night had been fine—better than fine. What could have happened in the few hours between the front door closing and now?

"Is he any better since I left?" Gabe asked.

"Nope, just digging holes like a maniac and ignoring our existence," Cole said, taking a long drink from his cup.

"Fucking great," Gabe groaned. "Sorry, Mary. I've heard worse out of your mouth, Evie, so don't look at me like that."

I punched him lightly in the arm.

"I don't know what you're talking about. I'm a lady." The other two at the table both gave incredulous huffs. "You're all obviously delusional."

I slid out of my spot to help Mary dish out eggs and toast, while trying to eavesdrop on the hushed conversation coming from the table. I was starting to get a little annoyed at being the only one out of the loop, especially when the conversation came to a stop after I sat down.

The subject changed to what needed to be done around the ranch today, who was doing what, and when Ben would be back from dropping Rodney off at the airfield. I had forgotten Rodney was leaving today; I must have missed his farewell dinner last evening. Nuts.

Breakfast finished and dishes cleaned, I headed out of the house toward King's enclosure. King had been putting on some weight since the first time I'd seen him, and his ribs were no longer sticking out. He still wouldn't let anyone close enough to get a good look at his cuts, but the vet had given Jack a general antibiotic to put in his food that would hopefully stave off infection.

"Good morning," I called to King, hoisting myself up onto the first rung of the fence. "Sorry I didn't come to see you yesterday. I had a bad migraine. You would not have wanted to see me with a migraine. It's not a pretty sight."

King's ears twitched, turning toward me and back again. Cole had explained to me that you can tell a lot about how a horse is feeling by watching its ears. According to Cole, King's forward-facing ears meant that he was paying attention to me. He took a couple of tentative steps in my direction before coming to a stop.

"I hate to break it you, buddy, but it sounds like you have pretty stiff competition for head drama queen today. It sounds like Jack may steal the crown from you. I know—shocking, right?"

King's tail gave the slow swish I knew was meant to swat at flies before he took a few more steps in my direction. I forced my face and voice to remain calm, trying to keep my excitement over his movements in check so I didn't scare him.

"I don't know what to think about his mood. I actually don't know what that mood is, but judging from everyone who's seen him today, it's not good," I sighed, resting my chin on my forearms. "It's weird. Yesterday when I was miserable, he brought me a ginger ale and checked on me. Then he sat with me on the porch swing and was all... I don't know... kind? So of course, I spent a ridiculous amount of time lying in bed this morning worrying about seeing him this morning. I mean, I don't have a great track record of not being awkward. Now I'm worried his mood is somehow my fault, which is stupid. What age do you think girls stop being stupid about boys?"

King was actually walking in my direction now—not taking tentative steps, but walking steadily toward me. I watched him carefully, pretty much holding my breath until my lungs were burning. He finally came to a stop so close to me I could feel his breath on my arms. Nothing had prepared me for this moment. I literally had no idea what I was supposed to do to not scare him away. I decided to play it cool, way cooler than I felt, and kept my chin on my crossed arms. *Baby steps. Baby steps.*

"Holy shit."

I heard Cole's voice from somewhere behind me, but I refused to turn my head around to look for him.

"I know. He's never gotten this close to me before. Maybe you should stay back there?" I said, keeping my voice at a normal volume.

No one said anything for a heartbeat. I just watched King, who watched me. I had no idea what Cole was doing back there. It was King who finally decided he'd had enough, and he walked to the other side of his pen, not bothering to look back. Honestly, I thought King and Jack might be soulmates. They both had that aloof, silent thing down to a science.

"Okay, well, I'll see you later then," I called, hopping down from my spot on the fence.

I turned around to find two stunned faces looking at me like I had just invented fire.

"What?" I said, raising both palms up toward the sky. "I told you he's walked toward me before!"

"Don't get all mad, now, but—I can't speak for Cole, but I thought you had maybe misunderstood the situation," Gabe said.

"Misunderstood?" I said, hands moving to my hips.

"I think what Gabe means is that we thought King was just moving around his paddock at the same time you were there, and you saw a connection between the two," Cole answered for Gabe, playing the role of peacemaker.

"Okay, rude, but I forgive you both. Do you believe me now?" I looked from one to the other; they were both nodding.

"Here's the thing, Evie. You've clearly got something going on between you two"—Gabe motioned between me and the general direction of King—"and I, we, are going to figure out what to do with it. But the timing is not great."

"Not great," Cole echoed.

"What does that mean?" I asked.

"Jack is just dealing with some things right now and he's probably not going to listen to what anyone says until he works it out," Cole said, a slightly nervous note punctuating his words.

"What kind of things?" I said, my voice taking on a slightly irritated tone.

The two men looked at each other, having some sort of silent conversation with their eyes and a few shakes of their heads. I huffed impatiently, more than a little annoyed at being left out of both this conversation and whatever was going on again. I was about two seconds from stomping my foot when they reached some sort of conclusion. Gabe rubbed the back of his neck and then adjusted his baseball cap. I knew this was his signature nervous move.

"Leigh called this morning," Gabe finally managed to say, with a slight edge to his voice.

"Leigh called this morning?" I parroted his words back to him in question form. They sounded bitter in my mouth. "Oh. What did she want?"

"No idea. Nothing good. That girl has always been nothing but trouble," Gabe answered. Cole nodded his head in agreement, his face uncharacteristically tense.

I swallowed down the awful feeling that had started to spread from the bottom of my stomach outward at the mention of Jack's former fiancée. I felt a strange sense of relief that these two men who I liked so much were obviously not members of the Leigh Decker fan club.

"Is Jack okay?" I tried to make my voice sound the right mix of concerned and curious, while shoving down the undeniable anxiety that was bubbling below the surface.

Cole answered this time. "He's taking his frustration out on the fence."

"So who the hell knows?" Gabe added, throwing his hands up before dropping them back down.

"Oh. Okay."

My mind was scrambling for a way to bow out of this conversation gracefully. I needed some time alone to process this information and overthink every single possible reason she might have called.

"We'll talk to him about King. I promise, Evie. Jack just needs some space right now," Cole said. Gabe grunted next to him.

"Okay." I shook my head trying to knock loose some actual words. "I understand. I think it's a good plan. Waiting to talk to Jack until he has some time to process the phone call, I mean."

We stood looking at each other for a few seconds. No one seemed to know what to say next. Finally, Cole—sweet, reliable Cole—broke the awkward silence.

"We need to head out and move some cows, but we'll come up with a plan later. You going to take Photo out this morning?"

"Yep! I was going to head over there now," I said, thankful for a reason to make my escape, and for an excuse to be alone. Jack was definitely not the only one who had some processing to do.

26.

With some final words of advice about my first solo ride with Photo, Gabe and Cole headed to the paddock where their horses were waiting, and I made my way to the barn where Photo was waiting for me. I stopped in the tack room to gather her gear before making my way to her stall.

"Hey, Photo, how would you feel about a little exercise this morning?"

Photo turned to look at me and gave me what I chose to believe was a head nod. I slipped on her bridle and led her out of the stall. Her warm breath hit my neck, making me laugh. I stroked her nose affectionately.

"We got this, huh? Just a couple of independent ladies today."

She nudged me gently with her nose, which I took as a sign of encouragement. I hooked her up to the wall leads and went through my pre-ride checklist. Once I was convinced everything was on right and her girth was tight enough, I led her out to the little dirt arena we used for lessons. I stepped onto the mounting block and took a deep breath before lifting myself up and onto Photo in one swift movement. My smile was so wide it felt like it might split my face in two. *I did it!* Photo was still wearing her saddle, and I was not on the ground! I leaned forward and wrapped my arms around Photo's neck.

"Thank you for being so great!" I said into her mane, thinking about how much I loved her and how much I loved this.

We went through all the skills I had learned: walk, trot, and canter. I felt my smile stretch wide again as Photo cantered around the ring smoothly. At first, I had been nervous every time I asked Photo to canter. It was fast and had felt a little wild for me, but it was my absolute favorite now. I loved the speed and feeling the cold wind rushing against us.

My thoughts drifted toward Jack and the phone call as I rode. My list of questions and what-ifs grew with each lap. What if she wanted to get back together with him? What if he wanted to get back together with her? Why did they break up in the first place? And the question that kept pushing its way to the front—did he still love her?

One question I didn't have to ask was why I was so bothered by the phone call. I was jealous, or some weird re-lative of jealousy. I felt a little bit like middle-school Evelyn, without the braces and frizz-control shampoo. I knew I had absolutely no right to be jealous. I knew it was stupid. And I knew, I *knew*, this crush that was more than a crush was so stupid. There was no way I wasn't setting myself up for dis-appointment. All those old insecurities about my appearance started weaseling their way back to the surface. I chastised myself, dismounting.

"I really am reverting back to middle-school Evelyn," I said to Photo, slipping the reins over her head and walking us out of the arena.

After Photo was brushed and settled back in her stall hap-pily munching on an apple, I made my way back to the tack room. My steps were wobbly under the weight of the saddle. The post-ride stiffness wasn't as bad as it had been after my first few lessons, but I still felt a little unsteady when my feet hit the ground. After I had put everything back in its place, I sat down on a small pile of straw that had been stacked just outside of the tack room.

I pulled out my phone, letting my finger hover over the screen before tapping out a single sentence.

Me: *Leigh called Jack this morning.*

My phone dinged with an incoming message almost immediately.

Elise: *WHAT?! Tell me everything.*

I sighed as if she were in the barn with me and not multiple states away.

Me: *I don't know anything and I HATE it. What if she realizes she made a huge mistake and wants to get back together? What if he still loves her?*

Elise: *Whoa, that was serious death spiral action, Evie.*

Corinne: *Yeah, maybe she just found a box of his CDs and wanted to return them?*

Me: *Nobody uses CDs anymore! Who is using CDs?*

Corinne: *I don't know! It was the first thing that came into my head!*

Elise: *So, are we just breezing past the fact that you aren't in denial about liking Jack anymore? This is a thing now.*

Corinne: *Awwww but Evie in denial is my favorite Evie!*

Me: *All right, yes, I admit it. I have a stupid, stupid crush on Jack and it is the worst. It's turning me into middle-school Evelyn without the braces.*

Elise: *Have you suddenly started wearing unicorn everything again?*

Corinne: *OMG yes! I forgot about the unicorn obsession! Do you remember the pink unicorn stirrup pants? So many bright colors!*

Elise: *LOL! What was that book series you were crazy about?*

Me: *First of all, they weren't unicor... you know what, never mind. Remind me why I still talk to you two?*

Corinne: *We're related. You have no choice.*

Elise: *You just need to put on your lady pants and ask him what she wanted.*

Me: *I can't do that! He doesn't owe me an explanation. We aren't dating and we never will be, so he can talk to anyone about anything.*

Corinne: *He's your friend and it's totally acceptable to ask your friend why they are upset. And why are you so sure you two will never date?*

Elise: *I have a feeling it's about to get real middle-school Evie up in here.*

Me: *Calm down. I know I'm not covered in warts. Jack and I are just in totally different leagues. He would never date someone who looks like me. That's just how real life works.*

Elise: *You are literally the dumbest smart person I know. Yes, you're shorter than the average human but who cares? You have the wavy hair people pay tons of money for at hair salons and, news flash, not everyone wants to date a twig.*

Corinne: *Yes to all of that. You have the prettiest green eyes ever. They are so unique! And your freckles are adorable. Plus, you're super smart and thoughtful. Oh god, I'm crying now. These hormones!*

Me: *Thanks for the pep talk but Jack and I just don't work. Even if you can get past the looks situation, his life is in Montana and mine's in Chicago.*

Corinne: *We're back to this again? You breaking up with him in your head before you even start dating? Newsflash, Evie, you can't plan everything. Plans are great unless you're so determined to stick to them that you start missing out on all the great things that fall at your feet along the way. Does that sound familiar? BE-CAUSE IT SHOULD!*

I lay back on the hay with a huff. I could almost hear Corinne hurling those words at me, hands moving around for emphasis. If anyone knew what it was like to have plans blow up in their face, it was me. This wasn't about making a plan and sticking to it, though. This was about being realistic. I could feel random pieces of straw poking me in the back and in my head. I shuffled forward trying to get more comfortable, my legs hanging off the end at the knee. Why did the movies always make lying on hay look so great? Sharp edges were poking me everywhere. I adjusted my position again, grumbling to myself a little about unrealistic expectations.

"What am I watching here?"

Jack's voice, deep and slightly amused, echoed through the space. I shot upright, face pink and eyes wide. I was startled and more than a little embarrassed.

"Jack, hey, hi!"

I watched him walk toward me, a pair of gloves tucked into his back pocket and his red hat on his head. My eyes scanned his face, looking for signs of stress or sadness or whatever had been there this morning. I had a sudden flash of anxiety that the Jack who had taken me to get boots and sat with me on the porch swing had been replaced by the old Jack.

"What are you doing?" he asked, taking a seat next to me on the stack of hay.

"Oh, uh, I was trying to get comfortable. You always see people lying on hay in the movies or TV, you know, but it's actually super uncomfortable. Hay is sharp and it pokes you everywhere. I can't believe people used to use this stuff in mattresses."

My eyes slipped from his face to pick at the straw. I was pretty sure my rambling gave away my nerves.

"Right. Why were you trying to lay on it?" His voice sounded curious, maybe a little amused.

"I don't know. I just put Photo's saddle back and sat down to talk to my sisters. I guess I was going to lie down and think about things. I don't really have a good reason. I just like it out here." I wrinkled my nose trying to come up with a reason to explain why I had decided to lie on the hay in the first place.

He turned to look at me, a small smile tugging at the corner of his mouth.

"You took Photo out by yourself?"

I think I would have been wary of answering that question after the whole 'city girl' conversation if Jack hadn't been wearing that small smile. I returned his smile with a wide one of my own, nodding my head, more than a little pleased that I had taken Photo out by myself and relieved that he wasn't going to linger on the hay-laying thing.

"I did! I got her tack on all by myself, and then practiced all my new moves. I even managed to mount her on my first try."

"I—" Jack began, but Cole's voice interrupted, followed by a high-pitched squeal.

"There you two are."

"Uncle Jack!" Letty appeared from behind her dad's legs and rushed toward Jack. He hopped down to wrap her in a hug before swinging her around. I moved to stand next to Cole, who was watching the little girl laugh with a smile on his face.

"Nice move," I said quietly, giving him a small smile. "Bringing Letty."

"I have no idea what you're talking about," Cole said, keeping his eyes forward. "But if I did, I'd say it was pretty genius but would have to give the credit to Margot."

Jack was obediently following Letty to go look at her pony, so Cole and I turned to head out of the barn. We totally just left a small child alone to deal with whatever grown-up problem Jack was struggling with. No shame in our game. It wasn't until we were walking through the front door that I noticed Cole had changed clothes from this morning.

"Wow, you look nice! What's happening? You don't normally get this dressed up for lunch," I said, taking in his clean-shaven face and slightly styled hair.

"It's part two of Margot's plan."

"That's not cryptic at all," I said, turning into the kitchen where Margot was helping Mary.

"Mission accomplished," Cole said, walking over to her and giving her a quick kiss on the head.

"I told you this was a great idea! Hey, Evelyn, how are you feeling?" Margot turned her smile in my direction.

"Much better, thanks. I think Mary's chicken soup cured me."

Mary laughed. "I'll have to make you some more then, just in case. Gabe snuck the rest home with him this afternoon," she said, taking the cutting board away from Margot. "Go sit down, Margot. Everything else is ready to go into the oven."

"I thought everyone could use a night out, and it just so happens that the Shepards are having their fall bonfire tonight. Mary and Dad are going to watch Letty, so I'm not taking no for an answer. From anyone," Margot said, taking a seat at the table. I didn't need to ask who 'anyone' meant, so I kept my mouth shut as I made my way to the sink to wash my hands.

My unofficial mealtime duties had been limited to tasks that didn't involve actually touching any of the food. I was pretty sure Mary had thrown in the towel after I massacred her tomatoes on the cutting board. There's a difference between chopped and diced; who knew? Not me. In my defense, I had warned everyone that cooking and I did not mix. Since then, I'd stuck to dish-related tasks: setting the table, washing, drying. I grabbed the pile of dishes Mary had set out on the island and started placing them around the table.

"So, are you excited?" Margot asked me. Cole rolled his eyes and let out a sigh. Margot responded with a playful nudge of her elbow.

"Excited about what?" I was genuinely puzzled by her question.

Margot gave me the universal face for '*duh.*'

"The bonfire!"

"Oh, sure. Very exciting stuff." I tried to infuse some enthusiasm into my voice, but it just came out sounding squeaky and unnaturally high-pitched. My acting skills were on par with my cooking skills.

"It's going to be fun, I promise." She must have picked up on the doubt in my voice. "And you have a designated driver so no drawing straws."

Her hand dropped down to rest on her slight bump, rubbing it fondly. Jack and Letty walked through the door, followed by Gabe the soup thief, before I had the chance to respond. I opened my mouth to yell at Gabe for taking the rest of the soup but I forgot the words, and the soup, and my own name, as I took in his appearance. He was wearing a pair of tight, tight dark jeans and a dark grey button-down that made his eyes seem unbelievably blue. The sleeves of his shirt were rolled up to reveal those drool-worthy forearms. I had to force my mouth closed and grip the plates with both hands to keep from fanning myself.

Because Gabe in those clothes was not enough, Letty stepped onto Jack's shoes, stretching her arms up to grab his hands. He walked toward the table, with Letty laughing as her little feet moved with his. I sent a silent prayer out into the universe: *Lord Jesus, have mercy on my ovaries.*

Margot waited until Jack and Letty were seated at the table before launching her attack.

"Hey, Jack," Margot said, shooting a smile his way. "Guess what? Grandma Mary and Grandpa are babysitting Letty tonight. Letty-Lou, are you excited to have a sleepover with Grandma Mary and Grandpa?"

"Yeah!" Letty bobbed her head enthusiastically.

"Mommy's excited too, because she gets to spend the night with her friends." Margot turned her attention back to Jack. "We're going to the Shepard's bonfire tonight. Me, Cole, Evelyn, Gabe, and you, of course. Ben is even going to try to meet us there."

"Oh, we are?' Jack asked, skepticism lacing his voice.

"Yes, we are. We haven't been able to hang out together in forever! And Evelyn hasn't seen the Pinehaven nightlife yet."

I opened my mouth to point out that Evelyn did not *need* to see the nightlife, but Jack spoke up before I got the chance.

"Okay." He said the one simple word like he hadn't even considered saying no.

I saw my last hope of avoiding this bonfire drifting away like smoke.

27.

The nervous butterfly that had taken up residence in my belly when Jack agreed to go to the bonfire had turned into an entire flock by the time I left the office a few hours later. I was hoping work would be a good distraction from thinking about the bonfire. Even a nice long shower did nothing to calm my nerves. By the time my hair was dried and resembled something tame, I was repeating affirmations to my reflection in the mirror.

"You can be outgoing. You're friendly. You made friends with everyone here. This will be fun. You love s'mores."

I pulled on a pair of dark skinny jeans and a deep green V-neck sweater that was somewhat fitted over my chest and then flowed loosely over my hips. Stopping in front of the mirror to give myself one last look before heading downstairs, I had to admit I looked nice. I applied some of the lip gloss Anna and Hilari had helped me pick out, slipping the gloss into my purse before leaving my room.

Laughter drifted down the hallway, acting as a soothing balm for my nerves. But I still found myself shifting my mass of hair over one shoulder as I walked into the room, my very own signature nervous move. Jack and Gabe were sitting on the couch with beers in hand while Margot and Cole were snuggled up together on a chair. Margot noticed me first and jumped up to wrap me in a hug.

"Hey, girl, you look great! I don't think I've ever seen your hair down, which is a freaking crime because it's gorgeous."

I tugged the ends of my hair self-consciously, feeling my

cheeks heat at the compliment. I kept my eyes fixed on Margot, not brave enough to seek out the other occupants of the room just yet. Not 'others,' if I was being honest. Just Jack. I wasn't sure what I would find when I did, but I knew what I wanted to see written on his face.

"That's because it's a total menace. I didn't mean to make you guys wait on me."

"It's all good, Evie. We had to wait on pretty boy over here to finish getting ready, too." Gabe pointed to Jack with his beer. "He didn't turn out as good as you did, though."

I laughed as Jack shook his head at Gabe, and used the distraction to take in Jack's appearance. My heart leapt in my chest as my gaze moved from that clean-shaven jaw to a blue and grey checkered flannel that pulled across those perfectly sculpted arms, then drifted lower to those jean-clad legs that didn't deserve to belong in this world.

I tried to swallow around a throat that was suddenly completely dry. Margot clapped her hands together, saving me from having to use my poor fried brain cells to think of something clever to say.

"All right, kids, are we ready to do this?"

Everyone rose obediently from their spots and followed Margot down the hall. She was clearly a woman on a mission. The guys dropped their beers in the kitchen while Margot and I pulled on our shoes at the door.

"So, Jack cleans up pretty good, right?" Margot said casually as she pulled on her second shoe. Her question made me lose my balance, sending me slumping into the wall.

"Ah... what... he... sure." I cleared my throat. "Yeah, he looks nice."

Margot was looking at me with a grin that I did not like at all. I narrowed my eyes at her. "Margot—"

Before I could let her know that she could forget about whatever was running through her scheming brain, we were rejoined by the rest of the group. Jackets and boots were slipped on and we headed out the door. I stopped a few feet from everyone when Margot opened the door to Cole's truck, doing the math quickly in my head.

"Are we all going to fit in one truck?" I asked, glancing at everyone and then back at the truck. I had a feeling I was not going to like the seating arrangements. A really bad feeling.

"We'll make it work," Gabe said, patting me on the head. "You're in the middle, Tiny."

I swallowed, looking up at the truck like it was a monster waiting to eat me whole. I hoisted myself up into it, scooting into the middle seat. I took a deep breath anticipating the two large, handsome bodies that climbed in next to me. Both sides of me were flanked by heat, which spread from the sides directly into my face. There was a real chance I wouldn't survive this car ride. I hoped the Shepards lived close. I frantically dug through my memory, trying to remember if I'd ever seen any houses around Pinehaven.

Jack reached into the very tiny space between my hip and his, sending my stomach down to my feet, and handed me the seatbelt. Then my hand brushed his, which sent my stomach up to my chest. I gave him a weak smile and turned toward Gabe to buckle myself in.

Gabe took the buckle from my hand and shot me one of his toe-curling grins. "I'm going to save us both the awkwardness and buckle your seatbelt for you."

I gave him a little laugh and a "Thank you," shifting my hip a little so he could reach the other half of the seatbelt. I was careful not too lean too far into Jack's side, especially when I could feel his gaze burning into the side of my face.

I settled into my spot after Gabe gave me the all-clear, trying to cram my short frame into the tiniest amount of space possible. Neither of the men beside me seemed to share my concerns about space. They sat with their legs spread comfortably, Gabe's elbow almost resting on my thigh. My eyes bounced from knee to knee to knee, and I felt a laugh bubble up from deep down inside. How was I living this life right now?

Margot turned up the radio and started singing along. Her voice was loud and happy, and it was impossible not to catch a little bit of her excitement. One of Cole's hands moved from the steering wheel to rest on her leg, making my heart squeeze.

A thought struck me suddenly, like a bolt of lightning appearing without warning. I wanted that. All my planning, all my dreaming—it had been about accomplishing something. It had been about building a career for myself that I could be proud of, one that checked off everything on my list. There was no room for anything or anyone else. It was hollow and empty and really sad, and it made me feel all of those things. This—being in the car with friends; Margot singing in the front seat, Gabe laughing every time she messed up the words; even being tucked close to Jack—this made me feel something so good. This was worth something.

I leaned back into the seat, closing my eyes. Taking a deep breath and smiling at the feeling of contentedness that came over me, I let myself believe that this was going to be a good night.

28.

The Shepards' house was not, in fact, close to Pinehaven. Forty-five minutes into the trip, I had given up trying to keep from pressing into either of the people next to me and was now melting onto both of them. Gabe was the safest option for my heart, so I shifted my numb butt until my back was pressed into his arm. I lifted my head to meet his curious gaze and gave a slight shrug of my shoulder.

"My butt is numb," I explained, nestling further into his side.

He lifted his arm, draping it across my shoulders so I had more room on the seat. The downside—or upside, depending on your perspective—of my new position was that I was now staring straight at Jack. He really did look so handsome with his hair styled back away from his face.

Jack was staring at Gabe's arm draped over my shoulder, a small crease between his eyebrows. I would have given a kidney to know what he was thinking about in that moment. Most of the time he was a complete mystery to me.

"Are you excited for your first Pine Hollow bonfire?" Gabe asked, his voice a rumble on my back.

"Yeah. It's been a long, long time since I've been to a bonfire," I answered, surprised that I meant it. "Will there be s'mores?"

Both men laughed at the question. I tipped my head back to look at Gabe who was smiling down at me.

"What? Everybody loves s'mores." I defended my question

with the universal truth of s'mores greatness.

"I'm not sure it's that kind of bonfire," Gabe answered. "Can't say I'm usually looking for s'mores though."

I scrunched up my nose. "That's a little disappointing, but I'm still excited. What are you usually looking for?"

Jack and Cole both made strangled noises and Margot let out a loud laugh.

"Wait!" I said, holding up my hands. "Don't answer that question. I can use my imagination."

Thankfully, we made it to the bonfire before I lost all the feeling in my lower half. I slid toward Jack's side of the truck, since that was the way my legs were facing. Inching forward, I tried to shake some feeling back into my legs.

"You okay?" Jack asked, his eyes roaming from my legs to my face.

"Yep, my legs were just starting to fall asleep. Middle seat problems."

I swung my legs out of the truck, then sat perched at the edge of the seat waiting for Jack to back up, giving me space to hop out of the truck. We stayed that way for one heartbeat, two heartbeats, before I accepted the fact that Jack wasn't going to give me any room to get out of this thing without his help. Why, why, why did I ever think anything with this man might be easy?

I huffed out a breath, eyes locked on the grey and blue pattern stretching across his chest, and launched myself off the seat. Two large hands shot out to land on either side of my hips. I heard the little gasp escape before I could stop it as his grip tightened, strong fingers digging into softer flesh. Startled, I tipped my head back slowly to peer at the man who probably held so much more than my hips at this point. He just stared back with that even, neutral expression on his face, and slowly lowered me to the ground.

He kept his hands firmly on me until he was sure I could stand on my own—which honestly would have been a lot easier if he had stopped touching me. I felt one quick squeeze before Jack turned and walked away without saying a word.

"What the hell?" I said to no one. My hands moved to the spots where his had just been, while my eyes tracked his progress through the crowd. Away from me.

Margot moved around the truck and slipped her arm through mine.

"You need a drink," she said, smiling at me and wiggling her eyebrows dramatically.

I nodded my head. "Yes, a drink. That's exactly what I need. Take me to the drinks, crazy pregnant lady."

Margot tugged me toward a folding table with a crowd gathered around it, laughing like the crazy person I had accused her of being. I looked around, trying to take in everything as we moved between row after row of pickup truck. The occasional SUV or car made an appearance, looking completely out of place here. Country music was playing from somewhere and there were people dancing off to one side of the fire. It looked like the low-budget version of every bonfire scene ever made for television. I scanned the surprisingly large crowd for Cole and Gabe, without luck. I was suddenly very grateful Margot had stuck behind to act as my unofficial tour guide.

"Oh em gee, Margot! I didn't know you were coming!" A brunette darted out from behind the table and wrapped Margot up in a hug.

"Hey, Katie! It was kind of a last-minute thing." Margot pulled out of her arms and steered me forward. "Katie, this is Evie. She's staying up at Pinehaven with the Danvers."

Katie gave me a friendly smile before pouncing on me. I *hmph*ed in surprise. Everyone in this state was a hugger. I also checked her left hand for a ring as she released me, because I did that sort of thing now. She had a ring, which meant she had a husband which meant she probably wasn't sleeping with Jack. The logic of a truly sad woman.

"It's nice to meet you, Evie. Where are you from? What brings you to Pine Hollow? Oh my gosh, listen to me! Let me get you a drink before I interrogate you. What would you like? We have lots of beer, some very fancy wine coolers, and something Boyd Smith brought in bottles, but I'd steer clear of that unless you're a professional drinker."

I smiled, trying to keep up with this firecracker of a human being whom I definitely liked already.

"Chicago. I came with Ben for work. And a beer would be great," I said, mentally checking off my answers to her questions as I spoke.

Katie bent down to rummage through a cooler, then walked to a smaller cooler. She handed me a beer and Margot a bottle of water.

"Thanks," I said, taking a big drink. Liquid courage didn't really call for moderation.

"So you came with Ben, huh? Are you two...?" She gestured between me and nowhere with her own beer bottle.

"No, definitely not!" I cringed at how loud my voice was, but Katie just tipped her head back, laughing. Margot was shaking her head beside me like she couldn't believe Katie had led with that question.

"Girl, good for you!" Katie clinked her bottle against mine. A lanky man with shaggy blond hair walked up next to her, slipping an arm around her waist. "Babe, this is Evie from Chicago. She came with Ben for work, but she is *not* sleeping with him."

I groaned at the same time Margot yelled "Katie!"

Katie just shrugged and took another drink. The man smiling indulgently at his wife stuck his hand out toward me, turning his smile my way.

"Nice to meet you, Evie from Chicago who is not sleeping with Ben. I'm Seth who is married to this already-a-little-drunk woman."

I laughed, despite the 'sleeping with Ben' insert, and slipped my hand into his. It was impossible to be annoyed with people who were so friendly.

"It's nice to meet you, too."

Seth said hello to Margot, pulling her into a one-armed hug and asked how she was feeling.

"Where'd your other half go off to?" Seth asked her, turning his head from side to side looking for Cole.

"He went to try to snag a couple chairs by the fire. That's my definition of partying these days." Margot held up her water bottle with one hand while the other landed on the tiny bump, just barely visible.

We lingered around the drink cooler while Katie and Seth asked Margot about how she was feeling. My attention was divided between their conversation and all the activity happening around us. I should have felt like an outsider, but I felt that strange sense of belonging that kept creeping up on me.

29.

Katie and Seth decided to tag along to find Cole. Margot hooked her arm through mine again, as if she knew I would need the extra support. She stopped along the way to introduce me to people curious about a new face—a Steve here, a Rachel there; a Pete and a Taylor. I tried to take a mental inventory of names and faces as she went, smiling and shaking hands or giving awkward waves, all the while saying a silent thank-you to the universe that Katie was too far ahead of us to include the "not sleeping with Ben" part of her introduction.

After what felt like a small eternity, we finally found Cole, who sat waiting close to what was actually a pretty big fire—like, a concerningly big fire. I had been to plenty of bonfires growing up, but they had been in backyards and contained to those little metal firepits. This was a raging inferno compared to those bonfires. If I'd seen this thing in Chicago, I would have immediately called 911 and then stopped, dropped, and rolled just to be safe.

Cole stood up when he saw us approaching and pulled Margot in for a quick kiss.

"Seats by the fire, as requested," Cole said, gesturing to the two empty lawn chairs behind him.

"Thanks, Cole," Margot said, raising up on tiptoes to place a kiss on his cheek. I felt that same strange tug in my chest that I'd experienced in the truck earlier. I shoved it down, then tried to drown it with another drink of beer. And then another drink just to make sure it was good and dead. I knew there was going to have to be a time and a place where I analyzed all these new things I was feeling, but it was definitely not this time or this place.

"Oh shit!" Margot exclaimed, eyes going wide. "I am a terrible, terrible wife. You went off to find me a seat and I couldn't even remember to bring you a drink."

"You *are* a terrible wife," he agreed, pulling her into his arms. "That's why I had Gabe grab me one before he goes off to do his thing."

"Oh, I didn't see it," Margot said, doing a quick scan for the elusive beer.

"Yeah, he left about fifteen minutes ago, so I'm not liking my odds here," Cole responded, with a little grin and shake of his head that told me exactly how he thought Gabe got distracted.

Right on cue, Gabe appeared with his arms full of beer bottles.

"Hello, ladies; Cole. Hey Seth, how's it going, man?" Gabe greeted us, carefully extracting one of the bottles to pass to Cole. "Who else needs refills here? Help me out."

Katie, Seth and I all shot our hands up into the air. Gabe chuckled and motioned for us to take the drinks cradled in his arms. I looked around for a trash can before following Seth's lead and setting my empty bottle on the ground. I cringed a little internally; it felt like littering. I was truly a rule-follower at heart.

A very pretty blonde appeared at Gabe's side and wound her arms around his waist. "Hey, handsome," she purred, batting her long lashes over deep brown eyes.

"Whit, I was just coming to find you." Gabe tugged her closer. He whispered something in her ear that made her giggle and sent her honey-blond hair cascading down her back.

I gagged. Was there anything worse than a giggle? I hated

the way her cheeks turned a light pink and made her even more attractive. When I turned red, it looked like I had a rash.

Katie must have seen me eyeballing the pair. "Gabe and Whitney have a thing." She clearly had confused my expression for curiosity instead of what it really was—a little disgust and a whole lot of completely unfounded jealousy.

"I'm not sure it counts as a thing if you're just sleeping with each other between relationships," Margot chimed in.

"Do we like her?" I asked. Cole and Seth had been joined by someone I thought was named John, or maybe Mike, and were busy with their own conversation.

"Eh." Katie shrugged. "She's fine."

"She doesn't really have much of a personality," Margot agreed.

"Which I think is what Gabe likes about her." Katie snickered. "I don't think he's in it for her great conversation skills."

I watched Whitney's hand snake across Gabe's chest, coming to rest on his biceps. She stretched up to say something clearly meant for only Gabe to hear.

"No, definitely not interested in the conversation," I echoed, watching her practically rub up against him.

We watched as they made their way toward a pickup truck playing country music nearby. The music was just loud enough that I could make out the unfamiliar words of songs I didn't know. Couples and groups of people were dancing in the open space between the truck and the throng of people hanging out around the bonfire. It reminded me of the few clubs I had gone to in Chicago—but the country version, obviously.

"Oh boy, look who decided she was good enough to show up tonight," Katie said, her voice laced with sarcasm.

I turned, trying to see who she was talking about, but there were too many faces I didn't recognize.

Margot cursed quietly beside me. "I didn't think she'd be here tonight," she said, casting a worried glance my way.

"Who?" I asked, still trying to figure out what was happening.

Then my eyes landed on a face I would have recognized anywhere. Jack stood just to the side of the makeshift dance floor, one hand holding a drink, the other hand holding onto the hip of a tall redhead. The mystery woman turned to plaster her backside against Jack, swaying a little to the music. The flames lit her face enough for me to recognize Shelly.

"Oh," I said, finally catching up. I stood still, watching them move together and feeling like a balloon that someone had poked a hole in. I was vaguely aware of Katie saying something and Margot responding, but the pressure in my chest kept growing like a living thing. I blinked hard, feeling a different kind of pressure building in my eyes.

I felt a strong tug on my arm, and Margot physically spun me around to face her.

"Listen, I know how it looks, but I swear Jack doesn't even like Shelly. Nobody likes Shelly," Margot said, squeezing my arms emphatically.

Katie looked from Margot to me with a concerned expression on her face. She stepped closer, making us into a little circle. I couldn't resist glancing back over my shoulder, trying to catch a glimpse of Jack.

"Let's go sit down," Katie suggested, already turning to walk toward the chairs. Margot followed Katie's lead, tugging me along after her. Once we were settled into the chairs Katie had moved into a half-circle, she cleared her throat.

"So who wants to tell me what that was?"

I took another long drink of beer, trying to numb the feelings that were starting to overwhelm me. A faint ringing in my ears alerted me to the fact that I was probably drinking too much, too fast. *Screw it.* I took another drink, embracing the warmth that had started to course through my body. This was a night to ignore warning signs.

"It's okay, Evie. Katie and I have been friends since we were kids. Fun fact: She was my maid of honor. You can trust us both," Margot urged. I wasn't sure what she wanted me to say.

"When you grow up in a small town in pretty much the middle of nowhere, you either learn to keep secrets or you become a huge gossip. I'm an excellent secret-keeper, right, Margot?" Katie looked at Margot for confirmation while I continued drinking.

"I wouldn't be friends with you if you were a gossip. I mean"—Margot motioned from herself to Katie—"we gossip together, because we're female and it's a small town, but we don't spread it. Katie kept my crush on Cole a secret for like five years."

"She did?" I smiled, thinking about a young Margot pining away after a teenage Cole, who had to have been a complete heart-throb.

"Yep, she did. Of course, she was also the one who told Cole I had a crush on him, but it worked out in the end so I forgave her."

"Hey! I only told Cole you liked him after I heard him say he wanted to ask you out but didn't think you were interested in him," Katie said defensively.

"Let's just stay focused on why Evie looks like she just found out Santa and the Easter Bunny aren't real." Margot reached over to rub my back soothingly.

I felt like this was turning into a weird interrogation where everyone was playing the good cop and I really didn't know whodunit. I sighed. God, I wished there were s'mores at this bonfire. I mean, what kind of bonfire doesn't have s'mores? Or hotdogs. A hotdog sounded really good.

Seth passed by, dropping a kiss on Katie's head and handing us all refills. I drained the rest of my current drink and set it down on the ground, not thinking about the littering situation—another clear warning sign, discarded like the empty bottle sitting by my chair. I didn't even bother looking at the label before taking a big gulp.

"Um, maybe you should slow down with the drinks," Margot suggested, sounding a little fuzzy, especially as the ringing in my ears grew louder. I shook my head trying to make the ringing stop, the movement causing the world to tilt briefly before doing a little spin. I blinked hard and listened for the ringing. Nothing. Perfect.

"Don't worry, I'm fine. Everything's fine," I assured them.

"Do you want to talk about what's inspiring this drink-fest?" Katie asked, taking a drink of her own beer. "'Cause I'll totally drink in support of whatever it is, but it would help me stay motivated if I knew why."

"There's nothing to talk about." I shrugged my shoulders helplessly. "I'm just a little in love with Jack."

Shit. Shit. Shit. How did those words sneak past my lips? Loose lips sink ships! I rubbed my forehead trying to figure out how to take it back. Apparently I had skipped right past phase one of Drunk Evie and gone straight to phase two, where I suddenly became super chatty. I eyeballed the bottle dangling from my hand. Phase three of Drunk Evie was what Hilari and Anna called the "so you think you can dance" phase. I set the bottle down on the ground. No way was I unleashing my dance moves. No one needed to see phase three.

I looked up to find Katie watching me with wide eyes, her mouth slightly open. I thought I saw her mouth "Wow." *Yeah, shocked me too, girlfriend.* Margot, however, was practically vibrating in her chair.

"Yes! I knew it!" She clapped her hands together gleefully.

I rolled my eyes at her. "I feel like you shouldn't be so excited about this."

"Are you kidding me? Do you even know how long I've been waiting for Jack to fall in love with someone I like?" Margot practically shrieked.

It took my beer-soaked brain a few moments to process her words. Katie looked like she was also trying to play catch-up.

"Hold the phone," I said, holding up a hand. "What are you saying?"

"You're super nice, we watch the same trash-TV shows, you would never have to ask if *To Kill a Mockingbird* is a field manual, you don't mind that my child is trying to steal your man." She ticked off each item on her fingers as she went. "This is perfect!"

"He's not my man! Not even close. Did you not just see Shelly climbing him like a horny, sexy, perfectly-proportioned vine?"

"I don't know what that was about," Katie said, apparently done absorbing all the new information. "No one likes Shelly. I mean, some people thinking with something other than their brain will sleep with Shelly, but no one actually *likes* her. I'm not sure that last part was actually helpful but you know what I meant."

"She's the worst. She's been trying to get Jack since before he even met Leigh. He's never taken her up on the offer, that I know of. I've heard him say he isn't interested more than once," Margot added.

Katie nodded her head in agreement. "I bet she snuck up on him before he could dodge her. She wound herself around him like a desperate boa and now he can't escape."

Against all the better judgment I possessed, I turned my head back toward the dancing. I was just in time to see Shelly whisper something in Jack's ear before placing a line of kisses down his jaw. I swallowed, the undeniable sting of tears making the scene in front of me blur. Shelly laced her hand in Jack's, pulling him off toward the parked trucks. I might not know much about Montana bonfires, but I knew enough to understand they weren't going off to discuss whether or not they shared the same taste in movies.

My shoulders slumped in defeat. A watery sigh escaped. I could barely force myself to make eye contact with Katie and Margot. What could be better than some humiliating rejection shared with new friends?

Katie popped up from her chair, wearing a smile in place of what I had thought would be pity mixed with sympathy.

"You know what? Fuck it. How ya feeling, mama? I'm feeling a dance sesh coming on."

Margot stood up from her chair and turned to face the boys. "Cole, watch our chairs!"

Cole's gaze bounced between all three of us, his expression morphing from concern to curiosity. "Do I need to warn you two to behave?"

Katie placed a hand on her chest and gave him a shocked expression. "*Moi*? Never."

I heard Seth mumble something that sounded like "Oh shit" before he shouted, "Make good decisions!"

Katie reached her hand toward mine, a mischievous smile tugging one side of her mouth up. "Don't worry, this is definitely a good decision. Ladies, let's go find something to loosen us up."

30.

"This doesn't seem like a good decision," I said, looking down at the shot of tequila in my hand.

"Whaaat? It seems like the best decision." Katie poured a little more tequila into her own glass.

Margot raised her shot glass of water. "Yep, this is the best possible decision."

I rolled my eyes at Margot, unable to keep from smiling. "You have water in that glass." I raised my shot glass to meet hers anyway.

"I'm greenlighting this decision, and I'm a parent so I'm super reliable with decisions." Margot motioned for Katie to raise her glass. "Okay, ladies, to great friends and great decisions."

We clinked our glasses together, letting out a collective "Cheers!"

I brought the glass to my lips and took a fortifying breath before tossing it back. The smooth liquid burned a hot path through my middle, and I gagged, then sputtered.

"Oh my God, I haven't done a shot in forever." I coughed again. "I think I need a chaser or something."

I looked around for a water or soda or something to stop the burning. Katie took the empty glass out of my hand and replaced it with a new one filled with more tequila.

"I got you covered," she said, nodding her head seriously, like she was actually being helpful.

"Um, not what I had in mind." The words were coming out sloppy.

My tongue felt heavy in my mouth. I followed Katie's lead and drank my shot with a quick tilt of my head anyway. The second shot went down much smoother than the first. This time I welcomed the fire that spread through me, and let it numb all the sadness still threatening to ruin my night. I looked over and saw Katie cringing, empty shot glass dangling from her fingers. Margot was laughing beside us, nursing her shot of water.

"Man up, lady." I motioned for Margot to finish her shot and ended up hitting myself in the mouth.

Katie and I started laughing like hyenas. She swiped at her eyes. "Okay, now we're ready."

Once again, Katie's hand found its way into mine, then she was dragging me behind her. My feet kept popping up in random places, making me stumble along the way. I laughed, tumbling into Katie's shoulder.

"You okay back there?" she asked, her words a little slurred. I nodded my head, a large, crooked smile spreading across my face.

She mumbled something I couldn't quite make out and pulled me to a stop at a truck near the dancing. Reaching inside the open driver's side door, she picked up a phone. Her fingers flew across the screen. Her face lit up when she found what she was looking for. "Here we go!"

Flinging the phone back onto the seat, she grabbed my hand and then reached for Margot's. A force of nature, she pulled us both to the dance floor just as the first notes of Demi Lovato's "Sorry Not Sorry" started playing from the speakers.

"Oh!" I clapped my hands together, jumping up and down. "I loooove this song!"

"Can't have this, can't have this!" Margot sang, already

moving to the music.

Katie and I joined her at the chorus, "Baby I'm sorry, I'm not sorry!"

We sang loudly, our words sounding slurred as they mingled with Margot's steady voice. The music mixed with the tequila flowing through me, making my eyes close and my hips move. Some switch flipped inside my head, turning off all the noise—even ignoring the evidence that Phase Three Evie had just been unleashed.

"Starboy" blared through the speakers, and I grabbed Katie's shoulders.

"I am totally in love with you."

Katie tipped her head back and let out another laugh, catching my arm in hers and spinning me around as my own laugh spilled out. It could have been all the alcohol, or the music, or the two women dancing along with me like we were the only people there, but something had silenced the little voice that played constantly on a loop in my head saying 'can't, don't, not for you.' I smiled to myself, letting the silence and the music flow through me as my body matched the rhythm coming from the speakers.

With our arms stretched toward the sky, heads back, we danced until I forgot that my heart was a little bit broken. When I saw Jack and Shelly reappear, I only briefly registered the flicker of hurt that flared in my chest as I watched Shelly storm off, because for the first time in a really long time, I felt completely weightless.

31.

Bottles of water in hand, we made our way back toward our seats.

"Seriously, she has the absolute worst ideas. Her freshman year, she was going to get her boyfriend's name tattooed on her back," Margot said, eyes wide in horror.

"A tramp stamp, with your boyfriend's name?" I asked, one eyebrow raised.

"It was going to be super tasteful!" Katie yelled, throwing her hands up. Her whole body moved forward with her arms.

Margot and I burst out laughing, reaching out to try and steady her. My eyes landed on the additions to the group we'd left to guard our spots. One in particular caused my smile to falter just a little. Jack's eyes landed on mine. Those eyes swept over my face and I looked away, focusing on Katie's defense of her tramp-stamp idea instead. I was not about to let him ruin the rest of my night. And in fairness to him, it wasn't like he was purposely ripping my heart out and stomping on it. It was negligent heart-stomping at most.

Seth and Cole turned at the sound of our laughter. Seth shook his head when he saw Katie leaning on Margot. He walked over and took his wife off of Margot's hands. Pulling her into his side, he smiled down at her. She looked up, returning his smile with a drunken one of her own.

"Hi I love you," she said, her words bleeding together.

"Yeah? Enough to get my name tattooed on your back?' he said, raising his eyebrows in a challenge. Katie tipped her head back on a laugh. "You smell like tequila. Please tell me you weren't doing shots?"

Katie vigorously shook her head 'no' just as a hiccup escaped my lips. I shrugged my shoulders as everyone in the little group chuckled.

"I'm extra glad you're pregnant right now." Cole placed his arm around Margot and gave her belly a little rub.

Everyone lapsed back into conversation, and my eyes bounced everywhere, trying not to land on Jack's face. His voice drifted all around me, though. I could make it out, low and rumbly and distinct from the others. The conversations drifted from a cow vaccination schedule to a football game, both topics I was equally clueless about.

"So I hear you're from Chicago?"

I turned toward the voice and immediately scrambled, trying to remember if we had been introduced earlier. I squinted my eyes, trying to make any connection at all happen. My brain felt like the little worm floating in a tequila bottle. I smiled, nodding my head and going for the 'act natural and not drunk' routine.

"Yep. I work for Ben Danver."

"Pretty big change, Chicago to Pine Hollow. How are you liking Montana?" nameless man asked.

I turned toward him, giving him my full attention. He was cute. Shoulder-length brown hair and brown eyes in a face that looked open and inviting. He had the kind of muscles that didn't come from a gym, the kind I was recognizing as a product of ranch life.

"It's definitely a big change, but I like it. A lot more than I thought I would," I replied honestly.

"Oh yeah? You're not begging Ben to let you fly back to civilization yet?" His tone sounded suspicious, and a little laugh burst out of me.

"No—I mean, I miss coffee shops being everywhere, but it's not awful here." I mentally high-fived myself for sounding way more sober than I felt.

He whistled loudly, causing a few heads to turn in our direction and heat to rush to my face.

"Wow, 'it's not awful.' That's some high praise right there." He rubbed a hand over his mouth like he was trying to wipe the smile off his face. "Is it the fact that there are more cows than people?"

"No but that's not exactly in the pro column." I leaned toward him like I was about to let him in on a secret. "It's the lack of pizza."

"Hey, now! We have a pizza place," he said, defending Pine Hollow's honor.

"One whole place?" The inflection in my voice gave away how unimpressive his argument was.

I felt heat cover my back like a blanket. Before I could turn my head to discover the heat source, a hand settled on the back of my neck, making me freeze. Goosebumps spread across my shoulders and down my arms, my body understanding before my brain.

"Jason, how's Fleet working out for you?"

Jack was standing so close that I felt the breath of his words rush past my ear. Every muscle in my body tensed.

"He's great, man. Fitting right in. He's turning out to be one of our best workers."
Jason's eyes moved to Jack's hand resting on my neck.

Jack's thumb began to trace a path up and down the side of my neck. I completely lost the ability to follow the conversation. All my concentration was focused on the movement of his thumb. Up, down. Up, down. A shiver traveled through me.

Jack's thumb stopped. He leaned his head down, his mouth almost kissing my ear.

"Are you cold?" His hands moved to my shoulder to turn me toward him.

"Yes. No. I don't know." I cringed.

Jack smiled, totally unfazed by my incoherent answer. Locking his eyes on my face, he tugged one arm out of his jacket and then the other. My heartrate accelerated to a level that had to be incompatible with life. Slowly, slowly, slowly he laid the jacket over my shoulders. On autopilot, I slipped my arms into the spaces his had just been. He grabbed the sides of the jacket and used them to pull me closer to him. In an effort to keep my heart from tearing out of my body, I focused my gaze on our feet. Somewhere near me, Jason made an excuse to leave and Jack answered for us both.

I held my breath as his hands tugged the jacket together, fastening the zipper, and then began tugging it up. I was literally being encased in his warmth. I fought the urge to inhale deeply, to breathe in that smell that was all uniquely him. His hands came to rest just under my collarbone, still clasping the zipper in his hands.

"Better?" His voice was so quiet that it came out as almost a whisper.

I almost told him that it was *not* better, that he had almost killed me. Instead, my hands moved of their own volition to cover his. I searched his face, looking for clues. I had no idea what was happening, why it felt like more than offering a friend your jacket. But I couldn't forget that these were the same hands Shelly had claimed earlier, and that this was the same man who had followed her to who-knew-where to do who-knew-what.

I sighed, pushing his hands away just enough to reach the zipper. I began dragging it back down reluctantly.

"I don't think I should be wearing this." My eyes had moved from his face to the path being traveled by the zipper.

His hands stopped my progress. "Why not?"

I summoned whatever was left of the tequila-fueled courage I'd had earlier. Dragging my eyes back to his, I tugged my lip between my teeth, trying to form an answer that didn't make me sound petty or jealous.

"I saw you with Shelly. I saw you leave with her. I don't think she would be happy you gave me your jacket." I tried to keep my voice void of emotion, as if I were simply stating a fact.

Jack's brows furrowed, the corners of his mouth tugging into a frown. He studied my face for what felt like forever, and then his frown transformed into a wide smile. The arrogant ass actually smiled, a bright flash of light against the dark.

"I don't really care what Shelly thinks."

I recoiled at his words, physically trying to distance myself from him. Anger quickly replaced the confusion and jealousy.

"Well, you should! And I do. You just… just went off with her alone to… and I don't want to be the kind of person who is okay with hurting someone's feelings even if I don't really like the person."

Every word that spilled from my mouth seemed to make his smile grow. He stepped into my space after a pause, making sure I was done with my lecture first.

"Nothing happened with Shelly."

His hands moved toward my hair, tucking the wayward strands behind my ears. He gathered up the unruly mass of waves tucked into his jacket and slipped them over the collar, sending them spilling past my shoulders.

Focus, Evie, I mentally chastised myself.

"I saw you with her." A little part of me begged me to shut up and stop fighting this. Okay, a big part of me. The biggest part of me.

"You saw me walk away with her, because it was too loud by the fire to talk. I needed her to hear me. We talked and she left. That's all." Sincerity radiated from him, and relief rushed through me.

"Oh." I forced the word out, looking down at my shoes while my brain and my heart warred over this new information. "What... um... what did you talk about?"

"How about I tell you later, when I'm sure you'll remember it the next day?" he said, a note of laughter in his voice.

My head snapped up and I stepped in closer to him, shaking my head furiously. It felt like his words had shifted something fundamental between us.

"No, I think now is good. I'm fine. I'm really good at remembering things. Well, except for everyone I met tonight's names. But there were a lot of them and I do remember a lot of them. Like that guy over there is Tom and the girl next to him is Sara."

I pointed at the first two people I saw standing just beyond us. Jack didn't bother turning to look. I was prepared to perform a field sobriety test if it got him to talk.

He smiled at me indulgently, moving back some of the hair I had shook loose. "I told her that I'm not interested, that whatever she thought was happening isn't because there's someone el—"

"Hey, are you guys ready to head out?" Margot's voice came from behind me.

I bit back a groan, refusing to break eye contact with Jack. I silently begged her to go away. I just needed a few more minutes in this moment.

"Yep, we're good," Jack answered.

I spun around and started walking toward Margot and Cole, feeling unreasonably annoyed. Jack caught up with me in no time, then Gabe appeared out of nowhere and joined our little procession.

"Where did you come from?" I asked him, noticing his shirt wasn't buttoned all the way up anymore.

He shot a boyish grin my way. "You don't want to know."

I shuddered. "Am I going to need a biohazard suit to sit next to you?"

Snickers erupted around us. Gabe chuckled, throwing his arm around my shoulder and dragging my body into his.

"Nah, it's all good, Evie. How'd you like your first Montana bonfire?"

"I liked it. I'm not sure it's safe to have a fire that big, though. I don't think Smokey the Bear would approve." I leaned into his body, suddenly feeling tired.

Cole hit the unlock button on his keys, and we all moved toward the flashing lights like insects to a flame. Gabe, Jack, and I slid into the back seat while Cole convinced Margot he was okay to drive us home.

Almost as soon as the truck started moving, my eyes started trying to close. It didn't help that I was sandwiched between two human space heaters. I stifled a yawn. My eyelids felt like they weighed a million pounds. Another small yawn managed to escape, and I gave up the fight and closed my eyes.

"No, I got her." Jack's voice stirred me. It sounded like it was coming from the opposite end of a long tunnel.

I was too tired to open my eyes when I felt myself being lifted out of the truck. I instinctively snuggled closer to the warmth. Jack's smell surrounded me. I felt myself being jostled, but didn't investigate—the pull of sleep was too strong.

Emily Mayer

I was perfectly comfortable in this cocoon. Then there was a warm, wet pressure on my forehead. The unexpected sensation made my eyelids flutter open, struggling against their own weight. They landed on a familiar form closing the door to my dark room.

32.

Hank Williams woke me up the next morning by shoving his wet nose in my face. I groaned and Hank whimpered.

I shoved myself upright, pausing to let my head catch up with the rest of my body. Stumbling into the bathroom, I flinched when I saw my reflection in the mirror. My hair was a tangled mess and my eye makeup was smudged all over my face, making it look like I was sporting two black eyes.

Hank headbutted my leg, drawing my attention away from the crime scene in the mirror. I slowly bent down to give him a reassuring head scratch.

"I know, buddy, I look like hot death. But hey, I actually feel worse than I look, so there's that."

I piled my hair on top of my head before scrubbing the makeup off my face. *Clothes, then coffee,* I promised my body. I slipped on the first pair of jeans I found on my floor and pulled on a sweater before I caught a glimpse of my boots sitting neatly next to my bed. Memories of the night before came flooding back to me: being lifted out of the truck, laid on the bed, what felt suspiciously like a kiss being placed on my forehead.

"Hank Williams, is there any chance you carried me to bed last night?" Hank walked past me and straight out the dog-sized crack in the door, which led me to my next question: How did this dog manage to get in and out of my room every day?

I decided I could overthink everything over a cup of coffee. Grabbing Jack's coat off my bed, I followed Hank out the door. At least I didn't need to worry about how I'd ended up in nothing but my underwear. I remembered waking up sometime in the middle of the night, fully dressed, and stripping off all my clothes.

The kitchen was eerily quiet for it being so late in the morning. Thankfully, there was still plenty of coffee left in the pot. I breathed in the smell, letting it rejuvenate me.

"She lives!"

Gabe's voice boomed behind me, making me jump and squeal. I whipped around to scowl at him, careful not to spill my coffee.

"Are you trying to kill me? My heart almost exploded," I grumbled, moving toward the breakfast bar. I sat on a stool and watched Gabe start moving around the kitchen.

"Feeling pretty good this morning, huh? I heard you and Katie went a couple rounds with a bottle of tequila last night," he said, pulling things out of the fridge.

"The tequila won. What are the odds that a McDonald's opened a convenient distance from this ranch overnight?" I would have given my remaining kidney for a greasy breakfast sandwich just then.

"Not good," Jack said from the doorway. My cheeks turned red as we made eye contact. I didn't know what the protocol was for the morning after someone carries you to bed and gives you a maybe-kiss on the forehead. Of all the things I'd slept through in my life, sleeping through that kiss was the worst.

Speak! a voice in my head urged me.

"A girl can dream," I sighed, turning my attention back to the steaming cup of salvation in front of me.

Jack poured himself a cup of coffee before joining Gabe at the stove. I watched as they began heating up two large skillets. I was genuinely curious about what was happening at the stove, and not just because I was hungry. I couldn't remember seeing either of them cook anything that didn't involve re-heating something in the microwave.

"What are you guys doing?" I asked, slightly concerned for my safety.

"Cooking," Gabe said, cracking eggs into a skillet.

Jack was buttering bagels like the two of them made breakfast together every morning. I really liked where this was going. I hoped they knew what they were doing, because my heart would be broken if this plan went up in flames. Literally or figuratively.

"Do you two know how to cook?"

Both men turned to give me a withering look. *Okay, then.*

"Yes, Evie, we know how to cook," Jack said, placing the buttered bagels on the other skillet. My stomach rumbled loudly. I was pretty sure I started drooling when I saw Jack hand Gabe a pack of ham. Holy hallelujah, they were making breakfast sandwiches!

"You guys look really domestic right now. It's kind of cute. You just need some aprons and it could be the cover of *Home and Garden*." I hid my smile behind my coffee mug.

Gabe reached over to swipe at me with the spatula. "Do you want this sandwich or not?"

I dodged the spatula, laughing. "That depends—will it have cheese?"

I heard Jack chuckle and I turned to smile at him. He held up cheese. My smile got bigger. He placed a gigantic sandwich on a plate and handed the plate to me. Without thinking, I said, "Oh God, I think I love you." My face flamed and I looked at the sandwich like it held the meaning of life. I hoped they both thought I was declaring my love to the sandwich.

I took a bite and groaned. I could really be in love with this buttery piece of heaven.

"Oh man, this is so good. Way better than McDonald's. I will never doubt your domestic abilities again."

Gabe and Jack joined me at the breakfast bar, and launched into a lengthy discussion about cows and whether they would need to burn a pasture this year. My attention was divided between the deliciousness I was inhaling and the maybe-kiss from last night.

"Do you want to help exercise the horses today?" I heard Jack ask.

I needed to get my phone out of my purse. I hoped the battery wasn't completely dead. There was no way my sisters would forgive me if I didn't tell them that Jack had carried me inside last night. Then a wadded-up napkin hit me in the head, forcing my attention to the two men.

"Yo, Earth to Evie," Gabe, the thrower of the napkin, yelled. "Do you want to help exercise the horses?"

My eyebrows shot up my forehead and I pointed a finger at myself. "Me? You were asking *me* if I wanted to help exercise the horses?" My disbelief was evident in my voice as I looked at Jack.

"Yeah, you. Do you want to help?" Jack asked, like that wasn't a life-altering question.

"Yes! I absolutely want to do that. I just have to help Ben with something this morning and then I'm all yours!"

I was practically bouncing in my seat with excitement. The wheels in my mind started turning, making all kinds of plans. Maybe if Jack trusted me more around the horses, he would be willing to let me help with King. Maybe there was a chance he could see me as more than some city girl pretending to belong here.

That last thought blindsided me. *Belong here?* Where had that come from? I was definitely the happiest I could remember being, here on the ranch, but I was on a quasi-vacation. Everyone was happier on vacation.

I reassured myself it was just the hangover and my intense love of this breakfast talking. But a small corner of my mind wasn't quite convinced.

33.

After breakfast, I took a quick shower and brushed my teeth. I headed to the office, and found Ben waiting for me.

"Hey, sorry I'm a little late."

I slid into my seat at the desk. Ben handed me a stack of folders I hadn't created. I stared at the pile in confusion, reading the labels Ben had made for each one.

"It's not a problem. Technically it's the weekend, so normal business hours don't apply. I also heard you got pretty cozy with a bottle of tequila last night."

I palmed my forehead in embarrassment. Information traveled at the speed of light around here. I cleared my throat. "That wasn't really my fault. I thought you were going to make an appearance?" I said, trying to change the topic.

"I was planning on it, but I started working on this and lost track of time." Ben motioned at the pile of folders sitting in front of me.

"What is all this?"

I was surprised and thrilled that Ben had come up with a project to work on. He was acting the way he had been before the board asked him to step away. When Ben was like this, he was totally in his element—unstoppable.

"I need you to help me find a new outside firm to work with us on the mergers and acquisitions we can't handle in-house."

My mouth dropped open. The calmness in his voice belied the enormity of what he was saying. It took me a couple of seconds to formulate the obvious follow-up question.

"Why do you think we need to hire a new firm?"

Alarms were going off in my head. Ben was going to fire Rodney's firm. This would be messier than a Kardashian divorce.

"I want to fire Rodney's firm, but I need to have every possible scenario planned before I bring it to the board," Ben said, confirming my suspicions.

"Why do you want to fire them? Sterling has worked with them for decades. This is going to be major, Ben." I tried to infuse some of his calmness into my voice.

This plan of Ben's could either prove how serious he was about running his family business well, or be one more thing to demonstrate to the board that he wasn't fit to lead the company.

"I do know this is going to involve an insane amount of planning and research, so it's a good thing I have a master planner working on it with me." He shot me a grin, and I rolled my eyes at his attempts at flattery. "Look, I did a little digging after it was brought to my attention that Rodney was getting a little handsy. The man's a serial sexual harasser, and some of his business practices are questionable at best. I might be calling the kettle black here, but I don't do business like that, and this is still my company."

I nodded my head, a spark of pride flaring in my chest. There was no way I wouldn't follow him on this.

"Okay. I'm assuming you've compiled all the complaints from HR, so I think we need to put that into some kind of comprehensive report. Chronologically would be best, to show that it's a long-term pattern. Next, we need to research what it would take to divest his firm." I started digging around in my bag for a notebook and pen.

"You read my mind. I'm going to go grab us both refills

while you start looking through the data I already compiled." Ben stood, grabbing a coffee mug off the desk.

I immediately outlined a plan of action, leaving space to fill in additional steps along the way. Ben reappeared with mugs in hand and explained how he had organized the folders in front of me.

I lost track of time, sifting through the information and organizing it into a more cohesive format. Jack's voice from the doorway drew my attention away from the computer screen.

"Hey, you ready for a break?" he asked, his gaze directed at me.

"Oh... um... I'm not sure—"

Ben cut me off. "Yes, go take a break. I need to take one too."

He didn't have to tell me twice. I took off my reading glasses and quickly tidied up my corner of the desk, making sure to mark the spot where I'd left off. Jack waited patiently for me at the door. I smiled up at him and apologized for making him wait.

"I don't mind waiting for you." His response was so casual, like he hadn't even had to think before answering. This poor heart of mine.

We stopped in the mudroom so I could slip my boots on. Jack disappeared and returned with a cloth bag.

"What's in there?" I asked, pointing at the bag.

"I thought we could take the horses out on a trail and find a spot to have lunch," he said, pulling his own boots on.

"Really? A trail ride and a picnic?" I sounded doubtful because it seemed too good to be real life.

"Yeah—is that okay?" He opened the door and motioned for me to go first.

I turned to look at him so he could see the sincerity written on my face when I said, "'Okay'? It sounds like the perfect day to me!"

I followed Jack to the barn and waited while he disappeared around the corner to get the horses we would be taking out. A few minutes later, he was leading two horses down toward where I stood. One of the horses was such a dark brown that it almost looked black except for a white stripe down the nose; the other's coat was white and sprinkled with brown spots. He hooked the dark horse to the wall, and walked a little closer to me before tying the second one. He motioned for me to join him.

"This is Gypsy. She's one of my favorite ladies here," Jack said, stroking her neck affectionately.

"It's nice to meet you, Gypsy." I held my hand out to her. "She's such a pretty horse."

Gypsy pushed on my hand with her nose in approval. I gave her nose a tentative stroke.

"She's an Appaloosa. They're known for their spotted coats. She's got a little more speed than Photo, but she's a much better trail horse. I think you can handle her."

My insides warmed at his compliment. Any nerves I had at taking a horse out on the trail for the first time were momentarily forgotten.

"I think so too. Should I get her all ready to go?"

Jack let out a whistle, a sly grin on his face that was nothing short of devastating.

"Look at you, city girl."

"Hilarious. Laugh it up now, cowboy; pretty soon I'll be riding circles around you," I fired back, already placing the saddle blanket on Gypsy's back.

Jack smiled back at me, lifting the saddle onto Gypsy's back for me before making quick work of getting his horse ready.

"Okay, I think I'm going to try to mount Gypsy without using a mounting block. I feel like I'm strong enough to haul myself all the way up there," I said, more to myself than Jack, once we were out of the barn.

"Uh, thanks for letting me know?" Jack was watching me, holding the reins in his hand.

"So can you please turn around?' I made a swiveling motion with my finger.

"You want me to turn around?"

"Yes, so…" I repeated the swivel motion. Visions of the first time I'd tried mounting a horse without help were playing on repeat in my head.

"Why?" he asked, looking at me with his head tilted a little to the side, like I was an abstract painting he couldn't quite figure out.

"I don't want an audience in case things go south, and there's a fifty-fifty chance this will end badly."

One of Jack's brows winged up skeptically.

"Fine, seventy-thirty," I said, amending my previous statement to more accurately reflect the odds of me ending up on the ground.

He seemed satisfied with the odds and turned around with a little huff. I waited to the count of five just to make sure he wasn't going to try to sneak a glance over his shoulder and witness me going down like the Titanic, then I placed my foot in the stirrup and hauled myself up. I wouldn't have won any awards, but I was up! I did a little happy dance in the saddle, careful not to upset Gypsy. I looked up to see Jack watching me. Gone was the inscrutable expression he normally wore, and in its place was one of genuine happiness.

"You looked!" I accused, not even a little bit mad that he

had seen me in action, complete with a happy dance.

"I didn't want to miss your first solo mount. I knew you could do it," he answered smoothly. He turned to place his foot in the stirrup and I leaned forward, watching him swing himself up into the saddle in one fluid motion that left me breathless.

He turned his head back and I shifted upright in the saddle, hoping there was no drool visible.

"You ready?" he asked, oblivious as always to the destruction he was wreaking on my body.

I motioned Gypsy forward and we set off side by side.

34.

Life was so weird. A couple of weeks ago if you had told me I'd be riding alongside a genuine cowboy on a trail in Montana, I would've said you were nuts. But here I was, riding next to Jack, feeling like there was absolutely no place else on earth I would rather be than in Pine Hollow, Montana. Except Paris.

"What?" Jack finally asked, after about the twelfth time he caught me staring at him.

I shook my head. "Nothing. I'm just happy to be here," I answered genuinely. "Thanks for inviting me."

He smiled at me, and I briefly wondered if this was the same man who, just a handful of days ago, I'd thought never did anything without a scowl.

"I'm happy you're here, too."

I just smiled like an idiot to prevent myself from spouting something ridiculous like 'I'm happy that you're happy I'm here.' Even though I totally was.

Jack, the consummate tour guide for the state of Montana, pointed out things he thought might interest me along the trail, until we reached a clearing in the trees. I looked around, realizing we were actually somewhere above the valley and we could see the river cutting through the mountains and fields below. I sucked in a sharp breath.

"Oh wow" were the only words I could come up with, staring in awe at my surroundings. "Jack, this is amazing."

"Not a bad place for a picnic." He swung down and secured his horse to a nearby tree branch. He walked toward us and took hold of Gypsy's reins, presumably so I could dismount.

I looked down at him from my perch. "We're eating here?"

"Yeah, is that okay?"

"Are you kidding? This place is amazing! We can eat every meal here." I executed a mediocre dismount and immediately reached for my phone. I snapped some pictures that probably could have been the next cover of a *National Geographic* magazine before sneaking a few shots of Jack securing Gypsy next to his horse. Those pictures could have been on the cover of a different type of magazine.

He pulled a Thermos and two cups out of one saddle bag, then moved around to retrieve the lunch bag from the other side. I smiled as he walked toward me, already sure this was the best picnic I had ever been, and would probably ever be, on. I hobbled to join him on the smooth rock of the overlook. We sat next to each other, looking out over the valley below.

Jack handed me a chicken salad sandwich from the bag and poured us each a cup of lemonade from the Thermos. I racked my brain trying to think up a topic of conversation that would be perfect for a picnic.

"So, bull sperm." Yep, that was what came out of my mouth. I closed my eyes in horror for a moment. If my sandwich wasn't so good, I might have jumped off the cliff.

Jack coughed a little, covering his mouth with his hand. He swallowed, clearing his throat. "Could you be more specific?"

"I saw the contracts you've been working on with Rodney and Ben," I rushed to clarify. "The ones for bull sperm."

"Oh, right. You caught me a little off-guard there. Cole and I are working on expanding our breeding program, which involves a lot more legal paperwork than it used to when things were just done the old-fashioned way," Jack explained, taking a bite of his sandwich.

"The old-fashioned way?" I asked, watching his jaw work.

"Just letting the bull loose in a pasture full of females and seeing what happens."

"And now?" I prompted. I had done a little bit of research about new bull breeding programs when I'd stumbled across the paperwork, but I'd been short on time and was left with a lot of questions.

"Now, bulls are selected based on pretty extensive genetic testing and their—" he paused, his cheeks turning red— "semen can be purchased and shipped all over the world. Bulls with superior genetics can go for upward of a hundred grand at auction."

"That's insane! How do they get it out? You know what, please pretend I didn't ask that question. I don't think I want to know." I was picturing little rooms with cow porn and a cup. "It seems like it's going well?"

"Yeah, my dad and grandad were pretty old school, but I wanted to take our program in a different direction. I got interested in the new genomic testing after hearing a talk about it at an auction, and got involved through the American Angus Association. DNA testing helps take a lot of the risk out of breeding livestock. It's not our entire breeding program, but I want to make sure Pinehaven is keeping up. Cole and I are using some of the same techniques with the horse program here, too. The horse-breeding community was using this kind of science a long time ago, though. Mom always says ranchers are as stubborn as their herd."

I listened to him talk about cattle and watched his entire being shift. It was obvious that ranching was his passion. I knew my face never looked like that when I talked about law. The law never inspired that kind of passion in me, and I was reluctantly starting to accept that it never would.

"You like working with horses more than cattle, right?" I

wanted to know every little thing that made him tick.

"I love working with horses, but being a cattle rancher is in my blood, you know? I mean, it's not always glamorous, sleeping under the open sky and all that, but I love working out here. I don't know how Ben does what he does. How you do." He shot a self-deprecating smile my way. "I swear I didn't bring you out here to talk about bull sperm."

Jackpot. Now we were getting to the good stuff.

"Why did you bring me out here?" I dipped my toe into the uncharted waters with a mix of caution and hope.

Jack turned to face me more fully, and I was once again trying to convince myself that I was really here having a picnic with this beautiful, surprising man in this equally beautiful, surprising place.

"I didn't really have a plan. I just wanted to spend some time with you." His eyes held mine, trying to judge the impact of his words.

I forced myself to maintain eye contact despite the pink creeping up my face. "I'm glad you asked me," I answered, offering him my own truth. "And I have something I wanted to talk to you about, actually."

I was laying all my cards on the table. The new and slightly improved Evelyn Irene Mercer did not need anyone else to fight her battles.

"What's on your mind?" Jack asked, sounding genuinely curious. Or maybe I was just hearing what I wanted to hear.

"Okay, promise you won't get mad? I don't think I could find my way back to Pinehaven alone. I wasn't paying very close attention to where we were going."

"I promise." Jack smiled indulgently, making an X over his heart.

I took a deep breath, trying to calm my racing heart. New

and slightly improved Evelyn was hard on my cardiovascular system.

"Let me help with King." I ripped the Band-Aid right off.

Jack's eyes searched mine again. "Why do you want to help with King?"

The lack of animosity in his voice bolstered my confidence even more. "Because I think I can."

My answer was simple and honest, and I hoped it was enough. I hoped *I* was enough for Kingpin—for Jack. He looked out over the valley before turning back to look at me.

"Okay." He said, just one word. Easy as pie.

Almost before he finished his sentence, I was on my knees and throwing my arms around him. A *oomph* left his lips when my body collided with his. He hesitated for less than a second and then I felt his arms wrap around me.

"Thank you! Thank you, Jack! You're not going to regret it, I promise." I pulled back from our impromptu hug to smile up at him.

His arms tightened, preventing me from completely breaking free of his embrace. His smile softened. "I'm sorry about the first time you asked." One hand moved to cup my face, thumb brushing across my cheek. "I should have at least heard you out."

I couldn't resist leaning into his hand, just in case this was the only chance I ever got to feel his hands on my face.

"So you didn't mean what you said? About me just getting in the way and you not having time to babysit some city girl?" I said, just in case he had forgotten the exact words he'd used to shoot me down the first time.

"Nah, I meant what I said." He laughed as both my hands came to rest on his chest and I shoved myself out of his arms with a huff. "I could have been nicer about it though, I guess."

"You guess," I grumbled, picking up what was left of my sandwich.

"I admit I might be a little rusty at the whole apology thing," he said, the corner of his mouth tugging upward.

"Well, you know what they say: Practice makes perfect."

This picnic was definitely going better than I planned. I had gotten a really good hug that was reciprocated, a lingering face touch that I would likely daydream about for the rest of my natural life, Jack had agreed to let me help with King, and this chicken sandwich was one of the best things I had ever eaten.

35.

I wandered into the kitchen the next morning to find all five men huddled around the table, looking at a large piece of paper spread out across the surface. I moved closer, trying to catch a glimpse of whatever it was that had captured everyone's attention, and wedged my way in between Jack and Gabe.

"What's going on?" I asked, peering up at Jack and then down at the paper, which looked like blueprints for a new house.

Jack wrapped an arm around my waist, tucking me in closer to his side. I fought to control the blush I could feel starting to work its way up my chest. This felt dangerously close to a public display of affection.

"It's a goat enclosure," he answered, pointing to the structure with a pencil. His voice sounded resigned.

"A what, now?" I leaned forward to get a closer look at the drawing, as if I might be able to understand the plans if I just looked a little closer.

"Mom wants to rescue a bunch of pygmy goats," Ben supplied, looking a little more amused than everyone else in the room.

"So, the most useless kind of useless animal," Jack added.

"I like goat cheese. A lot." I felt the inexplicable need to offer up some defense on behalf of the poor creatures.

"Do you want to build them a shelter, then? Because Mary has some very specific requirements." Gabe shot me a questioning look that placed him firmly in the anti-tiny-goat camp.

"No, I don't. I also don't think I could build anything. When are the little nuggets coming home?"

"Tomorrow," Cole said, his mouth tugged into a frown.

"Wow. Well, good luck with all this." I motioned to the paper with my hand, then let Ben know I was going to head to the office to get some work done on the proposal. Jack tugged me a little closer, catching me slightly off-guard. His fingers gently squeezed my hip, causing a chain reaction of squeezing in my stomach region and lower.

"We need to head out, too. See if we can get this lumber cut on short notice." Jack nodded at Gabe.

"Fingers crossed we can't." Gabe held up one hand with his middle finger crossed over his pointer.

"Man, you guys are really down on the tiny goats. I think they're going to be a great addition!" I meant it, too. Pygmy goats were adorable. I was already looking forward to sending videos to Celeste of the little nuggets hopping around, and Letty would absolutely lose her mind when she saw them.

Jack leaned down and planted a kiss on my head, rendering me momentarily stunned. "I'll see you later."

Kiss kiss kiss pinged around in my brain. His hand gave one last squeeze, obliterating the few brain cells I had left. I stood like a statue, "Girl Whose Brain Died by Kiss." My heart was pounding so fast in my chest that there was a real chance my coffee was now unnecessary.

"Okay yeah bye," I finally managed on a quick exhale. I shot furtive glances around the table to see if everyone else was as weirded out by that kiss as I was. I mean, it was the best head-kiss of my life and I definitely wanted more; I wanted to collect them like some people collect stamps. I just hadn't expected our second head-kiss to be in front of a group of people, especially when I had zero clue what we were doing. I darted out of the room before any of the remaining men could ask me any questions. I had no answers to give, and enough of my own questions to keep me plenty busy. Does he kiss all his lady friends on the head? I remembered him kissing Margot the night I met her, but he hadn't seen her in a while. I saw him every day! That made a lot of difference. And what did a girl have to do around here to get a kiss on the mouth?

I sank into the desk chair, mind still racing a little, and pulled up my inbox. My stomach let out an angry growl and I realized I forgotten to grab a muffin on my way out of the kitchen. Jack's kiss was so mind-blowing I actually forgot about food. If I ever did get that elusive full kiss, I'd probably be comatose. I grabbed my phone and sent Ben a text, begging him to drop off a muffin before he headed out to get in everyone's way building the goat house. I pictured being him just slightly handier than I was, in the sense that he could afford to hire someone else to build things. I was relegated to the least shady people I could find on Craigslist or begging my landlord.

The food situation handled, I pulled up Anna's latest email, Anna and Hilari were performing routine checks on my apartment to make sure I didn't have to evict dust bunnies the size of watermelons when I got home, or come back to find my television gone, and giving me all the important updates on life back in Chicago. Mainly hot-button issues, like Susan's reign of terror in the accounting department, which had started two months ago when she'd tried to give up smoking; whether my weird downstairs neighbor was trying to seduce the mailman (she was, everyone in our building knew it); and confirming their growing suspicion that the new "crazy-hot" spin instructor was gay. I clicked reply and watched the little dash blink while my fingers hovered above the keyboard trying to decide where to start.

Hey Ladies!

I miss you both! I'm sorry to hear that Paul's gay, but let's be real, we all saw this coming. Sorry for your loss, Hil. RIP Paul Jr., you were never meant to be, but I'm sure you would have gotten your father's drool-worthy pectorals and perfect bubble butt. Word on the street is that someone filed multiple complaints against Susan with HR for creating a hostile work environment, but you didn't hear it from me.

I added a couple of winky face emojis, because it just felt right.

In Montana news, something is happening with Jack. More specifically with me and Jack. I'm not exactly sure what that something is, though. I think we went on a date yesterday, but it's all pretty unclear, since the word date was never actually used. This morning there were two public displays of affection! Two! *Okay, so, when I type this out, it sounds like I'm just a crazy person, but I swear something has changed. Ugh, I wish I could just pass him a note that says "Do you like me? Circle yes or no." Also, we're getting pygmy goats! There will be a photoshoot.*

Evie

After I hit send, it dawned on me that I had used "we" instead of "they" or "Pinehaven." Even more startling, I'd meant it. This place was carving out a bigger and bigger piece of my heart with each passing day, and I had no idea how to go about getting it back. More importantly, it was becoming painfully clear that I didn't really want it back.

36.

There were people who actually enjoyed doing legal research, and no one would ever convince me that those were not the same people who never looked appropriately horrified when people discussed serial killers. I had been delving deep into the legal research database for hours, and was at the point where I was daydreaming about exciting things I would rather be doing, like getting a root canal or a Brazilian wax.

Ben had "taken a break" from helping with the construction of the goat house to join me in the office. Pretty sure he'd been voted off the island, but I wasn't going to kick the guy when he was down and also carrying an extra plate of lunch with him. I was feeling extra generous after my stomach was full, and let Ben put on his playlist. Less than an hour later, I was regretting my generosity and feeling restless.

Had I spent an embarrassing amount of time replaying the kitchen kiss in my head? Yes. Had I spent an even longer amount of time coming up with ways to trick Jack into kissing me on the lips? Also yes. Did I have to cross my legs and shift awkwardly in my seat, trying to relieve some of the friction when my plotting turned into some steamy fantasies? God, yessssss.

You'd think the fact that his brother was sitting mere feet away from me would have acted like a cold bucket of water, but it really, really didn't. Furthermore, this was mostly Ben's fault for choosing a throwback playlist featuring all the hits from when I had been a teen. It was clearly triggering all those long- dormant, now- raging hormones.

I closed my eyes and stretched my arms toward the ceiling, wishing I could make a latte magically appear. Then I heard footsteps getting louder and louder out in the hall. I opened my eyes to find Jack standing in the doorway, holding two to-go cups, and a little pink bag I recognized from our trip to Sweetheart's. I rubbed my eyes, convinced I had finally snapped and was hallucinating. When I opened my eyes, Jack was standing in front of me with a curious look on his face, like he didn't know quite what to make of me.

"Hi," I said, gazing up at him from where I sat. "I thought I was seeing things."

He chuckled, and then this wonderful, sweet man said the most beautiful thing: "I brought you a latte. There's a brownie in there, too."

I love you! "Thank you, Jack! This is amazing. I was literally just wishing I could make a latte appear."

"You're welcome. I thought you might actually kill me if I didn't bring you back one." He shot me a little wink that made me momentarily forget my own name. "Ben, I hope you still like Americanos."

"I like anything with caffeine in it right now," Ben said through a yawn, taking the cup from Jack's hand. "Though I am a little offended that you know Evelyn's order and had to guess about mine."

"Yeah, she's a hell of a lot prettier than you."

What? What?! He thinks I'm pretty!

Jack turned his grin my way. I sat in my chair with my mouth gaping, doing a pretty good impression of a deer in the headlights. I was picturing a billboard with the words *Jack Danver Thinks Evelyn Mercer Is Pretty* in some prime real estate located in downtown Chicago—something understated, that could be seen from space—when Jack swooped down and placed a kiss on my cheek. The cheek! So much closer to where

I really wanted to feel his lips.

"I'll let you get back to work. I need to help get that lumber unloaded before Mom drives everyone crazy."

"You're pretty... I mean you're welcome... I mean okay, thank you." Some not-insignificant part of myself was dying, listening to me botch what should have been an easy response.

Jack shot me one more mind-melting grin before heading back out the way he had come.

"Smooth," Ben said.

I spun around in my chair to face him with the wild, desperate eyes of someone who wanted to pretend the past few seconds had never happened. "That was bad, right?"

"Oh, yeah." Ben nodded his head in agreement.

"Will you fire me so I can go back to Chicago right now and pretend like that never happened?" I pleaded.

"Not a chance. I'm enjoying watching this way too much."

At least I had a latte to drown my sorrows in.

37.

The sound of saws and hammers echoed through the quiet house for the rest of the afternoon and well into the evening. Ben had eventually abandoned me to help the menfolk, leaving me alone with all my raging hormones. I didn't last much longer before making my way out to King's enclosure—at least that was the lie I was telling myself. I was just taking the long way there, to stretch my legs after sitting all day. If that route just so happened to take me past where the goat house was being built, it was just a happy coincidence, totally unplanned.

I followed the sound of hammering and country music until I reached the new enclosure. Two things immediately caught my attention. First, there was a herd of sweaty, tool-wielding men playing out some handyman fantasy I hadn't known I had until that very minute. Second, the goat house was freaking adorable! It was a surprisingly large two-story structure, with scalloped trim and a balcony in the works. It looked less like a shed and more like a playhouse.

My eyes scanned the group of men until they landed on the person I would've been looking for if it hadn't been just a co-incidence that I'd walked by the construction site. Hat backward, Jack was bent over a table with a pencil in his mouth and a ruler stretched out across a piece of wood. I watched, completely mesmerized, as he took the pencil out of his mouth to make several marks on the beam before lifting the saw and cutting along the marks. And then, *and then*, he reached for the bottom of his t-shirt and lifted it to wipe the sweat off his forehead. I caught a sliver of perfect abs and what I was pretty sure was the start of a tantalizing V that pointed directly to the promised land.

My ovaries exploded like two fireworks on the Fourth of July. Boom. Bang. Sizzle. By the time the bottom of his shirt had drifted back to its proper place I knew I would never be the same. I silently gave thanks for the unseasonably warm September evening.

"Enjoying the show?" The sound of Gabe's voice startled me out of my fantasy world.

I opened and closed my mouth like a fish flopping around on dry land.

"I just came to see if you guys needed any water because staying hydrated is important," I said, all on a single rush of breath and way too high-pitched to fool anyone.

"Sure you were, perv. I think I have a dollar if you want to shove it in his pants." Gabe reached toward the back pocket of his jeans. I swatted his arm away.

"Shouldn't you be…" I paused, searching the remnants of my brain for the name of a tool. "…hammering something?"

He shook a box of nails I hadn't noticed earlier. "Hard to hammer things without nails."

"Hey." The low rumble of Jack's voice made me whip my head around like a kid who'd just gotten caught with her hand in the cookie jar.

He gave me a crooked smile that had color flooding my cheeks and my head swirling as his boot-covered feet ate up the ground between us.

"Hi," I said, doing my best impression of a totally calm and unaffected human. I noticed his hair was getting long. It curled out from under his hat in a way I found inexplicably attractive. I wanted to run my fingers through those curls. It also confirmed my suspicion that I'd never actually grown out of my "backward hats are so hot" phase.

"Are you okay?" A furrow appeared between Jack's brows. His concerned eyes darted between mine and then performed a quick body scan.

So much for the calm, unaffected act. I could cross *actress* off my list of potential new careers.

"Evie is trying to earn her first-aid patch, so she came by to make sure we're staying hydrated. Right, scout?" Gabe inserted on my behalf. I elbowed him in the ribs, causing him to chuckle and Jack to look mildly concerned for our collective sanity.

"I just wanted to stretch my legs so I thought I'd come see how the goat shed was coming along. It looks awesome! Like one of those tiny homes on HGTV." I shot Gabe a look which I hoped he understood meant 'play along or I'll separate your balls from your body.'

"I can't believe this is for a bunch of goats." Jack lifted the hat up and ran his hand through his damp hair, giving a sigh that was echoed by the remnants of my ovaries.

Gabe announced he was delivering the nails to Cole, and sauntered off in that direction wearing a smug smile.

"Well, I think they're going to love their new home. I can't wait to see the looks on their little goat faces when they see it," I said, once again playing the role of goat defender.

Jack turned to face me more fully, placed both hands on my hips and gently tugged me closer to him. Warmth spread outward from where his hands were resting and traveled throughout my body.

"They would have been just as happy living in a shed." His eyes had that little shine to them that told me he wasn't really upset.

My gaze darted over his shoulder to the handful of men

who could clearly see Jack's hands on me again, and I wondered if they were as confused about the whole thing as I was. I recognized that the smart, mature thing to do would be to ask him for clarification, but that might mean an end to all the touches and almost-kisses. As it turned out, that was a risk I was not willing to take.

I turned my focus back toward the man standing in front of me and moved one hand tentatively up to rest on his chest. My fingers brushed lightly over his shirt at first, cautiously exploring the foreign territory. When I felt reasonably confident he didn't mind the first hand, I moved my other hand up to join it, marveling at the solid wall of muscle beneath them. I almost let out a pleased sigh.

"These poor goats deserve a cute little house after everything they've been through."

Jack smiled at my response. This variety of smile did not bode well for me. "Do you actually know anything about these goats?"

I searched my mind for any mention of their past, and came up empty. "They're pygmy goats? And... yep, that's it."

His smile morphed into a smug grin. Being this close to him, combined with the smell of sweat and leather and just a hint of something all man, was starting to make me feel a little drunk.

"They lived on a nice farm with a very loving family and a very ordinary shed," Jack informed me, hands squeezing my hips for emphasis.

"Oh. I thought you said your mom was rescuing these goats? It doesn't sound like they needed rescuing."

"They're an older couple, looking to sell their land and move into town. Mom heard about their plan to downsize at church and didn't want the goats to be split up. She's been going on about goats for years, so this was the excuse she's been waiting for."

"Aww, these goats are going to be going through a major life change. It's very important that they have a space where they can feel safe. You want them to feel welcome at Pinehaven, right?" My mouth was moving, but most of my attention was focused on my fingers dancing lightly across Jack's chest. Truthfully, I really didn't care that much about goats right now.

"Not really," Jack responded flatly.

I laughed, smiling up at him. "Okay, okay, you hate the goats. Your mom's really excited, though. She's cooking up a feast as a thank-you for getting their house together so quickly." I dragged the next words out of my mouth. "I should let you get back to work. I'm going to swing by and say hello to King."

I took a step back, letting my hands drop from the chest I wanted to burrow further into, but Jack tugged me closer before I broke free. He leaned in closer and placed a kiss on my forehead, making my breath catch. I glanced up at him, trying to figure out what was going on in that mind of his—and hoping whatever it was meant more of this.

"All right, I'll see you at dinner." He released my hips with a final squeeze, and started walking toward the enclosure. "Tell King I said hi."

And I did. I told King hi for Jack, and all about the kisses. When he didn't offer much insight, I convinced him to be my wingman, then headed inside to see what I could do to help Mary with the thank-you dinner. All the while, my head was busy dreaming up possibilities.

38.

Dinner was mostly the guys sweeping through the kitchen like a hurricane, stacking their plates insanely high with food and then heading back out to finish the goat house. I spent the remainder of dinner alone with Mary, rambling about absolutely anything I could think of in an effort to avoid any questions after she saw Jack drop a quick kiss to the top of my head on his way out the door. I had no answers to give, a fact made extra uncomfortable given that Mary was his mother. I imagined that conversation going something like Mary asking if Jack and I were seeing each other and me responding with "Visually, yes, we see each other."

I spent what felt like an eternity helping Mary do dishes while she snuck glances out the window to *ooh* and *ahh* over the goat house, then headed to the office to work a little more on the divestment project for Ben. I knew he'd want to present it at the next board meeting, which was scheduled for the end of the month—a deadline that was suddenly looming large in the back of my mind.

Now that Rodney was gone, I felt freer to wander the house in the evenings. The guys had finished painting the goat house about an hour earlier, and everyone had disappeared to their rooms or their own house for the night. The house was quiet, so I decided it was probably safe to wander downstairs in my grey sleep shorts and long-sleeved pajama top to investigate whether the TV in the living room had Netflix on it. I was tired of watching TV on my laptop; it felt like I was back in my college dorm room.

I flipped on the light in the living room and grabbed a

throw blanket off the back of the couch. I dug around for the remote control and confirmed that there was indeed Netflix on the TV. I clicked on my guilty-pleasure show of the moment, and nestled into the corner of the couch. A few minutes later, I heard soft footsteps padding down the stairs, coming to stop behind the couch. I tilted my head back to see Jack standing behind the couch, grinning down at me.

"Hi," I managed to squeak out, pressing *pause* and scooting myself upright. "I thought everyone would be asleep." I felt a little guilty and a whole lot strange, sitting on someone else's couch watching their TV, even though I was sure no one would mind.

"Couldn't sleep." His voice sounded raspy, tired.

Jack moved around the couch, and my eyes took in the flannel pajama pants slung low on his hips and the worn-looking t-shirt with *Pinehaven Ranch* stamped across it. He sat down next to me, close enough that our thighs were pressed against each other, and draped his arm across my shoulder. My body switched to autopilot, stiffening as soon as his arm met my shoulders and relaxing when he reached down to scoop up my legs and deposit them over his own. I sat like a limp noodle while he repositioned my body so that it was nestled into his side. I was tucked so close against him that I could feel the light scratch of the stubble lining his jaw on my forehead.

"Comfortable?" I felt the question rumble through his chest more than I heard it.

I nodded my head, mind racing as fast as my heart.

"What are we watching?" he asked, reaching for the remote and pressing play.

"Hmmm? Oh, the new season of *Queer Eye for the Straight Guy*." I turned away from staring at his profile to watch the show.

"What, now?"

"It's a makeover show, where a group of really awesome gay men help a blah straight guy get it together. I'm a sucker for a makeover show."

Jack chuckled. "This is what you watch?"

"I watch lots of things, and this is a great show." I gave him a gentle poke in the chest. "Who knows, you might even learn something!"

His head snapped toward me, a look of disbelief on his face. "Did you just call me a blah straight guy?"

I laughed, giving his pajamas a little tug.

"You do wear a lot of flannel, and you need a haircut."

He shook his head, a grin tugging up one corner of his mouth. "Rough crowd. I've never gotten any complaints before."

I rolled my eyes playfully at him. "Just watch the show."

Jack obeyed, turning toward the television. I was too busy listening to the sound of Jack's heart beating steadily to pay much attention to the show, but I felt slightly vindicated every time I caught him smiling or chuckling. Eventually, the sound of his heartbeat and the rhythm of his breathing started to lull me to sleep.

His shifting arm jostled my head a little, making me reluctantly peel my eyes open.

"Sorry, my arm was starting to fall asleep. I didn't mean to wake you up." His eyes searched my face, taking in my sleepy eyes and disheveled hair. I sent up a silent prayer that I hadn't been drooling.

"I can move." I started to sit up, but Jack's arm tightened around me, locking me in place.

"Stay. I like you like this," he said, his voice low and filled with something that sounded a lot like tenderness. It was my turn to search his face, looking for what 'this' meant. I was pretty sure he didn't mean half-conscious.

"You do make a pretty good pillow," I managed, my voice matching his.

A small laugh traveled through his chest. "I can see that," he responded, his hand moving to sweep a few stray hairs off my face. The backs of his fingers gently traced a path from my forehead to my chin, following the lines of my face. He reached up, tugging my bottom lip free of my teeth, then brushing the rough pad of his thumb across the freed lip. His eyes searching for permission, he cupped my face and touched his mouth to mine. He moved away just enough to press his lips against one corner of my mouth and then the other before capturing my lips.

All the thoughts racing through my head stopped, and my heart kicked a frantic rhythm in my chest as he urged my lips to move. I slanted my lips against his before tilting my head so I could deepen the angle. I heard what sounded like a growl coming from his throat, and then his tongue licked the seam of my lips. I opened my mouth on a sigh. He took full advantage of the access granted to him. His tongue swept my mouth before tangling with mine over and over again.

Suddenly, my body was too far from his, and I was scrambling to get closer. I shifted to bring one leg over his lap, and pressed my soft chest against his solid one. A moan escaped him when I rubbed my chest against his, relishing the contrast. His hands traveled up my back, one tangling into my mass of hair to hold my head where he wanted it. My entire body felt like it was electric, like it needed to move more than it needed the next breath. I rotated my hips tentatively at first, trying to relieve some of the friction building up in long-forgotten parts of my body. A growl came from Jack's throat, his hands traveling to my butt, pulling me more tightly against him. He tore his mouth away to trail wet kisses down my neck, nibbling on the hollow between my ear and neck and making my hips move faster.

Some part of me recognized that I was shamelessly grinding myself against this man in full view of anyone who happened to walk by, but that part was quickly silenced by the pulse beating between my legs. The next moan echoing through the silence definitely belonged to me. Jack lifted his mouth from my neck and rested his forehead against mine. We were both breathing heavily. He squeezed his eyes closed like he needed to catch his breath.

The heat created by his kisses and the feel of him pressed against my chest started to recede and my quiet mind started getting louder. Doubts sprang forward. Did he not feel the same way I felt? Why did he stop? What was I doing?

"We should stop." His voice was rough. It sounded like the voice he had used that day in the barn before walking away from me.

My heart plummeted as his words sank in, and I scrambled to get off his lap before he could see the tears starting to well in my eyes. God, I was such an idiot.

"I'm sorry, I should just go or—"

Jack cut me off before I could finish my train of thought, tugging me back onto his lap and winding his arms tightly around me. My head came to rest on his shoulder, and I turned to press my forehead into the nook between his neck and chin. His pulse was beating as wildly as mine.

"Don't run off on me now, Evie. I don't want to let you go yet." His hands traveled a soothing path up my back. "Not when you feel this good."

I sighed, content to be in his arms. The movement of his hand quieted the riot in my brain enough for me to think a little more clearly.

"Jack, what are we doing?" My voice was a whisper.

"I thought that was pretty obvious." I could hear the smile in his voice. "Making out on the couch."

"Why?" I hated how unsteady my voice sounded.

Jack lifted his hips up so I could feel his hardness pressing into the juncture between my thighs. "Because I want you, but not here where anyone could see. I want you to be able to look Ben in the eye tomorrow."

I needed more clarification. As much as I wanted this man, wanted to finish what we had just started, I knew I wasn't the one-and-done type. I couldn't sleep with someone and pretend like nothing had happened. I could try, or just flat-out lie to both of us, but somehow I knew that would just be setting myself up for a broken heart. My hormones might be begging me to pretend just this once, but I was smart enough to know better. It was who I was, and for better or worse, I would never change that for anyone.

I let out a miserable sigh. "I can't have sex with you. Not just sex. I'm not good at it."

Jack made a choking noise, his hands pausing briefly. "You're not good at it? I would have to disagree pretty strongly. You were doing great."

"What?" I said, confused. I played back my words and shook my head, realizing it had sounded like I'd just announced to this man who was walking sex that I was not good at sex. "Ugh, no, that's not what I meant. I meant that I can't *just* have sex with you, like a fling or one-night stand or whatever. I need more."

His hands resumed their leisurely exploration of my back. "I know."

I lifted my head from his shoulder to look him in the eye. My gaze was skeptical, but it didn't seem to bother him. All easy confidence, he just smiled at me.

"I don't understand." I needed him to spell it out for me.

"I know you're not the type for a one-time thing, and I don't want you to be a one-time thing." His gaze bored into mine like he was waiting to see how I would react to his confession.

"I'm so confused," I responded. The dam had broken wide open and I couldn't stem the flow of words now. "What do you want from me, Jack? Because honestly, a couple weeks ago, I was pretty sure you hated me."

His expression was pained for a moment as he watched the emotions play across my face.

"I never hated you, Evelyn. You got off that plane and I wasn't expecting you. When Ben said you were his personal assistant, I was out of my fucking mind with jealousy. I should've known you weren't his type, that you were better than that, after you tried to help me with the luggage. You're smart and kind and funny and so goddamn pretty that you wrecked everything without even trying. I tried to avoid you, put some distance between us. I'm sorry for being an ass, but I didn't want to be back in this situation again." The vulnerability I glimpsed in his eyes tugged at my heart. "I didn't want to fall for someone who didn't want to stay. But you're impossible to resist, and you're worth the risk."

A slow smile crept across my face as I listened. I didn't know if I wanted to laugh or cry, but I knew there was one thing I definitely wanted to do. I kissed him. He responded instantly, his mouth moving to catch up with mine. I broke apart before I forgot there were things I needed to say.

"I am really, really happy with that answer. We can figure this out together, if you want to. I mean, I didn't exactly plan for this either. For you."

His hands moved to either side of my head, gently moving my gaze from his mouth to his eyes.

"I want this. I want to try with you." His voice was so sure.

It did strange things to my heart. Strange things that I liked so much it scared me a little.

"Okay." I nodded, his hands still cradling my face. He smiled at me before placing a kiss on my forehead and releasing my face.

"Okay." He smiled, looking more than a little relieved. The realization that I made this beautiful man nervous stretched my smile impossibly wide. "We should get to bed. It's pretty late and we both have to be up early."

Heat pooled low in my stomach. I peeled myself off his lap, standing on wobbly legs.

"Yes, that's a good idea. You're just full of good ideas tonight."

Jack chuckled, standing to join me. I snuck a peek at the tent he was sporting in his pajama pants, and I wasn't disappointed. My cheeks warmed.

Jack cleared his throat and my gaze instantly snapped to his. He looked very amused—and very pleased with himself. "Let's go, before you get us into trouble." He adjusted himself with a smug smile.

I hoped he was as suffering as much as I was from his ridiculous self-control. I was fully prepared to rip his clothes off on the couch regardless of who might see us. At this point, Jesus could walk by and I would not care. Would. Not. *Care.* But I followed him up the stairs anyway.

Much to my disappointment, Jack actually meant go to bed—separately, to sleep. I tried to drag him into my room caveman-style, but he insisted we do things right, and proceeded to kiss me senseless. I closed the door reluctantly, thinking that it had been, without a doubt, the best goodnight kiss of my life.

39.

Despite last night's turn of events, I woke up grumpy to the sound of my phone buzzing on the nightstand. I'd been too restless to fall asleep after Jack left me panting in the hallway. My body seemed to have missed the memo that it wasn't going to see any action last night, and refused to calm down even after I'd splashed my face with cold water in sheer desperation. Turns out that trick only works if you're actually hot.

I looked at the screen to see a message from Elise.

Elise: *Do you know what I wish right now? That I had actually paid attention when Dad tried to teach us how to change a tire. Sitting in the coffee shop parking lot, waiting for the tow guy to come change my tire.*

Corinne: *Yikes. At least you have a cup of coffee while you wait! Here's a video of Celeste being Celeste to help pass the time.*

I clicked *play* to see a video of Celeste singing to herself in the mirror while wearing two tutus under her nightgown. I laughed. My mood was already brightening.

Me: *Omg, she is going to love you so much when you play that for her prom date.*

Corinne: *I knowwww.*

Elise: *That was perfect. I'm going to need about 50 more of those videos to keep me entertained.*

I briefly debated mentioning last night, my fingers hovering above the screen. A part of me was afraid Jack would feel differently this morning, but I decided to take a leap of faith.

Me: *So, fun fact, Jack kissed me last night. A lot. There was a lot of kissing. And then I kind of mauled him.*

Corinne: *OMG OMG OMG WHAT?! Tell me everything!*

Elise: *Why are we just now finding out about this? Please tell me you had sex with him.*

Me: *We were watching TV on the couch, and the next thing I know, he's kissing me. Sorry, Elise, there was no sex. I pretty much begged him, but he was said he "wanted to do things right" blah blah blah. I just wanted the D.*

Me: *I can't believe I just said that.*

Elise: *Send me a picture of you right now.*

Me: *What? Why?*

Elise: *JUST DO IT*

I snapped the world's most unflattering selfie.

Elise: *Oh thank God. I thought someone interesting had kidnapped you and was using your phone.*

Corinne: *I am honestly too stunned to fully appreciate this moment. You and Jack are a thing now?*

Me: *Yeah, we're a thing. I mean unless he changed his mind already, which is totally possible.*

Elise: *There's the Evelyn we know and love. Of course he didn't change his mind!*

Corinne: *So how do we feel about all this?*

I let my head drop back onto the pillows. It was a fair question. How did I feel about this? Physically I felt amazing. Beyond amazing. The memory of his kisses made my stomach flutter. But my brain and my heart were urging me to be more practical. I sighed.

Me: *I feel completely out of my element with him, and more than a little scared. Buttt mostly, I think I feel good about it. It feels right. He feels right.*

I was surprised to find that my response was the truth. Even as I got dressed and made the familiar walk to the kitchen, I couldn't shake the feeling of rightness that had started as soon as Jack's lips connected with mine.

Coffee seemed to jumpstart my mind—and with it, all the worries. After stopping to say good morning to King, I made my way to Photo's stall for a morning ride to clear my head. It might have been leftover bravery from last night that had me leading Photo away from the barn and down the path Jack and I had taken on our maybe-date. As I took in the scenery, I also tried to take inventory of my scattered thoughts.

For the first time, I didn't have a plan. Starting something with Jack was a complication I didn't need. I had no idea what I was doing with my life, and I knew my focus should be figuring out my next steps. Realistically, my life was at least two states away from his life, and I couldn't see that changing.

I also couldn't ignore the part of me that knew 'having a plan' wasn't a guarantee of happiness. I'd tried that once, and it had brought me nothing but a ton of student loans and a job I hated.

The undeniable truth was that I had nothing to lose but my heart.

All those thoughts fled when I made my way back to Pinehaven and found Jack walking toward me with a smile on his face. He held Photo's reins while I dismounted and then tugged me into his arms with his free hand.

"Hi," I said, suddenly feeling a little shy.

"Hi," he answered before covering my mouth with his. I sighed when he deepened the kiss. He pulled back, only to give me a slow kiss that left me clinging to his shirt. All my worrying about the future had been for nothing, because there was a real chance I would not survive this man anyway.

"Did you have a good ride?" he asked when we finally separated.

I may have been thinking more about the kiss than the ride when I answered, "Yeah, it was perfect."

"I like seeing you on a horse." Jack released me and started to lead Photo into the barn.

If I had responded honestly it would have gone something like, 'I can think of something else I'd like to ride.' But I stuck with the much safer, "Oh yeah? You don't mind seeing a city girl up on a horse without you there to babysit her while she plays cowboy?"

Okay, so maybe not that much safer. Jack took my small jab in stride, shaking his head with a self-deprecating grin.

"What are the odds you let me live that one down sometime this century?" he asked, taking down Photo's saddle and passing it back to me.

The things it did to my heart when he used words like 'century.' I *hmm*ed, pretending to give his question some thought. "Not great."

He chuckled. "That's what I thought. Are you hungry? I've got to get the goat enclosure ready before Mom and Gabe show up with them, but I've got time for lunch."

"Lunch sounds good."

We worked together to get Photo's tack off and settle her back into her stall. On our walk to the house, Jack reached out to take my hand in his, so casually, and I wondered if he felt how right this seemed. He kept my hand trapped firmly in his much bigger, rougher one until we got to the kitchen, only releasing it to peer into the fridge.

"What are you in the mood for?" His voice sounded muffled as he shifted the fridge's contents around.

"Um, anything is fine. Anything that's already been cooked by your mom, I mean," I added, just in case my inability to cook wasn't already obvious. I didn't think burning lunch would impress his pants off.

He turned around to smile at me, holding a pile of plastic containers and various ingredients. "How do you feel about paninis?"

"Ohhh, fancy. I like it." I slid onto a stool to watch him. "Do you need any help?"

"Nah, they're easy," he said, pulling out slices of bread and setting them on the counter. "So you don't cook? At all?"

"That depends," I said, wondering when I had started finding cooking such an attractive activity.

"On?" Jack prompted.

"On whether you think boxed mac and cheese is cooking. I can also make a mean microwavable dinner." When had he started smiling so much? This was the elusive man Margot had tried to assure me existed. "Where did you learn to cook? From your mom?"

"Yeah. I can't say I had much interest in learning until a couple years in on the circuit. After traveling started to get old."

"How so?" I was having trouble connecting rodeos to cooking.

"You do a lot of traveling, so it's a lot of shitty bar food or whatever you pass by or end up near. I learned a couple things to make on a hot plate. Nothing fancy." He reached for a pan, coating it with butter before placing it on the stove—all while I watched the muscles on his forearm flex, like a creep. "Plus, a grown man shouldn't have to ask his mom to make him a meal."

I laughed. "I don't know about that. Your mom's a pretty amazing cook. When I visit my family, my mom still sends me home with a ton of precooked meals and groceries, just like she did when I was in college."

The smell of butter melting and all the talk about food reminded my stomach that woman could not survive on coffee alone, and it gave an embarrassingly loud growl. Jack deposited a panini on my plate without breaking that easy grin. "Sounds like this is just in time."

The color in my cheeks deepened three more shades as a I smiled sheepishly up at him. "Thanks. This looks amazing."

It also tasted amazing. I hopped off my stool and poured two glasses of lemonade, feeling oddly at ease with this very domestic scene—so at ease, in fact, that I stopped to give Jack a quick kiss on the cheek on the way back to my spot.

Jack took the spot next to me, his thigh pressed close to mine. I silently willed myself not to choke.

"What are you doing tonight?" he asked, taking a bite of his panini.

I paused to stare at him, then cleared my throat, trying to sound nonchalant. "Nothing. I have no plans." Then I realized I had a mouth full of sandwich shoved into my cheek as I answered him, doing my very own impression of a human chipmunk.

"I have some ideas on how we should approach King. I really want to get him settled before we start getting snow. He's too exposed out there in that paddock, especially with his coat in the shape it is. I was thinking we could start tonight, if you have time."

We. We. *We.*

The word ricocheted around my heart, knocking things loose and just generally wreaking havoc.

I nodded my head in agreement, unable to keep the excitement out of my voice. "I have time."

The way Jack was looking at me right now made me wish

Emily Mayer

I had all the time in the world to give him. I just hoped what I had would be enough.

40.

After lunch, I shooed Jack out the door, promising I would clean up our lunch mess—but not before he pressed me into the counter for a kiss that left me hungry for more than a sandwich.

I made my way to the office to work on the project I had been so excited about before last night turned everything upside down. Finishing it would mean Ben and I were one step closer to leaving. I rubbed that spot just below my shoulder that ached a little at the thought of leaving. Somewhere down there was the truth, floating just below the surface. When I looked out the window and saw the empty goat enclosure surrounded by barns and fields, it was easier to grasp that buried thing.

"I don't want to leave." The walls were the only ones to hear my confession, but the weight of the words pressed down on me just the same.

After a while, Ben joined me, adding his own insights to the work I had done the previous evening. He seemed pleased with how much we had already accomplished, and suggested we start getting the material organized to present. I smiled through the anxiety I felt bubbling up, and agreed. It was the next logical step in the process.

But I couldn't stop myself from asking, "Are we both going back for the board meeting?"

Ben gave me an enthusiastic smile, because of course he didn't understand the real reason for my question.

"Yes, Evelyn, we're going back to the land of food delivery

and coffee shops on every corner. I managed to get in contact with everyone, and they're expecting us at the meeting. Peterson even agreed it was time for me to come back. It's time to get back to the real world."

His words left me hollow. It was the same feeling that had taken root in my chest the day I had finally handed in my resignation letter, a horrible combination of dread and uncertainty. Why did it feel like my world was right here?

The sound of the trailer bouncing along the gravel road had us both looking out the window to see if Gabe and Mary were back.

"This should be good." Ben turned, closing his laptop.

Without discussion, we headed for the door and got out to the truck just in time to see Gabe swinging down from the driver's side. His hat was missing part of its brim and the hem of his shirt looked like it had been torn in places. The easy smile that was almost a permanent fixture on his too-handsome face was missing; a frown tugged down the corner of his mouth.

I gave him a tentative wave, and he shot me a thunderous look that made my hand drop back limply to my side.

"What's going on?" My eyes flicked briefly away to Jack approaching us.

"These goats are a fucking menace," Gabe huffed, coming to stand next to me and placing both hands on his hips. It looked like he was making a visible effort to pull himself together. "I swear to God, Evie. Little fucking nightmares."

I heard Ben coughing to cover up a laugh. He cleared his throat before motioning up and down with his hand and asking, "Are they responsible for... whatever happened here?"

Even Hank Williams, who had just hopped out of the passenger's side, was looking a little frazzled. Mary was wearing a placating smile, following behind him. Hank made a hasty exit toward the porch. I watched him slump down into a shady spot before returning my attention back to Mary.

"Now, don't anyone worry, they were just a little nervous about the trailer." Her smile was starting to fray around the edges.

Ben, Jack, and I exchanged glances. Gabe made a huffing noise, but made no movement toward the truck. A bleating noise came from the trailer, followed by an entire chorus of bleating. Still no one made any movement. This was starting to feel like a bad horror movie. The bleating slowly wound down, leaving an eerie silence. It reminded me of the last few kernels of popcorn in the microwave.

Jack took a decisive step forward, then came to a halt when a metal pinging sound came from inside the trailer. Another ping followed close behind, then another. My hand shot out, grasping Jack by the arm and dragging him backward as the pings intensified.

Ping. Ping. Ping. Ping.

It sounded like someone was throwing a rubber bouncy ball violently against the trailer. We all stood in stunned silence as the trailer rocked from side to side on its wheels. The sound of the pings was joined by Hank's howling from the porch and the occasional bleat from inside the besieged trailer. I was pretty sure Gabe was mumbling something about 'fucking goats' next to me.

Jack's forearm tensed under my hand, which was still clutching his arm like it was a life preserver. I kept my gaze fixed on the trailer, waiting for Godzilla to burst out and start breathing fire.

"Shit." Jack managed to break free from my grasp, and once again moved toward the back of the trailer to release the ramp. I swear to God, this man who rode angry bulls on purpose, because he liked it, took a deep, fortifying breath before he unlatched the door and swung it open.

I let out a strangled, relieved laugh as five adorable goats casually trotted down the ramp, checking out their new surroundings.

"Oh my God, they're adorable," I gushed, watching them hop around their new home.

"Ha," Gabe barked, turning on his heel and storming off.

Mary joined the remaining onlookers at the fence, pointing to the goat closest to us.

"That's Saffron. And Ginger. There's Rosemary and Basil in the corner. And last but not least, the little explorer on the roof is Cinnamon."

"All spices! I didn't think I could love this anymore." I whipped my phone out of my pocket and started snapping pictures.

"That's great, Mom. So what the hell happened to Gabe?" Ben asked. Both boys turned to face Mary, clearly way more interested in hearing her answer than watching the frolicking goats.

"Well, the goats needed a little convincing about getting into the trailer and Hank Williams wasn't helping things, you know. They kept hopping away every time we tried to herd them in, so Gabe had to lure them into the trailer with some treats. It worked great—they rushed right in, but Gabe got stuck in the corner and they sort of mobbed him." Mary winced. "He must have gotten some of the treats on his clothes. Anyway, I don't think he'll be going near the goats for a while."

I looked over to see both men vibrating with suppressed laughter. As soon as our eyes met, Ben erupted, shoulders shaking, which seemed to trigger Jack's own laugh to burst from his body.

Mary and I stood shaking our heads in silent judgment. She swatted both boys on the shoulder. "Now, you leave him alone about this! It was very traumatic. Hank even barreled through the goats to get them off him."

Even I snickered, imagining Gabe being mobbed by goats and Hank Williams coming to his rescue. Mary turned on her heel, satisfied that the goats were settling in fine.

"I'm going to go make that poor boy a pie," she said, her statement leaving more laughter in its wake.

Ben was the first to recover, just shaking his head and staring at the goats. "I don't know, man. I know you were pretty against these goats, but they're starting to grow on me."

Jack turned to look at the little terrorists, shaking his head. "They might be okay."

I threw a fist into the air, giving it a little pump.

"Yes! Welcome to Team Goat! Letty is totally going to be on our team as soon as she sees these little nuggets. Pretty sure we have Margot too. Ooh, we should get shirts."

Ben looked at me like I was speaking another language. "On that note, I'm going to head back to the office. I want to get this done as soon as possible, before I start thinking goat shirts is a good idea."

"They are a good idea!" I fired at his retreating back.

Jack looped an arm around my shoulders, drawing me into him and dropping a kiss on my head. "I'd wear one of your shirts, baby."

I tried to focus on the other words, the ones that had come before "baby," but it was the only one my brain seemed to understand. The rest of them tumbled around inside with the rest of my organs.

"You would?" I gazed up at him, a ridiculous smile plastered on my face. I was mildly impressed I had managed to get out that much.

"Nope." He grunted when my elbow connected with his ribs, and tightened his hold on my shoulders. "We should make Gabe one, though."

I gave his ribs another playful jab. "Be nice to him. He was jumped by a bunch of tiny goats."

I felt Jack's chuckle vibrating through my side. "Man, I would've loved to have seen that. Still good for tonight?"

I nodded, soaking up this moment. "Yep."

"Good. I'll let you get back to work. See you at dinner." He dropped another kiss on my head and walked back in the direction he had come from.

I almost asked him for a real kiss. I had turned into a beggar —always greedy for more when it came to Jack.

41.

When the smell of pie drifted into the office, Ben and I abandoned work under the pretense of helping Mary in the kitchen. We were both chopping carrots and eyeballing the apple pie when Jack walked in, covered in grease. Thank God I had stopped chopping long enough to pop a carrot into my mouth, or I'd have been down a finger. No one seemed to notice my heavy breathing.

"Got the tractor running?" Mary eyed Jack's greasy hands, handing him some paper towels.

"I think so. Gonna get cleaned up before dinner." He dumped the mutilated wad of paper towels into the trash and walked out. The temperature in the kitchen dropped twenty degrees, and I assumed it was safe for me to start using sharp objects again.

Gabe walked in next, clothing all intact, and made a bee-line for the apple pie. Cole, Margot, and Letty followed, increasing the volume of the kitchen tenfold. Letty climbed up onto the island to help me chop the carrots and ask me about the goats. Sam was the last to arrive, and he had a tub of vanilla ice cream in hand, making him everyone's hero.

When Jack strolled into the kitchen, free of grease, sporting damp hair and a long-sleeved thermal shirt that wrapped around his biceps like a koala, he walked straight to me, ignoring all the newcomers, and kissed my cheek. His hand dropped to the small of my back when he leaned over to check out Letty's pile of carrot pieces. I snuck a quick glance in Margot's direction to see her eyes practically bugging out of her head.

She moved her head slowly from side to side, a wide smile transforming her face. I shrugged and shot her a sly grin.

Dinner was its usual circus, the boys taking thinly-veiled shots at Gabe, who took it all in stride in that good-natured way he handled everything. Letty chatted away in between bites of pot pie. Ben, Sam, and Mary carried on a conversation at the other end of the table, the sound of Mary's softer laugh mixing with the masculine voices floating around us.

I looked around the table, enjoying the chaos surrounding me and trying to commit it all to memory. A warm feeling spread through my chest that felt a lot like happiness and even more like love. I had a feeling that leaving this place was going to feel like losing a limb. The thought sent a wave of anxiety, tinged with what could only be called grief, crashing through me. I spent the rest of dinner pushing food around with my fork, my appetite gone.

Margot took Letty out to meet the goats, her mangled carrot pieces in hand, while Gabe, Sam, Cole, Jack, and I headed toward King's space. We were going to do this with an audience. Anxious energy buzzed around us as we approached the fence separating us from the horse of the hour. The rest of the group looked tense as we came to a stop, and Gabe actually shot me a thumbs-up.

Jack took me by the shoulders, forcing me to make eye contact with him.

"Here's how it's going to go. You're going to go in there, and you're going to do exactly as I say." I bristled slightly at his command, some of my anxiety falling away to be replaced by stubborn pride. "I mean it, Evelyn. You do exactly as I say. Got it?"

I nodded my head. "I got it."

"I don't want you getting hurt, so promise me you won't do anything stupid."

Geez, you'd have thought I was about to get into the ring with a bear.

"I promise, Jack. I'm not going to do anything crazy." I gave him a reassuring smile. "I don't really even know what would be considered crazy in this scenario."

Jack pressed a quick kiss to my forehead and let his hands drop. He huffed out a breath, taking off his cap to run his hands through his hair, his signature frustrated move. Seeing how concerned he looked for me melted some of my annoyance and made me want to comfort him.

"Hey, trust me." I bumped his shoulder with mine, trying to infuse some calm. "We've got this."

He shot me a quick smile before moving to the gate and unlatching it. "Just walk a couple feet in so we can judge his reaction. The whole point of this is to get him used to you being in there with him."

"Got it."

After a deep, calming breath, I took a tentative step forward. I willed myself to move slowly but confidently. I sneaked a quick glance over my shoulder when I heard the gate latch behind me. Jack was standing at the gate, looking ready to pounce. Cole, Sam, and Gabe were all leaning up against the fence. Cole smiled at me and gave a little nod of encouragement.

"Hi, King," I called in greeting. The horse was watching me curiously, swishing his tail back and forth. I kept moving forward, undeterred by the angry tail action. "So I thought I'd pop in and say hi tonight instead of our usual. I hope you don't mind."

I paused to gauge his reaction. His tail had stopped whipping around, and a soft snort was the only sign that he knew I was present. I took a few more steps in his direction, trying to keep my posture relaxed, my voice even and calm.

"It was time to take our relationship to the next level, don't you think?"

King turned his whole body to face me. Somewhere behind me I heard Jack telling me not to go any further. I released the breath I hadn't known I was holding and took another handful of steps. I heard Jack's soft curse and the clink of metal, followed by Cole's voice telling him to leave it. I kept my focus on King, trying to block out the background noise.

"Listen," I whispered, coming a little closer. "I'm going to need you to work with me here. I've been talking you up to the guys over there, so help a girl out. I'd really, really like to show them up—you know, girl power and all that good stuff."

I wasn't suffering any delusion that King actually understood the words I was saying, but I hoped he sensed, on whatever level was possible, that I wanted to help him. I hoped he could sense that I was good, and worthy of his damaged trust.

We stood staring at each other for a small eternity, only the sound of our breathing filling the air between us. I had resigned myself to the fact that this might be all we accomplished today—then King started walking. His stride was steady and unhurried. I stood still, fighting the urge to do a little celebration dance, although I lost the battle against smiling. But my smile didn't seem to upset King. He came to a stop less than an arm's length in front of me, blowing a little puff of air in my face that I chose to believe was a 'I've got your back' in Horse.

I tentatively stretched my arm forward, because I didn't know what else to do and my cheering section had gone quiet. I wanted to ask Jack what to do but that would require raising my voice. I couldn't risk scaring King away. There was no plan for this. The plan had stopped at 'walk inside a little ways and listen to me.' And since 'no plan' seemed to be the theme of my life lately, I did what I always did—swallowed my panic and improvised.

I laughed as his warm breath tickled my palm. "You're the best wingman ever! I'm going to give you so many apples for this, you know that, right?"

He nudged the back of my hand with his nose, and I moved it to gently stroke the soft part of his nose. When he seemed fine with my touch, I moved my hand to stroke his neck, taking inventory of his tangled mane and scarred coat. His muscles quivered under my hand, and I felt his breath on the side of my face, moving the loose strands of hair around. His tolerance ended abruptly, and he walked away as if the whole thing was no big deal.

I waited until he was settled into his corner, munching away on the patchy grass, before reluctantly making my way back to the gate. My gaze traveled from the smiling men on the fence to Jack, who was watching me with an intense expression I couldn't read. Was he mad at me for not listening when he'd told me to stop? I felt my smile slip a little as I neared where he stood holding the gate open.

I turned to face him, bracing myself for a confrontation. Jack slide the lock home and then walked toward me like a man on a mission.

"I—"

Before I could get any more words out, Jack's arms were around me, crushing me into his chest. He tightened his hold, forcing an *oomph* out of my throat. It took a second for the shock to wear off, but finally I wrapped my arms around his waist. Nose pressed into his chest, I breathed in the familiar scent of leather and sweat, and my whole body relaxed into him.

"I am so damn proud of you." His voice was like gravel. I glanced up at him curiously, surprised by his words. He dipped his head, bringing his mouth to mine for a soft kiss that was way too short.

"I told you King liked me." I couldn't resist pointing out that I was right, but I softened my words with a smile.

He kissed my nose. "Sorry, city girl."

I swatted his chest, earning a small laugh. Jack released me, but I was immediately pulled into Gabe's strong arms, and he lifted me off the ground and swung me around.

"Evie, you are a fucking champion!" He dropped me back on my feet, giving me the full dimple treatment with that devastating smile of his.

"Thanks." I felt my cheeks heat at the compliment or those dimples or some combination of both.

Cole and Sam were smiling at me. Happiness crashed into me as I stared at these four men, who were cheering me on and looking at me like they saw something in me that had been lost for a long time.

"I knew you had it in you." Cole's words confirmed my suspicions.

"You did?" I felt my eyebrows climbing my forehead. "Because I definitely didn't."

Gabe chuckled, throwing his arm across my shoulders, only to have it knocked off by Jack, who tugged me against his side. Jack shot Gabe a hands-off look that had me grinning like an idiot. Jealous was a great look on this man.

Gabe cheerfully ignored the warning, and shot me mischievous wink. "We never doubted you."

I thought my insides were going to explode as we walked back to the house. I didn't think it was possible for the human body to contain this much happiness. I was practically bursting with it.

I'd felt lost since I had walked away from my carefully crafted life. For a long time, I hadn't recognized myself as I stumbled through life without a plan for the first time. But here, I felt grounded. I felt like someone had woken me up. And more than anything else, I loved who I saw reflected back at me when I looked at this group of men, who had unexpectedly become my friends.

42.

Our little group settled in on the porch for a celebratory drink. I had declined a beer, worried about a migraine since my head was already teetering on the edge after all the excitement with King, and went with a ginger ale. Wild times, for sure. I enjoyed listening to the easy banter that flowed between the three men on the porch, occasionally adding my own commentary.

Letty darted around the corner of the porch, followed by Margot, who smiled when she saw us.

"Hey, how'd it go?" Margot asked me.

I shrugged my shoulders. "I think it went well."

Gabe made a strangled noise next to me, shaking his head.

"Okay, humble bee. King walked right up to her like it was no big thing and let her love on him."

I laughed at his nickname and his version of events.

"It was something," Jack added, smiling affectionately at me.

"That's great!" She turned her gaze to where Cole was seated. "Babe, why don't you take your child inside for some ice cream?"

"Ice cream?" Letty stopped in her tracks. "Ice cream ice cream ice cream!"

Cole reached for the bouncing child's hand, leading her toward the house. Gabe got up, rubbing his hands together.

"You think there are any sprinkles, Letty-Lou?"

"Well, I can't pass up sprinkles either." Sam rose, seeming to take Margot's hint.

As soon as the door closed behind them, Margot faced Jack, the last remaining male on the porch.

"Jack?" Margot said, her voice laced with sugary sweetness.

"Yes, Margot?" he answered, lifting one corner of his mouth in a small grin like he knew her tone meant trouble.

"Go away."

"Now why would I want to do that? I'm pretty comfortable right where I'm at, enjoying a nice cold beer. "

He tipped his bottle to his mouth, smirking around it as he took a pull. Margot grabbed him by his free arm and attempted to pull him up.

"Because I need to talk to Evie about you and that's going to be hard to do with you here."

My face instantly flamed. I sputtered, "Wh-what?"

Margot and Jack were too busy staring each other down, smiles plastered on their faces, to answer my question.

"I don't know. I think I might like to hear this conversation," Jack drawled, clearly enjoying this.

"Jack Danver, get gone!" Margot said in her best mom voice, pointing toward the yard.

Jack held his hands up, bottle dangling from his fingers. "Okay, okay."

He stood and shot me a wink that made the heat rush back to my face. Margot took the chair next to me, turning it to face me, really driving home the whole interrogation vibe she had going on.

"So, dinner was interesting huh?" she asked, taking the casual route.

"Not really. Nothing exciting about pot pies." Two could play this game. We were pretty well-matched, really. I had two older sisters and she had a toddler.

"Give it up, Evie."

I rolled my eyes playfully and gave her the same recap I had given my sisters, filling in a few extra details since I wasn't doing it over text this time around. Margot's expression had transformed from eager puppy to giddy and slightly deranged by the time I finished.

"I knew it!" She clapped her hands together. "This is so great."

I could actually see the wheels in her head turning.

"Okay, before you go planning the wedding, it's new. We haven't really talked about what this all means," I cautioned. "I mean, I still live in Chicago and he still lives in Montana and there's a lot of distance in between."

"So?" She scrunched up her nose, sounding genuinely confused.

"So, Jack obviously can't just pack up and move to Chicago, and I can't just move out here..." I let my voice trail off.

"Why not?"

"Why not what?" It was my turn to be confused.

"Why couldn't you move here? People do it all the time. You weren't happy in Chicago, but you're happy here." She held up a hand to keep me from interrupting. "You *are* happy here. I can tell. And you love Jack. You said it yourself. I don't see what the issue is."

"I have an apartment! And a job. And... people. I can't just pack up and move across the country," I said, offering the saddest defense in history.

"Wow, that's quite the list. Yeah, I can see why you wouldn't want to leave all that behind." Sarcasm dripped from her words. "Sublet your apartment, quit the job you're way overqualified for, and figure the rest out."

"I don't know, Margot. I feel like I'm too old to start over." She rolled her eyes. "I realize I'm not a senior citizen, but I should have it figured out by now, you know? Starting over just seems so much more daunting when you have student loans and health insurance and leases."

"Evelyn, no one ever has it figured out. I'm basically parenting on whatever Google tells me. I legitimately took pregnancy advice from Wikipedia the other day." She reached over and squeezed my hand. "But most importantly, it's never too late to be happy."

43.

Lying in bed later, Margot's words kept replaying in my head. My mind and body refused to settle. I rolled over, careful not to crush Hank Williams, and checked the time for what felt like the millionth time since I'd lain down. The clock read 11:26, exactly fifteen minutes from the last time I'd checked.

I got up and made my way to the bathroom to get a glass of water. Halfway across the room, I changed my mind. I knew what I needed, and it wasn't water. I cracked my door open and quietly padded down the hallway, coming to a stop outside Jack's door. I took a deep breath and knocked softly. I listened for any sound on the other side. Nothing. I waited another few breaths and then knocked again, just a little louder this time.

I shifted my weight from one foot to the other, second-guessing this plan. I had just turned to creep back to my room when Jack's door swung open. He stood there, one hand braced on the door, wearing nothing but a low-slung pair of athletic shorts. Involuntarily my eyes swept from his sleep-tousled hair across his broad chest, then down those abs that looked like they'd been carved. I swallowed.

"Evelyn?' Jack's voice sounded like gravel, and his eyes, heavy with sleep, swept over me, taking in my sleep shorts and cotton shirt. I felt overdressed and not covered up enough, at the same time.

"I couldn't sleep." I forced myself to stop fidgeting with the hem of my shirt. "Can I come in?"

It felt like a pit had opened near my stomach, and my heart dropped through it while I waited for his answer. He didn't know it, but he was witnessing what could be the boldest non-tequila-fueled moment of my life. I was terrified he would he say no.

He cleared his throat, stepping back into the room a little. "Yeah, of course you can come in."

I gave him a shaky smile as I walked through the door, aware of the heat coming off him as I passed. I took in as much of the room as I could in the dark. The king-sized bed with rumpled sheets immediately grabbed my attention. I stopped a few feet from the bed and turned to face him. He was still standing by the closed door watching me with a curious look on his face.

I took a deep breath, trying to steady my nerves. "I was thinking I could sleep with you. If that's okay, I mean. We don't have to do anything if you don't want to. We can just sleep."

Please say no, please say no, please say no. My thoughts were totally at odds with my words as I watched his chest move up and down where he stood across from me praying he was as uninterested in sleep as I was right now. I thought I might actually die if I didn't get to put my hands on all of that soon.

My words finally seemed to penetrate Jack's brain. I watched as his expression changed from sleepy and curious to predatory. His long legs ate up the distance between us. I sucked in a breath as his hands found my shoulders in the dark.

"Yeah, I don't feel like sleeping."

I barely registered the heated look in his eyes before his mouth was on mine. There was nothing sweet or soft about this kiss. I parted my lips, gladly granting his tongue access. His tongue swept my mouth again and again, making me dizzy. I lifted up on tiptoes so I could sink my hands into the too-long hair at his neck for purchase. Jack groaned, and started walking us back slowly.

My knees hit the bed, knocking my legs out from under

me. Jack looked down at me with hooded eyes, causing heat to pool low in my stomach. I had to fist the covers to keep from pinching myself.

"Is this okay?" Jack rasped out.

I nodded my head, way too enthusiastically to be anything close to sexy.

"Yes, definitely okay. So okay." My voice sounded unusually husky in my own ears.

Jack mumbled something about too many clothes, and then his hands were beneath my shirt. I felt a moment of panic when his rough hands traveled across the soft flesh of my sides and across a stomach that was not now and never had been flat. I was a normal human, and this man had been engaged to a model. I fought against the urge to stop him, to keep my arms trapped at my sides, as he slowly pulled my shirt up and over my head. The cotton dragging across my heated skin was replaced by cool air, the contrast causing shivers to dance across my skin. Jack's stare felt like it had weight as it traveled over my exposed chest. I felt my nipples harden into tight peaks in response, desperate for attention.

"God, you're so beautiful." His words instantly chased away my insecurities. One of his massive hands moved to palm my breast while the other went to work tugging the band out of my hair, sending it spilling down my back.

"Love your hair, baby."

His voice was just a whisper across my mouth, quickly replaced by his lips. He kissed me slowly, savoring the contact now that skin was touching skin. The rough pad of his thumb tugged at one nipple before cupping my other breast, sending sparks throughout my body. His other hand tangled in my hair, tilting my head to give him better access. I almost came off the bed when his mouth left mine and traveled to that hidden spot between my neck and ear. He bit the sensitive flesh gently before licking the sting away. My hands gripped his biceps, my nails digging into hard muscle.

"Jack. Jack, I need you," I begged, almost drunk with longing.

He stood back, his hooded eyes echoing the same need. In one quick movement, he shoved his pants down, and then his hands were on my shoulders gently pushing me back as he crawled over me. My heartbeat was frantic as my hands found his chest, exploring all those beautiful muscles I had been secretly admiring ever since I'd seen him standing at the airport. My mouth followed my hands, kissing every dip, every ridge I could reach.

I whimpered in protest when Jack sat back on his knees, grabbing my wrists and pinning them above my head. He gave me a grin that made me strain against his grip.

"My turn," he growled, grinding his hips into me. His head dipped down to dot kisses along my neck, sucking and nibbling a path to my collarbone. When the wet warmth of his mouth found my nipple, my entire body jerked at the contact.

"Jack, please."

Meaningless words tumbled from me as his tongue licked a warm path to the other breast, laving the neglected nipple with the tongue I was growing fonder of by the second. He let go of my wrists and caressed the ticklish skin by my ribs, his thumbs toying with the underside of my breasts.

I moved my hands to thread through his hair, tugging it roughly to get his mouth back where I needed it. He groaned, and I tugged a little more roughly this time, until his mouth found mine again. His hands were on my hips, lifting me just enough to shove my shorts and underwear off in one fluid move.

Panic tugged at the corners of my lust-fogged brain when Jack sank back on his heels to stare at my completely naked form. Goosebumps appeared every place his gaze landed. Almost unconsciously, my hands came up to cover the slight curve of my belly. Jack's gaze flicked to where my hands lay, in a position that was more appropriate for an exam table at a doctor's office than in the middle of sex.

"What are you doing?" His eyes traveled from my hands to my eyes. I could feel the blush start on my chest, rapidly spreading to my face. I groaned, mind racing with ways to avoid answering. I was completely naked, spread out like a freaking Thanksgiving feast for this man, and I was dreading giving him this one little truth.

I shook my head from side to side, slamming my eyes shut. "My stomach. It's not nice. I don't really... I don't like it."

I cracked my eyes open when I felt Jack's hands covering mine. He smiled down at me as he lifted each hand, turning them so our fingers were laced together. Pinning my hands by my head, he leaned forward until his mouth was next to my ear. When he took the lobe between his teeth, all thoughts fled my head. I squirmed beneath him.

"That's better." I felt the curve of his smile against my ear. He kissed a path straight down my middle, lingering a little in the valley between my breasts.

"For the record, I love every single part of your body," he said between kisses. "You don't even know what you do to me. You're fucking perfect, baby."

His hands deserted mine to wander down my body. My fingers found their way into his hair just as his fingers parted me. His thumb swirled around the bundle of nerves at my center, making invisible patterns that left me panting. His lips found that spot on my neck again as one long finger dipped inside. My hips moved to grind against his hand without conscious thought. He increased the speed to match my hips' frantic movements, and I almost exploded when a second finger joined the first, stretching me almost painfully. My muscles clenched around his fingers, urging him on, begging him for more.

"No, no no," I pleaded when Jack's fingers left me. I saw him reach for something on the dresser, followed by the sound of plastic tearing.

He chuckled, lowering himself onto his elbows so we were pressed chest to chest. One of those big hands swept down my side cupping my leg behind the knee. I felt his hardness pressed at my center, and I lifted my hips to meet him. Jack slid inside me, slowly stretching me, inch by inch.

I released a sound, some combination of whimper and moan, and I could hear Jack's rough curse near my ear. I dug my fingers into his forearms, the corded muscles there bunching as my nails carved little half-moons into his skin. Then his restraint snapped and he filled me with one quick thrust.

A startled gasp tore from me as long-neglected muscles came to life and adjusted to the welcome invasion. Jack's forehead dropped to mine, his breath coming in short bursts.

"Jesus, you feel so good, baby. Are you okay?" His eyes searched mine, looking for any hesitation.

I nodded, words escaping me. Satisfied with my nod, he started making wide circles with his hips until I was writhing beneath him and begging for more, more, more. I was always begging this man for more.

Jack began pumping into me with slow, languid strokes. The hand cupping my leg squeezed it roughly, and his mouth found one nipple, then the other, rolling them between his teeth. His pace increased when my hips moved to meet each thrust. He hitched my leg higher, fingers biting into my flesh, deepening the angle each time he drove into me. I felt release building in me like a wave, so intense that my hands grabbed onto those broad shoulders for fear it might sweep me away. With one more thrust, I exploded around him, coming so hard

I literally saw stars.

Jack's pace became more frantic, his strokes getting shorter until he buried himself inside me with one deep thrust that made my sensitive muscles spasm. He grunted my name as he came, giving me some weird primal satisfaction in my post-orgasm bliss. I smiled as his mouth found mine for a quick kiss before he collapsed on top of me, careful not to completely crush me under his weight.

I rubbed my hands over his back and up over his shoulders until they were buried back in his hair. He sighed, then rolled us over so I was draped over him like a blanket. I rested my chin on his chest and peered up at him. He wore a satisfied smile that made my heart do a happy dance I was sure even he could feel.

"How did I get so lucky?" he asked, one hand stroking a path through my hair. The vulnerability I heard in his voice told me he was genuinely curious.

I kissed the spot on his chest where my chin had just been resting. "I was just wondering the same thing."

I felt his laugh shaking my whole body. I smiled up at him, rolling off of him reluctantly. We lay in silence for a minute, just long enough for my mind to start racing. *What's the post-sex protocol if you live in the same house but aren't living together-together? Do I go back to my room? Do I stay here? Is this weird? Am I being weird? When can we do that again?*

I smiled up at him, rolling off him reluctantly. "I should let you get some sleep, I guess."

Strong arms wrapped around my waist, and I was on my back before my feet had even hit the ground. I huffed, staring up at Jack with surprise.

"Where are you going?" he asked, his playful smile softening the harsh tone of the question.

"Umm, back to my room?" My answer came out sounding

more like a question. Cool, confident Evelyn had officially left the building.

"Dining and dashing, huh?" He pressed kisses to each corner of my mouth. "I thought you wanted to sleep with me."

"I did," I pointed out, sounding a little breathless from the kisses. When he stopped to give me a confused look, I felt the need to clarify. "Sleep was code for sex. I wanted sex. Sex with you."

I felt that familiar rush of heat flooding my cheeks as Jack pressed his lips together, clearly amused by my explanation.

"Ah, thank you for clarifying." I swatted his chest playfully, eliciting a chuckle. "You should stay."

"Stay?" I parroted back like an idiot, because those little kisses had started again.

"Yeah, stay here with me. Actually sleep. I'm not ready to let you go yet."

There was absolutely no way I was saying no to that offer. "I like that idea better."

Jack pressed a quick kiss to my forehead and hopped out of the bed. I watched his perfect backside make its way toward the bathroom. It was hard to believe all that was mine. I wished I had my phone, so I could sneak a picture to memorialize this sight forever.

I snuggled under the covers, surrounding myself with his smell. I inhaled deeply, needing the reminder that this was real life. A few seconds later, Jack slid under the covers and pulled me into his side until my head was resting on the slab of concrete that was his chest. This man.

"Are you comfortable?" Jack's voice rumbled through his chest, making my head bob a bit.

"Yes," I lied. He leisurely stroked my hair with one hand, and I almost purred, every part of me humming with contentment. I listened as his breathing evened out and his hand eventually came to rest on my shoulder. I fought the urge to fall asleep, wanting to experience as much of being snuggled up against Jack, surrounded by his warmth, as I could. Hoarding up the moments for when I was alone in Chicago, wishing I could be right here. The *thud, thud, thud* of his heartbeat was the last sound I heard before sleep won.

44.

I yawned, slowly blinking open my eyes against the bright sun drifting in through the windows. My hand reached blindly for my phone on the nightstand. What time was it? I bolted upright when my hand landed on empty bed and tangled sheet. My gaze dropped down when cool air hit skin—naked skin. I looked down to confirm that I was, in fact, naked. Memories of the night washed over me, instantly heating my skin. Jack's bed. I was in Jack's bed. Did I caress the empty spot next to me and bring the pillow up to my nose to sniff, like a creep? I sure did.

My happiness was quickly replaced by the realization that I would need to find my pajamas and head back to my room. I groaned, dragging my hands down my face. How old was too old to do the walk of shame? The sun beaming in gave me a small jolt of hope that everyone would already be up and out working, allowing me to sneak back to my room. I didn't really want to have explain to Ben why I was leaving his brother's room in my pajamas.

I did a quick check in the mirror and smiled at my knotted hair. Once I had my hair de-sexed and my clothes straight, I paused in front of the door, listening for any noise before I opened it a crack. A quick glance down both ends of the hallway, and I was off. Montana Walk of Shame officially underway. A wave of relief crashed over me when my hand hit my room's door handle and I pushed the slightly cracked door all the way open.

Hank was still snoring happily on the bed, clearly unconcerned with where I'd gone or why I was slinking back mid-morning. I gave his belly a little good-morning rub before hopping in the shower. The warm water massaged the sore muscles I had earned in the best way.

Because I was very much still me, as I washed away all evidence of the previous night, I worried that Jack and I weren't on the same page. I closed my eyes, tilting my head back into the spray, and recalled all the words that I had committed so carefully to memory. His love of my hair, of all the soft flesh I constantly worried about. But I clung to the one word that had weaseled its way into my heart. *Stay.*

Dressed in yoga pants and the 'Bless This Mess' sweater my sisters had gotten me when I was studying for the bar exam (I was a mess—not a hot mess, just a mess), I made my way to the kitchen, following the smell of bacon and coffee. That smell was the stuff dreams were made of. The man standing at the sink wasn't bad either.

"Hi," I aimed at the back I'd gotten very familiar with very recently.

Jack turned, his face wearing a warm smile that was a balm to my anxious heart. He moved toward me with those confident strides that affected my heartrate more than five shots of espresso.

"Hey," he said, and then his lips were on mine for an unhurried kiss. "Sorry I snuck out on you this morning. I didn't want to wake you up."

"Smart man." I snuggled into his arms. "It's fine. I know how early you usually get up, and I clearly slept late."

He wagged his eyebrows, "Oh yeah? All that physical activity wearing you out, city girl?"

I swatted his chest, pushing myself out of his embrace and making my way to the coffee pot. Jack reached into the cabinet above me and handed me a mug.

I smiled, pouring the dark liquid necessary for life.

"I like this," I confessed, looking up at Jack leaning on the counter next to me.

He laughed. "I think we all know how you feel about your coffee."

"No, I meant this." I motioned between us. "I like us in the morning. I like coming downstairs and seeing you in the kitchen. And good-morning kisses. I like those too."

I felt my face flush as my eyes found his over the rim of my mug, waiting for his reaction to my quiet confession. At least if he didn't agree, I could blame my words on lack of caffeine.

He reached for the strand of hair that never stayed put, tucking it behind my ear. "I like that too. More than I probably should."

Before I could ask Jack what he meant, a throat cleared in the doorway. I whipped around to see Ben making his way into the kitchen, mug in hand.

"Morning, Evelyn. Jack." He came to a stop in front of us, his gaze darting to the small space between our bodies.

I prepared myself for the horror of explaining to my boss that I was sleeping with his brother. Silence filled the air between the three of us. My face grew redder and my heart beat faster as the silence continued, none of us apparently willing to start this conversation.

Ben lifted up his mug. "You're blocking the coffee pot. I need a refill."

I mumbled an apology as I shuffled away from the counter, feeling a strange pang of guilt. I snuck a glance at Jack, who looked completely at odds with the way I felt. He leaned casually against the counter, arms crossed loosely across his chest. He wore confidence like a zebra wears its stripes.

"So I received a calendar invite this morning for the next board meeting," Ben said, full mug in hand. "Due to a scheduling conflict, they asked to move the meeting up a few weeks. Looks like we're headed back to Chicago next Friday. We'll have a week filled with meetings, so I want to have the weekend to get settled in."

It felt like all the air had been sucked out of the room. I watched the expression on Jack's face darken.

"Wow, so soon." The words felt hollow in my throat. I hoped Ben thought the flatness of my response was due to surprise.

"I know. I bet you'll be glad to get us out of your hair." Ben directed the comment toward Jack, who stood looking like a thundercloud next to him. A familiar muscle in his jaw twitched, signaling his displeasure.

Jack's dark gaze stayed fixed on me. "Something like that, sure. I gotta get going. I'll see you two later."

I watched Jack shove off the counter and out the door, letting it slam behind him.

Seemingly unaware of the tension buzzing through the kitchen after he had casually burst the happy bubble I had been pretty content living in, the destroyer of perfectly good moments started making his way toward the office, motioning for me to follow him.

"We need to go over all the data, all the information we've compiled. I want this presentation to be flawless. Bulletproof."

I spent the rest of the day reading and re-reading all the words I already knew by heart while my mind wandered. My body was in the office, but my mind was worrying over the anger that had radiated off of Jack when Ben had said we were leaving sooner than expected. I was pretty well-versed in his angry body language, considering I had seen so much of it first-hand, but I didn't understand why he was angry. All I felt was a crushing sadness.

My skin was practically itching with the need to talk to Jack, so when Ben said we should call it quits, I flew out of my chair and straight out of the house.

"Hey!" I waved at Gabe, who was working with one of the young horses. "Have you seen Jack?"

Gabe grunted, turning his attention to me. "Last time I saw his grumpy ass, he was working on the tractor—"

I cut him off.

"Okay, great! Thanks, Gabe."

I heard him throw out a 'good luck' as I marched toward the barn where the tractor was kept. Gabe's words weren't enough to slow me down, but they didn't do anything to squash the rising anxiety in my chest. I needed to hear Jack say we were on the same page. I needed to feel the calm that being with him always seemed to bring.

I found him bent over the hood of the old tractor that looked like it was beyond saving. I stood quietly, watching him work for a minute, admiring the way his jeans hugged that oh-so-perfect butt and the way the muscles in his forearms bunched and jumped. There really should be a law requiring this man to always have his forearms visible.

"Hi." I moved to stand next to him, peering into the hood like it might have the answers I was looking for.

Jack looked up at me, a scowl marring that handsome face. He grabbed a rag off the work bench and started wiping grease off his hands.

"Hi." His tone was soft, so much softer than the expression he was wearing, giving me a burst of hope.

I moved my gaze from his hands to his eyes, taking in the deep green shirt he wore and the way it stretched across the expanse of his chest.

"Gabe said you were in a bad mood." He tossed the rag back

onto the bench and stepped closer to me. "Are you mad at me? About what Ben said? About us leaving?"

Jack's head reared back, eyes going wide with surprise. He pulled me into his chest, and my arms wrapped around his waist instinctively.

"Evie, no. Baby, I'm not mad at you." He let loose a sad laugh. "I'm mad at myself."

"You are?" I stared up into his face, loving the warmth in his eyes as they met mine.

"Yeah. I wasted so much time with you. I spent so much time trying not to let you get under my skin when you were already there. All that was time I could have spent with you."

I blinked back the tears threatening to overflow and snuggled closer to him. His arms tightened around me in response. I breathed in that smell of sweat and outside and all that was Jack, and the first tear slipped down my cheek.

"I wish we had more time." My voice cracked and another tear followed the first.

One of Jack's hands moved to cup my face, the rough pad of his thumb chasing away the rogue tears.

"We'll figure it out." His thumb traced over my bottom lip, tugging it free from where it was trapped between my teeth. "I know this girl who's pretty good at planning."

I laughed through a sniffle. "I think she could probably come up with something."

He smiled down at me, a gentle smile that made my heart ache. "I meant it when I said I wanted to try. I'm all in, Evie. Everything else we can figure out."

I let out a shaky breath. "I like the sound of that. I'm all in too. I have been for a while."

His lips covered mine for a long, deep kiss that promised we had all the time in the world.

When we finally came up for air, he pressed one more kiss to my forehead.

"We should go see King. Put some work in with him before dinner." He made no move to release me as he spoke. "We're going to have to spend a lot of extra time with him before you leave."

I dropped my arms, slipping one hand into his much larger one. A confidence I rarely felt these days pushed out the anxiety that had been my constant companion since I'd shoved all my personal belongings into a box and walked away from the legal department. We were in this together.

45.

The expression time "flies when you're having fun" has always held up, but as the days flew by, it seemed like time moved the fastest when you wanted it to slow down. Most of my days were spent working with Ben, and the evenings were spent with Jack. We worked with King until it got too dark outside to see, a job I was finding much more enjoyable than my office work. Margot, Katie, and I made lots of excuses for girl time—a day of shopping at the cute little boutiques in town, complete with a late lunch at Joan's, where I fought the urge to gloat every time Shelly walked by our table. We even visited the infamous Rowdy's one evening. Coming home to Jack might have been my favorite part of that evening, but it was a close contest between slipping into bed next to him and Katie teaching me to line dance.

The nights were all Jack's. We snuggled on the couch, watching Netflix and talking until we both agreed it would be a good idea to move to his bedroom. I spent every night with him in his room. Hank Williams and a large amount of my belongings moved down the hall with me.

We stayed up into the early hours of the morning, talking about anything and everything, taking breaks only to go another round. I was determined to learn as much as I could about this man who was taking up more and more space in my heart. I wanted to know everything—from his favorite food to how he knew he wanted to run the ranch instead of working at Sterling. I was equally determined to learn his body, what he liked and what made him crazy. I had more sex in that handful of days than I would have thought was possible. Jack was insatiable, and seemed just as determined to learn my body. Sometimes he made love to me slowly, worshiping my body until I couldn't tell where I ended and he began. Other times, it was almost frantic, like he wanted to brand my body so I would remember him when I was gone.

By midweek, lack of sleep had me nodding off at my desk, and once or twice at the table. One evening, I leaned my head on Jack's shoulder for five seconds too long, and slept through most of dinner. If I was sleeping through meals, the exhaustion was epic. I had no idea how Jack, who was up before the sun most mornings, was even alive. But I wouldn't have traded a single one of those early hours for the extra sleep. Especially moments like this, with my naked chest pressed up against his wall of muscles and our legs tangled under the covers. I traced every dip and valley on his glorious chest, following my fingertips with kisses. I felt Jack harden, pressing into my thigh.

"If you keep that up, no one's getting any sleep tonight." He squeezed my butt with one of those large palms.

I rested my head on his shoulder with a sigh. "I'm going to miss this."

Jack's hand moved the short distance from my butt to the curve of my back, leisurely sweeping up and down. Goose-bumps broke out with every pass of his hand.

"Me too. I like having you in my bed." He moved the hand resting on his chest down his flat stomach to cup his erection. "A lot."

I laughed into the side of his neck, giving him a light squeeze. "How is that even possible? It's been five minutes. You're insatiable."

"I am when it comes to you." His voice grew serious, making me shiver.

He guided one of my legs across his body so that I straddled him. My hair draped around us like a curtain, and all I could see were his eyes shining fiercely into mine. One hand cupped each side of my face, sweeping my hair back. I felt his eyes travel over every inch of my face.

"I love you." His voice was sure, leaving no room for doubt, and it sent my heart soaring out of my body. "I don't want you going back to Chicago not knowing how absolutely, completely in love with you I am."

"I love you too."

Giving voice to the words I had felt for so long was so natural that saying them was almost like breathing. I did it even without conscious thought.

The smile he gave me warmed me all the way through. He tugged my head lower so that our mouths were almost touching.

"Say it again." I felt his words on my lips, those warm eyes boring into mine.

"I love you." I brought my mouth even closer so that my lips moved against his. "Maybe even more than coffee."

His lips pressed lightly to mine, sweetly at first like he was savoring every pass, then with more urgency. His tongue slipped past my lips, tangling with mine over and over. He kissed me like he couldn't get enough of my mouth. He tore his lips from mine and nibbled a path down my neck, making a hot trail to my collarbone. I was panting when he lifted his head, his gaze sweeping over my swollen lips with a satisfied smile.

"Why did you stop? No stopping," I huffed, making sure to press my naked breasts against his chest. I smiled when I got the desired result and he let out a little groan.

"We should get some sleep. You have a long day tomorrow." His hand came up, tucking my loose hair behind my ear. His thumb swept over my bottom lip, which was forming a serious pout.

"I don't want to leave." The words tumbled out of my mouth before I could stop them.

He gave me a look full of sympathy, a sad smile tugging up the corner of his mouth. "I know, baby. I'm going to miss you like crazy."

I let out a watery sigh, feeling tears start to fill my eyes at an alarming rate. I laid my head on his chest, listening to the steady thrum of his heart. "But we can video chat every day," he said, "and you can send me naked pictures."

I swatted him playfully on the chest. "I swear to God if you send me a dick pic I will never forgive you. And I *will* show it to Ben."

He chuckled, bouncing my head where it was pressed tightly against him. "Nothing he hasn't seen before. He—"

"Please don't finish that sentence. I really don't want to think about Ben's... stuff... ever, and I need to be able to look him in the eye tomorrow without turning into a tomato." I traced the curve of one perfect pectoral muscle, trailing my finger over his ribs and loving the quiver of muscles as I went. "Can I ask you something?"

"You can ask me anything." He stroked my hair reassuringly.

"The day of the bonfire when Leigh called, what happened? You were upset."

I cringed when his hand paused.

"You've been holding on to that one for a long time, huh?"

I nodded without lifting my head, afraid to look him in the eye. His hand started moving again. "Leigh called to let me know her album was out and she was going to go on a promotional tour. She wanted to stop in Montana to see me. Wanted to talk."

"And that made you mad?" I was pretty confident that I wasn't in competition with a supermodel-turned-pop-star, but my heart needed confirmation.

"Talking to her usually does. It's not her fault." He let out a frustrated breath. "Hearing from her just takes me back to a bad time. But I don't still love her, if that's what you're wondering. I haven't loved her for a long time. If I'm being honest, I don't know if I ever did. Not the way either of us needed."

"Why did it end?" I pressed a kiss next to his heart, wanting to soften questions I knew were hard for him to answer, but that I couldn't seem to keep from asking.

"After the accident, I was in bad shape. Physically and emotionally. Doctors didn't know if I would walk right again and the therapy was awful. Our lives changed in seconds, and we didn't know how to handle it. I don't know. When something like that happens, all the cracks in your relationship just bust wide open and sometimes you can't fix them. And I was a miserable bastard for a long time."

"'*Was*'? As in past tense?" He smacked my butt with enough force to sting, making me squirm. "Hey! I'm just speaking the truth. I've been on the receiving end of your miserable-bastard routine. She didn't want to stay here?"

"No. Somehow we never talked about the future in those terms. I always planned on running Pinehaven. I can't see myself doing anything else. She needed to be in the city for work, and she barely tolerated being here just for visits as it was. She was not a country girl, that was painfully obvious."

His words unintentionally poked at a sore spot. "Like me."

Those big strong hands gently lifted my face until my eyes were forced to meet his. The resolve I saw in his expression made my heart pound in an uneven pattern.

"Nothing is the same with you, Evelyn."

I gave him a rueful smile, self-doubt creeping in. "I'm not

so sure what I am. I'm not a country girl and I'm not a city girl. I'm not a lawyer, not really, and I'm not an executive assistant either. I'm not an anything girl."

"You're right. You're not a city girl or a country girl." His thumb stroked my jaw, making a gentle line that stood in sharp contrast to the hardness in his tone. "You're an everything girl. When I look at you, I see my everything. Whether you're in Montana or Chicago or the goddamn moon, you are everything."

And I knew, I *knew*, that this Jack—who looked at me like I was everything, eyes overflowing with love and the quiet confidence that he took with him everywhere—was my favorite.

46.

The smell of coffee woke me up. Any other time, I would have loved waking up to one of my favorite smells, but today waking up meant I was leaving. I kept my eyes closed, snuggling into the warm body next to me, wanting every minute of this day to last hours.

"Morning, baby." His lips pressed against each eyelid before his mouth met mine in an achingly slow kiss that left tears streaming down my face. He kissed each errant tear, whispering soothing words as he pulled me tighter against him.

"I better pace myself." I gave him the saddest smile in the history of sad smiles. "I don't want to run out of tears before Margot gets here."

Jack laughed, the sound rough from sleep. "She'd be pretty disappointed if she had to cry alone, but something tells me that's not going to be a problem."

A few kisses later, I stood in my room for the last time, taking in the neatly-made bed—which hadn't been slept in lately. It felt a lot like standing in my childhood bedroom when I went home to visit. I was not the same girl who had lived there, but the memory of her was still there, haunting it like a ghost.

I showered, then put the toiletries I hadn't packed last night into an open suitcase, fighting tears the entire time. I took a deep breath before opening the door, trying to brace myself for walking to breakfast for the last time. The effort was wasted when I finally opened the door and saw Hank Williams lying outside my room, waiting for me. His tail wagged when he saw me and I let out a choked sob before throwing myself on him and gathering him into my arms. A wet tongue licked my face furiously. I loosened my grip and pressed a kiss to his head.

"I can't believe how much I'm going to miss you, Hank Williams."

Together Hank and I marched down the stairs like we were going to our own funerals. Even the smells wafting from the kitchen weren't enough to improve my mood. I stopped just inside the room, observing the flurry of activity in front of me. Food was spread out across the breakfast bar, buffet-style, and wine glasses stood empty at one end next to a pitcher of orange juice. Jack, Cole, and Sam were seated around the table talking, empty plates in front of them. Ben was standing next to Mary, scraping eggs onto a serving dish.

Mary's eyes were red when they found mine, just as Gabe walked in holding a bottle of champagne. He made a beeline toward me, wrapping me in a hug despite the bottle of champagne pressing into my back.

"You look like shit." He gave me a one-dimple smile. God, I was going to miss him. And those dimples.

"I'm going to forgive you because you have a bottle in your hand that I'm pretty interested in."

"Oh, this?" He waved the bottle in front of me. "I was told mimosas were all the rage with the basic bi—brunch crowd."

"You heard right." I threw my arms around him for another hug. "Thank you."

He squeezed me back. "If you start crying, I'm not giving you any of this."

I laughed, grateful for the comedic relief, since this moment was definitely headed toward tears. We made our way to the glasses and pitchers with only the occasional sniffle from me. Gabe uncorked the bottle and poured a generous amount of champagne in a glass. Just before the orange juice hit the bubbles, the front door burst open and Letty's voice called out to announce her arrival. Margot's laughter drifted through the open door, followed by two familiar voices I hadn't expected.

Katie and Seth, covered dishes in hand, walked into the room. "Surprise!" Katie set her dish on the counter and pulled me into a hug. "We couldn't let you and Ben leave without saying goodbye."

"Thank you." I swallowed the lump in my throat. "I'm going to miss you all so much."

Katie gave me a final squeeze, speaking so low I could barely hear her words. "You won't be gone long enough to miss us."

Gabe shoved two mimosas into our hands. "Just take a drink of this every time you feel like crying. It'll be like a drinking game."

I scrunched my nose, eyeing the glass that looked like a whole lot of champagne with just a hint of orange juice. "I'll be drunk in ten minutes if I drink this that fast."

"That's the idea." He clinked his glass with mine. "Bottoms up, ladies."

A strong arm wrapped around my waist. "You doing okay?"

Jack pressed a kiss to the side of my head, concerned eyes searching mine.

"Yep." I gave him what could pass as a cheap imitation of a smile. "Let's get something to eat."

47.

I managed to get through the rest of breakfast without tears. The food was beyond amazing, as always, and the company made being sad impossible. It wasn't until the last dish had been cleared and Katie and Seth had said their goodbyes that the full realization that I was leaving soon—so soon—barreled into me like a summer storm, fast and without warning.

I slipped onto the porch, hoping for a second alone to pull myself together. I sat in the swing, pushing off with my feet, and looked out over Pinehaven. The red barns, looking like they belonged on a postcard, stood out against the green of the fields and the bright blue of a perfect fall sky. I closed my eyes, breathing in the cool air and listening to all the noises that had seemed so foreign but now sounded like home. Warm tears ran down my cheeks.

Notes of laughter and conversation from inside drifted through the air around me, reminding me that it wasn't just the beautiful scenery I would miss. At the soft thud of the door closing, I opened my eyes with a sigh. I was an endless parade of sighs and tears today. Jack took the spot next to me without saying a word, his arm stretched across my shoulders. I leaned into him, resting my head on that spot between his neck and shoulder that was made for these moments.

We stayed that way until the gentle sway of the swing had soothed away the last of my tears. I was too much of a chicken to admit I was terrified that as soon as I stepped onto the plane, some type of spell would be broken and I would turn back into a pumpkin. Part of me—the part that still believed there was no way this man could possibly love an ordinary, slightly rounded pumpkin—worried that he would forget about me after a couple of days. I worried that there was no way he could love me enough, not as much as I loved him. If the things I whispered to myself were true, I would have no reason to come back to Pinehaven again. And that thought was what broke my heart the most.

"You ready to see Photo and King?" Jack interrupted my depressing train of thought, his voice sounding a little hoarse.

I peered up at him, taking in brown eyes that looked suspiciously shiny.

"I'm ready," I lied.

I would never, ever be ready.

We walked the short distance to the stable, hand in hand. I let go of his hand to offer Photo an apple slice, the other hand stroking her neck.

"Thank you for being so patient with me. I'm going to miss our rides so, so much. Don't forget me, okay?"

She let out a soft huff of breath, nudging my now-empty hand with her nose. I pressed a kiss to her cheek. I turned, wiping a palm across damp skin.

"Sorry, I can't stop crying. I feel so stupid. I just can't stop."

Jack gathered me into his arms before the last word was out of my mouth. "You don't have anything to be sorry about, Evie. This is just a goodbye for now, just a 'see you later'—you know that, right?"

I nodded into his chest, fully aware that I was leaving wet spots on his shirt.

"Good, because I will fly to Chicago and drag you back here if I have to. I'm not letting you go. No one else will put up with this miserable bastard."

I laughed. "You're right. Thank God you look so good in

jeans."

It was his turn to laugh. "Glad to know I have some redeeming qualities."

His hand slipped down into mine, his long fingers weaving through my smaller ones. The rough pad of his thumb stroked back and forth over my knuckles.

"One more stop." Every word was dipped in the same sympathy that shone from his eyes.

"One more stop," I echoed, sounding like someone facing the gallows, not a flight back to Chicago. I promised myself this wouldn't be the last time. I told that voice inside my head to be quiet. I forced myself to believe Jack's threat was the truth as we unlatched the gate and stepped into King's paddock together, something that would have been unfathomable a week earlier.

I waited for King to come to me, confident that he would, because we had done this same dance for over a week now. Sure enough, King stopped munching on the grass at the far corner of his enclosure and made his way over to me after hearing the metal clinking of the gate. I watched him walk the short distance, amazed at the transformation. His coat was starting to grow back a healthy shade of black, and he had put on so much weight. It was the lack of hesitation as he came to stand in front of us that did me in, though. He was no longer the scared, broken creature he had been the first day I'd seen him standing in the corner, looking as lost as I'd felt.

Jack's hand slid into mine and gave it a light squeeze, a reminder that he was here, before releasing it. I trailed my hands over the smooth hair at King's neck and then brought my arms around him in the best embrace I could manage. His strong muscles tensed for a minute, but relaxed after a few seconds. I was always pushing this poor horse, and he was always giving in to me. I pressed a kiss to that soft hair.

"Today's the day. I'm leaving, going back to Chicago. I'm going to miss you so much. I wanted to say..." I swallowed down the tears, taking a shaky breath. "I wanted to say thank you. You made me brave. We made each other brave."

I felt him turn his neck and snort out a breath that blew through my hair. One of Jack's hands made a soothing path up and down my back while he spoke reassurances to us both.

"Don't worry, buddy. She'll be back." His words were meant as much for me as for the horse who was just learning to trust him.

"I'll be back. I'll be back," I chanted into his neck, like saying it could make it true. "Jack is going to take good care of you until then."

I released King and took a step back, taking him in through watery eyes. Waves of hysteria were trying to claw their way out of me. I fought against the surge of emotion and turned to make my way out of the enclosure, aware of Jack following my retreat. As soon as the gate was latched, Jack pulled me into his arms.

"I don't know why I'm so sad," I mumbled into his chest. "I'm not usually this much of a wreck, I swear."

"It's okay. I'm not happy about you leaving either." He pressed a kiss to the top of my head. "I'm going to miss you so damn much."

We held onto each other for a few more seconds, then made our way to the goat pen, where I proceeded to hug each one. Without tears—it was almost impossible to be sad around tiny goats. By the time we made our way back to the house, our luggage was stacked next to the truck, signaling it was time to leave, and for my tears to return.

Gabe walked through the door and gave me a sad grin as he came down the stairs. He shoved his hands into his pockets, looking more unsure than I had ever seen him.

"So this is it, huh? Goodbyes aren't really my thing, so go easy on me." He cleared his throat as if he was trying to find more words.

My arms were around him, trapping his arms to his side. "You're basically my best friend. I'm going to miss you so much. Promise me you'll text me, okay? Or at least respond to my texts. Promise me, Gabe?"

"Jesus, Jack, control your woman." Gabe struggled to free his arms from where I had them trapped. Jack just patted him on the back, walking past us into the house. "I promise, Evie. I'm not going to ghost you. I can't breathe. You're surprisingly strong for someone half the size of a normal person."

I laughed through my tears, a watery noise that sounded a little more sad than happy. "I'm a normal height."

"Sure you are. Oh God, are you crying?" he groaned, giving me an awkward pat on the back. "Come on, now, you know you'll be seeing us all again. Do you think I'd work that hard getting you two to pull your heads out of your own asses just to watch you both throw it all away?"

"What?" I loosened my grip to look up at him, fully aware that snot and tears were making a home on my face.

"Evie, Evie, Evie. Do you think I agreed to give you riding lessons in exchange for helping out around here for my own health? 'Cause I can guarantee you that watching you try to use a wheelbarrow shaved a solid five years off my life."

"I have no idea what you're talking about." I wrinkled my brow in confusion.

"Of course you don't." He gave his head a slow shake, like he was trying to explain long division to a baby. "I knew Jack had a thing for you but was trying not to, just like I knew you belonged here. You both just needed a shove in the right direction."

Pieces of the puzzle came together, and my head jerked

back in surprise and my tear-soaked eyes regarded him in a new light. "Is that what you were talking to Cole about the day I asked you to give me lessons?"

He nodded, looking pretty pleased with himself. "I knew that if Jack could see how well you fit in, he would eventually stop fighting himself on this. And it was pretty obvious you fit in here."

"How could you possibly know all that? I'm the opposite of every woman Jack's ever been with." I couldn't keep the skepticism out of my voice.

"I know, Evie. That's how I knew. All those other girls didn't have any staying power. They were just temporary. You've got staying power in spades, babe. Don't ever doubt it."

"How'd you get so smart?" I was genuinely in awe of this man, who really saw the people around him and quietly plotted to help them.

"Aunt Evie, I made you something!" Letty's voice called out, followed by the sound of the door slamming.

I squatted to meet her, reaching out my hand to receive the paper she was waving in front of her.

"Look." She smiled at me, pointing to the paper, filled with lots of unidentifiable shapes. "This is Daddy. This is Mommy. And this is me!"

"Oh wow, Letty, this is beautiful!" I gushed, smiling genuinely. "Thank you so much! I'm going to hang this up as soon as I get home."

"You can look at it if you're missing us and then you won't be so sad." Her little voice was so filled with concern that it made my heart swell in my chest.

Margot and Cole were waiting for me when I stood up. Margot's eyes were red.

"I know this is stupid but I can't help it." She wiped under her eyes. "I'm blaming the hormones."

"I can't stop crying, and I have no excuse." I gave her a quick squeeze. "I'm really going to miss you all."

"We got you something." Cole held up a forest green crewneck sweater, with the word *Pinehaven* stretched across the middle and the ranch's logo below it. "You're officially a ranch hand now."

"Does this mean I don't have to muck out stalls anymore?" I never did get the hang of wheelbarrows, and the smell of horse poop was on the short list of things I would not miss.

"Not a chance." Cole laughed, handing me the sweater.

"You ready, Evelyn?" Ben walked out the door, followed by Mary and Jack.

"Yep," I lied, clutching the sweater to my chest, careful not to crinkle Letty's drawing.

The luggage was loaded into the truck, and there was nothing left to do. No more goodbyes to say. We drove to the tiny airport in silence. My eyes ate up the scenery when they weren't sneaking glimpses of Jack. The trip seemed so much quicker than last time.

Ben hugged his mom goodbye, promising not to stay away so long this time. She reminded him that Thanksgiving was still mandatory. He moved to Jack next, and gave him a manhug complete with lots of back-patting. I watched him hop up the plane stairs before I turned to Mary.

"Thank you for everything, Mary. I really enjoyed my visit and your cooking."

She pulled me into her arms. "You take of yourself, sweetheart." She gave my cheek an affectionate pat. "We'll see you soon." She gave me a knowing smile, then walked back to the truck, leaving me and Jack alone.

I didn't know how to do this. I didn't know how to leave

him. I would have laughed at the absurdity of that knowledge if I wasn't so unbelievably sad. My foot bounced on the ground as Jack's hands cupped my face, gently tipping my head up. His eyes ate up my face like it was his last meal, and then his mouth was on mine. His lips moved against mine hungrily, and then he was gone.

I watched him walk away without another word. I watched him until he was standing beside Mary, and then I boarded the plane that would take me back to the real world.

48.

I slipped back into my old routine, my city routine, pretty easily. It helped that Jack had sent me the first of many text messages while we were still on the plane. As soon as we landed, I had turned airplane mode off, and found a text message from him reminding me to let him know when I got home safely and that he loved me. It eased that tight knot of dread that had formed in my chest somewhere between Montana and Illinois.

My initial excitement about being back in the city had faded by the end of the weekend. I really tried to muster up some enthusiasm about all the things I had loved before Pine Hollow, Montana, had turned my world upside down. A sentence I'd never thought I would utter.

Everything felt a little hollow since I'd returned. Well, everything but the availability of coffee shops and the food delivery situation. Pizza being delivered to my doorstep was never going to get old.

By Monday morning, I was ready to go back to work just so I didn't have to sit in my empty apartment all day looking at pictures from Pinehaven. Anna and Hilari were waiting at my desk with a latte, and a flower arrangement was sitting on my desk, making it look more inviting.

"Evelyn! We're so glad you're back." Hilari handed me the latte.

"Girl, we have so much catching up to do." Anna sat down on the edge of my desk, like we were going to start right now.

"Thanks, guys, this was so nice." I motioned to the flowers

with the latte. "We should get dinner tonight. Are you free?"

"We are not responsible for the flowers. Those were here when we got in. I think there's a card though. It's probably a thank-you from all the other executives for keeping Ben out of trouble." Anna reached for the card, handing it to me. "And I'm definitely in for dinner."

"Same," Hilari added. "What are you in the mood for? Any place you've been missing since you left?"

The list of restaurants I missed was actually pretty long. I had to put dining on the list of pros for Chicago. That list consisted of mostly food-related items—no surprise there—and my two friends. It was a really depressing list.

"Sushi." I settled on the least likely item to be had in Montana. "I missed sushi."

We made plans for dinner, and then they headed back to their own desks. I opened the card and smiled when I saw who the flowers were from.

Have a good first day back. Love you. Jack.

I pulled my phone out and thumbed through the text messages to the one with Jack. I already had one from Corinne and my mom wishing me a good first day back.

Me: *Thanks for the flowers. They're beautiful.*

I was surprised when the three little dots appeared almost immediately.

Jack: *Glad you liked them. How's your morning been?*

Me: *I've only been here for ten minutes, so okay. I made dinner plans with Anna and Hilari so I'm looking forward to catching up with them. And sushi. I'm also looking forward to sushi.*

Jack: *That's good, baby. I have to get going, the cows are getting excited about breakfast. I miss you.*

Me: *Miss you too. Love you.*

I tucked my phone into my desk drawer and got to work, making a short list for Ben of things that needed to get done before the end of the day and putting notes together for him on all our meetings today.

The rest of the week was just an endless string of meetings broken up by meals and sleep. The best parts of every day were the text messages from Montana, or what I now referred to as 'back home.' I had no idea when I'd started referring to Pinehaven as 'back home,' but there it was.

My phone's background picture was a selfie Jack had sent of him holding Saffron and Basil while Rosemary photobombed them over his shoulder. Gabe kept his word and sent me multiple text messages a day. He sent me updates about King's progress, knock-knock jokes, and videos of the goats. He refused to admit they were growing on him, but he'd bought them a soccer ball that resulted in the best video I'd seen in my life. Goats playing soccer should be mandatory viewing. Everyone sent me pictures of Hank Williams. I even forced Jack to FaceTime me, because I was worried Hank would forget the sound of my voice.

Friday morning's board meeting seemed like merely an obstacle to my video date with Jack. It went off without a hitch. The board was horrified and impressed with the information we had compiled, which was the exact reaction we were going for. They agreed to move ahead with the dissolution, and expressed their gratitude to us for bringing this to their attention. I accepted their praise with a smile, then got out of there as fast as I could without being inappropriate.

It was almost dark by the time I got home. I changed out of my suit and into a pair of leggings and the sweatshirt I'd stolen from Jack. I had slept in it every night since I left. I poured myself a glass of wine and settled onto the couch, picking up my phone to order Chinese. My laptop started buzzing with an incoming video chat invitation from Elise. I hit *answer* and held up a finger, silently asking her to hang on a second while I finished ordering.

"Hey, sorry about that. I was ordering dinner. What's up?"

"Nothing, we thought we could do a little video date. Are you expecting company? We can try this tomorrow." Elise adjusted the screen so I could see her better. I did not miss the way her eyebrows rose when she took in my oversized sweatshirt.

"Nope, I'm not expecting anyone," I reassured her.

"All that food was for you?"

"I haven't had Chinese in over a month, Judgey McJudgerson! Also, I only had time to scarf down a yogurt for lunch."

I was saved by Corinne's request to join our chat.

"Hey ladies, happy Friday! What's going on? How was the board meeting, Evie?" Corinne's smiling face filled the other half of my screen.

"Evie just ordered enough Chinese food to feed a family of five," Elise informed Corinne.

"I did not order that much food." I rolled my eyes. "And the meeting went really well. They accepted our proposal, and even seemed genuinely happy to have Ben back."

"That's great." Corinne shot me a thumbs-up. "I don't know why I just did that. Feel free to pretend like it didn't happen."

I chuckled, giving her a thumbs-up in return. "You got it."

It was her turn to roll her eyes.

"You don't seem that excited about how well the meeting went. Why aren't you out celebrating?" Elise leaned into the screen, as if she could find the answer to her question by examining my face on her screen.

I shrugged. "I don't know. I just feel meh about the whole

thing. I was completely plugged in during the meeting, old-school Evelyn style, but after it was over, I just couldn't get that excited about it."

Corinne sighed, thoughtfully running her hand up and down her very large stomach. "Everything's been meh since you got back."

I nodded, because I couldn't disagree. "I know. Not to sound pathetic, but I don't think I realized how lonely my life was until now."

Elise gave me a reassuring smile. "That's a little sad, Evie. But the not-sad part is that you know now and you can change it."

I blew out a breath. "I know you're right. The problem is I don't want to fix it."

"What do you mean?" Corinne's forehead was scrunched in concern. "You want to keep being lonely?"

"No. I mean..." I searched for the words to explain how I was feeling. "I've only been back a week, but I don't think I want to do this anymore."

Elise's voice rose with alarm. "What are you talking about here? Because I'm about to hop in my car and drive to Chicago. That sounded real doomsday."

I would never understand what I did to deserve these two. "Calm down. I'm fine. I just feel like, in Chicago I'm always trying to fit myself into this *idea* of me. I didn't have to do that in Pine Hollow. I was just *me* there, and that was good enough. Does that even make sense?"

Both women were watching me with small smiles on their faces. Corinne was the first to speak.

"That makes perfect sense."

Elise nodded her head in agreement. "It totally does."

"It does?" I was a little surprised that they were both

agreeing with me on this one.

"Evie, I haven't seen you that happy and confident in a really long time." Corinne wiped under her eyes. "Sorry, everything makes me cry right now."

"And I think you left a really big chunk of your heart in Montana," Elise added with a soft smile. "I almost said 'hunk.' Hunk of your heart. It still would have worked."

I laughed, feeling relieved that they understood the feelings I was doing a pretty terrible job of giving voice to. "I just need to figure out what to do with all this."

"Well, if you want any pointers on what to do with Jack—" I heard Ted yelling at Corinne in the background. "Okay, okay. I was totally serious though."

"Anyway, what I think Corinne was trying to say is, and I agree with her, you already know what to do about it."

Corinne nodded her head. "Yes, that is what I meant to say. Before you start to argue with your older, wiser sisters, just think about it okay? Remember that your heart is just as big as your head, and just as important."

We chatted for a little bit longer about what was going on in their lives. Texting all day meant that there wasn't really much to fill in, but it was just nice to see their faces sometimes. I said goodbye when the delivery guy buzzed up.

I was making my way through the Chinese buffet on my coffee table when my computer dinged with another incoming video chat request. This one I was expecting. I accepted the request, and Jack's handsome face filled up my screen. He looked tired. Stubble lined his jaw, and his hair was still damp from a shower.

My ovaries sighed. "Hi. You look tired."

"Long day. You look good, though. I like your shirt." His voice was rough and the gravelly tone made my heart dip down toward my toes.

"Me too." My greedy eyes ate up his face, making me forget all about the food. "I miss you."

"I miss you too, baby." He smiled, settling back onto his pillows. "How'd your meeting go?"

I filled him in on the meeting, and he told me about his day. The last time I looked at the clock, it was past midnight. I fell asleep listening to Jack's voice, my head resting on a throw pillow.

49.

Monday morning came and went. By Tuesday, I was looking at plane tickets. Flying commercial to Montana for a weekend was expensive, and somehow involved a lot of driving. Wednesday found me seriously considering asking Ben what the company policy was on borrowing the corporate jet. It seemed like a reasonable employment benefit. Health insurance, paid time off, use of the corporate jet—same thing.

When I got to work Thursday morning, there was a note stuck to my computer telling me to meet Ben in his office. I grabbed my notes for the day and made the short trip to his door, knocking lightly.

Ben's head popped up. "Evelyn, come on in. Do you have the notes for the meeting with Van Horn's this afternoon?"

I passed him one of the files in my hand. "Yes, I had the legal department verify some of the clauses in the contract that weren't included in the first draft. Their notes are highlighted, but everything checked out."

"Great." He pushed back from his desk, standing up. "Walk with me for a second."

I followed him out of his office and down the hall. He came to a stop outside an empty office, in the part of the executive floor where general counsel was located. Incidentally, it was where I had planned on being one day. Ben flipped on the light and motioned for me to follow him inside.

"What do you think?" His hand swept around the space, a big smile on his face.

It was a dream office. One wall was all windows, and a floor-to-ceiling bookcase covered another wall. The office was spacious enough for a large desk and some fancy chairs.

"It's a great space." I smiled back at Ben, unsure what we were doing here.

"It's yours if you want it."

My jaw dropped. "What? What do you mean, mine if I want it?"

"The board was impressed with all your work on the dissolution. They've been impressed with all your work as my assistant. Beyond impressed. We're offering you a general counsel position. You've been a great executive assistant, Evelyn, but we both know you were meant for more."

My heart started beating erratically. *More. More. More.* The walls felt like they were closing in on us, pushing the oxygen out of the room. Sweat beaded on my forehead. I pictured hours and hours of my life spent in this space, in this building, and it felt like I couldn't breathe.

Fifteen minutes later, I walked out of the office and toward my desk on wobbly legs. I felt a little nauseated, and there was a real chance I would need to make a detour to the bathroom to throw up my bagel. It took me longer than it should have to notice all the whispers and glances in my direction. I thought I was just being paranoid at first, but by the time I turned the corner I was sure the whispers were about me.

I discreetly swept my hand down the back of my skirt to make sure I hadn't tucked it into my underwear again. Nope, underpants were still safely hidden under my skirt. I was puzzled. There was no way everyone could have found out so quickly about what had just happened with Ben.

I picked up my pace, anxious to reach the security of my desk. Heart hammering already, I turned the corner and saw the last person I had expected to see, sitting in my chair.

"Jack?"

His head shot up from his phone and a smile slowly stretched across his mouth. Mystery solved. Standing in front of me was the cause of the whispers.

"Surprise."

I crashed into him and his lips found mine. He kissed me like we had been apart for years, not weeks. My cheeks were flushed when he finally broke the kiss. "I'm sorry. I shouldn't have done that. This is your workplace."

I placed a quick kiss on his lips, smiling up at him. "No, it's not."

"It's not what?" He ran his hands down my hair, his eyes searching mine.

"It's not my workplace. At least it won't be in two weeks." Jack looked stunned. I was still processing it myself.

"You quit?"

I nodded, panic warring with relief. "I did. I was hoping you might need another ranch hand at Pinehaven."

His hands came up, bracketing my head between them. "Evelyn, what are you thinking? Did you just wake up this morning and decide to quit?"

"No." I shook my head as much as his hands would allow. "I decided to quit when Ben offered me a general counsel position. It didn't feel right, the idea of working in that office when my heart was somewhere else. You feel right. Pinehaven feels right. I don't want to be anywhere else."

Jack's eyes searched mine almost frantically, like he couldn't believe the words coming out of my mouth. His lack of reaction started making me rethink the thing I had put no thought into originally. This was why I didn't do things without a plan first. Tears started building in my eyes and I took in a deep breath, reminding myself that I was going to be okay no matter what happened next.

My hands moved to wrap around each of his wrists, trying to tug them away from my face. "You don't have to worry. I saved up to quit but then I didn't quit. I mean the first time I quit. You know what I mean. So I'm fine. I'm more than fine. Really, I—"

Jack mouth silenced my nervous rant. He kissed me until I forgot what I had even been nervous about. Then he lifted his head, a smile transforming his face. He let go of me and walked around my desk, grabbing my coat and bag.

It was my turn to be confused. "What are you doing?"

He slid my jacket onto my left arm, then the right, before handing me my bag. "You're taking the rest of the day off."

"I am?"

"Yeah. We have a lot to get done in two weeks." He zipped up my jacket. His hand moved to the small of my back, gently pushing me toward the elevators. "We need to get some boxes, unless you have those. How long was your lease? We'll probably need to find a subletter. And we should probably get you one of those fancy espresso machines for the kitchen."

The elevator dinged and he guided me through the open door.

"For the kitchen?" My mind was struggling to keep up with him. To keep up with this whole morning.

"I figure you aren't going to want to drive all the way to town anytime you want a latte, which we both know is pretty much all the time." He pressed a button on the panel, never taking his eyes off me.

I nodded my head. "I like that plan. It's a really good plan."

He smiled at me. "You taught me everything I know."

EPILOGUE

Three years later

I heard Jack's worried voice calling from somewhere behind us. "Evie! Slow down!"

I tugged lightly on King's reins, slowing him down to a fast walk. I sighed, already missing the feeling of the wind rushing past me. I leaned forward so that my mouth was lined up with King's ear.

"I promise we'll find a way to sneak in our runs. At least for the next couple months." I stroked his neck before steering us to the disgruntled man standing just beyond the fence with his arms crossed. I didn't need to see his face to know he was wearing his signature scowl.

He uncrossed his arms to take King's reins as I dismounted.

"I'm fine," I reassured him. "Dr. Blower said it's perfectly safe for me to keep riding during the first trimester. You were there with me, so I know you heard her."

"She said to be careful, try to keep it to a walk or trot." He turned the full force of that stormy expression my way. "That was not a walk or a trot."

Unfortunately for him, I had become immune to the full array of his fierce expressions about two years ago.

"Jack, I'm fine. Baby Danver is fine. And we both trust King."

I'd picked up with King as soon as I got back from Chicago, and over the years we had formed a strong bond. I trusted King like I trusted Corinne to let me know if I looked bad in a pair of jeans. She hadn't let me down yet, and neither had King.

I trailed behind Jack as he led King back to his stall, grumbling the entire way. I had become fluent in Jack-grumbles and Jack-grunts, so I knew this particular session was from a place of love. I still had a hard time believing this man was my husband. *Husband.* It was less new than the baby I was brewing, but still new enough that the title made me do a little happy dance on the inside.

My hands settled on my stomach, cradling the little bump I was sure you could see from the right angle if you looked really, really hard.

"I know it's hard to believe, listening to him right now, but your daddy is actually a totally rational person. Mostly."

"And your mama is going to be the death of me." Jack pressed his lips to my stomach, and I fell in love with him all over again. "Mom and Sam are here. They brought dinner."

About six months after I moved in, Mary moved out to live with Sam. That was a twist I hadn't seen coming, but it was the best kind. I think she was just waiting to make sure Jack was settled before she flew the coop. Thankfully, she hadn't gone far, because my cooking skills had barely improved. My stomach grumbled on cue.

"Do you think she brought pie?" I sighed dreamily. I handed King an apple, hoping any fruit I consumed this evening would be covered in a buttery, flaky crust.

Jack chuckled. "I'm sure she got the hints you've been dropping all week. Subtlety is not your strongest suit, babe."

"I know. She said to let her know what sounds good to me and Baby Danver, but it feels like I'm taking advantage of the whole pregnancy thing if I ask her to bake for me." I leaned into Jack's side when he slipped his arm around my waist.

"So you trick her into doing it instead?" I could hear the humor in his accusation.

"When you say it like that..." I trailed off as we stepped through the front door and were immediately greeted by Letty.

"Uncle Jack! Aunt Evie! I was looking for you." She wrapped her little arms around me and added in a hushed voice, "Grandma made pies."

At almost six, Letty wanted to be a rancher just like her dad and uncles—and she was absolutely fearless, too.

"Best news ever! Are you keeping Uncle Gabe away from them?" I gave her tiny frame a squeeze. Letty may have been all about her uncles, but I could always count on her to be my co-conspirator.

She giggled, reaching to take my hand and attempting to drag me toward the kitchen. "Yes, but you have to hurry. I can't keep him away much longer!"

We all moved toward the sounds of laughter and conversation coming from the kitchen. Sunday night dinners were my favorite, and not just for the cooking. I loved it when we all got together. These people were a huge reason why I had fallen in love with Pinehaven in the first place. They were also the ones who had known I belonged here even before I did.

When I'd decided to take the Montana bar exam so I could practice law here if I wanted, they were the ones who tolerated my intense level of crazy. It was how I knew Jack was really, truly in love with me. If he could handle me at my bar-exam-studying worst, it had to be love. And they welcomed my family with open arms when they came to visit, which made me love them even more.

"Stay away from that pie!" I yelled at Gabe, who was hovering dangerously close to it. His hands shot up in a defensive pose.

"Have you been telling tales, Letty?" he said, feigning innocence. "You know I would never touch your baked goods, Evie.

Who are you going to believe here, me or this rugrat?"

I *hmm*ed, tapping my lips as if I was giving his question some thought. "I choose Letty."

Letty jumped up and down in celebration. Gabe marched over to me and leaned down until his mouth was inches from my stomach.

"This is your Uncle Gabe speaking, Baby D. Your handsome, funny, and charming Uncle Gabe."

I laughed. "What are you even doing?"

"I'm getting it right with this one. I'm starting in the womb," he said, giving me the two-dimple treatment. "How long did you make it on King before the mother hen stopped you?"

"I snuck out of the office after I got the last contract finished up. I knew he wouldn't be back for another twenty minutes, so I managed to get in a solid fifteen minutes."

Gabe chuckled. "That's about ten more minutes than I thought you'd get away with."

Mary ushered us all to the table. I slid into my usual spot next to Jack, careful not to step on Hank Williams, who was waiting patiently for scraps. Jack's hand found mine under the table, like it always did. He gave my hand a gentle squeeze, leaning over to ask a question, low enough for only me to hear.

"Are you happy, wife?"

It was the same question he asked me every day, like he still couldn't believe I was here with him in Montana instead of in a high-rise in Chicago. I gave him the same answer I always did.

"Very happy, husband. How could I not be?"

And I was happy. Sometimes it seemed like my heart was so full that my chest couldn't possibly contain it. The day I walked out of Sterling for the last time was the day I became so much more than I could ever have planned on. I had become the office manager of Pinehaven, an aspiring horse rehabilitator, a rancher, a bull sperm contract expert, a dog owner, the sister I always should have been, the friend I always wanted to be, a wife, and now a mother. I wasn't just one thing anymore. I was an everything girl.

Printed in Great Britain
by Amazon

46272486R00199